Praise for the novels

The Good W...

"Porter does an excellent job of capturing the not-always-smooth bond between sisters . . . and the dynamics of guilt, silence, and strength in a large Irish Catholic family . . . It is an honest story of a woman making her first real mistake."
—*Booklist*

"Porter writes with honesty, warmth, and compassion about the uncomfortable issues that may arise in one's life. Anticipate a good series as each sister explores different paths and different outcomes that are challenging and real." —*Library Journal*

"Porter portrays family relationships with insight and fairness. Her characters are compelling individuals who quickly grab your heart. Intense family scenes are balanced with moments of quiet reflection. The interaction between the characters blends high emotion with realistic events and choices that can turn a person's life upside down. This beautifully written story sends readers on an emotional roller-coaster ride that twists and turns right to the end." —*RT Book Reviews*

She's Gone Country

"I've always been a big fan of Jane Porter's. She understands the passion of grown-up love and the dark humor of mothering teenagers. What a smart, satisfying novel *She's Gone Country* is."
—Robyn Carr, *New York Times* bestselling author of The Virgin River Novels

"A celebration of a woman's indomitable spirit. Suddenly single, juggling motherhood and a journey home, Shey embodies every woman's hopes and dreams. Once again, Jane Porter has written her way into this reader's heart."

—Susan Wiggs, *New York Times* bestselling author

"Richly rewarding." —*Chicago Tribune*

"Strongly plotted, with a heroine who is vulnerable yet resilient . . . engaging." —*The Seattle Times*

Easy on the Eyes

"An irresistible mix of glamour and genuine heart . . . *Easy on the Eyes* sparkles!" —Beth Kendrick, author of *The Pre-nup*

"A smart, sophisticated, fun read with characters you'll fall in love with. Another winning novel by Jane Porter."

—Mia King, national bestselling author of
Good Things and *Sweet Life*

Mrs. Perfect

"With great warmth and wisdom, in *Mrs. Perfect* Jane Porter creates a richly emotional story about a realistically flawed and wonderfully human hero who only discovers what is important in life when she learns to let go of her quest for perfection."

—*Chicago Tribune*

"Porter's authentic character studies and meditations on what really matters make *Mrs. Perfect* a perfect summer novel."

—*USA Today*

"The witty first-person narration keeps things lively in Porter's latest. Taylor's neurotic fussiness provides both vicarious thrills and laughs before Taylor moves on to self-awareness and a new kind of empowerment . . . a feel-good read." —*Kirkus Reviews*

Flirting with Forty

Basis for the Lifetime Original Movie

"A terrific read! A wonderful, life- and love-affirming story for women of all ages."

—Jayne Ann Krentz, *New York Times* bestselling author

"Fits the bill as a calorie-free accompaniment for a poolside daiquiri." —*Publishers Weekly*

Odd Mom Out

"Jane Porter must know firsthand how it feels to not fit in. She nails it poignantly and perfectly in *Odd Mom Out*. This mommy-lit title is far from fluff . . . Sensitive characters and a protagonist who doesn't cave to the in-crowd gives this novel its heft." —*USA Today*

"[Porter's] musings on balancing work, life and love ring true." —*Entertainment Weekly*

"The draining pace of Marta's life comes across convincingly, and Porter's got a knack for getting into the heads of the preteen set; Eva's worries are right on the mark. A poignant critique of mommy cliques and the plight of single parents." —*Kirkus Reviews*

The Good Wife

JANE PORTER

BERKLEY BOOKS, NEW YORK

THE BERKLEY PUBLISHING GROUP
Published by the Penguin Group
Penguin Group (USA)
375 Hudson Street, New York, New York 10014, USA

USA I Canada I UK I Ireland I Australia I New Zealand I India I South Africa I China

Penguin Books Ltd., Registered Offices: 80 Strand, London WC2R 0RL, England
For more information about the Penguin Group, visit penguin.com.

This book is an original publication of The Berkley Publishing Group.

BERKLEY® is a registered trademark of Penguin Group (USA)
The "B" design is a trademark of Penguin Group (USA)

Library of Congress Cataloging-in-Publication Data

Porter, Jane, date.
The good wife / Jane Porter.
pages cm
ISBN 978-0-425-25367-0
1. Married people—Fiction.   2. Adultery—Fiction.   I. Title.
PS3616.O78G66 2013
813'.6—dc23
201301520

PUBLISHING HISTORY
Berkley trade paperback edition / September 2013

PRINTED IN THE UNITED STATES OF AMERICA

10 9 8 7 6 5 4 3 2

Cover design by Rita Frangie
Cover photo © Andreas Gradin / Shutterstock
Book design by Laura K. Corless

This is a work of fiction. Names, characters, places, and incidents either are the product
of the author's imagination or are used fictitiously, and any resemblance to actual persons,
living or dead, business establishments, events or locales is entirely coincidental.
The publisher does not have any control over and does not assume any responsibility for
author or third-party websites or their content.

For Megan Crane

You are a wise woman
Safety net
And glue.
I love you!

Acknowledgments

Books are work. This book was especially demanding. I tore the story apart over and over to make it into what I wanted it to be. The process was hard and scary but ultimately I wrote the story I wanted. But I didn't get this story without help.

So, first and foremost, thank you to my amazing editor, Cindy Hwang. You give me such freedom to find my stories and push the boundaries of what I know, I believe, and what I can do.

Thank you to Megan Crane for discussing this story endlessly. Your friendship has changed me, and given me strength to live, love, and create even in the middle of messy.

Thank you to Lilian Darcy for being willing to read this story in various drafts, and give me your insights so I could make it even better. Your input made such a difference. You are a truly gifted writer, a dear friend, and I value you immensely.

Thank you to Lee Hyat. You work so hard for me, and have for years. I'm deeply grateful. You've made a significant difference in my life, and career.

Thank you to Kari Andersen, Kimberly Field, and Marlene Engel for being Beta readers. You girls rock! Thank you also to my awesome Street Team. You know who you are. Thank you for being part of my world and making each book launch fun!

Thank you to Shevawn Maida for all your care, compassion, friendship, and love. We are so lucky you agreed to become part of our family.

And last, but not least, thank you to my husband, Ty Gurney. You always have my back, and you make me feel like I can do anything. Thank you for being my guy. I love being your girl.

One

All you have to do is get through this, Sarah told herself, gulping down wine from her mom's Waterford Lismore goblet.

She didn't have to like it. Didn't have to be at the door, greeting every single person as he or she arrived. Didn't have to know the right thing to say, or the right thing to do, because that was Mom's job. Dad might be the rock in the family, but Mom was the glue.

Mom.

Jesus.

Sarah drank more wine, blinking back tears as she dodged yet another well-meaning guest, trying to avoid her family at the same time, which was even more challenging as the Brennans were a large family, and she the youngest of five, with aunts and uncles and cousins in every corner of the house.

Normally she loved her close, opinionated family, but right now she didn't want to talk to any of them, unable to deal with them. They'd spent the past few days monitoring her eating, her drinking, her parenting skills, and then bombarding her with unsolicited suggestions and advice, forgetting that at thirty-five, she was an adult, a woman, not little Sarah, the charming, good-natured baby of the family.

It'd been years since she had thought of herself as charming or good-natured. Sarah was also certain that Boone, her husband of thirteen years, wouldn't call her good-natured either. No, he'd probably describe her as intense, emotional, demanding. Maybe even a little unstable, but honestly, what professional athlete's wife wasn't?

Once upon a time, a long time ago, she'd been the athlete, playing soccer, basketball, and softball in elementary school, and then volleyball, basketball, and softball in high school before going on to play volleyball at UCLA. A tall, strong athlete, Sarah had been a physical player, and she'd been blessed with mental toughness, too. After UCLA, she'd planned on going on to law school to take on the bad guys in the world but instead met Boone and gave up law school to be his wife.

She'd never thought it'd been a mistake—trading her dreams for his—until her world fell apart a couple of years ago, and she'd been fighting to rebuild her marriage, and her self-esteem, ever since.

Sarah drained her glass as she eased through the crowd, wobbling ever so slightly in her black heels as she entered the dining room to refill her glass from the collection of wine bottles on the sideboard.

The pale gold bottle, newly opened, felt damp and cold in her hand. The weight of the bottle felt good. It was a familiar feeling, and reassuring. It was a new bottle, recently taken from the refrigerator. Sarah liked newly opened bottles of wine. It meant that there would be plenty more if she wanted another glass.

And she'd want another glass.

Soon.

Replacing the golden bottle on the silver coaster, Sarah felt her father's gaze from the other side of the long dining table. He'd been watching her ever since she entered the room, but Sarah pretended to be oblivious—something she'd perfected as the youngest—and slipped from the room without making eye contact.

Being the youngest did have advantages. Sarah had learned how to manage Dad from watching her older sisters and brother. First of all, you never directly challenged him. He was old-school; a sixth-generation San Francisco firefighter, he was all about serving and protecting his family and community.

Second, even if you totally, absolutely disagreed with him, you didn't ever tell him so. It was a disaster to pull a Brianna. Far better to at least appear to consider his advice, reflect on his wisdom. Even if it was archaic.

Mom had always been so good at managing Dad; whether it was handling a situation before it became a crisis, or smoothing Dad's feathers once they were ruffled, she knew he needed to feel secure and respected.

Mom had never been shy about admitting that Dad had double standards. His son could do things he didn't want his girls doing. Like drinking. Tommy Jr. could have a beer or two every night when he wasn't at the firehouse, but it made Dad uncomfortable to see his daughters drink. A glass of champagne at Sunday brunch, or Christmas Eve, was nice and festive, but regular drinking? Bad.

Speaking of daughters—where was Sarah's daughter, Ella?

The last time she'd seen her five-year-old, Ella had been with Sarah's sister Kit, but that had been . . . oh, at least thirty minutes ago. Maybe longer, and that wasn't good. Sarah couldn't abdicate responsibility for her children just because one of her sisters had offered to keep an eye on the kids.

Entering the family room, Sarah scanned the crowd, spotting Uncle Jack and Aunt Linda with Tommy and Cass, but there were no kids anywhere in sight. Gulping her Chardonnay, she let the cold, crisp wine warm in her mouth for an extra second before swallowing, then retreated back to the hall, where she stood on the bottom step of the staircase and listened for her daughter's high voice upstairs. Nothing.

She wasn't panicking yet, but she took a swift step down and teetered, which didn't help her sense of self-control.

Maybe she should stop drinking. Maybe she needed to pay a little more attention to her own family.

Weaving through the guests packing the entry hall, she was heading to the living room when a hand reached for her.

"Sarah."

Sarah turned and felt herself be drawn against a big, maternal body, enfolded into a particularly uncomfortable hug.

"I'm so sorry, my dear," the woman whispered in Sarah's ear as she patted her back. "So very, very sorry."

"Yes," Sarah murmured, juggling the wineglass while attempting to detangle herself.

But the woman wasn't ready to release Sarah and the hug continued, as did the firm pats on Sarah's back. "I just adored your mother. She will be very missed, my dear."

Sarah sighed inwardly, giving in to the hug, because that's all she'd been doing for days. Accepting condolences. Speaking of her spirited, wickedly funny mother in hushed, reverent tones. Speaking of her lively, loving mother in the past tense.

I absolutely adored her . . . She was just wonderful . . . She will be so missed . . .

Sarah blinked hard, willing the lump in her throat to go away. "Thank you for coming," she said huskily, successfully pulling away even as she injected the right note of warmth and appreciation into her voice. As the youngest, Sarah had been able to watch her mom in action the longest, and her mom, a nurse who had returned to school to earn her MBA in Hospital Administration, was brilliant with people. She had a soft touch that belied her steely core.

And then the woman was gone, and Sarah was back on her mission to find her daughter, and she squeezed through the crowd, into the living room, searching chairs and small corners in case Ella had found a quiet spot to sit.

But no Ella here either, and trapped as she was by the mantel with its profusion of flowers and framed photos of Mom, Sarah's head spun, her stomach churning from too much wine on an empty stomach and the cloyingly sweet scent from the Stargazer lilies filling her nose.

My God, but the living room smelled like a mortuary.

Suddenly the tears were falling and Sarah faced the mantel so no one could see her cry. She couldn't bear it if someone approached her now, trying to comfort her. She didn't want to be comforted, not when she hadn't even truly begun to grieve. And how could she grieve with hundreds of people reaching for her, talking to her, trying to keep her from feeling whatever it was she was feeling?

But maybe funerals weren't for grieving. Maybe funerals were just a thing you did, a way you marked an occasion, passed time.

Maybe once she returned home to Tampa Bay, maybe once she was with Boone, she could let herself feel . . . let herself hurt . . . let herself need . . .

"There you are," Meg Roberts said, pushing through the crowd to reach Sarah's side, with another sister, Brianna, in tow. Sarah had three sisters and Meg was the oldest and married with three kids, while Sarah's fraternal twin sisters, Brianna and Kit, were both forty, single, and committed to their respective missionary work—Kit, teaching Catholic school in Oakland, and Brianna, working as an infectious disease nurse in Africa.

"Kit was looking for you earlier," Meg added, tugging gently at the severe neckline of her black dress and fanning herself. "She wanted you to know that she's taken your two and my Gabi to the park, thinking it would be good to get the younger kids away from the house for a while." Meg exhaled hard, cheeks flushed. "Is it hot in here, or is it just me?"

"It's hot in here," Brianna said. "Somebody needs to turn down the heat."

"Good to know it's not just me," Meg muttered, lifting a hand to wave at a couple across the room. "Can't remember their name. Friends of Mom. I think the woman used to work at St. Mary's—"

"Lorraine O'Neill, and her husband, Charlie," Brianna said, glancing over her shoulder. "I've already spent a half hour talking to them today. Lorraine is taking Mom's death really hard, and she's quite emotional. If she nabs you, you'll end up comforting her."

"Don't want to do that," Sarah said. "Don't want to do any of this. When are people going to go?"

"Soon, I hope," Meg said. "I've got a terrible headache."

"I do, too. I think it's the flowers." Sarah slid her empty glass onto the mantel, where it clinked against a vase, and then against a metal frame. All week Aunt Linda had been gathering pictures of Mom, turning the living room into a shrine. Mom, the swaddled newborn. Mom, the wary toddler on a red tricycle, and then again as the serious, knobby-kneed five-year-old in her plaid uniform on the first day of kindergarten.

And then there was Mom, in her stiff white dress and veil in the all-important First Communion photo, and again at the beach house in Capitola at thirteen with her three brothers, and later as the high school graduate in her velvet shrug, with dark red lips and high arched brows.

Sarah reached out to touch her favorite, the photo of Mom as a slender, stunning, twenty-year-old bride just about to walk down the aisle, with the sun shining around her from the stained-glass windows behind her, silhouetting her, making her look like an angel.

"I love this one," she said, adjusting the eight-by-ten frame. It was the picture Dad kept on his nightstand, the one Sarah used to stare at as a little girl, dazzled by the beauty of her dark-haired, dark-eyed mother in her beautiful white dress.

"I do, too," Meg said, her voice cracking. Impatiently she reached up to wipe her eyes. "This has to stop. I can't cry anymore today. I've had it with tears."

"Me, too." Sarah glanced toward the crowded room and beyond to the hall. "It's been a long day. I had no idea the reception would last this long."

"Poor Dad. He's been surrounded all day. How does he do it?" Brianna asked.

"Must be his training, all those years as a fireman, keeps him focused." Meg's brow furrowed. "But what about later tonight? When everyone's gone? I think it's going to be hard then."

"But I'll be here tonight," Brianna said. "And Tommy and Cass. They're staying over, too."

Meg nodded. "That's good. Makes me feel better."

But Sarah shot Brianna a cool look. She was glad Bree was staying with Dad for the next few days, but she wasn't happy with her. Wasn't sure when she'd stop being angry with Brianna for her power play when Mom was dying.

"What?" Brianna demanded, eyebrows arching as she noted Sarah's expression.

Sarah shrugged, refusing to engage, and turned to Meg. "Can Kit manage three young kids on her own?"

Brianna groaned. "Kit's a teacher, Sarah."

Sarah ignored this, too.

Meg seemed oblivious to the tension between her younger sisters. "Kit's not alone. She has Jude with her."

"I don't find that in the least bit reassuring," Sarah answered. She didn't like Kit's new boyfriend, biker Jude Knight. Jude claimed he'd hung out with Sarah and a friend of Sarah's years ago, but Sarah didn't remember him and couldn't imagine ever hanging out with someone like him. It wasn't just his tats and piercings that put her off; it was his whole I-don't-care-about-anyone vibe, and Sarah just couldn't understand how kind, compassionate, bookish Kit could be attracted to someone so completely opposite her in every way. "I don't trust him," she added. "And we know nothing about him—other than the fact that he works part-time as a mechanic at a garage in Oakland—and frankly, I don't think he should be around our kids until we do know more."

"Kit adores her nieces and nephews. She's not going to let anything happen to them," Meg said.

Sarah didn't have the same confidence, and her wine-fueled imagination was taking flight. "But what if he's a child molester? What if he tries something when Kit's not around?"

Meg glanced from Sarah to Brianna and back again. "I really doubt he's a child molester. Jack talked to him a few days ago and thought he was interesting."

"But interesting and safe aren't the same thing. And we want safe around the kids."

"Sarah's right," Brianna said quietly. "One shouldn't take chances. You really never know. But, on the positive side, I do think Kit is . . . sensitive . . . to that sort of thing."

"Okay. You've got me convinced. I'll go give her a call," Meg said, before slipping through the crowd to look for her phone.

Sarah watched Meg go, wishing she had taken Brianna with her instead of leaving Brianna here. Meg knew Sarah was upset with Brianna. Meg knew that they weren't talking—

Oh.

That's what was happening. Meg had just engineered this moment, leaving Brianna with Sarah, hoping that the two of them might finally talk. Sort things out. But Sarah felt far from conciliatory, and she turned away from Brianna, reaching for one of the little cards tucked in the nearest floral arrangement.

Tom, our thoughts and prayers are with you and the children. Love, the Deluceys

"Nice card?' Brianna asked.

Sarah eased the little card back into the equally tiny envelope. "Yes."

"Who was it from?"

Sarah tried to give her the envelope but Brianna wouldn't take it.

"How long is the silent treatment going to last?" Brianna asked, her naturally husky voice sharp with exasperation and mockery.

Sarah looked down her nose at her sister. Brianna might be older, but she was tiny, barely reaching Sarah's shoulder. "I have nothing to say to you, Bree."

"You're being such a drama queen."

"Go away. I'm sure there is someone in the house you can torment."

"This is stupid. You do know that, Sarah?"

"Of course it's stupid to you. You were the one who was there with Mom. And you were the one who got to say good-bye."

"Mom needed to go. She was in pain."

A thick knot filled Sarah's throat. She swallowed hard, but it just grew bigger. "Please just go away."

Brianna's delicate features tightened. "I wasn't trying to hurt you, Sarah. Wasn't trying to hurt any of you. I was just focused solely on Mom that night, wanting what was best for her—"

"Death?"

"She was *dying.*"

"And you hurried it along."

"*What?*" Brianna's voice spiked, echoing too loudly in the period living room, momentarily silencing all other conversation.

Sarah saw the Martins, Hughes, and Keegans—all friends of her parents—glance at her and Brianna before quickly looking away.

Brianna leaned toward Sarah and dropped her voice. "You make me sound like Dr. Kevorkian!"

"If the shoe fits . . . ?"

"All I did was hold her hand, and tell her how much she was loved—"

"And what a good job she'd done, a *great* job, but she'd fulfilled her responsibilities, and now she was free to go." Sarah blinked, clearing her vision, furious, so furious. "And she did."

"She *needed* to go. She was hurting."

"I get that. But you should have called us. You should have given us a chance to say good-bye, too." Her voice broke. "At the very least, you should have called Dad. You owed it to Dad . . . to all of us."

Brianna jerked her chin up. "She couldn't have gone, not with us all around the bed, hanging on to her for dear life."

"You don't know that. We will never know that—"

"Get over yourself!"

"Myself? *Myself?*" Sarah clapped a hand to her forehead and laughed. "You're the one who lives on the other side of the world, only flying in for the big moments, and then only on Mom and Dad's dime—"

"I have never taken their money," Brianna snapped, folding bony arms across her thin chest. She'd returned from Africa two weeks ago emaciated, her slender frame downright skeletal. Everyone had been alarmed, and no one more so than Mom. There had been endless discussion about Bree's health, behind Bree's back: Did she have cancer? Was she dying? What had happened to her in the Congo?—even as Brianna insisted she was fine. "Nor have I ever asked for financial support, not even to go to college, unlike you, who had them pay for your undergraduate education, as well as law school."

"I didn't go, but they'd hoped I'd go, and they wanted to do it for me. They were proud of me—"

"Let's just hope you don't ever need a real job—"

"I *have* a job, Bree. I'm a wife and a mother—" She broke off, silenced by the pressure of her brother's hand bearing down on her shoulder.

"What's the matter with you two?" he demanded curtly, his broad shoulders rigid inside his black suit jacket. "Everyone can hear you. Dad can hear you. I bet even Mom can hear you."

Brianna managed a tight-lipped apology and walked away, leaving Tommy with Sarah.

He glanced toward Brianna, who was rounding the living room corner to disappear into the entry hall, and watched her a moment before turning to Sarah. "What's going on? You and Bree are usually thick as thieves."

"Not anymore."

He frowned. "Have you been drinking?"

She flushed. Was it that obvious? So annoying. "I just had a glass. But I need to eat. Haven't eaten today."

"Then don't drink anymore."

"I'm not."

"Good." He glowered down at her, his expression bemused. "So when did Bree stop being your favorite sister?"

Sarah groaned inwardly, wanting Advil. Three of them and a huge glass of water might help the pounding in her head. "I hope you don't say that sort of thing in front of Meg or Kit. It'd hurt their feelings."

"No, it wouldn't. They know it's true."

"Even if it *used* to be true, it's still not something you should say in front of them." She ran a trembling hand down her hip, lightly smoothing the black velvet fabric. She'd found the dress with the burnout design and three-quarter sleeves on Amazon. It'd looked comfortable and was affordable, which was good, because Sarah didn't intend to ever wear it again.

"I think I know why you're fighting. Cass told me. And I can't believe it's true. Hope it's not true that you're blaming Brianna for Mom dying when you weren't there."

"First of all, it's none of your business, and secondly, I'm not blaming Brianna for Mom's death. I'm just really pissed off that Brianna wouldn't call any of us when she saw that Mom was getting ready to go. She could have called us. We were just minutes away—"

"So you *are* blaming Bree."

"I just don't think it's fair that Brianna was the only one who got to say good-bye—"

"But life isn't fair! You of all people have to know that by now."

She stiffened, shoulders drawing back as she pressed her fingers against her throbbing temple. "What do you mean, me of all people?"

"Being married to Boone. His career as a major league baseball player. The whole professional sports world." He gave her a puzzled look. "What do you think I meant?"

"I don't know." She rubbed at her brow, starting to feel sick. "I don't feel so good."

Tommy's gaze rested on her face. "You need to eat."

"I do."

"Do you want me to get you something?"

"No, I'll find something."

"Most of the food has been put away, with just desserts now in the dining room. But you don't need a cookie. You need a sandwich, or some lasagna, something—"

"I know what I need," she said, gagging at the idea of eating lasagna. That would make her throw up. But maybe a sandwich, or a toasted bagel. Something light, something to cut the acid from all that wine on an empty stomach.

Entering the kitchen, Sarah found Meg's husband, Jack Roberts, at the old farmhouse-style sink, elbow-deep in hot sudsy water.

"Hey, look at you," Sarah said, surprised to see him alone. "Where is everyone? Who is helping you? You shouldn't be in here by yourself."

"I'm fine. I don't need help," he answered, rinsing the pan he'd just washed and placing it on the counter to his left, where it joined a dozen other Pyrex dishes, ceramic casseroles, and wooden salad bowls. "If you're looking for something to drink, I think there's an unopened bottle of wine in the fridge—"

"I'm good," she said, cutting him off, embarrassed. Make that horrified. Did everyone associate her with wine these days? "Actually I wanted something to eat. But let me give you a hand first—"

"Don't. Honestly. I'm good, Sarah. I really don't want help. I like doing this, makes me feel"—he broke off, his expression suddenly wistful—"better. I need to do something. For your mom. Your family."

Sarah went to her brother-in-law and gave him a swift hug. He endured it with good grace. Jack wasn't particularly touchy-feely. According to Meg, his family hadn't been very affectionate. "I appreciate you," she said, giving him another quick squeeze before going to the refrigerator to see what she could find.

The refrigerator was packed. Plastic containers of every size and shape filled every shelf. So that's where the leftovers from all those casseroles and salads and pasta dishes had gone. Dad would have food for days. "Can you recommend anything?" she asked Jack, wondering what would be good.

"The chicken Caesar salad and the lasagna. But I think the lasagna is gone now."

"Tommy was pushing the lasagna."

"I'm not surprised. He was the one who ate it all."

"I think I'll just do toast," Sarah said, closing the fridge door and opening the breadbox. She popped a slice of cinnamon bread into the toaster and reached for the kettle on the stove. "Want a cup of tea?"

"Actually, I'd love one," Jack answered, taking the kettle from her and filling it.

Once the kettle was back on the stove, Sarah went in search of tea bags and told Jack his options. "Green, black, chamomile, mint, peach mango, orange something?"

"How about orange something?"

"You got it," she said, flashing him a crooked smile. She liked Jack, always had. He was smart, funny, with a dry sense of humor. So different from Boone. Boone was Southern, born and raised in New Orleans's fabled Garden District; he oozed warmth, charm, and oh, how women loved that warmth and charm . . .

"Am I really just supposed to stand here and watch you?" she asked, once the mugs were filled with steaming water and she'd set his at his elbow.

"No. You're supposed to sit and watch. Your feet have to be killing you in those shoes. Four inches. Ridiculous."

She glanced at her feet as she pulled out the counter stool. "I always wear heels."

"Why?"

"They make me feel pretty."

"You *are* pretty. So stop crippling your feet."

Sarah blew on her tea. "I'll keep that in mind next time I have a date night with Boone."

"I can't believe Boone cares about what shoes you wear," Jack said, glancing at her over his shoulder.

"He doesn't. I just want to look hot for him. Remind him that he's already got his number one fan, and she's right at home waiting for him."

Jack frowned and seemed as if he was going to say something before shaking his head. He rinsed off a platter and then a wooden salad bowl, and placed both on the counter. "So how is Boone?"

Her heart ached a little. "Good." It killed her that Boone had to leave right after the service at the cemetery. She'd wanted him here for the reception at the house. She'd needed him here. But he'd already missed two days of games, so he jumped on a plane and was rushing back to Florida for the end of spring training.

"It's good he came for the services," Jack said quietly, as if he were able to read her mind.

Sarah swallowed around the lump in her throat. "I'm glad his manager let him come."

"Your dad was glad to see him."

She nodded. Dad loved Boone. But then, Boone was a man's man. Big, tough, uncomplaining. Dad always said Boone would have made a great fireman.

"I just wish he could have stayed for the whole day and gone home tomorrow or with us on Sunday. It's so much easier flying when Boone's along. He's so patient with the kids and he can manage all the bags—" She broke off, hating that she was beginning to sound pathetic. She had a great life, a great husband, great kids—so much to be thankful for—but she did wish she had more time with Boone. It was the one thing she couldn't seem to get enough of, with him always packing and unpacking, his suitcase a constant on the bench at the foot of their bed.

But it wouldn't be long before he retired. He'd be thirty-nine soon, in just a couple of weeks, and that was ancient in baseball. Grandpa, the rookies called him. The rookies weren't far off. There weren't many players Boone's age in the majors who could still hit the ball like Boone. But then, Boone was special. He always had been.

"Heard he had a great spring training," Jack said.

She nodded, relaxing a little. "It was a great spring training."

"JJ said Boone had three home runs last week."

"He hasn't hit this well in a long time," she said, wanting to be excited about the new season but dreading it, too. There was always so much to worry about. Team politics, trades, injuries, Boone's performance at the plate, the fickle fans, the groupies.

Sarah shuddered and stopped herself there, not wanting to think about the girls or groupies tonight. They were part of baseball—a fact of life—but they didn't have to bring her down tonight. It'd been such a hard week . . . a hard year . . .

"How's your dad holding up?" Jack asked, glancing at her as

he rinsed a massive Pyrex bowl that had been filled with potato salad.

"Okay. I think he's reverted to his firefighter role—focus and get through it."

"I've been amazed at his composure."

"So have we," she said, remembering the noon funeral Mass at St. Cecilia, and the graveside service after. The church had been packed, and almost everyone followed over to the cemetery. Dad had been quiet and attentive during both services. It wasn't until the end of the graveside service, when the casket was lowered, that he went down on one knee, bent his head, and cried.

Those who'd remained left for the house then, everybody moving on to the reception, except for Boone and Tommy Jr., who stayed behind with Dad. Eventually they'd accompanied him back to the house for the reception, and then Sarah had just enough time to give Boone a quick hug and kiss before he jumped in a cab and took off for the airport.

Jack reached for a damp dish towel and dried his hands one final time before crossing the floor to toss the wet towel into a white plastic basket in the laundry room next door. "I think that's it," he said.

"You deserve a medal of valor," Sarah said, sliding off the stool and stretching.

"I'm a hero?" he teased.

"You are," she answered. "Absolutely. You've been there for Meg, and that's what counts."

"I don't know about that."

"I do. Meg told me how amazing you've been. You've canceled your trips to D.C., and you've been managing the house and kids so Meg could be with Mom as much as possible. That's pretty cool."

He shrugged uneasily. "I cared about your mom. And I care about Meg. It's the least I can do."

Sarah frowned, thrown by the way he said "I care about Meg." It didn't sound right. Shouldn't he have said, "I love Meg"? "You and Meg okay?"

He hesitated. "What do you mean? As a couple?"

She nodded.

His shoulders twisted. "I don't know. Things are what they are."

That definitely did not sound good. "Still rocky?"

He made a face as he shrugged again. "We have our ups and downs. Sometimes it feels like more downs than ups."

"But you haven't thrown in the towel yet," she said, trying to be encouraging.

"Not yet."

"That's good."

"Is it?"

Sarah heard the weariness in his voice and her chest tightened. "I think so," she answered, knowing that she and Boone had been through a difficult couple of years, but she couldn't imagine life without him. He was as important to her as oxygen—not that her sisters thought she should love any man that much. "Boone always says—" She broke off as Kit entered the kitchen carrying Ella, who was crying inconsolably.

"There's your mommy," Kit crooned, kissing Ella's wet, flushed cheek. "I told you we'd find her. Your mommy didn't go anywhere. No need to cry. She's right here talking to Uncle Jack."

"Come here, baby," Sarah said, taking her daughter from Kit. "What's wrong? Why such a sad face?"

"I want Daddy," Ella wailed. "I want my house. I want to go home. And I hate Brennan. He's so mean."

Checking her smile, Sarah cuddled her five-year-old. "What did Brennan do this time, sweet pea?"

"He said he was going to bury me like Grandma—"

"He's not!" Sarah interrupted, looking at Kit over her daughter's head. "That's a terrible thing for him to say."

"I told him the same thing," Kit said with mock sternness, her blue eyes warm. "He's with Dad, having a time-out in the dining room right now."

"I don't want to get buried!" Great crocodile tears rolled down Ella's face. "I don't want to be covered up with dirt. Why did they cover Grandma with dirt?"

"Because Grandma died," Sarah said gently.

"And so she went to heaven to be with God and Jesus and Mary and all the saints and angels," Meg added, entering the kitchen and leaning against the doorframe.

"Is Grandma with angels now?" Ella asked, looking into her mother's eyes.

Sarah nodded. "Yes, and they're going to keep Grandma company and make sure she won't be lonely."

Ella reached up to touch Sarah's face, her small hand gentle on her mother's cheek. "Can we go see her?"

"Someday." Sarah kissed Ella. "But not now, because Daddy would miss us, and Grandpa needs us. Maybe we should go see Grandpa now?"

"And then we can go home?"

"Not to our house. But maybe to Aunt Meg and Uncle Jack's. We're staying with Aunt Meg and Uncle Jack for a few nights, remember?"

"Without Daddy?"

"Daddy had to go back to Tampa, but we'll see him in a few days."

"I want to go home now."

"I think you're tired, sweetheart. I know I'm tired. It's been a really long day." Sarah glanced at Meg, and then Jack. "Do you think we could leave soon?"

Meg glanced at Jack, and he nodded.

"I'll round up the kids," Meg said. "Let Dad know we're leaving."

"Great." Sarah kissed Ella's cheek, snuggling her closer, needing her sweet girl's warmth tonight. "I'll get Brennan and we'll say our good-byes."

Two

An hour and a half later, Sarah was in her pajamas in bed in the guest room on the second floor of Meg and Jack's big shingled house in Santa Rosa. Ella slept next to her, and eight-year-old Brennan was on the floor in his sleeping bag, wearing headphones and watching a movie on his laptop.

"Need anything?" Meg asked, hovering in the doorway. "Water, tea, something to eat?"

Sarah shook her head and pushed heavy honey-blond hair from her face, wishing she'd pulled it back in a loose ponytail for bed. "I'm good, Meg."

"You're sure? I can go make you something—"

"I'm fine. Really. Don't worry so much."

Meg's shoulders lifted and fell. "I just want you comfortable."

"And I am." Sarah glanced down at Ella where she slept curled on her side, facing Sarah, her thumb popped into her mouth. Ella only did that when she was stressed and it made Sarah's chest ache. "What a strange, long day."

"And a strange, long year," Meg agreed, her voice husky. "This time last year we thought everything was wonderful. Mom was healthy. We were all good, and then just weeks later at our Girls' Getaway, we found out the cancer was back and there was nothing to be done." Suddenly she crossed the room, adjusted the heavy pale green velvet drapes, which had been drawn for the night, making sure there was no crack between fabric panels. "It was brutal . . . all those months waiting for Mom to die."

"Praying for a miracle," Sarah added.

"She deserved one," Meg said, exhaling hard as she crossed her arms over her chest.

Sarah reached out to her. "Come, sit," she insisted, waiting for Meg to take her hand and then take a seat on the edge of the bed next to her. "You okay?"

Meg blinked away tears. "No. You?"

Sarah's throat and eyes burned as she shook her head. "No. Miss her, Meg. Miss her so much already—" She broke off, sucked in air, tears trembling on her lashes.

"She was my best friend. She gave the best advice. And even though I live on the other side of the country, she still managed to be part of everything. Calling, sending cards, little texts, and her Facebook messages . . . those updates . . . hilarious." Sarah wiped away tears, trying to smile through her tears and failing. "What are we going to do without her?"

Meg's lower lip quivered. "Try to make her proud."

"Yeah." Sarah was quiet a moment, thinking about her mom, her sisters, the whole family. "What do you think Dad's doing right now?"

"Probably watching TV with Tommy," Meg said.

Sarah nodded. It's how she pictured him right now, too. Dad was a simple man. He liked his routine. "I wonder how he feels . . . not having had a chance to say a last good-bye."

Meg shot Sarah a swift glance. "It was probably hard for him, not being there at the very end, but I don't think he blames Brianna."

Unlike me, Sarah thought fiercely, meeting Meg's gaze. "Yes, I am upset with Brianna. Yes, I feel cheated. I needed that final good-bye. I wanted to be there at the end with Mom, too."

"But maybe Brianna was right," Meg said carefully. "Maybe Mom couldn't let go when we were all there. Maybe it was too hard for her to leave us, when we were around the bed, hanging on to her for dear life."

"Of course we were hanging on to her for dear life. We loved her." Sarah drew her knees up to her chest, defensive, even as the ache filled her chest, heavy, suffocating. "I just can't believe she'd want to . . . go . . . without me there." There was a defiant note in her voice but she didn't care. "I thought I'd be the one, holding her hand, at the end." *Not Bree.*

"We'll never know why Mom chose to let go then, but she had to have a reason. You know Mom never did anything by chance."

Suddenly Sarah didn't want to do this anymore, talk about Mom anymore, talk about death and dying and letting go. She'd spent so much of her life letting go, saying good-bye, leaving friends, starting over in new cities with new teams. Since she'd married Boone he'd been traded five times, which meant five huge moves. But even when they were settled with one team, she wasn't. Because Boone wasn't settled. He was constantly traveling and training and nursing a real, or perceived, injury. And when he was home, she fluttered around him, alternately thrilled and resentful. And when he was gone, she was constantly trying to stay busy, trying to kill time, trying to feel stable and content even though in her heart, she was lonely and empty and just getting emptier . . .

"It doesn't matter," Sarah said roughly, collecting her long hair and drawing it over her shoulder. "It's not as if we can bring her back. All we can do is move forward."

Meg reached out to cup Sarah's cheek. "You were always

Mom's baby. She absolutely adored you, Sarah. You know that, don't you?"

Uncomfortable, Sarah pulled back, leaning away from Meg's touch, but not before she saw the flicker of hurt in Meg's eyes. "Sorry, Mags," she mumbled. "Just . . . overwhelmed."

"I understand," Meg said, rising, smiling, and yet the shadow remained in her eyes.

Sarah's chest squeezed tight. "You're a great big sister, you know that, don't you?"

Meg was silent a moment. "I've tried. But I don't think I've always succeeded. Like last year when I—"

"That's the past."

Meg's brow creased. "Is it?"

Sarah nodded, definitely not wanting to go there either, since the whole affair thing was still a sensitive topic for everyone. "Jack was really helpful tonight. He did all the dishes at Mom and Dad's . . . mountains of dishes."

"I saw."

"You don't think it's good?"

"It's great. And it's what you or I or any of us would do at a family member's funeral."

"What's wrong?"

Meg shook her head. "Nothing. Just tired. I should probably go check on the kids and go to bed."

As if on cue, Sarah's phone vibrated on the nightstand. "Boone," she said, reaching for her phone, reading his one-word text. *Here.*

"He's landed," she added, glancing up at Meg, feeling as though an immense weight had tumbled from her shoulders.

"That's good. I know you never relax when he's in the air."

"It's silly. I know nothing's going to happen," Sarah answered, quickly texting Boone back. *Yay! Glad you're on the ground. Call me when you can.*

Meg smiled indulgently as she watched Sarah text her husband. "You know air travel is so safe these days. There hasn't been a big accident in the U.S. in years—"

"Don't say that. You'll jinx him for sure that way."

"Come on, you're not superstitious."

Sarah looked up, eyes wide. "Of course I am!"

"Since when?"

"Meg, I'm married to a professional baseball player. Ball players are incredibly superstitious—"

"But that doesn't mean you have to be."

Sarah's phone rang. "Boone," she said, grinning.

Meg rolled her eyes. "Take the call. I'm heading to bed. See you in the morning."

Sarah blew her a kiss. "Sleep good. And thanks, Meg. For everything."

In the hall, Meg quietly closed the guest-room door so Sarah could have some privacy and headed toward her girls' rooms. Tessa and Gabi were both already asleep, but sixteen-year-old JJ was at his desk, Skyping with his girlfriend, Heather. When he spotted his mother in the doorway, he tersely signaled for her to leave.

"Simply saying good night," she said mildly. "Just making sure you're okay . . . with the funeral and all."

JJ's glare suddenly softened and he said something to Heather before hitting the disconnect on the computer. Springing from his chair, he went to his mom and wrapped his arms around her in a quick, guilty hug. "Sorry. And I'm sorry about Grandma," he muttered. "Sorry for you, too. It must be awful losing your mom. I would hate to lose you."

Meg, who'd kept it together for much of the day, blinked to clear the hot, stinging sensation from her eyes. "Well, I have no intention of going anywhere, and Grandma was a really good mom."

"I loved Grandma."

"I know. And she loved you."

JJ pulled away and folded his arms across his chest. He'd grown five inches in the past six months and had filled out through the chest and shoulders, showing an early hint of the Brennan brawn. Not that he was a Brennan, but he had her brother's and father's athletic ability and he hoped to make it to the pros, like Sarah's husband. "Why did she have to die?" he demanded.

Meg shrugged. "Something about God's plan."

"Don't get mad at my language, but I think it's a fucked-up plan."

"Can't disagree, babe, but let's not use foul language."

"But it is. She suffered so much—" He broke off, took a step away, and rubbed at his watering eyes. "So not right."

"No."

"Grandpa's going to really miss her, won't he?"

Meg swallowed around the lump filling her throat. It'd been such a long, hard couple of months, but hopefully Mom was in a better place. Or at least, a place without pain. "Yeah. They've been together a long time."

"And they were happy, weren't they? They always seemed to be in a good mood when they were together. Always laughing and joking around."

She nearly reached out to touch his jaw with the straggly chin stubble, his facial hair still light and thin, but crossed her arms instead, not wanting to invade his space. She'd learned that it was better to let him come to her, to reach for her, otherwise she could end up rejected. "They definitely enjoyed each other."

"Did they ever fight?"

"They had their moments. Grandpa isn't always easy to live with and Grandma was never a pushover, but they were committed to each other, and very committed to the family. It's why their marriage worked."

"They were best friends, weren't they?"

"Yes."

JJ's forehead creased and he stared across the room, to his desktop computer. "Were you and Dad ever like that? . . . Best friends?"

Meg's mouth opened, then closed. It took her a second to think back, to the early days of her marriage, and her first thought was how new and exciting it had all been, that big move with Jack to California, her state, which then made her reflect on how different it'd been for him and how uncomfortable he was with her large family. From the start he'd been overwhelmed by her tight-knit Brennan family and resisted their many traditions—family summers and holidays in Capitola at the beach house, big gatherings for Thanksgiving, Christmas, and Easter, winter ski trips to Tahoe, brunches every Sunday, Saturday barbecues, baptisms, and ball games, never mind casual family dinners.

No, Jack hadn't enjoyed her family holidays and traditions. He'd never come out and said so, but she'd suspected that he found them a little too loud, a little too blue collar, a little Catholic. The Roberts family, which could trace its ancestors to the *Mayflower,* had been educated, affluent, and aloof, as well as fractured by a highly contentious divorce and custody battle that lasted for years, scarring Jack permanently.

Meg had loved Jack anyway, adoring his brilliant mind and his talent for sensitive architectural preservation and design. She'd learned that he needed his space, and he was most creative when left to himself, and so she gave him his space and told herself that the space was good for her, too. She was, and always had been, very independent. She didn't need a lot of attention. Mary Margaret Brennan Roberts excelled at self-sufficiency.

"Your dad is still my best friend," she said now to JJ, which stood for "Jack Jr." "He's amazing. There aren't many people as smart as he is."

"I thought Aunt Kit was your best friend."

Megs suddenly felt the weight of the last week settle in her gut and burn in her chest. There were few people as loving and supportive as her sister Kit. "We are really close."

"So she is your best friend?"

"Can't a girl have two best friends?"

"I guess."

Needing to escape, she kissed JJ's cheek. "I'm going to bed. Don't stay up too late, okay?"

"I won't. I can't. I've got the last SAT study session and still have to take a pre-test in the morning."

"You mean, after Mass."

"I'm taking the test in the morning."

"JJ, it's Palm Sunday tomorrow."

"So?"

"It's a holy day."

"Went to church today, don't want to go tomorrow, and technically it's not a holy day, but the start to the Holy Week."

Meg stared at him for a long moment, flattened. She was too tired to do this. Too tired to do anything but go to bed. Sleep. "Fine. Stay home, and take the test. You just better ace the SAT."

He grinned a lopsided grin. "I'll do my best."

"Night, JJ."

"Night, Mom."

In her bedroom, Meg discovered that the lights had been dimmed and Jack was already in bed, on his side, his back to her.

She gently closed the door, retreating to the master bath to wash her face and brush her teeth. She performed her nightly routine swiftly without looking at herself. She was too tired to look at herself, not interested in seeing her face, not wanting to see her fatigue, or her sadness.

Impossible to believe Mom was gone. Mom couldn't be gone. There was still so much life ahead. Still so much time. Baseball games and ballet recitals and high school graduation and weddings . . .

Her girls would one day walk down the aisle and her mom

wouldn't be there to see it. Her mom wouldn't be there for any of it.

Meg cried, bent over the bathroom sink, splashing water on her face. Tired. She was just so tired. And sad. But that was natural. This was all natural. Part of life. Birth and death and change. She didn't have to like it, just accept it. And adapt.

In bed, she quietly slid into her spot, carefully fluffing and adjusting her pillows as she eased under the duvet. The sheets were cool and smooth, the softest, lightest cotton. Her favorite indulgence. She didn't care about expensive clothes or jewelry or cars, but she loved quality sheets. Good sheets made a great bed.

"You were gone awhile," Jack said, breaking the silence. His voice was clear, firm. He hadn't been asleep.

"Talked a long time to Sarah, then to JJ," Meg answered, rolling over to look at him. His eyes were open, his gaze fixed on her.

"Everything okay?"

"Sarah's a wreck, and JJ just wanted to talk."

"What did he have to say?"

Meg hesitated, studying Jack's strong, patrician features and unsmiling mouth. He didn't smile much anymore, and suddenly she wondered if he ever had. "He talked about Grandma and Grandpa, and how much Grandpa would miss Grandma. He said they were best friends. I agreed. And then he asked . . ." Her voice trailed off as she struggled to voice JJ's question. "He asked . . . if we had ever been like that. Best friends. And I told him yes."

Jack didn't say anything. His expression didn't change. But Meg felt that acidic knot return to her stomach, the one that seemed to live there all the time, making her reach for Tums and Rolaids several times a day.

"What?" she prompted, trying to see into Jack's brown eyes, trying to read what he was thinking.

"A long time ago," he said finally.

She pressed the pillow closer to her cheek. Her face felt so hot, and yet on the inside she felt so cold. "Not that long ago."

"Seems like forever."

"We've had a hard year."

"It wasn't good before that."

He was referring to her affair. Her affair, her fault, her responsibility. And it was no one's fault but hers. She'd be doing penance forever, not because anyone asked it of her, but because she owed it. She'd messed up, badly; and nine months later, she still found it impossible to forgive herself. Maybe one day she could. Maybe when she and Jack were good again, solid again. She looked forward to the day. Prayed for the day. It was hard living with so much self-hatred. "It'll get better."

"I'm not happy."

Meg exhaled slowly. "I'm sorry."

"Are we working?" he asked.

"I'm not unhappy."

"But are you happy?"

Her eyes stung and the acid from her stomach seemed to be bubbling up her esophagus and into her throat. "This is a kind of tough time to be talking about happiness. Mom's just died. The funeral was this morning. We had two hundred and fifty people over to the house—"

"But that's the point. We're all going to die. Death is inevitable. In fact, some would say we're dying every day."

"I disagree. As long as you're alive, you're alive. When you're dead, you're gone—"

"Unless you're not really alive. Unless you're just going through the motions." Jack's mouth flattened, and a small muscle pulled and popped in his jaw. "Like we are."

You mean, like you are, Meg silently corrected, closing her eyes, shoulders rising up toward her ears.

"This isn't working with us, Meg."

She didn't want to hear this, not now, not today. She was too sad. Things had been too hard. "We're tired, Jack, worn out—"

"I leave tomorrow for D.C., and I think we need to really think about the future and what we want. We're not getting any younger. We deserve to be happy. You deserve to be happy—"

"I'm not unhappy, Jack!" she cried, sitting up, knocking away a tear before it could fall. "I'm just tired. It's been a rough couple of weeks, and a very long day, and I will not lose you now, not after everything we've been through. We're good together. We have the kids. We have a history. We have a future."

"But maybe it's not the one I want," he answered quietly, his voice cutting through the dark room, and her heart.

Meg's lips parted but no sound came out. She balled her hands into fists and pressed them against her thighs. She wouldn't cry. She wouldn't. Things would work out. They always worked out. She just had to be strong. "Have faith, Jack! We *will* get through this."

"I don't think so."

"*Jack.*"

"I'm not trying to be mean, Meg. I'm just being honest."

Palm Sunday.

A beautiful Palm Sunday, too. Cloudless blue sky. No breeze. Seventy-two degrees. How could it be better than that?

Thirty-four-year-old Lauren Summers laughed softly, a low, rough laugh. Pure irony.

At least she'd made it here. That was something. It'd been months and months since she'd come. But today . . . today she'd made the drive to the Napa cemetery from Alameda. No traffic. Ninety minutes. *Easy.*

More irony.

God, she was funny. Full of gallows humor. And why not? If you couldn't laugh at yourself, what was left? Nothing. And nothing begets nothing . . . leaving one with . . . nothing.

Lauren ran her hands up and down and all around the steering wheel. Her stomach cramping, hurting, already wishing she hadn't agreed to meet her parents here today.

She should have just met them in town for brunch. Gone somewhere public, somewhere loud, somewhere with lots of distractions. She still needed the distractions.

The air caught in her throat. Her eyes burned.

She missed him. Missed him so much. People said it'd get easier. People said it was just a matter of time.

Squeezing the steering wheel tightly, Lauren clamped her jaw, teeth grinding. She wasn't going to lose it today. Wasn't going to cry.

Blake had hated it when she cried. She remembered how as a little boy he'd put his fingers into the corners of her mouth and lift her lips. *Smile, Mom.*

The lump in her throat grew, filling her chest. She swallowed, hard. She wouldn't crack. Today she was going to be strong. Today she was going to get out of her car, and walk across the expanse of grass to his grave and . . .

And then what?

Lauren frowned. What would she do once she reached his grave?

Her phone rang, breaking her concentration. Reaching for her phone, she saw it was her mom, Candy Summer. The family ranch was a fifteen-minute drive from the cemetery. Her parents were supposed to meet her here. They were all going to do this together. Visit Blake. Bring him flowers. Her mother had the flowers.

"How far away are you?" Candy asked.

"Still a little way out," Lauren answered, needing more time. This wasn't easy doing this . . . coming here. She hadn't wanted to come. Her parents asked. They liked to come see Blake, their grandson. They didn't understand that for her it was so much harder. Make that impossible.

He was just a boy.

How could she outlive her son?

"Did you hit traffic?" Candy asked, concerned.

Lauren closed her eyes and lifted her face to the sun beating through the glass. "No."

"But you left almost two hours ago."

She couldn't do this. Wasn't ready to do this. "I'm turning around." Her voice was low, tight. If she wasn't careful, she'd start crying. "I'm heading home."

"How far away are you?"

"I can't do this, Mom. I can't."

"But we made plans."

"You and Dad can still come. Bring the flowers—"

"Lauren."

"I love you, Mom. I'll call you later."

"At least come to the house. Come see us. Have lunch with us."

"I'm already on my way home. But I'll see you soon. Okay?"

Lauren hung up quickly. She dropped the phone into her lap. She stared blindly out the window. Blake.

And then from nowhere a voice whispered, *Love doesn't end.*

Tears prickled the back of her eyes. Lauren drew a slow, deep breath. *That's right, baby,* she whispered. *Love doesn't end. And I will love you forever.*

Lauren numbly started the car, eased into drive, and headed for home.

A half hour away in Santa Rosa, Jack and JJ remained at the house while Meg and Sarah took the younger kids to the Palm Sunday service.

Sarah secretly wished she had stayed behind, too. In Tampa, Sarah rarely went to Mass. Her kids didn't attend Catholic school either, or Sunday school, and as she watched Ella and Brennan during the service, she knew they didn't really understand what was going on. Over the summer her parents had talked to her about getting Ella and Brennan enrolled in her local parish programs, thinking that both children were of an age at which they'd benefit from Catholic education, but Sarah had been bored silly by her years of such schooling and wasn't in a hurry to sign the kids up.

Now, as they fussed and whispered and stared up at the ceiling, she felt guilty for not doing more.

Maybe it was time her children learned more about their faith. Or maybe she'd continue to wait until Boone retired and they moved somewhere, and were settled somewhere, for good.

After Mass, they returned to the house, where Meg made brunch and the girls helped Sarah set the dining room table.

During the meal, Gabi and Ella talked about Easter next week, and dyeing eggs, while Meg's son, JJ, said he was looking forward to Opening Day of baseball season on Thursday.

"How does Uncle Boone think Tampa Bay will do this year?" he asked, between enormous bites of a Belgium waffle dripping with strawberries and whipped cream.

"He's hopeful, as always," Sarah answered, reaching over to place a restraining hand on Brennan's arm to stop him from flicking any more bacon bits across the table at Tessa, who—judging from her annoyed expression—had had enough.

"What?" Brennan demanded, pushing Sarah's hand off his arm.

"Stop," she corrected him under her breath.

"Why?" he asked, preparing to launch another bacon bit from his spoon.

"It's not appropriate," she answered firmly, taking the spoon from him and tucking it onto the far side of her plate. "Boone had a great spring training—" She broke off as Brennan flung a strip of bacon with his fingers. *"Brennan!"*

"What?" he said innocently, smiling at her so broadly that his dimples flashed on either side of his wide mouth. Boone had the same dimples. Ella had inherited them, too.

"Knock it off," she whispered. "You know how to act at the dinner table."

"But this isn't the dinner table. It's breakfast."

Sarah's eyes widened, and before she could say anything, Meg suggested that the kids who had finished eating clear their plates and be excused.

All the kids but JJ left, carrying their dishes with them. JJ reached for another waffle and doused it with mounds of strawberries and cream.

"Starving," he said cheerfully, cutting the waffle into quarters and stuffing one into his mouth.

"Boys," Meg said indulgently, leaning back in her chair.

Sarah lifted her coffee, which had gone cold a long time ago. She wrinkled her nose as she drank it. "Exhausting," she said. "I don't remember JJ being this hyper at this age."

"JJ was busy," Meg said. "And so we learned to tire him out before he tired us out. By the time he was in first grade, he was playing five sports a year, and some of them overlapped."

"Not my call," Jack interjected. "I didn't think it was necessary to have JJ play so many sports, but Meg disagreed."

"I never made him," Meg corrected. "JJ loved anything to do with a ball. Football, basketball, baseball—he wanted to do it all."

"But it was up to us as parents to provide some guidance," Jack retorted.

Meg's brows tugged. "We did provide guidance. And we're still providing guidance—"

"Really? Because it doesn't feel like it. Seems to me we've allowed the kids to do whatever they want in life. The girls have had no exposure to art or culture—"

"That's not true," Meg interrupted. "Tessa dances. She eats, sleeps, and breathes art."

"Fine, but they don't play instruments." Jack shrugged. "And JJ doesn't do anything but play sports."

JJ stabbed his fork hard into another wedge of waffle. "You make that sound like a bad thing, Dad, but I like playing sports."

"You would have benefited more from music lessons. Would have helped make you a well-rounded person."

JJ shrugged as he chewed. "I'm happy the way I am," he said, around his food.

"I just want you to know that I'd do it differently next time," Jack said, looking at JJ, acting as if JJ was the only one in the room. "I wouldn't acquiesce to your mom so much. I'd make sure you learned the things I wanted you to learn, the things you needed to learn—"

"Next time?" Meg interrupted, eyebrows arching ever so slightly.

Incredibly uncomfortable, Sarah glanced from Meg to Jack, thinking now would be a good time for someone to make a joke, ease the tension.

"Our kids aren't academic," Jack added. "I would have liked to have one child who cared about art, literature, history, culture—"

"Hey, Dad," JJ said, swallowing his bite and waving his fork, "you know I'm still here, right? I can hear everything you're saying."

"I'm not blaming you, JJ. It's not your fault you don't know anything about the world but what you've learned off the Cartoon Network and ESPN, because we've allowed it to happen. I'm just as guilty as your mom. I should have stepped up earlier, insisted you learn something of the world, something that mattered."

JJ wiped his mouth with his napkin. "Sports matter, Dad. They're a metaphor for life. They symbolize man's struggle to survive and the need for people to believe in something and to belong to something. And yes, I did say 'metaphor' and 'symbolize.' I may like sports but I'm not an idiot. I'm taking three AP classes right now and getting A's in almost everything, so lay off.

Your bad mood is just bringing us all down." Then, with a nod at his mom, he stood up, lifted his plate, and carried it to the kitchen.

"Smart-ass," Jack muttered as JJ disappeared, before glancing at Meg. "Does he really have straight A's?"

"He has a B right now in physics, but the rest are A's," Meg said evenly, her expression serene.

"His grades weren't that good last year, were they?"

"It's his junior year. He's taking school seriously this year."

"It's about time."

Meg opened her mouth to answer, but closed it without speaking, shaping her lips into a small, pleasant smile.

Jack stared at her moodily a moment, fingers drumming the table, before abruptly rising and stalking out.

"Wow," Sarah said quietly once Jack was out of earshot. "That was . . . weird."

Meg's serene expression melted, leaving her features naked and sad. She swallowed and picked at a bit of frayed lace in the tablecloth. "It's . . . uh . . . yeah."

"What's going on?"

She shrugged. "This."

"For how long has it been going on?"

"Months."

"How do you stand it?"

Meg made a soft sound, her shoulders lifting, falling. "I love my kids. I love my family. I want to keep us together."

Sarah glanced toward the door, making sure everyone was gone. "Do you still love Jack?" she whispered, remembering Jack's words last night in the kitchen at her parents' house. "I care for Meg," he'd said. Not "I love Meg," and it'd been bothering her ever since. But this wasn't a conversation she'd want any of the kids to hear, particularly Meg and Jack's. JJ, Tessa, and Gabi had been through enough this past year.

Meg hesitated, thinking, then nodded. "I do."

"Romantically? Sexually?"

Now Meg squirmed. "He's the father of my children."

"But do you want him?"

"Yes." Meg frowned. "I mean . . . if he wants me. But I don't think he does. And I don't think he has. Not for a long time."

"Since your . . . affair?"

Meg stared off across the dining room, her brow knitted. "Since before. It's like he's lost his . . . drive. It's been gone awhile. Couple of years maybe."

"Do you think he's having a midlife crisis? Apparently men's hormones change around forty, too."

"My friend Farrell said the same thing. Her husband went out and got Botox and joined a gym and bought a new car at forty. She was convinced he was having an affair."

"Was he?"

"Not that she knew, and she hired a PI to follow him."

"She didn't!"

Meg nodded, smiled wistfully. "The PI found nothing. Apparently Jeremy just felt old, and he didn't like it."

Sarah studied her sister for a long moment, thinking it'd been months, maybe years, since she'd seen Meg really, truly happy. "Does Jack still love you?"

Meg fiddled with her knife, and then her teaspoon, and then touched the frayed thread in the tablecloth again. "I would hope so."

"That doesn't sound very confident."

Meg looked quickly at Sarah and then back down. "We have children. They deserve stability. I'm trying to focus on what they need."

"But the kids—"

"*I know*," Meg interrupted fiercely, staring Sarah in the eye, her expression almost defiant. "You're right. I should have remembered them before. I should have thought about the consequences then. But I didn't. I didn't." She swallowed, shrugged, her expression no longer defiant but regretful. "And they're paying the price.

We are all paying the price. But I can't give up, Sarah. Won't. I can fix this. Us. And I will."

"What if . . ." Sarah paused, struggling to voice what had been bothering her all night and morning.

"What, Sarah?"

"What if . . . Jack . . . doesn't want it fixed?"

Meg jerked upright. "Did he say something to you?"

Sarah flushed. "No. But I also know, from being on the . . . other side . . . of things, that it takes two to make a marriage work. You can't do it alone. You need him to meet you halfway."

Meg said nothing, her lips pressed tightly together, but Sarah felt her pain, and she reached across the table to cover Meg's hand.

"I'm not judging you, Meg," she said softly. "Maybe last year I did, but I was caught off guard. Shocked, and surprised that you of all people would cheat—" Sarah broke off as Meg winced. "Affairs are just so hard on a relationship. They shatter trust and make you question everything. Like your commitment to this other person. As well as your desire. Do you really want to be with him or her forever? Do you need to be?" Sarah shrugged. "I went through all of that with Boone after I found out about his affair. I'm still going through it. It'll be three years this summer, and I'm still struggling, but I'm also still with him, because I love him. I'm crazy about him." Her smile wavered. "Maybe too crazy."

Meg squeezed Sarah's fingers. "I love that you love him so much. It's the way it should be." She released Sarah's hand, leaned back in her chair. "Maybe if Jack and I had some of your passion, we wouldn't be in the situation we're in now."

Sarah drew a slow breath, counting to ten before asking, "Is Jack going to forgive you?"

Meg took an even longer time to answer. "Have you been able to forgive Boone?"

Sarah thought about it, then shrugged. "I've tried."

"And Jack's trying to forgive me, too." Meg hesitated. "But it may not happen. And if that's the case, then he may want something . . . someone . . . else."

"But you and Jack . . . you've been together forever. Since I was in high school."

"I know." Meg stood up and began stacking dishes on top of platters and adding cutlery to that. "And I can't imagine life without Jack in it."

Three

In her small one-bedroom apartment close to Alameda's historic downtown, Lauren pushed aside the frosted chocolate layer cake she'd just made and reached for the stainless-steel mixing bowl to start over.

Third time was a charm, she reminded herself, turning her back on the two abandoned cakes on the counter. She didn't feel sorry for them. They'd soon find a home. Her neighbors loved it when she baked, especially the college kids on the third floor. Those boys were always hungry.

With the mixing bowl clutched to her middle, Lauren studied her recipe on the counter, a recipe she'd been editing and marking up all afternoon. This was the chocolate cake that had always sold well in Napa at the bakery and café she'd started with her sister. But when she'd baked it last week for Mama's Café in Alameda, it'd disappointed her. It didn't matter that the cake had sold out by early afternoon. It'd tasted a little dry to her—and that could very well be due to the ovens at the café—but it'd also tasted bland. *Boring.*

True, it was her great-grandmother's chocolate cake recipe, which made it old and old-fashioned, but she'd made tweaks to the cake recipe over the years, improving it. Or so she'd thought until earlier in the week.

So here she was, spending what was left of her Sunday trying to make the perfect chocolate cake, and it'd been a good decision to bake. It occupied her hands. Kept her mind busy so she wouldn't think about Blake and her drive to the cemetery this morning.

She'd cried driving back from Napa, the loss feeling fresh again. Fresh, and shocking, and heartbreaking.

Coming back to her cramped little apartment made her just feel worse. She missed her life in Napa. Missed her family. Missed being a mom.

Unable to handle the pain, she marched into the kitchen and reached for the bowls and pans, swiftly lining up ingredients on the counter. Cake . . . a cake . . . strawberry or chiffon, spice with salted caramel frosting, chocolate or maybe banana . . .

Chocolate won.

So she cracked eggs and stirred and whisked and baked. *Don't think*, she'd tell herself when she rinsed the mixing bowl at the sink. *Don't think*, she'd repeat, sliding pans in and out of the oven. *Don't think*, she'd chant every time her thoughts turned inward, turned to home. *Don't think*, just bake.

Baking gave her a sense of purpose. Purpose was good. Purpose got her out of bed in the morning. Purpose would get her through the day.

Sarah spent part of the afternoon helping Meg tidy the house. She was in the middle of adding water to the four floral arrangements in the living room when a small card fell from the lavish purple and lavender arrangement. She was tucking the card back into the plastic holder when the message caught her eye.

To Meg & Family,

From all of us at Dark Horse Winery

Craig, Chad, Jennifer, and Victoria

So Chad knew Meg had lost her mother. Or someone at Dark Horse Winery knew.

Sarah felt the corners of the small, heavy card stock in a silvery cream. It wasn't your usual cheap florist enclosure, and somehow it felt weighty and thick. Sincere.

But perhaps she was reading too much into it. Perhaps Jennifer, the winery receptionist, or this new Victoria, had ordered the flowers and purchased the elegant card. Perhaps Chad had nothing to do with it.

But looking at the darkly lush arrangement in deep, passionate purples and delicate violet, Sarah felt emotion, as well as love and loss.

Someone cared for Meg. Someone cared enough to send something beautiful. Meaningful.

Someone like Chad.

Feeling ridiculously emotional as well as conflicted, Sarah grabbed a bottle of wood polish and a dustrag from the mud room and tackled the dining room furniture, dusting and polishing everything made with wood. She needed the work to occupy her hands and distract her thoughts from Meg's affair with Chad.

Sarah didn't like Chad Hallahan. Didn't respect him. Couldn't respect a man who'd make a move on a married woman, threatening her marriage and family. Marriage was sacred. Families were to be protected.

But as she rubbed and polished the dining room buffet with the enormous arrangement of orchids, hydrangeas, calla lilies, and sweet peas, she tried to picture Meg smiling, laughing, but couldn't. It'd been a long time since Meg had been happy.

Sarah couldn't even imagine her as light, or joyous, never mind bubbly.

What had Chad seen in her? What had they been like together? Had Chad been able to make her laugh? Was Meg happy when with him? Had he made her feel good? Girlish? Beautiful?

Sarah snapped the dustcloth in frustration. She didn't even know why she was thinking these things. Meg was married. Married to Jack. Chad didn't factor into the equation. He didn't.

And yet . . .

Jack didn't seem to want to be with Meg, not now, or in the future. And if that was the case, if it was true that he'd soon be out of the picture, then Sarah wanted Meg happy. She wanted to see Meg smile, and hear her laugh, and know that someone loved her deeply. That there was a man who wanted her, and would protect her, and stick with her through thick and thin.

But even more importantly, she wanted Meg to feel the same love and desire. She wanted Meg to run to her man the same way she herself still ran to Boone.

Heart heavy, thoughts tangled, Sarah moved into the living room and tackled the end tables before going to the piano with its half-dozen framed photos. Family shots, individual portraits, and a picture of Mom that immediately caught her attention.

It was Mom the night of her fortieth birthday, and she was smiling up at the camera, glowing in her bronze metallic gown, her dark, glossy hair tumbling over one shoulder. She was smiling with her mouth and her eyes and the photograph radiated joy. Joy and love. *My God, how Mom loved Dad. And life.* She knew how to live. She'd known what mattered. Faith, family, friends, community.

Hearing footsteps behind her, Sarah blinked hard and turned toward Meg with a shaky smile. "I love this one of Mom," she said.

But it wasn't Meg in the hall, it was Jack in shorts and a T-shirt, flushed, sweaty, tan following his run.

"I like that one of Marilyn, too," he answered, mopping his brow. "Meg said it was taken the night of her fortieth birthday."

Sarah nodded and put the photo back on the piano, surprised to see Jack in running shoes, looking fit and trim. She'd thought of him as academic, unathletic, but there was nothing soft about him today. "I didn't know you ran."

"Started to in D.C. Needed something to do when I wasn't working." With his hands on his hips, he surveyed the elegant living room with its high ceiling and thick white molding. "We never use this room. Such a waste of space."

"I think it's pretty."

"But nonfunctional. I have a problem with that." He reached up to catch a bead of perspiration on his temple. "I'm sure I reek. I better go shower and then pack."

"When do you leave?"

"Tonight. I'm on the red-eye."

Sarah watched him climb the stairs two at a time, whistling as he went. Strange to see this lean, tan Jack practically bounding up the stairs. He had so much energy. He looked downright boyish, which was such a contrast to Meg, who'd put on ten to fifteen pounds in the past six months, weight she didn't need.

Meg entered the living room, her low heels clicking on the hardwood floor, her dark hair pulled back in a haphazard ponytail. "Did I hear Jack?"

"He's showering," Sarah said, increasingly concerned about her oldest sister. Meg wasn't a classic beauty, but she'd learned to cultivate an elegance and sophistication that made her beautiful, but that elegance and beauty wasn't in evidence today. "He'd apparently gone for a run."

"Good. He should be in a better mood now." Meg tucked a strand of hair behind her ear as she entered the living room to take the bottle of furniture polish and dustcloth from Sarah. "Let's get out of the house. Go do something fun with the kids."

"What do you want to do?"

"Whatever your kids would enjoy. It's your last day here. Let's make it fun."

"They like everything. We could go to a park . . . a movie—"

"How about a movie? I need to relax. Escape."

"I'll check Fandango and see what's playing."

Twenty minutes later, Meg, Sarah, and the four younger kids climbed into Meg's Lexus wagon and headed off to see *The Lorax,* which was still playing at one of the smaller theaters in Santa Rosa. Jack stayed home to finish packing, and JJ went to hang out at his girlfriend's house.

They got to the theater almost a half hour before the movie started, so Meg gave Tessa money for snacks and sent her and the kids out to the concession stand while Meg and Sarah camped out in the virtually empty auditorium, saving their seats.

"No one's here," Meg said, scanning the rows of empty seats.

"The movie has been out for months, which I like. I love having the theater to ourselves," Sarah said, propping her feet up on the seat in front of her. "When it's empty like this, I don't have to worry about Ella annoying people by talking or Brennan bouncing in his seat."

"Your kids are still so little."

"Ella's easy. A little clingy, but she's so sweet, I don't really mind. It's Brennan who pushes my buttons. He just doesn't listen."

"He's only eight."

"Almost nine."

"But that's young."

"Dad expected us to listen and follow directions by the time we were three."

Meg shrugged, unable to disagree. Obedience was as important as respect in their family. If you were told to do something, you did it. The first time you were asked.

Well, unless you were Brianna, because Brianna had her own rules. Probably because Brianna was her own species. Sarah laughed.

Meg glanced at her. "What?"

"I was just thinking about Bree."

"Thought you were mad at her?"

"It's hard to stay mad at Brianna forever. She's just so . . . Bree. Free Bree. Doesn't listen to anyone. Not even Mom or Dad."

Meg didn't answer, and for several minutes neither said anything, both looking at the screen, reading the parade of movie trivia, before Meg broke the silence. "What do you think is wrong with her?"

"Besides being certifiably crazy?"

"Sarah!"

Sarah rolled her eyes. "I'm joking. Come on. You're the one always feuding with her."

"We've called a truce."

"Is that because she looks like she's dying?"

Meg suddenly looked stricken. "Don't say that!"

"I was *joking*."

"But she does look terrible. She's skin and bones."

"And jaundiced."

"What do you think it is?" Meg asked.

"I don't know. Dad told Kit he thought Bree had malaria."

"Malaria?"

Sarah chewed on her bottom lip. "Kit thinks it's hepatitis."

"And Brianna won't say." Meg sighed. "That's the part that worries me. If it was nothing, she'd tell us. But she's not talking about it, which makes me wonder if it isn't more serious."

"Like what? Cancer?"

"Or she's HIV positive."

"Meg, stop." Sarah jerked upright. "That's not . . ." Her voice drifted off as she considered the possibility. Brianna did live in the Congo. She was a nurse specializing in infectious diseases. Brianna was the family wild child and admitted to experimenting with drugs, as well as enjoying . . . "adventurous" . . . sex. But

Brianna was also street-smart. She knew how to take care of herself. Didn't she?

The kids returned just then, their laughing voices echoing in the hall just before they emerged into the dimly lit theater, carrying buckets of popcorn and cold drinks with boxes of candy tucked under their arms.

Sarah watched Tessa stop and help Ella up the stairs. What a good cousin Tessa was, she thought, before glancing at Meg. "Do you really think it could be HIV?" she whispered.

Meg whispered back, "I don't know, but my gut says it's serious."

After the movie, they stopped at a playground so Brennan could burn off some energy before they returned to the house. The late afternoon gleamed gold with the lingering sun.

"Love the longer days," Meg said, taking a seat on the park bench closest to the swings where Tessa was pushing Ella while Gabi and Brennan raced up and down the slides. "Have been craving more sunlight." She looked at Sarah, who was standing next to the bench. "You don't get a shortage of light in Florida, though, do you?"

"No, but I miss the light here in Northern California. It's different. And you still get seasons here, and none of our humidity."

"Do you think you'll stay in Tampa when Boone retires?"

"Hope not." Sarah saw Meg's expression and hurriedly added, "I've made good friends there and Tampa's a great city, but I miss being near family."

"Will you come back here, then?"

"I don't know. Boone doesn't love the Bay Area. It doesn't feel like home to him."

"Where would he like to go?"

"Back to New Orleans. He loves the big mansions in the Garden District."

"That's where he grew up."

"Yes, but in a smaller house, at the outskirts of the Garden District. He'd love to return and get a proper house . . . a real Southern mansion."

"What do you think?"

"I think it'd be great, provided the house doesn't come with any ghosts."

Meg laughed. "I don't think I'd want a haunted house either."

Gabi suddenly let out a piercing squeal and then Brennan was crying as Gabi flung herself on top of him, punching him for shoving her off the top of the slide.

"Hey!" Sarah practically leaped over the bench to get to the kids. "Brennan, don't push Gabi, she could have been hurt. And Gabi, no punching," she said, hauling Gabi off Brennan and setting her firmly on her feet. "Brennan is still a couple of years younger than you."

"I could have broken my leg," Gabi said, brushing bark chips off her knees and butt.

"But you didn't." Sarah turned to Brennan and picked him up. "Brennan, what were you thinking, pushing your cousin off the slide like that?"

"Just playing," he said, smiling angelically.

"That's not playing, that's dangerous. Don't do it again," she said, wagging her finger in his face. "Hear me?"

"Yes."

"Yes, what?"

"Yes, ma'am."

"Now go play nicely, you've only got fifteen minutes left and then we're heading home to make dinner." Sarah watched as Brennan chased after Gabi, who no longer wanted to play with her cousin and was telling him so in no uncertain terms.

"They're fine," Meg said.

Sarah turned to look at Meg, who was sitting bathed in late-afternoon light. "Are you?" she asked softly.

"What?" Meg asked, folding her arms across her chest.

"I'm worried about you, Meg."

"You don't need to be. I'm a tough girl."

"That's not the same thing as happy."

"Happy is overrated."

Sarah studied Meg's tense expression, trying to work up the courage to ask her the question that had been burning inside of her since their conversation in the dining room. "Did Chad make you happy?"

"Oh, Sarah, why?"

Sarah dropped onto the bench next to Meg and faced her. "Because I want to know. I want to understand. Were you happy when you were with him?"

"I don't know."

"You don't know?"

"I've closed a door on all that. What happened was so hurtful, I'm better off not remembering."

"But if you loved Jack, what was Chad?"

Meg groaned and looked away, focusing on Tessa and Ella, who were now swinging together in one swing with Ella on Tessa's lap. "A diversion," she said flatly.

Sarah glanced around to be sure there were no little bodies around and that they wouldn't be overheard. "Didn't you love him?"

"Not the way I love Jack."

"But you . . . you slept with Chad for weeks. Had this torrid affair with him. And you're telling me it meant nothing?"

Meg turned her head, met Sarah's gaze. "I won't say it meant nothing, but it certainly wasn't love and marriage and a baby carriage."

"Why?"

"I just never saw myself with him. Not long term. And I tried, but I couldn't picture him with the kids, going to their events, or living in our house, or me living in his."

"So what was he? Just a fling? Sex?"

Meg grimaced. "I guess."

"You guess?"

Meg looked back to Tessa and Ella, who were swinging high now, and Ella was laughing uncontrollably. Meg's lips curved, her expression softening. "They're so sweet together," she said softly. She continued to watch them another few moments before glancing at Sarah. "Affairs aren't what you think they are. At least, my . . . relationship . . . with Chad wasn't what I thought it'd be. When it started, I felt so many emotions. I felt so much. I . . . loved feeling so much. When you've been with someone for a long time, you forget what those other emotions feel like, and then all of a sudden they're back, and intense, and they, uh . . ." Her voice drifted away.

Sarah stared at her sister's profile, holding her breath, waiting to hear the rest, because it was important. She needed to hear this, understand this. Because maybe if she understood how affairs happened, and why they happened, maybe she could prevent one from happening again. Maybe she could figure out how to keep Boone faithful, and keep her marriage safe. "They what?" she prompted.

"Seduce you." Meg made a soft, bruised sound of pain laced with regret. "Destroy you."

"But you're not destroyed. You're strong. Remember?"

"That's right. I'm tough." Meg smiled faintly, and yet the expression in her eyes was one of defeat. "I'm Mary Margaret Brennan. I can do anything."

"That's right."

Meg's eyes watered. "But if I could take it all back, and undo the damage, I would. In a heartbeat."

Jack grilled steaks on the patio for dinner, and even though the temperature dropped the moment the sun set, they still ate outside at the wrought-iron table, bundled up in sweatshirts and sweaters, Meg's rustic yet expensive lanterns flickering, casting yellow and orange light across the table.

"Our first meal of the spring al fresco," Jack said, lifting his wineglass. "To spring. And family."

"And family," Sarah and Meg chorused, lifting their wineglasses while the kids toasted with their water glasses.

"And to Grandma," Gabi said, lifting her glass again. "We will always love you."

"To Grandma," the children echoed.

"That's right," Sarah murmured, grateful that her niece had remembered Mom.

Brennan shuddered. "Just hope the maggots aren't eating her," he said.

Sarah's eyes bugged out, but before she could say a word, Gabi slugged him in the arm.

"Oh my God, Brennan!" Gabi cried, slugging him a second time. "How can you say that?"

"So gross!" Tessa said.

"What are maggots?" Ella asked, glancing from her brother to Tessa, and then to her mother.

"Nothing," JJ muttered, disgusted.

"Worms," Gabi answered precisely.

Ella's face crumpled. "Worms are eating Grandma?"

"No," Sarah answered even as she shot Brennan a you-will-soon-die look.

"Well, they will," he answered, unconcerned.

Tears filled Ella's eyes. "I thought Grandma was in heaven with angels and the saints and Mary—"

"She is," Meg said quickly. "And Grandma loves heaven."

Ella looked at her brother. "Then why did Brennan say Grandma is being eaten by worms?"

"Because Brennan is a boy, and boys like to say gross things," Tessa said, leaning over to hug Ella. "So don't listen to him. He just wants attention."

"Really?" Ella asked hopefully.

"Really," Tessa said firmly.

And with that, Tessa restored harmony to the dinner table.

After the meal ended, JJ and Tessa did the dishes, and Jack, Meg, and Sarah went to the family room to talk. Jack and Meg sat on the couch next to each other, and Sarah took the chair across from them.

Jack was in a good mood, just as he'd been after his run, and he talked animatedly about a new exhibit opening in D.C. at the Smithsonian Museum, and how he'd heard that later in the year, right around Thanksgiving time, that there'd be an even more impressive exhibit focusing on the Civil War and American art.

"Works by Winslow Homer, Frederic Church, Sanford Gifford, and Eastman Johnson will all be part of the exhibit," Jack said. "I'm really looking forward to the show, as it's a period in history I find particularly fascinating."

"It does sound like a wonderful exhibit," Meg agreed, smiling. "Maybe we can take the kids back to D.C. for Thanksgiving, see the exhibit, and visit some of the historic sites together."

"Maybe," Jack said.

Meg's smile faded. "You don't think we should?"

Jack shifted on the couch. "I said maybe."

"But maybe isn't yes—"

"You're right. It's not."

"So why can't we take the kids?"

Jack sighed and rubbed his forehead, as if he suddenly had a massive headache. "Because I don't want to commit to something that far in advance."

"Why not?"

Sarah exhaled, feeling uncomfortable, wishing she wasn't here, witnessing a marriage unraveling. But Jack and Meg continued on, as if Sarah wasn't present.

"You know why," Jack said grimly.

Meg leaned toward him, equally fierce. "Can't you give us a year, *please*?"

But Meg's "please" wasn't sweet or conciliatory. It was angry and sharp, colored with a bitterness that made Sarah wince.

Sarah sank lower in her seat, trying to decide if she should leave or stay, wondering if it'd help, or make things worse, to leave, wondering if she could help things by staying.

"It's almost been a year and it's just gotten worse," Jack retorted.

"It hasn't been a year, it's been nine months—"

"Which is a hell of a long time when you're miserable."

"Jesus, Jack!" Meg glanced around, expression wild. "That's cruel."

"What do you expect me to say? You just push and push. It's all you do. It's all you know how to do—"

"I'm trying to save us."

He was off the couch, staring down at Meg. "And I keep telling you there is no us. Not anymore."

"Jack."

"No."

"Meg, yes." Jack glanced at Sarah, his gaze narrowed, his expression tortured. "Sarah, help me."

Sarah pressed her hand to her mouth, unable to speak, feeling as if she was about to be sick.

His eyes met hers, held, his brown depths pleading. "Make her understand," he added. "I'm finished. Done. I want out. I want to get away."

And then he was walking out and Meg covered her face with her hands and cried.

JJ stepped into the living room a few moments later, his face pale, his jaw hard. "Mom?" he said uncertainly.

But Meg's back was bowed. She kept her face hidden.

"Mom, he didn't mean it," JJ said, moving toward her slowly, cautiously. "He's just in a bad mood because he's flying out tonight."

When Meg didn't answer, JJ looked at Sarah and mouthed the word *help*.

Sarah joined Meg on the couch and wrapped an arm around her. "People fight," she whispered, picking her words with care, wanting to calm Meg, soothe her. "People say things they don't mean when they're angry."

"He means it, though," Meg choked from behind her hands. "He's done. Done with me."

JJ swore and ran out of the room to race up the stairs. Suddenly voices were raised upstairs, JJ shouting at his father, cursing him out, and then Jack was shouting back.

Meg lifted her head, her face wet, eyes wide. "Oh no. JJ can't. No." Before she could move, more feet sounded on the staircase and then Tessa's high voice could be heard, crying, "Stop it. Stop it, both of you, right now!"

There was another shout that had Meg flying to the stairs. She was halfway up the staircase when Jack came storming down with his suitcase, briefcase, and heavy traveling coat. "This is bullshit," he said, facing Meg on the stairs. "I don't want to be here. There's no reason for me to be here."

"You have children here," Meg said hoarsely.

"You've turned them against me."

"I haven't."

"My son doesn't respect me. My daughter is screaming at me—"

"They were just trying to help," Meg said, reaching out to him.

He backed away so he couldn't be touched. "I hold you responsible, Margaret. You did this."

"No."

"You've robbed me of my family—"

"That's not true."

"It is true."

"Jack, your family is here. You're the one leaving."

"My work is in Virginia."

"But your family is in Santa Rosa."

"*Daddy!*" It was Tessa at the top of the stairs, leaning over the railing. "Daddy, please don't leave. Please don't go mad at us."

"I'm not mad, Tessa," he said, glancing up at her and, seeing her troubled face, he softened his voice. "And I'm not upset with you. Okay?"

"But you're upset with Mom, aren't you?"

"This is between your mom and me," he said, before swearing under his breath. He looked into Meg's eyes. "This is just what I didn't want," he said quietly. "This is just what we didn't need."

Then he was gone, his old Saab roaring out of the garage and down the driveway, tires squealing as he took the last corner fast.

Within seconds of Jack's departure, Ella appeared at Sarah's side and grabbed hold of her leg, wanting reassurance. Brennan slunk into the hall moments later and nervously asked why Uncle Jack left in such a bad mood.

Meg's kids were even more emotional and Meg just looked lost. Baffled. Sarah's heart went out to her.

"Should we see if there's a show on TV?" she suggested brightly, patting Ella's head and smiling at the others. "Or a movie we could all watch together?"

"Don't want to watch TV," Brennan said. "I'm bored."

"A puzzle?" Sarah suggested.

Brennan and the girls shook their heads.

"How about we make cookies?" Meg asked, pulling herself together. "We could do roll sugar cookies and then decorate them. I have sprinkles and icing."

The kids agreed enthusiastically, with the four younger ones trailing after Meg into the kitchen while JJ skulked away, heading upstairs to his room.

Sarah followed JJ, knocking on his open door. "Hey," she said, when he turned around. "Can I come in?"

"Oh, sure, Aunt Sarah." He pushed his jacket to the foot of his bed and moved his mitt to his desk.

"You don't have to clean up," she said as he made a half-hearted effort to tidy the top of his desk. "Just wanted to make sure you were okay."

"I'm fine." He straightened, arms folding across his chest. "Just sorry you had to hear all that. My dad can be such a dick."

"I think he's stressed."

"He's not the only one. We're all stressed. Grandma's dead and Mom's working almost full-time, even though they're just paying her for part-time."

"How do you know that?"

"'Cause they fight about money nonstop."

Sarah frowned. "Is money a problem?"

JJ shrugged. "I don't know. Hard to say. Dad says we spend too much, but I think money wouldn't be so tight if Dad didn't have a house and a car in Virginia."

"He has a house?"

"Just bought one. Says he'll use it for his office, too, but he'll still need electricity and water, which is just more bills, you know?"

Sarah tried to hide her shock. Meg must know about the new house in Virginia, but she hadn't mentioned it. Sarah couldn't imagine that her sister was happy about it either. Her curiosity got the best of her. "Is your mom okay with him buying the house?" she asked, delicately probing.

"Mom's afraid to fight with him. Doesn't want Dad leaving."

Wow. Sarah sucked in air, shocked again. If JJ was aware of all of this, did Tessa and Gabi know, too? "There's a lot going on here," she said. "Can't be fun."

"No. It's pretty shitty—" He broke off, winced. "Sorry about the language. But I'm kind of over it. Ready to go. Get away. Hoping I'll get a good scholarship so Mom won't have to worry so much. Or work so much." Suddenly his eyes were bright and he looked away. "I will feel bad, leaving her, though. Who knows, maybe I'll stick close to home for college. Maybe Cal or Stanford might want me."

"How's it going this year? Your mom said you guys had your first game last week."

"We've had three now, but I missed two yesterday 'cause of the funeral."

"You had a doubleheader yesterday?"

"Yeah, but it's okay. Coach knew I was going to miss, and I played Thursday in our opening game and got a home run and a double. Pretty sweet." He grinned a lopsided grin. "Was strong defensively, too. I think all the training I did this winter helped. You know Uncle Boone set me up on a conditioning program. Had me doing weights and sprints and stuff. My legs are a lot stronger."

"That's great. I'll tell Boone the exercises helped."

"Yeah, do. And let him know I can't wait until June when I can come out and see you guys and watch him play. He's said I can go to the park with him while I'm there. He'll take me to the locker room and onto the field, and introduce me to some of the scouts, too."

"He said he'd invited you out. We'd love to have you."

"I'm coming, for sure, this year. I'm already looking at flights, trying to find a cheap ticket."

"We've got miles, JJ—"

"No, I'm using my own money. I'm saving up." He fished out his phone, glanced at the time. "Hey, uh, Aunt Sarah, you mind if I run? Heather keeps texting me. She wants to know where I am. We're supposed to be hanging out."

"Go. Have fun." Sarah kissed his forehead. He'd grown this year. He was as tall as her now, five ten, and still growing. "Just drive carefully."

He flashed her another grin. "I always do," he said, grabbing his coat, checking for his wallet, and then disappearing into the hall.

Back downstairs, Sarah found Meg in the kitchen, surrounded by kids. They were rolling out the dough in vigorous puffs and poufs of flour.

"You've got a lot of action in here," Sarah said, approaching the big island to inspect the trays filling with bunnies and chicks and frolicking lambs, which were also, tragically, missing legs, due to the difficulty of peeling thin dough off the floured cutting board.

"It's kind of a mess," Meg admitted, wiping her chin, leaving a dusting of white behind. "But everyone's having fun."

"And that's what's important," Sarah said firmly, filling the kettle for tea and then pulling out two mugs, one for her, one for Meg.

Once all four trays of cookies were in the oven, the kids settled in the family room to watch cartoons, and Meg wiped down the floured surfaces while Sarah washed up the beaters and mixing bowl. Neither of them talked while they worked, and Sarah was thinking it was a companionable silence, and was enjoying the peacefulness, until Meg joined her at the sink to rinse out her floury rag.

"Don't say it," Meg murmured, holding the cloth under the faucet.

Sarah glanced at Meg, who still had the swipe of flour on her chin and two bright spots of color high in her cheeks. "Say what?"

"Anything about anything."

"Not planning on it." Sarah struggled to understand what was happening. "Did I miss something?"

"No. You were there."

Oh. Jack. Sarah sighed, suddenly very glad she was flying home to Tampa tomorrow. She needed to get home. Needed to get back to normal.

Meg wrung out the rinsed cloth, giving it an extra-firm twist before glancing at Sarah. "There's nothing you want to say?"

"No."

"This is my fault, isn't it?"

"I didn't say that, and I don't think it either."

"You don't want to tell me 'I told you so—'?"

"*No,* Meg. I don't blame you, and what's happening here is brutal, painful. I don't know how you do it. I couldn't do it. If Boone talked to me the way Jack talks to you, I'd kill him. I would—"

"You wouldn't," Meg interrupted flatly. "You'd hate prison. It wouldn't be your thing at all."

Sarah laughed, wiped her eyes. "You're so deadpan."

"What can I say? I'm just funny."

Sarah snickered and then choked on a smothered laugh, and when Meg giggled, Sarah impulsively threw her arms around her big sister and hugged her tight.

Sarah had cried more this week than she'd cried in her entire life—no, not true. She'd cried for weeks when she first found out about Boone and that Atlanta woman. That had brought her to her knees—but suddenly she needed to laugh, and needed to make Meg laugh, and needed to bring love and hope back.

"You *are* funny," she said. "And wonderful. And absolutely my favorite oldest sister in the world."

Meg snorted. "And your only oldest sister."

"See? Don't you feel good about yourself now?"

Meg started to laugh and then the laughter turned to tears, and she was crying hard, sobbing against Sarah as if her heart would break.

Swallowing hard, Sarah rubbed her back, murmuring soothing things even as the whole week came flooding back. Mom dying. Mom gone. The nurse from hospice returning Mom's pale pink bed jacket and the beautiful, soft knit blanket the color of Mom's favorite roses that Aunt Linda had made for her at Christmas. Dad on one knee at the cemetery, his big shoulders shaking, and Ella scared that Grandpa was crying and pressing herself into Sarah's legs while Brennan stood stoic at her side, a rare event for this usually hyperactive child.

But those intense, painful memories were balanced by the memory of Boone's arms around her just before he left for the airport yesterday, and just sitting with Meg, talking in the empty movie theater, and then the kids at the park, playing, and the kids here in the kitchen, rolling out the dough and working in tandem, as if they were performing a delicate medical operation instead of making cookies. It was good, this life. Even at its messiest.

"It's going to be okay," Sarah said firmly, more briskly. "You're amazing, and you have an amazing family."

Meg suddenly looked up at Sarah, face wet, nose streaming, and made a yelping sound. "How embarrassing!" She stepped away, turned around, looking for a tissue. "I'm a disaster!"

"We all are. That's just life."

Meg grabbed a paper towel and blotted beneath her eyes. "So. Do I call Jack? Text him? What do I do?"

Sarah pictured the scene she'd witnessed an hour ago, remembered the slam of the door behind Jack, the way he'd walked out, seething. "Give him space."

"I feel like I should apologize."

"I'd wait. He needs to cool off, and you don't need to chase after him. It'll just make you appear clingy and weak."

"So I wait."

"Yes. Wait. Let him call you."

While the cookies cooled on top of the stove, Sarah slipped up to the guest room and phoned Boone, hoping he was still awake.

"Not asleep?" she asked when he answered the phone.

"Nope. Just in bed, watching the news. What are you doing?"

"About to help the kids frost cookies."

"That sounds fun."

"Yeah."

"So it was a good day?"

"Pretty good. Overall." If she didn't think about Mom, or Meg and Jack, or the fact that Boone was about to start a new season of ball, which meant he'd be traveling a lot again, and in and out of hotels, with girls and groupies camping out in the lobby, hoping to snare a player for a quick lay. Or longer. "Jack and Meg are having some serious problems," she said, not wanting to think about girls or groupies tonight, or giving her imagination any power. There was enough real drama happening as it was.

"Jack's not happy," Boone said.

"Did he say that to you?"

"Yeah."

"He told me the same thing." She drew a breath. "He bought a house in Virginia. JJ told me tonight. I guess it's a new thing."

"What does Meg say about it?"

"She hasn't brought it up, and JJ implied that Meg hadn't made a fuss because she's afraid Jack will leave if she does."

"That's ridiculous. Jack's not an ogre. He loves Meg, and the kids."

"You should have heard the fight tonight. It was crazy. Jack lost it. Meg was crying, and the kids were all upset—"

"They heard?"

"They couldn't help but hear. Jack and Meg were screaming at each other in the living room and on the stairs."

"Were our kids there?"

"Yes."

"You should have got them out of there."

"I wanted to, but there was nowhere to go . . . and it all happened so fast. Jack wants a divorce—"

"He said he wants a divorce?"

"No. But he did say he wants out."

"Just like that?"

"Yeah."

"Not good."

"I know." They were both silent a moment and then Sarah sighed. "I can't wait to see you, Boone. I miss you. And I hate this. It's stressful and scary for the kids."

"I hear that."

"I wish we were flying home tonight."

"You'll be on the plane tomorrow. You'll be back here, in your own beds tomorrow night."

"Tomorrow seems so far away."

"It's been a rough month, babe."

"It has. But, Boone, everything's easier when I'm with you."

"I know it. And I miss you, too, hon. I'll be very glad when you're back home with me, where you belong."

Four

Lauren was in bed, staring at the clock, watching the minutes tick by. 9:23. 9:28. 9:35. 9:36. 9:48. 10:00.

She needed to sleep. Her alarm went off early every morning. She wasn't good on her feet all day without rest but tonight, the moment she tried to relax, her past returned, haunting her.

Torturing her.

This is why she'd moved. This is why she'd left Napa in the first place. She'd needed the change of scenery. Needed new activities and routines to give herself something else to think about . . . something else to do.

But at night she struggled. At night she had only time on her hands and it was too easy to lie awake in the dark, replaying that last morning with Blake over and over in her head . . . wondering if she could have done something to prevent the accident from happening . . . wishing she'd known it was her last morning with him. . . .

Unable to go there tonight, she grabbed her phone and texted her sister Lisa to see if she was still awake.

Lisa, a night owl, phoned immediately. "I was just thinking about you," Lisa said. "Mom told me you bailed on meeting them at the cemetery."

"I couldn't do it."

"What point did you turn around?"

Lauren swung her legs out of bed to sit on the edge. "When I couldn't get out of the car at the cemetery."

"So you made it all the way there."

"And then I didn't want to be there. Didn't want to put flowers on his grave. I don't want to see his grave. He was seventeen. He shouldn't be in the ground."

Lisa didn't speak for a long minute. "No," she said heavily, breaking the silence. "He shouldn't be. And I don't blame you for not wanting to go. I've gone with Mom once, and I cried myself sick. I don't know how they do it. But it's important to them."

"I'm glad they go. Makes me feel better knowing that someone is keeping an eye on things there, but I can't see the stone. Can't see his name and his birthdate—" Lauren bit hard into her lip, holding in the grief.

"So what did you do when you got back to Alameda?"

"Made cakes." Lauren laughed and wiped beneath her eyes. "Three of them."

"What kinds?"

"Chocolate. Grandma's old-fashioned chocolate cake recipe. Made the same cake over and over trying to perfect it."

"I thought it was already pretty good."

"It is good. I just think it can be better."

"So you've got the perfect recipe now?"

"Not yet. But I haven't given up." Lauren left her bed, paced the room, ending up at the window overlooking the street. The street lamps shone yellow through the leafy trees. Cars lined both sides of the street. "So how are you? How are you feeling?"

"I'm good. Ready to have this baby. I'm sick of being pregnant."

"Just another six weeks."

"Which seems like forever when you're getting up half a dozen times a night to pee."

"And then soon you won't be sleeping because you'll be nursing every couple of hours."

"Which freaks me out since you know I need my sleep."

"You'll get used to it."

"Will I, really?"

Lauren thought about it. "No," she said, smothering a laugh. "You won't. It'll suck. You'll survive."

"Wonderful," Lisa retorted dryly. "And just so you know, you're not the only one baking. I've had such crazy cravings lately that when I can't sleep, I head to the kitchen and throw together something sweet. I've been on a cinnamon and sugar kick this last week . . . cinnamon rolls, coffee cake. Last night it was miniature donuts." Lisa made a rough, mocking sound deep in her throat. "Which I then ate, all *eighteen* by myself, at three in the morning."

"Lisa!"

"I know . . . I'm horrified. But I can't sleep and then for some reason, I start thinking about food. . . ."

"But donuts? You hate donuts."

"Not when I roll them in a cinnamon-sugar coating. Then they're delish."

"Lisa, you have to stop. That's not good for you."

"But it gives me something to think about, besides giving birth. Because I have to tell you, I'm beginning to panic about how the baby gets out. I'm not sure I want it coming from *there*."

"It's supposed to come from *there*."

"Can't they just take it from my stomach?"

"You're not getting an elective C-section."

"No, I'm not. It just seems really painful."

"Eating donuts and cinnamon rolls in the middle the night

won't make birth any easier. And you'll just hate yourself if you put on a lot of weight now."

"Too late for that," Lisa muttered. "I'm huge. Can't even fit in my extra-large maternity jeans anymore."

"I'm sure being on bed rest for so much of your pregnancy didn't help."

"That's what Mom said . . . before she found out about my cinnamon and sugar fetish." Lisa snapped her fingers. "Speaking of Mom, she and Dad were here last week. I made them my blueberry pie for dessert. My best pie yet. Same crust—love that crust—but I tweaked the filling, doubling the amount of cinnamon and added an extra squeeze of lemon juice and it was perfect."

"Okay. Now you're making *me* hungry."

"Wish you were here. We could go bake something right now."

Lauren felt a pang. "What would we make if I were there?"

Lisa sighed. "Something easy, because I'm tired." Then she giggled. "And something yummy that we could eat warm, because I don't have the patience to wait for anything to cool anymore."

"One of your cobblers or crisps. Maybe your apple crisp."

"Or maybe my new favorite crisp. Peach-mango."

"Peach-mango?"

"I made it earlier in the week. It was supposed to be a peach cobbler, but the peaches hadn't ripened enough, and I had mangos from the farmers' market and they were ripe, so I threw them together and it worked out perfectly."

"And let me guess . . . you put cinnamon in that one, too?"

"Of course."

Lauren laughed. "Well, if it's as good as you say, it might be another good one for our cookbook."

Lisa was silent a moment, before asking carefully. "Do you still want to do the cookbook?"

"Of course. Why not?"

"We've done nothing on it in years."

"Not years. A year maybe. And that's only because we've had

other things come up. The move to the new location, and then Blake—" Lauren broke off, and clamped her jaw tight, holding her breath, and the bruising emotions in. She loved her sister so much, but Lisa didn't understand how hard it was for Lauren to negotiate the past and the present, the dreams they'd had, the plans they'd made. A year ago Lauren felt like she had everything. Then it was gone. And gone was a scary, dark place. Lauren drew a quick breath. "I'm sorry to make everything about Blake. I know it's not fair to you—"

"No. No," Lisa interrupted hurriedly. "I shouldn't have said it like that. Obviously, the timing isn't good for me, either, not with the baby, and everything I have going on."

Lauren battled the lump in her throat. "We'll still make it happen. We'll just wait until the time is right for both of us."

Hanging up, she hastily wiped her lashes before the tears could fall. There would be a right time someday. There would. She didn't know it, or see it, or feel it. But she had to believe it. Faith was all she had left.

Sarah needed to turn off her Facebook app on her iPhone and sleep. It was late, nearly midnight, after a very intense day. It felt good to be on Facebook, reading all of her friends' updates. Made her feel almost normal again. As if life would one day be normal again.

She switched off her phone, put it on the bedside table, and slid down beneath the covers. She wasn't sleepy. How could she sleep?

Meg's life sucked. Jack was, as JJ so eloquently put it, a dick. And Boone's birthday was coming up on the twelfth, which was just eleven days away, and she hadn't bought him anything yet, or planned anything, either, because he'd be gone on his birthday, in Detroit on a ten-day road trip.

Ten days.

She wasn't ready for him to be gone, nor was she looking forward to being left alone with the kids again. Ella was easy—clingy but easy—while Brennan was always a little bit out of control. Sarah suspected that her son might have ADHD, but every time she brought up her concerns to Boone, he shut her down, saying that Brennan was just a boy, and boys were active.

How about hyperactive?

Sarah flopped over onto her stomach, looked down on Brennan where he slept at the side of the bed. He'd started out at the foot but had wriggled closer to her side before finally passing out, exhausted.

She smiled down at him. He was so sweet when asleep. Almost angelic.

Gently, she reached down and pushed his mop of dirty-blond hair back from his forehead. Such a handsome boy. And sometimes a really good boy. And sometimes not good at all, but she knew he didn't mean to get into trouble all the time. It just seemed as if sometimes he couldn't stop himself. That's the part that worried her most.

With a last tender pat on his head, Sarah settled back in bed, plumping the pillow behind her head, hoping that one day Brennan would be like his cousin JJ. JJ was a really good kid. A sweetheart. She loved him, and Tessa. Gabi, too, but Gabi was a handful. Kind of like Brianna.

And Brennan.

Oh God. Maybe it was genetic, and maybe Brennan's wild side came from her family.

Good thing Boone loved her family. Like Jack, he'd been raised in a small family, but unlike Jack, Boone had taken to the boisterous Brennans right away. He liked her family so much, it was Boone who suggested they name their son Brennan, in honor of them.

Just thinking about Boone made Sarah restless. She missed him, was still crazy about him. Boone was hot. The hottest man she'd ever met, with a gorgeous face and an amazing body, and he continued to rock her world, even after twelve years together. At six four, Boone was all muscle, all man, and hung well . . . like a man. A big man.

She smiled in the dark, thinking about that body, and how he used it, and how it felt to be with him. Her skin loved his skin. Her body loved his body. It was more than the size of his dick, or the way he made love, it was something else . . . something deeper, less tangible.

His smell. His taste. The rightness of it all.

Pheromones. Hormones. Soul mate.

Sarah reached under the covers, touched herself, trying to see if she could possibly arouse herself. Wasn't working. It was just her hand and her parts. Even waxed and trimmed, it was all rather boring. She didn't need an O. She needed Boone. And there was no way she could come if her children were around her. Sarah left the bed, headed to the bathroom to find something that might help her sleep.

As she filled a glass with water, she caught a glimpse of herself in the mirror.

For thirty-five, she was still remarkably pretty. But it wasn't a bragging kind of thing. Sarah wasn't vain and saw no point in cultivating excessive ego since she'd done nothing to earn the bone structure that had made her a UCLA calendar girl. It was all genetics. She'd been born with good skin, great cheekbones, long arms and legs, a slim torso, great hair. They were gifts given to her as a baby and the only thing she did to maintain her looks was exercise and a decent moisturizer. Doing more would have felt wrong. And she didn't want to tempt fate.

Rifling through her travel bag, Sarah dug out the bottle of Tylenol PM and popped one, needing to sleep. She returned to bed, hoping the sleeping aid would knock her out. It did.

She was sleeping deeply when the repeated ring of a bell woke her. Opening her eyes, she listened. The house was quiet. Perhaps it was just a dream, she thought. She was closing her eyes when she heard footsteps in the hall and then down the stairs.

Not a dream.

Someone was at the front door.

Groggy, Sarah pushed back the covers and crept into the hall.

The lights were on downstairs, the chandelier in the entry hall glowing yellow. Meg was unlocking the front door, drawing the dead bolt and removing the chain.

Sarah leaned over the balcony railing. "Who's at the door?" she whispered to Meg, not wanting to wake the kids.

"I think it's the sheriff," Meg answered.

Sarah's head cleared. *"Why?"*

"I don't know."

"Hang on. I'm coming down," Sarah answered, returning to her room and stepping over Brennan to grab her robe, catching sight of her bedside clock: 3:05. Quickly, quietly, she closed the bedroom door behind her.

She was halfway down the stairs when she heard Meg's voice. *"No!"* Meg cried.

The hair rose on Sarah's nape and she took the stairs two at a time. "What's happening?" she demanded breathlessly, her sweeping gaze taking in Meg and the two uniformed officers on the front porch.

But all three were quiet, with Meg staring at the officers in their brown-and-khaki uniforms, her eyes wide, her mouth slack.

Sarah's heart skipped. "What's happened?" she repeated, this time directing her question to the officers.

"There's been an accident," one of them said, his voice quiet, respectful.

Meg made a low, gurgling sound and Sarah knew then that something terrible had happened. "Jack?" she whispered, reaching out to touch Meg.

Meg drew away. Her lips trembled. *"No."*

"I'm so very sorry, Mrs. Roberts," the officer added carefully. "I realize it's a shock—"

"It's not him," Meg interrupted, teeth chattering. "There's a mistake."

"We don't believe so," the second officer spoke. "The Saab is registered to Jack Roberts, and we were able to recover the wallet, with his driver's license. That's how we were able to find you."

"He can't be dead," Meg said, straightening. "He's on a plane now. To Arlington. Call United. They'll tell you. It's the eleven fifteen flight to Reagan National Airport."

"Ma'am, he didn't make it to the airport. He crashed less than two miles from here."

Impossible, Sarah thought.

Meg shook her head. "It can't be. He left here hours ago. And Jack is a good driver. A great driver. He's never even had an accident."

The first officer looked regretful. "We need you to identify the body. We can drive you there, if you'd like."

Meg simply stared at him.

"I know this isn't easy, Mrs. Roberts, but due to the nature of the accident, and the resulting trauma . . . we need a positive ID for the body. We could wait for dental records—"

"Do you hear yourself? Do you know what you're saying? He's not a body. That's my husband. My *husband*." Meg's voice cracked. "And we have three children together. Two are just young girls still. They need their father. They need a father. They—"

"I'll go," Sarah volunteered. She turned to Meg, put her hands on Meg's shoulders. "Is that what you want? For me to go with them? If that would be easier for you, Meg, I'll do it, and you can stay here with the kids."

Meg stared up at her, her expression agonized. "What if it *is* him? What if Jack didn't make the plane—" She broke off and pressed a trembling hand to her mouth as her eyes filled with tears.

Sarah wrapped an arm around Meg. "I'll get my coat and shoes and go find out. I'll see him and I'll know, and as soon as I know, I'll call you. Okay?"

"Mom? Aunt Sarah? What's going on?" JJ asked gruffly, his voice thick with sleep as he came down the stairs.

Sarah looked over Meg's head at JJ, who was crossing the hall, still buttoning the fly of his jeans. He wasn't wearing a T-shirt, and his pale skin stretched tight over his broadening shoulders.

Sarah stepped away so JJ could reach Meg.

"Mom?" he said, looking at her, his brow creased. "What's happening?"

Meg sank her teeth into her lip and shook her head.

"There's been an accident, JJ," Sarah said huskily.

"Who?" he asked, scanning faces,

"Dad," Meg said quietly. "At least they say it's Dad."

JJ exhaled hard. "How do you know?" he asked, looking from his mom to the officers.

"The '71 Saab was registered to a Jack Roberts at this address, and the vict—man—had his wallet on him, and the car's registration in the glove compartment."

JJ shook his head disbelievingly. "But how? What happened?"

"Looks like he lost control, went over the guardrail on Fountain Grove Parkway, and ended up down in one of the ravines."

Fountain Grove Parkway was a route they used to get to the 101, which meant Jack had crashed not long after leaving the house.

Eyes stinging, air bottled in her lungs, Sarah heard again the squeal of tires as Jack screeched down the driveway, leaving angry. The parkway was new, but the terrain was hilly and there were steep drop-offs on either side of the road. You couldn't make a mistake on Fountain Grove, but apparently Jack had.

"It took him a long time to be found," Meg said, shivering and rubbing her arms.

"A motorist noticed the damaged guardrail and called 911. It took a couple of hours to reach the car and recover the body."

JJ looked from his mom to the officers. "Do you think he suffered?"

"No, son. He probably died on impact."

Meg pressed her fist to her mouth. "My fault," she murmured, still shivering. "We shouldn't have argued. Shouldn't have fought. He left upset, because of me."

"That's not true, Mom," JJ said sharply, shoving his hands in the front pockets of his jeans. "Dad and I were fighting—"

"No," Sarah said, her voice low, rough, unable to listen to them do this. "It's no one's fault. Not yours, Meg, or JJ's. It was an accident. A tragic accident—"

"But if we hadn't been fighting," Meg protested.

"Everyone fights, Meg. Everyone argues. But it was Jack's choice to walk out of the house and get into the car and climb behind the wheel. Nobody made him go. Nobody wanted him to go."

"But normally he's such a good driver," Meg whispered. "Normally—" And then she was crying and JJ reached for her, holding her, and Sarah turned away as she saw Meg's tears splash onto JJ's bare shoulder.

One of the officers cleared his throat. "We still need someone to come identify the body."

"Let me get my coat and shoes," Sarah said.

"No." JJ patted his mom's back. "We'll do it. Mom and I will go together."

"I don't know if it's a good idea for you to go, son," the officer answered. "The Saab was destroyed, flattened in the fall."

"But he's my dad," JJ said roughly. "I need to see him. And I need to be there for my mother."

Meg wanted to drive, and so she and JJ rode together, and they followed the officers into town to the morgue.

As the cars disappeared down the long, winding drive, Sarah went upstairs to retrieve her phone to call Boone.

Her teeth were chattering as she waited for him to answer. It was almost six thirty in the morning in Florida. Boone would be sleeping. He hadn't gone to bed until late, but he wasn't picking up. She left him a message, asking him to call, and headed to the kitchen to make something warm to drink.

She'd just turned on the burner beneath the teakettle when he called her back.

"What are you doing up? Are the kids okay?" Boone asked when she answered.

Sarah sat down on the nearest kitchen stool. "Jack's dead," she blurted, her hand shaking as she pressed the phone to her ear. "Meg and JJ have gone to identify the body."

"Say that again," Boone demanded, his voice louder, harder.

"Jack's dead."

"When? *How?*"

"Car accident. Lost control on the parkway and went over the edge of the hill." Her teeth chattered together. She crossed her arms over her chest, feeling chilled to the bone. "How can he be gone just like that? How can he be dead?"

"I don't know. I don't understand what's going on. Who told you? How did you find out?"

"Two officers came to the house to break the news. I guess a motorist saw the guardrail—it was bent or broken or something—and called 911, but because Jack's car was way down in the ravine, it took them a while to get to him. And now Meg and JJ have gone to identify the—" Sarah broke off, unable to say "body." Her eyes filled with tears. ". . . Identify Jack." She blinked and a tear fell. "I was going to go do it, but JJ said they should, and he went with her. But Boone, the girls don't know yet. They're upstairs sleeping. They have no idea what's happened." She abruptly stopped talking, unable to say another word because she'd just realized that everything had changed for Meg's children, forever.

"Does the family know?" Boone asked.

"No." Sarah rose to turn on the gas beneath the kettle. "Meg only just left now with JJ, and it's still the middle of the night here." She leaned against the stove, squeezing her eyes shut. "How do I go home tomorrow, Boone? How do I just leave Meg here, like this?"

"You don't, babe. You stay. Meg's going to need you now."

* * *

Meg and JJ returned to the house just as dawn was breaking. Sarah had made coffee and she poured Meg a cup when she entered the house. Meg didn't drink it, though. She wandered around the kitchen, touching things, adjusting things, moving continuously while JJ went up to his room.

Sarah stood next to the coffee machine, watching Meg pace, understanding her need to move. Sarah didn't want to walk. She wanted to run. She wanted to run as far away from Meg's house as she could, dreading the moment the girls woke up and needed to be told what had happened.

She dreaded telling her own children what happened, but they were younger, and Ella wouldn't really grasp the significance. Sarah was glad. Glad that Ella and Brennan would be shocked and sad, but grateful that Jack's death wouldn't impact their lives. They only saw their Uncle Jack now and then.

But Meg's kids . . .

Sarah shuddered inwardly, anticipating their grief.

"It was him," Meg said abruptly, sagging against the kitchen island, her hands on the marble counter. "I didn't look at his face, though. They warned me. I'm glad they did. I didn't want—" She broke off, swallowed. "But I saw his hand. It was his hand. He was wearing his wedding ring." She drew a deep breath, struggled to smile. "He always had beautiful hands. An architect's hands. He was such a brilliant architect, too."

"Have you told his parents yet?"

"Haven't called anyone. I was waiting to tell the girls, but maybe I should phone his parents now. It's eight thirty on the East Coast. They'll both be up." Meg closed her eyes, shook her head. "He's their only child. They're going to be devastated." She opened her eyes, looked at Sarah, the brown irises shimmering with tears. "If God wanted to punish me, He should punish me, but oh God, this hurts the children."

Meg wouldn't let Sarah comfort her, going instead into the family room to phone Jack's parents, who'd divorced when he was a boy. The calls were short as there wasn't much Meg could say after breaking the news. Both Jack's mother and father wanted to know about services, and Sarah heard Meg say that Jack had wanted to be cremated, and she thought that probably on Friday or Saturday they'd have some kind of memorial service for him, but that was all up in the air.

Meg returned to the kitchen, wiping away tears. "That was awful," she said, reaching for the coffee Sarah had poured twenty minutes ago. "Beyond awful."

Sarah clutched her cup, needing its warmth. "Because it *is* awful. Meg, I can't believe any of this is happening."

"I can't either. I keep thinking it's all a dream, and any second now I'm going to wake up, and Jack will be here, and everything will be good—" She bit down into her quivering lower lip. "But it's not, is it?"

"No."

Tears filled Meg's eyes. "I just don't understand how it all fell apart. I did love Jack. Very, very much. I loved his mind and his wit and the way he saw the world . . . as something beautiful and creative. I loved his creativity, and his passion, and his ability to get lost in his work. And then somewhere along the way, I got frustrated that he lived in his head, and that his family . . . his children . . . were less interesting to him than his ideas and designs. I couldn't understand how he could let his kids grow up without wanting to be more involved."

Meg paused for breath, and Sarah said nothing. There was nothing she could say.

"And now he's really gone and he will never know them, and they will never know him, and I just hope to God they remember him the way he was—brilliant, creative, loving." She drank her coffee quickly, sloshing a little onto her shirt. She glanced down at the stain, blinking back tears. "It's going to be horrible, telling the girls."

"I know," Sarah murmured.

"Need to call Dad. He's going to be upset. He'll be so worried about all of us, but this is the last thing he needs right now."

"Dad will be fine. And in a weird way, it'll be good for him. It'll give him a sense of purpose. Helping you. Being here for the kids. I guarantee he'll make every one of JJ's games. In fact, he'll be the one behind the dugout, shouting the loudest."

Meg nodded, exhaled slowly. "I can't handle telling him, though. Just want to focus on the girls. Be ready when they come downstairs." She hesitated. "Would you call him? Let him know I just can't . . . can't . . ."

"He'll understand."

Meg nodded again. "And Kit. Call Kit. And I'm sure Dad and Kit will call the others."

"I'm sure they will."

Sarah stepped into the mud room, and then outside, to make the call to Dad. It was still early, an hour before he normally rose, but when he answered, his deep voice crisp and clear, she flashed back to the days when she was younger and would call him at the firehouse.

"Firefighter Brennan," he'd answer, booming into the phone.

She'd loved it. Loved that her daddy was a fireman. A handsome one, too.

"Dad, it's Sarah," she said now, knowing that he liked his facts up right up front. "Jack was in a car accident last night. He died at the scene. Meg and JJ have already gone to identify his body."

For a moment there was silence. Then he spoke and his voice was deeper, rougher. "Is Meg at the morgue now?" he asked.

"No, she's home."

"How is she?"

"Shocked."

More silence. "Died at the scene?" he said a moment later.

"Yes."

"Must have been some accident."

"I can't even imagine," Sarah answered. "This is crazy. It's a nightmare. And now Meg's just waiting for the girls to wake up to tell them the news."

"Gabi and Tessa don't know yet?"

"No."

"How's JJ?"

"Haven't talked to him since he returned from the morgue. But he insisted on going with Meg. And he was the one who drove them home."

"He's strong. He'd make a great fireman."

"He'll make a great ballplayer, too."

He sighed. "What a terrible thing . . . losing Jack like this."

"I know."

"I'll go tell Brianna, and then I'll be on my way." He paused. "Do you think Meg wants everyone there today, or do you think she'd prefer for the family to stay home?"

Sarah pictured Meg in the kitchen, and the way she'd tried to drink her coffee, only to slosh it onto her top. Sarah's chest ached. "I think it'd be good for her to have everyone here. I think she needs to know she's not alone and that she's got everyone's love and support."

Hanging up, Sarah called Kit next. Kit must have still been sleeping and answered only after the fifth ring. "Hello?" Kit said, groggily.

"It's me, Sarah."

"What's up? Everything okay?" Kit asked, still sounding sleepy.

"There's been an accident." Sarah took a deep breath. "Kit, Jack . . . he died."

"*What?*"

"It was a car accident. On the parkway. They say he lost control and went over the guardrail. The sheriff came to the house in the middle of the night and asked Meg to go identify the body."

"Jesus," Kit whispered, and coming from her, it wasn't an oath, but a prayer. "How is Meg? Where is she? Do the kids know?"

"She and JJ just returned from the morgue. Meg's waiting for the girls to wake up to tell them. JJ's in his room. And Meg phoned Jack's parents a few minutes ago to break the news, but Meg asked me to let our family know. I just called Dad. Now I'm calling you."

"Thank God you're there. I can't imagine Meg having to go through this alone. And not so soon after Mom—" Kit swallowed. "Now another funeral. Wow."

"Jack's parents asked Meg about arrangements. Meg told them she hasn't made any yet."

"I'll help Meg with that stuff. I helped Dad with Mom's arrangements and know what needs to be done."

"You coming up today?"

"Just need to get a sub to cover my classes and I'll be on my way."

Sarah returned to the kitchen and sat with Meg at the kitchen table, neither saying much of anything for a few minutes. Unable to sit still, Meg jumped up, heading for the laundry room to start a load of wash.

A half hour later they were both back in the kitchen when footsteps sounded on the stairs. Meg looked up at her, her expression stricken.

"I don't want to do this," she whispered.

"I know. And I'm sorry, Meg. I am." Sarah went to her sister, gave her a hug. "Do you want me to go? So you can have some privacy."

Meg squeezed Sarah's hand. "No. Stay. Just in case."

Sarah had no idea what "in case" meant, but of course she'd remain and she crossed the kitchen, finding a position next to the wall, needing something solid behind her.

And then Tessa entered the kitchen, with a grumpy Gabi behind her.

"Gabi refused to get up," Tessa said sharply, going to the refrigerator, opening the door, and taking out a container of milk. "She hasn't even showered."

Gabi made a face and reached past Tessa for the orange juice. "I showered yesterday. I don't need to shower today."

"You're hitting puberty," Tessa said with a sniff, closing the door hard, almost catching Gabi's hand. "You don't want to stink."

"I don't stink."

"You will if you don't bathe, and use deodorant."

"Girls!" Meg's voice rang out in the kitchen.

Tessa and Gabi both stopped and turned at the same time to look at their mother.

Meg shot Sarah another panicked glance. Sarah gave her a small nod, trying to encourage her, even though on the inside, she wanted to throw up.

What a terrible, terrible day and night it'd been, and it was just going to get worse.

"Girls, I have something to tell you," Meg said, gesturing to the chairs around the kitchen table. "Please, sit down."

Tessa glanced at Gabi. "Are we in trouble?"

"No." Meg took a seat in one of the kitchen chairs, facing her daughters. She drew a slow breath, and then another. "Your dad was in an accident last night, driving to the airport. It was a very bad accident—" She paused, held her breath, before adding, "He didn't make it."

The girls just stared at her. Tessa looked confused. Gabi was still. But then it was Gabi who grasped the implications. "Daddy's *dead*?" she asked.

Meg nodded.

"How do you know?" Tessa asked, voice wobbling.

"I went and saw him earlier this morning. JJ went with me. It's Daddy." Meg took a breath and swallowed hard. "They say that he died instantly. He didn't suffer." Her voice broke. "He probably didn't even know what hit him."

Five

The Brennan family had descended, Sarah thought wearily, listening to the din coming from the family room, where everyone had gathered late Monday morning.

Dad, Bree, Tommy Jr. and Cass, Kit, Mom's brother Uncle Jack and his wife, Aunt Linda, as well as two of Dad's three brothers.

At noon Dad, Tommy, and the uncles rounded up the five kids and took them out to lunch to give Meg some quiet so she could focus on making decisions for Jack's service.

Meg wanted to schedule the service for Saturday noon, allowing friends and family on the East Coast to fly in, and giving them Sunday to get home again. Brianna agreed with her, but Kit gently reminded them that Sunday was Easter, and it might be a difficult and expensive travel day.

"But we can't have a service on Good Friday, can we?" Meg asked.

"Not a Mass. But you probably could have a prayer service." Kit hesitated. "But Jack wasn't Catholic. He was Episcopalian.

Would the Episcopal church in Santa Rosa be willing to hold a service for him on Friday?"

"I can call and ask," Meg said.

"Or I can call for you," Cass offered.

Meg nodded gratefully. "Could you?"

By noon, word of Jack's accident had spread, and flowers began arriving at the house.

By two, most of the big decisions regarding the funeral arrangements had been made and Meg went upstairs to take a bath and lie down and rest before the kids came home.

By three, when Dad, Tommy, and the kids returned to the house after hours walking around Santa Rosa Plaza, the house was full of people and flowers and food piling up in the kitchen.

At four, Sarah cracked open a bottle of white wine and drank a glass fast, standing in the mud room by herself, then poured herself another, bigger glass to take with her into the family room.

Even with the wine to take the edge off, Monday evening felt endless, as Jack's accident made the evening news, and the phone wouldn't stop ringing, and flowers continued to arrive what felt like every fifteen minutes.

Dad's brothers left before dinner, and then Uncle Jack and Aunt Linda left immediately after eating a dish of Aunt Linda's warm berry crumble, which she served à la mode.

Meg hadn't eaten more than a couple of bites all day and passed on dessert, but she gratefully accepted a cup of tea from Dad. While Meg sipped her tea, Dad, Kit, Tommy, and Cass kept her company in the dining room, with Dad and Cass making most of the small talk so Meg didn't have to.

Brianna joined Sarah in the kitchen, drying the dessert plates as Sarah washed, since the dishwasher was already full and running.

Brianna reached for the next rinsed plate and, glancing behind her to make sure no one else was in the kitchen, asked, "Has there been any explanation as to why Jack crashed?"

Sarah shook her head. "I haven't heard anything."

Bree dropped her voice even lower. "Had he been drinking? Was he distracted by something? Maybe texting, or on his phone?"

"I don't know. No one has said anything." Sarah's stomach churned. "But you know he left angry last night. They'd been fighting. Meg and Jack. And then JJ got involved, and Tessa, too—"

"Seriously?"

"Yeah. And Jack said some pretty harsh things to Meg before taking off. And he literally took off . . . racing down the driveway like a bat out of hell."

"Shit. I hadn't realized he left upset."

"I'm worried about Meg and the kids. It was such a scene—" Sarah stopped talking as footsteps sounded behind them.

"Tommy and Cass are leaving," Kit said. "I might as well head out now, too, as I've got to teach in the morning."

"I'm almost done. Have them hold up a moment so I can say good-bye."

"I'll tell them," Brianna said.

"Let me take the towel," Kit said. "I can finish drying. It'll give me a chance to talk to Sarah."

Sarah glanced at Kit, hearing her sister's serious tone. "What's wrong?"

Kit didn't immediately answer, taking her time to find the right words. "Did you tell Meg that you didn't want Jude to join me for Jack's service on Friday?"

Sarah turned the water off and swallowed, blindsided. "I . . . uh . . . may have."

"*May* have? Sarah, you either did or you didn't."

Sarah wished she could just vanish into her room with the rest of the white wine. "I did, but it wasn't a big deal—"

"If it wasn't a big deal, then why did you say it? Because Meg just pulled me aside and asked me not to bring Jude on Friday as he made *you* uncomfortable." Kit enunciated each vowel and consonant so clearly that the words seemed to bounce, even as her blue eyes blazed, her gaze holding Sarah's. "I can't believe you'd say such a thing. I'm honestly hoping that in Meg's grief and exhaustion she misunderstood." She paused, waiting, one dark eyebrow arching higher. "Did she misunderstand?"

Sarah winced. "No."

"No."

Sarah drew a deep breath. "I don't think it's good to have Jude around the kids. And that's what I told Meg."

"*Why?*"

"I . . . don't . . . like him."

"You don't know him."

"True."

"Nor have you even tried to get to know him."

"Kit, he doesn't talk. And he doesn't smile. He just watches people, and I'm sorry if it hurts your feelings, but I find him . . . creepy."

"Jude's not creepy."

"Then scary?"

"He's not scary either. He's a really, really nice guy. You just have to give him a chance. Like the kids. They all love him."

"But I'm . . ." Sarah closed her eyes, screwed up her courage, and blurted, ". . . not good with him being around the kids. At least, not around my kids."

"*What?*" Kit's voice rose a full octave.

Sarah shuddered inwardly, hating that they were doing this but thinking it better to at least get it out now before something happened later. "Try to see it from Meg's and my point of view. We don't know anything about him—"

"I do!"

"Okay, but do you know everything about him? Is it possible he has a criminal record?"

"No."

"How do you know that? Have you run any reports, bought one of those search things on the Internet? He might have a record." Sarah silently added, *He certainly looks like he has a record*. "You should at the very least find out."

"I have. And he's not a criminal, or a pedophile, or whatever you think he might be." Kit drew a short breath, eyes too bright, cheeks flushed pink, making the smattering of freckles on her nose seem to pop. "Just because he has tattoos and a motorcycle—" She exhaled sharply. "Christ, Sarah! Do you think I'd ever, ever put your kids, or Meg's kids, or *any* kids, in danger?"

Sarah held her breath, aware that Kit wanted children and a family badly, but she didn't have kids yet. She didn't understand how one had to be constantly vigilant, especially when one had young children. "No, but—"

"*No,*" Kit interrupted. "And I get that you don't like Jude. But I do. He's a good person. Someone *I* love. Someone *I* trust. And that's all that matters."

"You're right."

"Yes, I am." Kit tossed the dish towel onto the counter and walked out, back stiff, lips pressed into a thin, hard line.

Sarah sagged weakly against the edge of the sink.

Kit was pissed.

Meg was a widow.

Mom was dead.

Awesome. Things were going really well.

With Jack's funeral service set for Friday and the formal obituary sent off to the paper, Meg spent Tuesday morning tackling the reception that would follow the service. She'd been going back and forth about having it at the house. She really didn't want to hold it at the house, in part because they were a good ten-minute drive from the church and parking would be a hassle. And then there was the real issue of having people filling the house Friday afternoon, eating, drinking, and then leaving . . .

Sarah helped her call the various hotels and event spaces in

Santa Rosa, but either nothing was available or the space was too small, or the room was too plain, and finally Meg had had enough. "Forget the reception," she said, pushing away from the kitchen table to take care of the laundry in the mud room. "I don't care anymore. It's stupid. And I don't even want to talk to people. I don't want to hear how they're sorry, and how wonderful and inspirational Jack was . . ."

Her voice faded and Sarah followed her into the mud room, where her sister began shoving wet towels into the dryer.

". . . but he wasn't all that wonderful," Meg continued breathlessly, furiously. "He was selfish and self-absorbed and couldn't lift a hand to do a lick of housework. I don't think he unloaded the dishwasher more than a half-dozen times during our marriage, and if he ever did the laundry, it was because he was out of socks! It wouldn't have crossed his mind to do any of the kids' laundry, or my laundry. My God, he'd rather die than do my laundry. No, that was woman's work. My work. Even though I had a full-time job and three kids and meals to prepare!"

Sarah heard a door open and shut and could see Dad outside through the mud room window, dragging all five kids with him onto the driveway, a basketball under his arm.

Good old Dad. He was going to make the kids exercise.

Sarah began folding the clean, dry load of colors piled on the marble counter. Small purple T-shirts and pink-and-white-striped shirts and boys' boxers and men's dark T-shirts.

Meg made a soft choking sound as Sarah reached for a brown knit collared shirt. "Jack's," she said, taking it from Sarah. She balled it against her chest. "He just wore it Saturday."

Sarah hated feeling so helpless. "I'm sorry, Meg."

Meg nodded and walked out of the mud room, still clutching the shirt. Sarah continued to fold clothes, her hands moving even though the rest of her was numb. It was time to go home. She wanted to go home. She wanted to hug Boone and never let him go.

Sarah folded until the pile was gone and then stayed in the mud room, watching Dad and his five grandkids shooting hoops. Ella was too small to get any shots in, but Brennan was surprisingly good. Really good. He was nailing the baskets, one after the other, and Sarah could tell from JJ's expression that he was impressed, too.

Good for Brennan. He was far more often criticized or corrected than praised, and so it was really wonderful to see him getting pats on the back and enthusiastic high fives from JJ and his grandpa.

Sarah couldn't wait to compliment him. But she didn't get the chance. Just minutes later she heard loud voices, angry voices, and the kids were in a knot, fighting.

By the time Sarah got outside, Gabi had Brennan on his back, on the driveway, in a headlock.

"Shut up!" she was shouting at him, her knees on his chest. "Shut up about my dad. He's my dad, not yours. Don't talk about him. Not one more word!"

Everyone was still yelling. JJ, Dad, Tessa, Ella. It was an absolute zoo.

"Let him go, Gabi," her dad said.

"Get off my brother, Gabi!" Ella shrieked, bordering on hysterical.

"What are you doing, Gabi?" Sarah demanded, pushing through the kids and trying to lift Gabi off her son, but the girl refused to let go of his neck.

"Shutting his mouth," Gabi said. "He keeps talking about Dad. Saying he got smashed like a pancake—"

"Well, he did!" Brennan cried, wiggling fiercely beneath his cousin. "The car was flat, so he had to be flat—"

"Brennan!" Her dad's roar silenced everyone.

Dad didn't usually roar. He rarely raised his voice. The fact that he just had was not a good omen.

Gabi meekly released Brennan.

Brennan silently stood up.

Everyone stared at Tom Brennan, waiting for whatever would come next.

"Next one that lets out a peep will be doing laps up and down the driveway for twenty minutes, understand?"

Five heads nodded.

"Now go wash up and settle down."

"Yes, Grandpa."

The kids headed toward the house. Sarah's dad grabbed the basketball and started dribbling and shooting. Sarah opened her mouth to ask if he was okay, but judging from his fierce expression, he wasn't. He was probably missing Mom. Probably wondering what the hell had happened to his family.

Sarah understood. She was wondering the same thing herself.

The kids lined up in the mud room to wash their hands. Sarah stepped around them, thinking she'd go check on Meg, but Gabi and Brennan were still having words.

"I hate you," Brennan said under his breath to his cousin.

"Good," Gabi sneered, "because I hate you, too."

Gabi sailed out, shoulders back, head high, and Brennan kicked the wall and burst into tears. "I want to go home! I hate it here. I want to see Dad."

Sarah grabbed him before he could kick the wall again, and wrapped him in her arms. "Easy, bud. This isn't our house. We don't want to put dents in the wall."

"I want to go home!"

"We are going home this weekend."

"How many days until the weekend?"

"Four. Five."

"I don't want to be here for five more days. I want to go home *now*."

"But I've got to stay for Uncle Jack's funeral."

Brennan struggled in her arms. "I don't want to go to another funeral. I'm sick of them."

So was she, but that didn't matter when you were an adult. "Let me talk to Dad," she said instead. "We'll see what can be done."

That evening, after talking it over with Boone, she bought Brennan a ticket back to Tampa in the morning, booking him as an unaccompanied minor.

Brennan had never flown alone and Sarah wasn't sure how he'd handle a five-hour flight without anyone familiar next to him, but he didn't seem concerned when she told him he'd be flying out in the morning.

"Good," he said, snapping some Legos together. "I'm sick of my cousins. They're stupid and mean."

Sarah rolled her eyes. "They're not stupid or mean. But I do want to be sure you understand that I'll drive you to the airport in the morning, and check you in, but when it's time to board the plane, the gate agent will take you on without me."

"Will I have my DS?"

"Yes. And the laptop with your movies."

"So?"

"You're not scared?"

"Why would I be scared? Dad's going to come get me. And I'll have food, right? Goldfish, Oreos, stuff to eat?"

"Yes."

"Just make sure there are lots of Oreos. That's all I really need."

The next morning Dad and Brianna left as soon as commuter traffic eased, and then Sarah headed out with Brennan while Ella stayed at the house with her cousins.

At the airport, they played cards at the gate while waiting for his name to be called for early boarding.

Brennan jumped to his feet when he heard his name. "That's me," he said.

"Yes." Sarah gave him a big hug. "I love you. And Dad will be there at the gate when you land."

He looked nervously at the agent who was waiting for him. "You really aren't coming with me?"

"No. But I'll be home this weekend."

Suddenly tears filled his eyes. "I don't want to go without you."

"You'll be home in hours. And you've got your DS and movies and Oreos—"

"But I won't have you."

Sarah's eyes burned and her throat ached. "There's nothing to be sad about. Dad said the Neeleys can't wait to have you come over, and the day after tomorrow you'll go to the opening night game with them."

"Against the Yankees?"

She nodded, and caught the eye of the gate agent, who gestured that it was time.

The lump in her throat grew and Sarah gave Brennan one more quick hug, kiss, and then stepped away, handing him his backpack even as she steered him briskly toward the agent. "Your games are in the front pocket. The DS is in the middle pocket, and the computer and snacks and juice are in the back."

The agent took him from her.

"Love you, Brennan!" Sarah cried, waving.

He looked back at her, small, forlorn, and lifted his hand to wave, but the agent was moving him forward, herding him into the jet ramp way.

Sarah pressed her fist to her mouth, struggling not to cry. He was going to be fine. He was. It was just five hours and then he'd be with Boone.

Her vision blurred and she drew a quick breath and wiped her eyes dry. To distract herself, she reached for her phone and texted Boone. *He's on the plane. Text me as soon as he lands.*

Her phone rang. It was Boone.

"Hey," she said thickly.

"You're not crying now, are you, babe?"

She exhaled in a whoosh. "No."

"He's a big boy. He's flown hundreds of times."

"But he's never flown alone."

"There's a first for everything."

True. And there would be a lot more firsts ahead of them. "Promise to call me the moment you have him?"

"I promise. Now relax. Everything's going to be fine, darlin'."

Her chest squeezed, heart aching. God, she loved him. Loved her family. Loved the four of them together. They were good together. A family.

Sarah was just fifteen minutes from Meg's house when her phone rang. It was Brianna. "What's up?"

"What happened last night between you and Kit? Because she just texted me that due to a situation you created, she won't be able to attend the funeral Friday."

"That's ridiculous," Sarah snapped. "She can attend. I just told Meg it would be better if Jude didn't."

"How do you even have a say in the guest list for Jack's funeral?"

"There's no reason for you to get involved, Brianna. This is between Kit and me."

"You have no right to dictate who should, or shouldn't, attend Jack's services."

"I'm not comfortable having Jude around my kids."

"What do you think he's going to do? Molest them?"

"Maybe."

"Jesus."

"You don't have kids, Bree, you don't understand."

"Tell me you didn't say this to Kit."

"Which part?"

"Any of it. That she wasn't a mom, and therefore she wouldn't understand that little girls can be hurt by men."

"Not hurt. Molested."

"Got it." Brianna's voice hardened. "Sarah, if this gets back to Kit, I swear I will tear you apart limb from limb—"

"You're half my size and weigh about ninety pounds—"

"Kit was molested as a little girl."

Sarah nearly missed her exit and slammed on the brakes.

"I was, too," Bree added flatly, "but that's neither here nor there. The important thing is that you figure out how to fix this so Meg can have her family with her on Friday."

Brianna hung up.

Sarah dropped the phone into the car console, stunned, shattered.

For five minutes she just drove, unable to think, absolutely reeling. And then she grabbed her phone and called Brianna back.

"What?" Sarah choked, panicked, unable to say more than that.

"What do you mean, what?"

"What you just said. That . . . Kit . . . and you . . ." Sarah shook her head, trying to clear the fogginess in her brain.

"Were molested?" Brianna supplied.

"Yes."

"And . . . ?"

Sarah's eyes burned. "Why did you say it like that? Why did you tell me like that?"

"Because it's true. And you hurt Kit—"

"I wasn't trying to hurt her. I was trying to be a good mom!"

Brianna said nothing.

Sarah blinked, her throat aching. "I'll call her after school. I'll apologize. Okay?"

Still reeling, Sarah entered Meg's house only to discover that things were in absolute turmoil.

Meg was in the living room with JJ. She was pacing back and forth while JJ slouched in a chair next to the sofa.

"How do you think I felt, going into your room and finding it empty?" Meg demanded. "Your bed not slept in? What do you think I thought happened?"

"I sent you a text that I was staying at Heather's," JJ answered shortly.

"I didn't get it," Meg snapped.

"Well, I sent it."

Sarah slowly put her purse down on the hall table, listening for a moment, before heading for the stairs, thinking she should probably go check on the girls.

"Why didn't you come home?" Meg asked as Sarah slunk up the stairs.

"Because I didn't want to."

"You're sixteen, JJ."

"Almost seventeen."

"And way too young to be staying out all night."

"I thought it was better staying there than drinking and driving."

"You've got to be kidding!"

"Just a couple of beers."

"You're sixteen!"

"You know I drink. And smoke—"

Meg let out a shriek and Sarah quickly turned around and came right back down, entering the living room in time to hear Meg say, "I expect more from you, JJ. A lot more, considering the fact that you are *almost* seventeen."

JJ rolled his eyes. "You're losing it for no good reason—"

"No good reason? Maybe you weren't aware that I just lost my mom, and your dad, and I really don't need you, Jack Jr., being a smart-ass when my life has fallen apart."

"Well, my life isn't any better, Mom. It was my dad who died, and I can't get that picture of Dad lying there on that metal tray or bed or whatever it was, with just half a face—"

"*Jack Thomas Roberts!*"

"So yeah, I had a couple of beers last night and then made out with Heather and decided to camp out with her because when I'm with her I feel good. Sorry you didn't get my text. Sorry you don't like me drinking. Sorry I'm not the perfect, stand-up son you wanted, but this is me, Mom. This is who I am."

JJ stalked out of the living room, passing Sarah in the doorway, to tear up the stairs three at a time.

Sarah heard his bedroom door slam shut and turned to look at Meg, who was standing, shell-shocked, in the middle of the living room.

Sarah didn't know what to do, or say. "Teenagers are fun, huh?"

Meg's eyes shimmered with tears. Shaking her head, she exhaled slowly and then tried to speak but couldn't.

"Meg, he's a great kid. He loves you so much—"

"Sure has a funny way of showing it."

"It's only been two days since Jack died. He's reeling."

Meg swiped at the tears, drying them before they could fall. "We're all reeling."

"Exactly. So don't take it personally. He probably doesn't even know what he's saying."

"Great."

"Where are the girls?"

"Upstairs watching a movie in Tessa's room."

"Has everyone had lunch?"

Meg nodded. "That's how I found out JJ wasn't here. Sent Gabi in to wake him up for lunch."

"But he's back now, and safe, and you deserve some time to yourself."

"Ha!" Meg's voice quavered.

"You won't get much time once Jack's parents arrive tomorrow. Why don't you go lie down for a while . . . or take a bath. I'll manage the kids."

"I was going to boil some eggs. The girls want to decorate them later."

"You go upstairs. I've got the eggs covered."

*   *   *

hree hours later, Sarah and the girls covered the farm table in the kitchen with a layer of newspapers and then Tessa measured out the vinegar and water for the dye while Gabi showed Ella how to organize the plastic cups and tablets of dye. "Orange goes with orange," Gabi said. "Blue with blue. And green with green. See?"

Ella wrinkled her nose. "But that pill doesn't look green."

"They have to dissolve, and it's not a pill. It's a tablet."

"A tablet," Ella repeated.

"Yes."

Ella frowned. "What is a tablet?"

Gabi shrugged. "It's like a pill."

Ella said nothing, even more confused than before, and Sarah reached over to hug her. *Welcome to the world,* she thought.

The two dozen eggs were drying in the open cardboard cartons and Sarah was at the sink, rinsing out the extra glasses they'd used for some of the dye, when her phone rang.

She quickly wiped her hands and reached for her phone in the back pocket of her jeans. Boone. Which meant Brennan had landed.

"I've got him," Boone said when she answered.

"Wonderful. Now I can relax."

"Now you can relax," he agreed. "How is Ella?"

"Good. She just finished dyeing two dozen eggs with her cousins. Ella made one for all of us."

"What did she put on mine?"

" 'I heart Daddy.' " Sarah crossed the kitchen, glanced into the family room to make sure the kids were doing all right. The three girls were crowded onto the couch watching the Disney Channel. "So what are you doing now?"

"Driving home."

Sarah pulled out one of the stools at the island and sat down.

"Can't believe that Friday is opening day and I'm missing it. Against the Yankees no less!"

"Wish you could be there."

"Me, too. Can't wait to come home."

"What day will that be?"

"Saturday. I'm hoping."

"That's not too soon?"

"I can't stay here forever."

"No, I hear that. And it'll be good to have you home."

"I've been looking into flights. Ella and I would get in around ten. If you're still at the park, we will just cab it."

"You don't need a cab. If I'm still at the park, I'll have a car sent for you."

"How did Brennan do on the flight?"

"He said it was fine. He's looking forward to the game tomorrow. Alyssa is going to take him to the park with her kids."

"That's nice of her," Sarah said, grateful that Alyssa Neeley always included Brennan. Her husband, Jeff, was the Rays' new shortstop, joining the team a year ago, and when the Neeleys moved to Tampa Bay, they bought a house on the same cul-de-sac as Sarah and Boone.

"Alyssa has offered to watch Brennan until you're back."

"She's a sweetheart," Sarah said.

"We owe her big-time."

"Remember that when I treat her to a spa day later."

Boone laughed. "I promise I won't complain, 'cause, baby, you've earned it."

Sarah closed her eyes, savoring the way Boone's deep voice rumbled through her. She loved his voice, both the tone and the Louisiana drawl. She didn't know how he did it, but when he laughed he managed to sound sexy and innocent all at the same time. "Excited for tomorrow night?"

"Men don't get excited, babe."

She grinned. "Looking forward to tomorrow night, Boone?"

"Yeah, I am. The Yankees have CC Sabathia on the mound and we've got to take Shields. Should be a good game."

"Nervous?"

"Nah. Just ready to get the season going."

"Come on. No butterflies? None at all?"

"Shields is probably feeling a little puky, but not me. I'm good. I just want to get out there and hit the ball."

"That's what I love about you."

"That's it?" he asked innocently.

She laughed softly, amused. "Well, there is something else . . ."

"Really?"

"Uh-huh."

Ella suddenly appeared next to the kitchen island, blue eyes wide, worried. "Mommy?"

Sarah covered the phone. "Yes, sweetie?"

"I'm sorry."

"Sorry, why?"

Ella wrinkled her nose. "'Cuz Gabi told me I'm supposed to tell you I had an accident."

"Oh." For a second Sarah just looked at her and then she stood up. "Boone, I better go."

"What's happening?"

"Ella had an accident."

Boone laughed, a low, husky laugh, on the other end of the line. "It's all you, babe."

"I know." Sarah held out a hand to Ella, uncertain whether she should laugh or cry. "It usually is, hon."

Six

Meg lay in bed, eyes open, eyes burning, chest burning, feeling dead. No, not dead. She hurt too much to be dead.

She'd been doing this for the past couple of nights, all night. Lying awake. Feeling too much. Thinking too much. Thinking of Jack and the previous weekend, and that last night they were all together. Replaying that final scene over and over in her head, wondering if she could have stopped him from leaving angry, wondering if he'd be alive now if she'd smoothed things over . . . made amends.

But how many ways were there to make amends? How many times did you apologize before the words just didn't mean anything anymore?

And now he was gone and tomorrow his parents would arrive—they were staying in two separate Santa Rosa hotels—but they'd both come to the house for dinner, and then there was his church service and reception on Friday.

Except she still hadn't booked anything for the reception and she was beginning to run out of options . . . never mind time.

Just this morning she'd called her favorite caterer, Summer Bakery & Café in Napa, and practically begged Lisa Summer, the older of the two Summer sisters, to cater the reception, but Lisa explained, most apologetically, that with Lauren moving to the East Bay for the year, and with so many of the café staff gone for spring break, she was shorthanded.

"I hate saying no to you, Meg. You're one of our favorite people, and definitely our best client—"

"It's okay." Meg gently cut her short. "I understand. And it's a lot to ask of Lauren, even if she hadn't gone. Although I hadn't realized she'd moved away. When did that happen?"

"Last fall. September. But it's just temporary."

"That's good. Napa wouldn't be the same without her."

"And that's what we keep telling her." Lisa drew a quick breath. "Meg, honestly, I'd cater the reception myself, if it weren't for this darn pregnancy. It's been difficult and I've been on and off bed rest the entire time."

"You're pregnant, Lisa?"

"Eight months."

"How wonderful!"

"Thank you. Matthieu and I are really looking forward to meeting our little one." Lisa paused and the silence stretched over the line. "I'm so sorry, Meg, about Jack. I can only imagine how difficult this time is for you. Please know that our thoughts and prayers are with the whole family."

"Thank you," Meg whispered, her voice failing her.

"I'll make some calls. Talk to my friends who are in the business. Maybe I can find someone who can help you on Friday."

"That'd be great."

"It will come together, Meg."

"Yes. It will. And thank you."

That had been twelve hours ago, and so far, nothing from Lisa, and no nibbles from any other caterers.

Too bad Jack hadn't checked his calendar before crashing,

realized that spring break wasn't a great time for dying . . . far better to wait a couple of weeks.

Grimacing at her gallows humor, Meg left her bed and walked to the window with the view of the hills and valley, the sky a black canvas dotted with stars.

Looking up into the sky, she thought of her mom, and wished desperately that Mom were here with her now.

Meg sat down on the upholstered cushion of the window seat, amazed that just a year ago everything had been calm, uneventful. Mom had been healthy. Meg's marriage had been solid. Life was good.

Maybe too good, because she hadn't even known it. Hadn't appreciated it. Hadn't realized that she was living a fairy tale, because now it was a nightmare.

Forgive me, Jack.

Help me, Mom.

Her eyes stung, and her insides felt sore, shaken, broken.

Across the room, on the nightstand, her phone suddenly buzzed.

God calling, maybe?

Meg retrieved her phone. A text from Lauren Summer, Lisa's little sister. *Have you found a caterer yet?*

Meg suppressed panic as she texted back, *No.*

Moments later her phone rang. It was Lauren. "Meg, I am so sorry."

Meg gulped a breath. "Thank you."

"I didn't know. I only found out this evening when Mom forwarded me the obituary from the paper. I called Lisa and she told me you'd asked us to help—"

"It's fine," Meg said in a rush, embarrassed. "I didn't realize you'd moved to the East Bay."

"I'm managing a little place called Mama's Café in Alameda. It's different from our restaurant in Napa, but it's what I needed."

"Change," Meg said.

"Yes." Lauren paused. "So. The reception. What time is? How many people are you expecting, and what would you like for the menu?"

"You're not serious, are you?"

"Yes. So . . . how many? What time is the reception? What do I need to know?"

Overwhelmed, Meg closed her eyes. "It's a noon service," she said huskily, "very short, approximately thirty minutes. Everyone is invited to the house immediately after. I'm thinking we'll have at least one hundred people, maybe one fifty, although it could be more, so a buffet, and maybe something sweet."

"Will you want to serve alcohol?"

"I'm Irish, and it's a funeral, so my family will definitely drink. But I think we should just stick to beer and wine."

"Anything else?"

"Maybe your soup, salad, and sandwich buffet . . . you did it for me a couple of years ago at Halloween, and everyone thought it was wonderful."

"You want soup?"

"Since it's Easter . . . I was thinking carrot might be nice." Meg hesitated. "It was Jack's favorite."

"Right."

"Do you mind handling the rentals, too?"

"We've got it covered."

Meg could suddenly breathe again. Finally. Something good. "You're a godsend."

Lauren made a soft, rough sound on the other end of the line. "I'll see you Friday. Take care of those kids."

Hanging up, Lauren Summer sat higher in bed, curled her legs under her, thinking and not thinking, feeling and not feeling, hoping she wasn't in over her head.

This wouldn't be easy.

This wouldn't be fun.

This wasn't something she wanted to do.

Reluctantly she called her sister. It was late, but Lisa was a night owl. "I talked to her," Lauren said, when Lisa answered. "One hundred and fifty people. Twelve thirty start time. We'll do a buffet and offer cold drinks, dessert, and a simple bar of beer and wine."

"I thought you were calling her to offer sympathy, not agreeing to cater the event."

Lauren rubbed the back of her neck. "She needed us."

Lisa was silent, struggling to choose the right words. "You can't even come home to see us, hon. How are you going to come home to cater a funeral?"

Sighing, Lauren pressed the comforter down over her legs, thinking Lisa had a good point.

She didn't know how she'd do it. She'd been to Napa only once since leaving in September, and that had been for Thanksgiving, and just sitting at the table with her family had been more than she could handle.

"And I'm huge, Lauren," Lisa added. "I'm not going to be able to get out of the kitchen."

"Hope you're not that big. You still got six weeks to go, which means you could be putting on a pound a week from now—"

"Don't go there. Can't even fit into maternity extra large as it is."

"You'll lose the weight later."

"I better," Lisa said. "But you know, I mean it about not being able to do a lot. I've been on and off bed rest. I won't be able to do more than man the kitchen on Friday."

"That's okay."

"And the prep, and the cooking, and the—"

"Yes."

"Why?"

Lauren swallowed, remembering how devastated she'd been last June when Blake had died, remembering the shock and the grief, which had been so consuming. "This is Meg. How could I tell her no?"

Lisa had nothing to say to that, because really, it was the bottom line. They'd both worked with Meg frequently over the past six years, catering numerous events at Dark Horse Winery as well as holiday parties at the Robertses' house. But Lisa knew that for Lauren, Meg wasn't just a customer, she'd become Lauren's friend, stopping by the bakery every week to pick up something special to take home to her family—flaky dinner rolls, warm, gooey cinnamon bread, or one of their special-occasion cakes—and when Meg came in, Lauren always came out from behind the counter to sit with her at a table by the window. They'd sip coffee and talk about life and work and kids. Meg had a son just a year younger than Blake and he played baseball, too. JJ was an outfielder, while Blake had been a pitcher. And how Blake could pitch. Scouts had been watching him for two years—

"So what are we serving?" Lisa asked quietly.

"A selection of our miniature sandwiches on our homemade breads. Soup. Salad. Dessert tray. But I really don't think we should do soup."

"Then don't," Lisa answered.

"But Meg requested carrot soup. Apparently it was Jack's favorite."

"Oh. Soup it is." Lisa hesitated. "This is just so much work for you, Lauren."

"It's fine. I'm used to it. I'm on my feet all day at Mama's Café."

"How is that going?"

"It's an experience."

"Still in the red?"

"Hoping we're going to start turning a profit soon."

"How?"

"Going to make some changes to the menu starting Sunday—"

"This Sunday?"

"Yep."

"But you'll be in Napa this weekend, catering Jack's reception."

"On Friday. I'll drive back to Alameda Friday night, or Saturday morning."

"That's too much. Honestly, Lauren. When do you rest?"

"I don't. But that's because I don't want free time. I don't need free time. I'm better off being busy."

"So, what changes are you making to the menu?"

"Cutting back on some of the Cajun items. Going to serve a little less blackened chicken and fish. Make just one kind of gumbo each day, instead of three. And add some appealing entrées, make Mama's a little less regional and a lot more mainstream."

"But Mama's is supposed to be a New Orleans–style restaurant. People expect Creole and Cajun."

"And they'll still find sausage and gumbo and biscuits and think it's fun, but I guarantee they'll come back for the prime rib, grilled half chicken, and barbecued steaks we'll soon be serving."

"You're offering prime rib for lunch?"

"No. For dinner."

"You're not open for dinner."

"We are now, starting Sunday."

"You said a month ago you can barely afford to pay the staff you have. How are you going to stay open even later?"

"I'll work the evening shift."

"And cook, too?"

"Not everything, no."

"Lauren!"

"It's going to be okay, Lisa. I've got it figured out." *Kind of, sort of,* she silently added.

"And what if it isn't?"

"Then we'll go back to just breakfast and lunch."

Lisa made a tsk-tsking sound. "I can't believe Mimi signed off on something like this."

"She doesn't care, provided the café makes money."

"But she's paying for the extra staff, right? She's paying for the new menus and extra overhead."

"Um . . ." Lauren tugged on a strand of her long hair. "Not exactly."

"Oh my God. Lauren!"

Lauren winced. "Mimi's promised to reimburse me. If we turn a profit."

"*If.*"

"I like the challenge."

"It's insane. You're insane."

"The café is in a good location, and the concept of a Southern, New Orleans café is cute, but it could be a lot more appealing. A lighter, brighter décor, better hours, better service, better food—"

"Hello! Hey, sis, remember? We already own a business, you and me. If you want to sink some money into a business, sink it into ours!"

Lauren blinked, taken aback, unable to think of a single response. Because Lisa was right. Lauren couldn't argue with her.

"I just don't get it," Lisa said, her voice sharp with frustration. "We've got a great restaurant, one that's written up in every travel guidebook on Napa, and yet you've abandoned it to go slave away at a decrepit little café in the East Bay!"

"I haven't abandoned our place. I'm just . . . taking a break."

Silence stretched, an uncomfortable, long silence that put a knot in Lauren's stomach.

"I hope you mean that," Lisa said quietly.

"I do."

"Because Summer Bakery and Café is our business. You can't be gone for good."

"I'm not."

"You're sure? Because if you're out, tell me now—"

"Lisa, I'm not. Okay? It's a sabbatical. That's it. I promise."

"Okay."

But when they hung up, Lauren buried her face in the crook of her arm, heartsick. She didn't lie to Lisa. She'd always been honest with her sister. But she hadn't been honest just now.

Lauren wasn't sure she'd be back. She wanted to return to Napa. She hoped she could return one day. But she didn't know when that would be. All she knew for sure was that it wouldn't be soon.

Lauren slept badly that night, repeatedly waking up and then falling back asleep, with Lisa almost constantly on her mind.

Lisa was right.

Lisa was right.

But Lauren didn't know what to do with the knowledge. What was she supposed to do?

Turning on the light, she went to the kitchen and poured herself a bowl of Lucky Charms, her secret weakness.

She ate the cereal at the small kitchen table and stared at the plain white refrigerator. Such an ugly old refrigerator. But then, her one-bedroom apartment was rather ugly and old, which is probably why it was so cheap.

But it's close to work, she reminded herself. *Convenient,* she added, pouring a second bowl of cereal, this time for the marshmallows.

She loved marshmallows. Peeps, chocolate-covered marshmallows, stale marshmallows, marshmallow whip. All good and that's because she wasn't a gourmet. She'd never planned to be a baker or a cook. But after she'd graduated from high school and delayed the inevitable by putting in two years at the community college, it was time to get a job.

Her parents had already helped her with Blake for three years. She couldn't sponge off them any longer. So she juggled part-time jobs and parenting and it was hellish, trying to work twelve hours a day and still find time to be Blake's mommy. There were only two good things about those two hard years: Blake, and her parents, who'd insisted she continue to live at home so they could help care for Blake when she worked.

Her parents were awesome.

Her sister was awesome, too, but Lisa hadn't come home after college, choosing to remain in L.A., working as an administrative assistant for a law firm specializing in the entertainment business. Lauren envied her sister's glamorous life and the adventures that awaited her. It'd been hard becoming a mother at seventeen. Lauren knew she'd missed out on so many opportunities.

Lauren was twenty when her mom said it might be okay for her to start dating again.

She was twenty-one when her dad casually mentioned that the valley was full of decent young men who might make good husband and father material.

Lauren wasn't interested. She couldn't imagine dating anyone.

Her grandmother sat her down one day after church and, holding Lauren's hands, told her not to hate, that it wasn't good for her to hang on to anger. "Let the bitterness go, dear," Grandma Summer had said. "Don't let it fester inside."

Lauren let her grandmother talk, keeping her expression blank. How little her family knew her.

Lauren didn't hate John. No, at twenty-one, she was still hoping John would come back and claim her, and their son.

He didn't. But she hoped. And dreamed.

Lisa moved home almost a year later, after an office romance soured, leaving her brokenhearted.

Dad and Mom welcomed her home. For a summer they all lived together: Dad, Mom, Lauren, Lisa, and Blake. By fall they were all getting on each other's nerves.

Lauren had her jobs in town, and Lisa had been working with

Dad on the ranch, but the small farmhouse just wasn't big enough for them to continue as they were.

One evening in late October, after Blake and their parents had gone to bed, Lisa and Lauren sat bundled in jackets by the outdoor fire pit talking smack and drinking wine.

It felt good to let their hair down a little. Things had been stressful all month. Lisa had begun missing the freedom she knew in Los Angeles and Lauren was exhausted juggling two jobs and an active little boy.

"Something has to give," Lisa said restlessly, holding up the wine bottle and discovering it was nearly empty. "Can't stay here much longer. But don't really want to go back to L.A."

"Are you thinking of moving?"

"I'm twenty-four, almost twenty-five. It's embarrassing being back home, living with Mom and Dad."

Lauren sighed, shoving a hand through her long hair to push it off her face. "I feel the same way."

"Would you want to move with me to Los Angeles?"

Lauren couldn't imagine taking her son away from Napa. "Mom and Dad would miss Blake, and he'd miss them."

"So you're going to just stay here forever?"

Lauren didn't answer immediately. "I'm thinking when Blake starts kindergarten next year, I'm going to try to get my own place."

"Can you really do that . . . financially?"

"I'm hoping. It's a stretch."

"Kind of hard on part-time jobs, huh?"

"Yeah. But it is what it is. And at least this way I get to spend a big chunk of each day with Blake."

"You're a good mom."

"He's a good boy."

Lisa glanced over her shoulder, back at the house, where everyone was tucked in bed, sleeping. "Yes, he is. And he's beautiful, you know. His dark hair, those blue eyes."

Lauren smiled wistfully. "He looks like his dad."

"Hopefully that's all he inherits from his dad, because Meeks is a first-class asshole."

Lauren shrugged. "People change."

"John Meeks hasn't changed."

"We don't know that."

"Oh, has he finally called? Decided to acknowledge his four-and-a-half-year-old son?" Lisa caught sight of Lauren's unhappy expression and groaned in exasperation. "What? It's the truth!"

"It's just . . . harsh."

Lisa swore under her breath and kicked at the fire pit with the toe of her boot. "I've tried to respect your feelings. I try not to judge, but, Lauren, come on. He's not a good guy. He's given you nothing but heartache, and he's not ever going to magically transform from jerk into prince!"

"Maybe not."

"Maybe?"

"I don't know, Lisa. I just can't help thinking that if John saw Blake, if he saw how amazing Blake is, and how sweet he is, he'd want to be part of his life—"

"You mean, John would want to be part of *your* life."

Lauren flushed and closed her eyes, tucking her chin into the collar of her coat, not saying anything.

Lisa couldn't stand it. She swore and leaned forward. "John Meeks is a self-centered asshole who can't love anyone but himself. You deserve better. You and Blake both deserve more."

"I just want Blake to have a family," Lauren whispered.

"Blake has us. What more does he need?"

The pressure grew in Lauren's chest, making it difficult to breathe. "A father."

Lisa didn't answer. She couldn't. She refilled her wineglass and took a sip, and then another, and another, struggling to contain her anger.

"I had no idea you were still so hung up on him," Lisa said when she was finally able to speak.

"I wasn't. Not until this last summer, when all the local papers when nuts about him, you know, making the jump into the big leagues, and I think . . . I think . . . it got to me." Lauren stared into the fire, watching the flames dance. "I sent him a picture of Blake. In a card."

"Tell me you didn't, Lauren!"

"It was of Blake's T-ball photo from spring, you know, the one where he's wearing his little blue baseball T-shirt, and he's got the bat on his shoulder?" Lauren bit down her lip, working it over. "I thought, maybe John would see it, and . . . care."

"You're killing me, Lauren," Lisa whispered.

One of the logs in the fire pit cracked, shifted, popping and falling, sending up a shower of orange and red sparks. Lauren blinked back tears and sipped her wine, watching the bright hot sparks shoot high and then burn out and disappear. She had waited all summer for John to e-mail or call. She waited for him to do the right thing. "He didn't respond," she said, voice faint.

"Of course he didn't." Lisa grabbed a poker and savagely jammed the end into a glowing log, twisting it. "That's because he's a piece of shit." She jammed it again, ferociously crushing the log. "And I hate, hate, *hate* that you contacted him, but"—she took a breath, and looked at her sister with tears filling her eyes—"I understand why you did. You want the fairy tale. You want the happy ending. I get it. I do, too."

Lauren struggled to smile and Lisa poked the fire once more.

"So," Lisa said slowly. "I don't know if this is the right time to talk about this, but I think we should go into business together."

This was a rapid shift and it took Lauren a second to follow. "You do?"

"Yeah. We need to be our own bosses. Call our own shots."

Lauren could feel the wine in her veins. She was definitely

buzzed, but not drunk. "What would we do? Mow lawns? Clean houses? Open a day care?"

"Good God, no." Lisa shuddered and dropped back into her chair, crossing one cowboy boot over the other. "Have a shop. Something upscale and trendy."

Lauren eyed her sister's tattered Wranglers and scuffed-up boots, knowing she was wearing the same outfit. Neither of them had ever been fashionistas. "Trendy and upscale . . . you and me?"

"Not talking clothes or shoes. Talking cupcakes."

Lauren coughed, choking on her mouthful of wine, thinking her sister had to be kidding.

Lisa's chin jerked up and the crackling flames cast a golden, flickering light over her face, revealing the set of her jaw and her determined expression.

Oh, dear. Lauren recognized that expression. Lisa was serious about her proposition.

Although they were two years apart, even as children, Lauren and Lisa had looked so much alike that people thought they were twins with their long, light brown hair, blue-gray eyes, and their stubborn mouth and chin.

"Yes, cupcakes," Lisa repeated firmly. "They're the big thing in Los Angeles right now. Big, fat, beautiful cupcakes with lots of big, fat, pink frosting."

It crossed Lauren's mind that Lisa had been living in L.A. too long. "Lisa. This is Napa. New York and Los Angeles are big cities. Maybe they can handle a cupcake-only business, but there's no way we'd survive on just cupcakes here."

"We could make cakes, too," Lisa said, reaching for the wine bottle but discovering it was empty. "Damn." She looked at Lauren. "Should I open another bottle?"

"Good God, no. I think we've had enough."

Lisa pursed her lips, disappointed. "It helps with brainstorming."

"We've got to keep it real, though. We need to make money, Lisa, and cupcakes aren't going to pay the bills." Lauren gave her glass a swirl, watching the rich red liquid spin. "Furthermore, where would we do this? And do you have any idea what commercial spaces go for?"

Lisa dropped her feet. "I've already found a spot." She smiled. "And it's free."

"Where?"

"Grandma's."

Lauren pictured her grandmother's little Victorian on First Street and started shaking her head. "No. No."

"Why not? First Street is already being developed into a commercial district. Two of the bigger historic houses near Grandma's are B-and-Bs and another one is an art gallery."

"That makes it okay to kick Grandma out?"

"She's moving in with Mom and Dad later this year. She needs help and Dad's not going to put his mom into a nursing home. He'd cut off his right arm first." Lisa rose, headed for the house. "I'm going to get another bottle."

"Not going to drink it," Lauren called after her.

Lisa turned, marched back. "Grandma is leaving her house to us. It's going to be ours anyway—"

"I just can't kick her out, and where would she live here anyway? I've got a room with Blake. You've got a room. Mom and Dad have the master."

"We'd go live there. We'll live in the back and operate the business from the front. We'd need to make changes to the living room and kitchen, but it'd work. Think about it. It could work. Our bakery would be small, inviting, easy . . . it's perfect."

Lauren was thinking about it, and her head, already fuzzy from the wine, was beginning to buzz with something else. Curiosity. Possibility.

"There's no mortgage," Lisa added. "The house is paid for. Grandpa made sure of that years ago."

Lauren wasn't ready to admit it, but she could see the bakery, could see the possibilities, and Grandma's house would be perfect. But they'd need start-up money and there was risk, and God help her, she didn't like failing, and people talking. "If we do this, it's got to be legit, Lisa. Can't do handouts and massive loans we can't pay back. I hate owing people, you know it."

"This is a John Meeks thing, you know that, don't you?"

Lauren pressed her lips together. "Maybe. But I won't go through life apologizing anymore."

"Totally a John Meeks thing."

"Great. We've established that. But I'm serious. If we're going to do this, we're going to do it, you and me. Our money, our muscle, our tears, blood, and sweat."

Lisa grimaced and dropped back down into her chair by the fireplace. "You're not making it sound very appealing right now."

"You know what I'm saying."

"I do. But we're going to need some help, Lauren. At least in the beginning. A loan to help us get on our feet. Construction help to make changes to the kitchen and living room. New appliances for Grandma's kitchen. Commercial ovens and stove. Dishwasher. Big refrigerator."

Lauren snuggled deeper into her jacket and drained what was left in her glass. "Cupcakes won't do it, though. No one is going to line up at our door at eight or nine for a cupcake. We've got to offer something in the morning that has substance. Something folks can grab on their way to work or school." She set her glass down on the ground, stared into the fire, lost in thought. "Remember that place in Fresno you loved when you were going to school there? You loved their sweet cream-cheese croissants."

"And their scrambled-egg-and-cheese ones." She made a face. "I think I gained fifteen pounds that year eating at Le Croissant all the time."

"Le Croissant," Lauren repeated, still thinking. "They were popular, weren't they?"

"Very. Both breakfast and lunch. Always drew a crowd. Plain croissants, chocolate croissants, breakfast ones, lunch ones—"

"That's what we should do." Lauren sat forward, held her hands out to the fire. "Not cupcakes, but croissants. We could open early for breakfast, and make croissant sandwiches for lunch, and then we could close midafternoon and I'd have the rest of the day free with Blake."

Lisa mulled it over. "I like the idea. But I think we could do more than just croissants. Maybe a variety of breads and baked goods to give people options and a reason to keep coming back."

"Cinnamon rolls."

"Grandma's coffee cake."

"Aunt Virginia's lemon meringue pie."

"Would she share her recipe with us?"

"Wouldn't hurt to ask."

Lauren rubbed her hands, getting excited. "We could do this."

"The Summer Sisters' Bakery and Café," Lisa said.

" 'Summer' for Dad and Grandma, who have been here forever."

"Summer for *us*," Lisa retorted.

Lauren grinned. "I think we might want to open another bottle of wine after all."

Bottle open, glasses full, they toasted new ideas and opportunities. "To the future," Lisa said, clinking glasses.

"It's going to be good," Lauren said.

"It's going to be bright."

And it was.

Thirteen years had passed since that Halloween night and the Summer sisters had succeeded far beyond their wildest dreams.

Owning a business with Lisa had given Lauren flexibility and income.

But even more important, it'd gone a long way toward restoring her self-respect.

But now, as she rinsed her empty cereal bowl before leaving it in the sink, it crossed her mind that the restaurant had served its purpose.

It'd been a wonderful experience for the first twelve years, but a big part of her was ready to move on.

Seven

Lauren woke at four, just as she did every morning to be at Mama's Café by five. She needed to be there early to get her cakes and pies in the oven before the café's doors opened to the public at six. Mama's Café had never featured homemade desserts before Lauren started working there, but she couldn't stand the idea of ordering cakes and pies and serving them as her own, and so within a month of starting at the café, she'd taken over the baking, adding her signature desserts from Summer Bakery, and it'd given her a sense of accomplishment, offering something truly fresh and delicious made with her own recipes, with her own hands.

Today, Lauren worked the morning shift, stayed through lunch, made sure her staff was fine closing, and then packed her favorite knives and cooking utensils into a cardboard box and headed to her car to make the drive home.

Just before pulling away from the restaurant, she sent a group text to her mom and Lisa. *Leaving Alameda now.*

It was the middle of the week, and there was no traffic. Leaving the city, Lauren rolled down the window, welcoming the fresh air.

The afternoon was sunny and warm, and it felt good to drive with the breeze blowing through the car, catching at her hair. Now and then she reached up to untangle the long brown strands that snagged on her eyelashes or the tip of her ear.

The drive from Oakland wasn't particularly interesting, not until she'd reached Sonoma County and then cut over to Napa. It was around Sonoma that the land turned into undulating hills with secret valleys, hiding and then revealing farms and ranches, turn-of-the-century farmhouses, and dark green vineyards. Lauren smiled at one of the weathered farmhouses tucked back off the road, shaded by the massive gnarled limbs of a majestic oak tree. As a girl, she'd thought oak trees ugly; now they represented home. For many, Napa was synonymous with wine, but for her it was farmland, cattle, and trees, funny, bumpy, ugly-beautiful oak trees. The cattle would lie beneath them, seeking shelter from the sun, and rub up against them, scratching their backs.

Her parents, Rick and Candy Summer, owned sixty-five acres just outside downtown Napa. Her dad ran cattle on part of the land, and the rest had been turned into fruit and nut orchards. A couple of years ago he had been approached about planting grapes on one hillside. He wasn't interested. The ranch had been in his wife's family for two generations, and he thought they already had a good thing going.

They did, Lauren agreed, crossing the big iron cattle guard marking the entrance to their property just as the sun went down behind the hills. It was twilight as she pulled up in front of the house, and the lavender and gray shadows made the old single-story, three-bedroom house look even smaller and plainer than it usually did.

Her parents weren't fancy people. They didn't spend money on luxuries. Their biggest splurge in years had been adding some premium movie channels to their cable package.

Dad was on the porch waiting for her. Mom came bustling out when Lauren's tennis shoes touched the front steps.

"How was the drive?" Dad asked, giving her a quick hug and taking her overnight bag from her.

"Easy. No traffic," Lauren answered, turning to kiss her mom. "How are things here?"

"Good. I've a roast in the oven. Dinner's almost ready." Mom opened the screen door leading back into the house. "Lisa and Matthieu were going to join us, but Matthieu called a little bit ago saying Lisa wasn't feeling so good and has gone to bed."

"Is she okay?" Lauren asked, following her mom into the kitchen, where she appeared to be in the middle of mashing potatoes.

"Just overtired," her mom answered, adding some more melted butter to the potatoes and turning the mixer back on.

"Two people didn't show up for work today," her dad added, entering the kitchen behind them. "So Lisa had to cover."

Lauren peeked into the oven, spotted the garlic-studded roast, admiring its rich brown color. Mom was a great cook. She'd taught Lauren almost everything she knew about food and flavor. "I wish she would have called me. I would have come up earlier."

"She didn't want you worrying," Mom said, adding a good shake of salt and pepper to the bowl. She looked up at Lauren. "The salad's in the refrigerator, honey. Would you mind putting it on the table?"

"It's time she cut back," her dad said. "It's not good for her, or the baby, to have that kind of stress."

Her dad wasn't looking at her, but Lauren knew the comment was directed at her. Meant for her. He was not happy she'd moved to Alameda last September, and even unhappier that she'd stayed. No one could believe she'd just up and left Napa. She had so much history here, as well as a thriving business. But she did go, and it felt good to go, and honestly, Lauren didn't know if and when she'd ever come back.

"I'll be at the restaurant early tomorrow morning," Lauren said as she carried the salad bowl to the dining room table. The table was already set for five. Lauren went about removing Matthieu's and Lisa's settings. "I can handle everything so she can take the day off and just rest and stay in bed."

"And what about this event you're catering tomorrow?" her dad demanded gruffly, following her into the small, plain dining room with its faded lavender-sprigged wallpaper and oak trim. "How are you going to do that?"

"Easily." She put the extra dishes in her mother's china hutch, the silverware in the chest, and was sliding the place mats into the hutch's drawer when she glanced at her father over her shoulder. His broad, weathered face was creased, his bushy gray eyebrows drawn. "I'm serious, Dad." She softened her tone, went to him, putting a hand on his arm. "The shopping's done. Everything's organized. I've got the staffing—"

"Not the restaurant's servers?"

"No. My catering staff. The ones I use for outside events."

"And the rentals?"

She squeezed his arm. "Booked and being delivered tomorrow morning right to Meg's house."

"What about all the cooking?"

"I've got that under control, too." Lauren rose up on tiptoe, kissed his cheek. "Relax. This isn't my first rodeo."

No, it wasn't her first rodeo, but she wasn't entirely comfortable doing all the cooking and prep for the reception without Lisa to assist her. Things, though, were what they were, and Lauren, not Lisa, had been the one to make the commitment to Meg.

She would make it work. She'd find a way. And no matter how stressful it might be tomorrow, it was only a day. It'd pass. She'd survive. Experience had taught her that.

After dinner, Lauren washed the dishes and stayed up late, making small talk with her parents. Her mom was the first to turn in.

"Aren't you tired?" her dad asked as the clock on the mantel chimed eleven. "You've been up since four."

"I'll go to bed soon," she answered, kissing him good night and then listening as he locked all the doors and walked down the hall to his room.

Lauren changed the TV channels, trying to find something to watch.

Her eyes felt gritty and dry. Her head ached. She was tired. She'd slept badly last night, but she dreaded turning off the TV and going to bed in her parents' house. It was easier here than at Grandma's house, which was actually still her house, filled with her clothes and Blake's things, which was why she was staying here and not there.

But still . . .

Still.

Lauren changed the channels again. No murder programs. No scary horror things. She needed safe, she needed soothing, she went to the Food Network.

But she couldn't stay focused. Her attention wandered from the cake competition on the TV to the framed pictures on the wall of the living room.

Lisa's baby picture.

Lauren's baby picture.

Blake's.

Christ.

She forced her gaze back to the TV, aware that there were other framed photos on that wall, too. Lisa's high school graduation photo. Lauren's. But not Blake's. Because Blake would never graduate.

Lauren turned off the TV and headed to her room, knowing that there were no photos there to haunt her. She'd made sure of that earlier.

In her pajamas, she turned out the lights, climbed into bed, willing herself to sleep.

Instead she thought of Blake. This had been his room, their room. Her dad had painted it yellow and put the Toys "R" Us crib in the corner.

For four years she and Blake had shared this room. It had been so hard for both of them, getting him used to his own room when they moved to Grandma's house. Lauren missed sleeping near him. Missed the sounds he made in his sleep. Missed hearing him breathe at night.

Lauren turned over in bed, dragged the pillow against her chest.

It'd been such a shock to find out she was pregnant. It was still the beginning of her junior year in high school, and she'd only just turned seventeen a few weeks earlier. She hadn't been worried at first when she was late. She was often late. But as the weeks passed, she got nervous. Scared. She didn't tell anyone, not even Lisa, who was away at college, a freshman at UC Irvine. Just hoped against hope her period would come.

It didn't.

Lauren took the pregnancy test the day before the big homecoming parade and game. Positive.

She wanted to call John Meeks, her boyfriend, immediately, needing to talk, needing his support, but she knew even before she called him what he'd tell her to do.

John Meeks wasn't familiar with compromise. A senior at Napa, he was a standout in football, basketball, and baseball, having lettered in each sport his sophomore year, and Division I schools wanted him for both football and baseball, dangling scholarship offers, but John had his eye on something greater. He didn't want to go to college. He wanted to go pro right out of high school.

Lauren used to listen to him talk, awed and impressed by his vision for his future. He was going to be big, and he was going to make a lot of money, and nothing and no one would stand in his way.

She'd never dated anyone like John before.

In fact, when he'd first asked her to the winter formal the year before, she'd laughed nervously, thinking he was joking. Even as a junior, he was a big man on campus. Girls loved him. Guys wanted to be him. And Lauren couldn't believe he would be interested in her.

He was, he insisted, telling her he loved that she was sweet and natural, thinking it cute she did all the aggie stuff like 4-H and Future Farmers of America. Then, once they were a couple, he immediately set about changing her.

Gone were her boots and Wranglers. Gone were the silver belt buckles she'd worn with everything. Gone were the long ponytails. John liked his girlfriend to be feminine, pretty, which meant that every morning Lauren fussed with her hair before school, and wore shoes that hurt her feet. It was a lot of work being John's girlfriend, but it was also exciting.

People knew John, they followed him, keeping track of his stats and what he'd achieved in his last game—the points, the turnovers, the plays—and now they knew who she was, too.

And her parents, who weren't easily impressed, liked John. A lot. He was tall, handsome, polite. A star.

A polite, charismatic star, he charmed the pants off his teachers, his coaches, even the school administration.

It wasn't long before he charmed the pants off Lauren, too.

It actually took more effort on his part than he'd anticipated. Lauren was shy and conservative. But John was persistent. After spending all June and much of July trying to put brakes on John's advances, she gave in one day late in July, and they made love for the first time in the tiny shed that reeked of the chlorine and chemicals the Meekses used for their pool.

They'd done it standing up, not the most comfortable position for a first time, but he'd gone down on her and made sure she was wet, and Lauren wouldn't say it hurt badly. It just wasn't fun. He kissed her after, assuring her it'd be better next time, and he was right. When they did it the next day, back in the hot, sweaty, chlorine-drenched shed, it was . . . okay. She didn't come, but neither did she bleed. A definite plus.

For the rest of the summer, the pool house was "their spot." It was set back from the house, and John even added a padlock to ensure they had privacy.

Lauren liked kissing, and got used to the sex, but sex was never the romantic thing romance novels and movies made it out be.

It was a relief when school finally started in September. Lauren loved John, but she was finding it tough studying and helping out on the ranch when she was always so tired.

The exhaustion became almost all-consuming. Lauren couldn't stay awake. She started to doze off in class. She played hooky one day just to stay in bed and catch up on sleep.

"This isn't normal," her mom said, inspecting Lauren's eyes, touching her face and then her forehead. "Good."

"Why?"

"I wondered if you had mono."

"Mono?"

"The kissing disease."

But no, it wasn't the kissing disease. It took a home pregnancy test to rule that out.

John didn't take the news well.

He liked Lauren—she was a very pretty, sweet girl, a very pretty, sweet, accommodating girl—but he wasn't about to settle down, and had absolutely zero interest in fatherhood.

His parents agreed with him. The Meekses offered to pay for the abortion.

Lauren's parents told the Meekses to back off and let Lauren decide what she wanted to do.

The Meekses offered her some serious money if she'd end the pregnancy soon.

"John doesn't need this distraction right now," Mr. Meeks

had said, appearing at the Summers' house one October evening. "This has to be handled immediately."

But Lauren couldn't get an abortion, and after a week of sleepless nights, she announced she'd give the baby up for adoption instead.

Mr. Meeks worked with a prominent attorney who handled adoptions, and a couple was found for John and Lauren's baby.

Everything went as planned.

Lauren attended school until Christmas break and was then homeschooled her second semester. She went into labor, a week and a half early, on April 25. After twenty-six hours of labor, the baby arrived, weighing six pounds eight ounces and measuring twenty inches long.

Lauren had been warned not to hold the baby. She'd been warned that it would make the good-bye so much harder. But once she heard her baby's cry, there was no way she could let him go.

She was his mom.

He was her sun and moon.

The Meekses were furious. The baby had to go. The baby was supposed to go. Lauren had promised.

Mr. Meeks threatened legal action.

Her dad threatened to do serious damage to Mr. Meeks's face.

Mr. Meeks stormed out, and Lauren never heard from any of the Meekses again. John included.

By the time she returned to school in the fall, John was already off playing football for some college in the Midwest.

And even though he was gone, Lauren knew that one day she would hear from him, because how could he not care about his son?

Four thirty the next morning Lauren was in her car, heading for downtown Napa. It was dark, still pitch-black, and she was thankful she'd grown up on the ranch's winding country roads as there were no streetlights here, just sharp curves and deep valleys, and her car's headlights only illuminated so far.

She reached downtown before it was even five and parked on South Main Street, deserted at this early hour. Leaving her car, she cut down Third Street to the riverfront and walked along the river, under the streetlights, listening to her footsteps and the gurgle and rush of water.

She could do this, she told herself. She could handle this. Just go to the restaurant. Unlock the door. *You'll be fine.*

So she turned around, retracing her steps, hands thrust deep into her coat pockets, head down, putting one foot in front of the other, before taking a shortcut down Main Street and over another block.

Crossing the quiet street, Lauren glanced up at the dark building. It was a handsome brick corner building, a former bank, three stories high, with big windows on two sides and lots of trim. While she admired the building's aesthetics, she'd never been comfortable here, in this new space.

It was too much square footage, and the elegant ceilings Lisa adored were too high and impersonal in Lauren's eyes.

They were here, in this new spot, because of Matthieu.

He'd been the one to insist they needed the change. And while Lauren knew they were outgrowing her grandmother's Victorian, she wasn't ready to relocate. The timing was all wrong, for one thing. Blake was a junior in high school. He was studying hard for his SATs. It was also baseball season and he had games almost every night of the week.

But Matthieu owned the bank building, and he'd poured over a million dollars into renovations, and he was anxious to fill the space. He offered to ready the ground floor, covering the costs of adding a kitchen and making the other necessary changes if Lauren and Lisa would handle the lease.

Lauren said no.

Lisa said yes.

The sisters were at odds for weeks, barely speaking at one point, which didn't help in running the restaurant or their catering business. Lauren didn't want to be financially stretched, not when Blake would be going away to college soon. But Matthieu had insisted the move would be profitable, with better parking, signage, and increased foot traffic.

Blake, who absolutely adored his Aunt Lisa, had sided with her and Matthieu, and Lauren, cornered and outnumbered, caved in.

So Lisa and Matthieu went to work, teaming with a local architect to remodel the ground floor, dividing the old bank lobby into sections, added partitions, creating hallways, bathrooms, and storage closets. One fifth of the sunlit bank lobby became an old-world bakery with a huge mahogany glass display case for all the cakes and pastries and sweets, another chunk became a modern, efficient kitchen, and the rest was turned into a sophisticated café with dozens of round marble-topped tables, black-lacquered chairs, big mirrors in thick gilded frames, and a long gleaming white marble counter paired with tall, red leather stools.

It was beautiful. Stunning.

Très chic.

The new, improved Summer Bakery & Café was written up everywhere, and the reviews were brilliant. Matthieu and Lisa did tons of interviews, too, and the publicity ensured there was immediate traffic. From the first day they opened their new glossy door, business boomed.

Matthieu had been right about their location. Parking was plentiful and foot traffic excellent. The compliments poured in from both old customers and new. The comments on Yelp and TripAdvisor were glowing. The café was delightful. Excellent food, impeccable service, and a comfortable but stylish interior.

Matthieu and Lisa were delirious with happiness. Lauren less so, but even she saw that this new location was a positive, that people enjoyed all the light and the location close to the new riverfront development.

Lauren had been here, that morning last June, the morning everything changed.

Here, she silently repeated, fishing her keys out of her purse to let herself in. She held her breath as she unlocked the front door, the air still bottled in her lungs as she locked it behind her. Little spots danced before her eyes as she switched on the overhead light.

Come on, now, she told herself, *breathe.*

She did. Exhaled, inhaled, and repeated.

You can do this, she told herself. *You can. Just walk, one foot in front of the other. Through the dining room, to the kitchen.*

And that's what she did, walking through the hall into the restaurant, switching on lights as she went past the hostess stand, winding through marble-topped tables on her way back to the kitchen.

Everything looked good. Surfaces sparkled.

Her gaze swept the interior, over the pale marble tabletops and counter, the creamy-white stone flecked with gold and shots of gray and black. The dark, polished wood gleamed. Inhaling, she smelled citrus and thyme in the air, and then turning the corner, heading for the kitchen, she spotted a potted lemon tree by the window, the dark green leaves dotted with milky-white blossoms.

Ridiculously emotional, Lauren stopped and gently touched one of the white citrus blossoms, then bent to sniff the scent. Sweet, so very sweet.

Eyes stinging, she peeled off her coat and hung it up on a hook in the massive broom closet before turning around to face the giant kitchen.

She was in here that morning, working, when she got the first call. June 13.

Heart twisting, pulse racing, Lauren reached out, put a hand on the counter, needing something solid next to her, feeling the past rise up, huge, so huge, so horrible.

But she hadn't even known that first call was bad, hadn't known it was the start of the end.

It seemed so innocuous. Napa High's attendance office phoning to let her know that Blake had been marked absent that morning.

The second call came not even two minutes later, buzzing in as Lauren was trying to reach Blake on his cell phone. It was the mom of one of the girls in Blake's car pool. Paige had just been marked absent. Was Paige maybe doing something with Blake? Mrs. Garrett knew they were just a few days away from summer, a few days from the kids becoming seniors . . . had they planned something today? Were they playing truant to go to the beach or lake?

I don't know, Lauren had answered, trying to stay calm. *I'll let you know as soon as I talk to Blake.*

But hanging up, she tried Blake again. He didn't pick up.

She shot him a text next. *Where r u?*

And then another, still trying not to panic. *What's going on?*

Lauren pulled the miniature banana cakes from the oven, set them aside to cool, and then tried phoning Blake again, this time leaving him a message. *Blake, call me. This isn't funny. I'm getting worried.*

He didn't call.

She didn't know what to do. Blake, a serious student and a competitive athlete, didn't ditch. He cared about his grades. He rarely partied. He had big plans for his future. But finals were over. His big paper was done, turned in last night before midnight at turnitin.com.

She mixed up the icing, her thoughts racing as the beaters whipped the powdered sugar into the softened cream cheese.

Maybe the kids were off to Santa Cruz for the day. Blake's friends surfed and they'd been teaching Blake last summer.

They could be in an area without good cell reception.

It was going to be fine. Blake was a good kid. Responsible. He'd call as soon as he saw her messages.

And then her phone rang. It was Dad. He'd heard there had

been a bad accident on Highway 112, a 1987 Camaro, which they both knew was Daniel Avery's car, and Dad called, wondering if Daniel had maybe picked up Blake for school that morning . . .

Lauren's legs buckled. She didn't remember fainting. Didn't remember waking up on the floor with Lisa and the kitchen staff around her, didn't remember Matthieu in the hall on the phone himself, trying to get the facts after hearing on the news that there had been a horrific accident on Highway 112 involving four teenagers. The car had caught fire, and early reports had it that only one teenager had been airlifted to the hospital. The other three died at the scene.

It would be another hour before Lauren learned that Blake was one of the three who died at the scene.

It would be days before she believed it.

Months before she accepted it.

And now it was almost a year . . . almost a year since her boy had been taken, and Lauren hated this restaurant that wasn't her restaurant but Lisa and Matthieu's . . .

She hated it because it wasn't Grandma's Victorian house. She hated it because it didn't have old wooden tables covered in white linen clothes embroidered with cheerful red thread. She hated that the little glass vases of miniature roses and daisies had given way to chic, potted citrus trees.

Their old café had been cheerful and comfortable, inviting one to relax over a cup of coffee and a generous slice of coffee cake.

They didn't even serve coffee cake at this new location.

No, this new location was all about new. New look, new menus, inventive new foods—with a French twist.

And Lauren understood, she did.

Lisa had fallen in love with a Frenchman and had embraced his culture. There was nothing wrong with being chic . . . or having an elegant café. It just wasn't Lauren.

She was a country girl, fond of flea markets, thrift stores, vintage anything, and shabby chic.

Once upon a time Lisa had been the same. But that was back before she fell in love with a Frenchman from Bordeaux who happened to have grown up in a five-hundred-year-old château. (Although, apparently, growing up in a château wasn't such a big deal in France, as Bordeaux was full of them.)

And honestly, it didn't matter if Lisa loved the glamorous background or not. Because she could have fallen in love with him for his charming French accent.

Or possibly his style. He had his own unique style, and he wore his dark brown hair long, as if he were an international soccer star.

And he had brown eyes—warm, smiling eyes—and a masculine chin beneath a strong, Gallic nose.

So no, Lisa hadn't fallen in love with Matthieu Roussel for his money. But good God, it helped.

"Lisa said you'd be here." Matthieu's deep voice suddenly sounded in the shadowy hall, startling Lauren.

She jumped, turned, slamming her elbow on the counter. "When did you arrive?" she demanded, rubbing her elbow and glaring at him as he emerged from the dark hall into the kitchen.

"Just now."

"I didn't hear you."

"I will bang on the door with a hammer next time," he answered, his brown eyes warm, smiling at her.

Lauren refused to be charmed in any size, shape, or form by Lisa's attractive and charming husband. "That would be nice. What brings you here so early?"

"I've been sent here on a mission." He extended a hand, a big stainless-steel thermos in his hand. "Your sister said you'd be here and that you'd need coffee. *Vite.*"

He'd come bearing gifts. Coffee, specifically. Okay, maybe Lauren would allow herself to be just a little bit charmed. "Thank you."

He smiled benevolently. "Or should I say *'schnell'*? Since I believe you studied German in school."

She wasn't going to laugh. She hadn't had coffee and she was in this kitchen she detested. "Or you could just say 'fast,' Matthieu, since we are in America and I speak English."

"I didn't think of that."

She rolled her eyes at him, and yet it was all an act. It was impossible to dislike Matthieu.

Gratefully, she unscrewed the top of the thermos and watched the steam escape from it. Lauren inhaled deeply, greedily, letting the aroma fill her nose. She took a cautious sip. The coffee was hot and strong and perfect. "Really good."

"Not too strong?"

"No. It's heaven." She took another sip, grateful for small blessings. "Tell Lisa she hasn't lost her touch."

He leaned against the counter. "I made it."

"*You* did?"

"Ever since Lisa became pregnant, she can't stomach the smell of coffee."

"So she didn't wake up and make me coffee?"

"No. She woke me up and told me to make you coffee."

Lauren laughed and shook her head.

Matthieu might be a gorgeous, wealthy Frenchman born in a five-hundred-year-old château, but she couldn't hold that against him forever. Not when he was truly nice. And so devoted to his wife.

"So what do we do first?" Matthieu asked her, going to the sink to wash his hands.

Lauren swallowed her coffee and looked at him vigorously soaping up his hands as if he was about to perform surgery or deliver a baby. "You're . . . helping . . . me?"

"*Oui.*" He flashed her a smile. "I am here to assist you."

"So you can cook now?"

"Not cook. But I can chop and mix and stir and watch things in the oven to make sure they don't burn."

"Since when?"

"Since you were gone." He saw her baffled look and added with an apologetic shrug, "Lisa was lonely when you left."

Lisa was lonely. Lonely. Good God, Lauren had never really thought about that, had she?

"So I'd come in and help her," he added with another half smile. "And I warn you, I'm not a cook, not even close, but I've learned how to be good company."

Lauren stared at him for an endless moment before going to him and giving him a fierce hug. "Thank you," she whispered. "Thank you for being there for her."

"I love her."

Lauren's eyes stung. She stepped back and smiled a watery smile. "I'm glad."

He clapped his hands on her shoulders, held firm. "And I love you."

Suddenly she couldn't hang on to her smile. She looked up into his face, and yet he'd gone all blurry with her tears.

He squeezed her shoulders again then let go. "So. Let's get to work. What do I do first?"

Eight

After spending all morning cooking, Lauren was ready for the reception at Meg's house on Friday afternoon. She was also ready for it to be over so she could head back to Alameda.

She loved her family, and beautiful Napa, but her tiny little apartment in Alameda was easier. Quieter. Free of all these complicated relationships and even more complicated emotions.

Lauren and Lisa were in Meg's kitchen, warming everything and still setting up the buffet when Lauren heard the first of the cars approach.

A series of dark limousines pulled up before the door. One limousine, two, three, four.

The Roberts and Brennan families were back, returning from the brief, formal funeral service for Jack at Santa Rosa's oldest Episcopal church, the Church of the Incarnation. Lauren knew the small 1873 church well, as one of her friends from high school had been married there and Lauren had decorated the church and hall for them, donating her time, as well as the flowers, to help Allie save on expenses.

"They're here," Lauren said, quickly drying her hands and removing her apron. She'd be serving the late lunch, and cleaning up with two other girls hired for the occasion while Preston handled the bar and Lisa manned the kitchen. "They'd said it would be a brief service. Didn't realize that meant under thirty minutes."

"They're back way too early," Lisa answered, bending awkwardly at the stove to remove three cookie sheets of sourdough rolls and cheese biscuits from the oven, one after the other, all while being very careful not to bump her belly. "Nothing's ready."

"The bar is ready. The wines are uncorked, and the lemonade and iced tea are already out. What more do we need?"

Lisa wiped her damp brow. "Um, food?"

Car doors slammed outside. Voices echoed as people approached the house. Lauren glanced outside and spotted Meg walking toward the front door, her arms around her daughters, her black coat draped in the crook of one elbow. Her black dress was simple, almost severe, and her dark hair was scraped back in a low, unattractive knot, but as she focused on her girls, her expression was kind.

Lauren's chest ached and she turned away from the window, not wanting to see more, because it would just make her feel more, and feeling wasn't something she could, or would, do today. "People can wait," she said crisply. "They'll drink. They'll talk. They'll be fine."

Lisa shot her younger sister an incredulous glance. "I can't believe you're so calm. You used to be the queen of panic, Miss Type A, always stressing out."

Lauren shrugged as she opened the refrigerator and drew out two of the silver trays filled with miniature sandwiches and peeled the plastic wrap off each. "I've learned that not everything is life and death because there is real life and death."

Lisa cringed. "Oh God. Sorry—"

"Why apologize? You didn't say anything wrong. You asked why I'm chill, and so I told you. Now sit for a second. Catch your breath. It's about to get crazy."

Sarah was grateful to be back at Meg's house. The service, surprisingly similar to the Catholic Church's funeral service, did not include a Eucharist, due to its being Good Friday, which kept things brief.

Pleasingly brief.

Carrying Ella into the house, Sarah felt a little guilty for being happy that the service was short, but the last week had been beyond grueling, with everyone unraveling beneath the stress and grief of two deaths, and two funerals, in a little more than a week. Sarah, by being the youngest, had never really been caught up in the family dramas until this last year when she'd been shocked and outraged that Meg—*Meg*—had cheated on her husband with her vintner boss, Chad.

But now Sarah found herself struggling with Brianna and Kit, too.

It didn't help that today in the church, she had sat behind Meg, her kids, and Jack's parents, squished into her pew with Ella on one side and Kit and Jude jammed against the other.

Tommy and Cass were supposed to be sitting with Sarah and Ella, but at the last second Brianna claimed Cass and Tommy, forcing Jude, Kit, and Sarah into the same pew.

Nice, Brianna. Thanks.

Just because Sarah had gone to Meg the other night and asked her to please ignore what she had said about Jude didn't mean everything was okay between Sarah and Kit. It wasn't. Kit was still angry with her and Sarah didn't know how to process what Brianna had said about the whole molestation thing.

Sarah shuddered. She didn't want to know more, didn't want

any of the details. It was too horrifying, too overwhelming to imagine her sisters going through it, living with it, but then, on the other hand, she *ought* to know. Weren't sisters supposed to know these things?

But after two weeks of being here in California, with her *sisters,* Sarah was tapped out. Families, especially big Irish-American families filled with opinionated sisters, were a lot of work.

Meg's voice in the entryway caught Sarah's attention. She glanced at Meg, who stood surrounded by her kids as people pressed toward them, offering condolences.

Sarah didn't know how Meg did it. Gabi had been hysterical during the funeral service, lying across her mother's lap, sobbing uncontrollably.

Jack's parents had been clearly uncomfortable with Gabi's grief, and Jack's mother, Abigail, even said something under her breath to Meg about the girl's excessive display of emotion. Meg had simply looked into her mother-in-law's eyes until Abigail dropped her gaze.

Score one for Mary Margaret, Sarah had thought.

Meg was just as amazing now with the people gathered around her. She was Mary Margaret at her best, talking, listening, warmly thanking people for coming. It's what Mom would have done. But then, as the oldest child, Meg had learned from the best.

Sarah put Ella down. "Let's find you something to eat," she said, taking her daughter's hand.

"I'm not hungry," Ella said, backing closer to Sarah as two big teenage boys passed by. Ella was always more clingy when strangers were around. Sarah hoped she would one day develop more confidence, but she hadn't yet.

"I bet those are JJ's friends," Sarah said, smoothing her daughter's dark hair. "Do you think they play baseball like JJ and Daddy?"

Ella barely glanced at the boys. "I don't know." She tugged on her mom's hand. "Can I go upstairs? Play with Molly?" she asked, referring to the brown-haired, blue-eyed American Girl doll she got for Christmas and insisted on taking everywhere.

"Do you want to get her and bring her downstairs?"

Ella's gaze scanned the room. "I just want to go upstairs."

"Okay. I'll be down here if you need me."

Twenty minutes into the reception, Lauren moved through the crowded living room, doing her first sweep for dirty plates, discarded, lipstick-smudged wineglasses, and balled-up cocktail napkins that would inevitably hide a toothpick or two. But most people hadn't eaten yet and she succeeded in rescuing only two wine goblets and one lonely plate.

She couldn't wait to escape the living room, though, and focused on breathing through her mouth to avoid inhaling the fragrant lilies, roses, and gardenias used in the lavish floral arrangements that covered every flat surface.

So many flowers.

So many people.

So much like Blake's funeral.

But she wouldn't think about Blake, not today. She was just going to work, and stay busy, and get through the day so she could return to her little apartment in Alameda tonight.

A firm hand reached out, stopping her. "Lauren."

She looked up into Chad Hallahan's eyes. "Hi," she said, surprised, and yet not surprised to see him, as the Hallahans had insisted on donating all the wine for the reception today, and Chad had personally dropped the bottles off this morning. He'd worn jeans and a T-shirt earlier. Now he was dressed in black trousers and a white dress shirt, open at the collar, and looked as blond, bronzed, and ruggedly handsome as ever.

"How's Meg doing?" he asked.

She shook her head. "I don't know. Haven't really talked to her today. There are always so many people around her."

He looked away, his brow creasing. "Hate this," he muttered.

"It's horrible," she agreed, thinking that tongues would soon be wagging. Over the summer, even though Lauren had been grieving Blake's death, she'd still caught some of the gossip about Chad and Meg. Napa was a small town and all the locals knew one another's business, good and bad, and so through the hot summer months, people discussed Meg's affair with her boss, Chad, speculating about what had happened, as well as what would happen in the future. Would Jack Roberts divorce his wife or would he take her back? Would Meg leave her husband for Chad? Would Meg and Jack be able to work it out?

And now Chad was here, which would result in more gossip.

"I'd heard you'd moved to Berkeley," Chad said.

"Alameda," she corrected. "Moved in September. I'm managing a little New Orleans–style café there."

"Beignets and café au lait?"

"And lots of omelets, grits, and biscuits, too."

"A breakfast place?"

"Breakfast and lunch. We close at three, and I'm usually out of there by four, but we're toying with trying to stay open, see if we can draw a dinner crowd."

"Where is it?"

"On Park Street, just down from Books, Inc."

Chad looked apologetic. "I don't know Alameda."

"The downtown's cute. It's got a little historic district and I live close enough to ride my bike to work."

"So you're just back for today?"

Lauren nodded. "Meg needed help." She stumbled a little over Meg's name, feeling strange to be talking about Meg with him, even though she'd catered a dozen different events at the winery during the past six years, and she'd always been comfortable around the Hallahans and Meg.

"Thank you for handling the reception," he said. "I'm glad it's you, although I know it can't be easy."

Lauren shrugged, not wanting to go there.

"I hope you won't stay away forever," he added. "We miss you in Napa."

She nodded, forced a smile. She'd gone to school with Chad and Craig, who was older, just as their parents had gone to school together. The Hallahans, like the Summers, were an old ranching family that dated back to the late nineteenth century. She knew Chad lived in his great-grandfather's farmhouse now.

"I haven't left for good," she said briskly, smiling, keeping her voice strong. "Just a change of scenery."

But Chad saw past her tough-girl facade. He reached out, touched her shoulder. "How are you doing?"

She couldn't let him in, couldn't let his kindness shatter her control. "Fine."

"He was a really good kid, Lauren."

She felt a little crack in the ice around her heart. It couldn't happen. She didn't want to feel. Didn't want to feel anything at all. "Don't," she gritted. "Can't."

"We all miss him," he added. "And I never drive past your old place on First without thinking about him."

"Thank you," she whispered.

"Meeks blew it. Blew it in a big way."

Her smile faded, and she looked away, suddenly dizzy and nauseous. "Lisa's here," she said, her voice sounding faint to her own ears. "She's pregnant. Due next month. Have you seen her?"

"No. Where is she?"

"In the kitchen. Come say hello to her before you leave."

"I will."

She flashed a smile, hoped it *was* a smile, and then murmured something about needing to get rid of the dishes, before disappearing into the crowded hall; she slipped past Lisa in the kitchen, put everything in the heavy plastic trays in the mud room, and then stepped outside, hands on her hips, gulping air to keep from bursting into tears.

How hard.

How hard all of this was. Life and death, loving and losing, and trying to move forward, because what else could you do? She was only thirty-five. Too young to lie down and die. No, she'd fight through this, fight to make it, not merely for her own sake, but for Blake's. He deserved to be remembered. He deserved to be cherished. And as long as she lived, he'd live in her heart, and that's all she could do now. Keep him in her heart. Love him with all her heart.

"It's too much, isn't it?" Lisa asked from the doorway.

Lauren turned around, hands knotting. "People want to talk about him. They want to tell me he was good, and wonderful, but I can't handle it. I can't."

"That's because everybody here knew him, and loved him."

"Everybody but his own father!"

"Oh, Lauren, don't even go there!" Lisa put a hand on her belly. "John was a seed, a spark, not a father. We all adored Blake. He was our boy, too."

Lauren nodded, knowing it was true. She'd been sixteen when she'd gotten pregnant, seventeen when she had her baby, and her family helped her raise him the first couple of years while Lauren finished school.

"If you want to go, I can manage the rest," Lisa added.

Lauren straightened, squaring her shoulders. "I'm not leaving you."

"I can see this is killing you."

"It's hard, but it's not killing me. I'm a Summer. Tough, thanks to our hearty German DNA."

Lisa stepped back so Lauren could enter the house before closing the door behind her. "It is good to see you. I've missed you."

Lauren patted Lisa's belly. "I can't believe how big you've gotten."

Lisa's eyes widened. "She just kicked!" she said, grabbing Lauren's hand and putting it back on her belly. The baby obliged by kicking again, hard.

"Feisty little thing," Lauren said.

"Just like her Aunt Lauren." Lisa held her sister's gaze. "'Cause Aunt Lauren's inspiring. Strong. And beautiful—"

"Stop."

"You are."

"Don't feel very strong. Feel pretty damn broken."

"Fortunately, feelings aren't reality. They're just feelings." Lisa's gaze rested on her sister's face. "Meg told me how much she appreciates you coming home to do this. I appreciate it, too. It's nice working with you again. Have missed it."

Lauren felt a pang of regret. "I abandoned you, didn't I?"

"You'll be back."

"That's right."

"Because if you don't come back, I'm not sure I want to continue Summer Bakery and Café without you." Lisa held Lauren's gaze. "It's not as much fun without you."

Lauren felt a sharp twinge of guilt. Lisa wasn't just her sister, she once had been her best friend, but since Blake's accident, Lauren had virtually shut her out. "I miss working with you, too," she said softly. "I miss not seeing you every day. It's weird not seeing you. And now I've missed nearly all of your pregnancy."

"Better to miss the pregnancy than miss the baby's birth." Lisa smiled uncertainly. "You *are* coming home for the birth? She should be here in the next month."

Lauren nodded. Lisa had been her birthing partner when she had Blake. "Absolutely."

"And you'll be the godmother?"

Lauren struggled to hang on to her smile. "Of course."

"I know this isn't easy, but it'll be good for us. Good for the family. New life . . . new hopes and dreams."

Lauren kept smiling, aware that Lisa had no idea how much

her words hurt. New life . . . new hopes and dreams . . . as if Blake could be replaced that easily. And of course that wasn't what Lisa meant, but it was how it felt.

"I'll need your help and advice," Lisa continued. "You were such a great mom. You'll be able to tell me what I'm doing wrong—" She swallowed nervously. "I'm saying all the wrong things, aren't I?"

"Yes." But Lauren softened the words by leaning forward and hugging her sister. "But it's okay. I don't know what the right words are anymore. I'm just glad your little one is almost here. I can't wait to meet her."

Lisa held Lauren tightly. "You mean that?"

"I do. You're going to be a wonderful mom—" Lauren broke off, sniffed the air. "Something's burning. Smell that?"

"The tartlets!" Lisa screeched, racing for the oven.

Sarah spent a half hour hanging out with her dad and his brothers in the living room before going upstairs to check on Ella.

She found her in Tessa's bedroom, in front of Tessa's old dollhouse, which was actually a miniature of Monticello, made by Jack for his daughter's eighth birthday. Tessa was sitting on the floor next to Ella, pointing out all the dollhouse's architectural details.

"This is basically Roman neoclassical architecture," Sarah heard Tessa explain to Ella. "This is called a portico, and this is a dome. It's made out of glass, just like the real Monticello. See?" Tessa lightly tapped the delicate dome of her dollhouse and then gestured to the ceilings. "See how the ceilings are different heights? Jefferson's real house was like that, too. And look at these little rooms. These are the privies. That's what they called the bathrooms in those days. Although Dad said Thomas Jefferson called his bathrooms air-closets and they all had skylights. Pretty smart, huh?"

Sarah quietly stepped out of the bedroom and was heading back down the hall for the stairs when she passed JJ's room and caught a whiff of something that stopped her short. She sniffed again. Marijuana.

Boone didn't smoke it, and Sarah didn't anymore, but she had in college. Lots of kids had smoked it in Capitola, too. But marijuana, here, in Meg's house? Not good,

If Meg caught JJ smoking in his room, she'd have a fit.

Sarah put her ear to the door, heard music. He must be in there. She knocked lightly, once. He didn't answer.

Uncertain as to what she should do, she opened his bedroom door a crack and peeked in.

The sunlit room revealed skin. Naked teenage skin. And lots of it.

Boy and girl parts, too.

Arms, legs, butts, breasts.

Arms, legs, butts, and breasts moving, rocking, groping, *groaning.*

Christ!

Sarah closed the door quickly, quietly, praying that they hadn't heard her. Or seen her.

But maybe she should have made a noise. Maybe she should make them stop.

Sarah was massively conflicted. Meg would freak if she thought JJ was having sex, in her house, during Jack's funeral reception.

But . . .

It was also JJ's dad's funeral reception, and apparently this was how he felt comforted.

But Sarah wished she hadn't seen it. JJ naked, orgasmic, his room reeking of weed . . .

If Meg discovered them . . .

No, Sarah wouldn't go there, and she most definitely wasn't going to get in the middle of this one.

She was halfway down the stairs when she spotted Kit at the foot, arms crossed over her chest, expression worried.

"Everything okay?" Sarah asked, aware that things with Kit were still on the tense side, and still not totally sure how to fix them.

"Yes."

But Kit looked stressed and it troubled Sarah. "Are you sure?"

Kit hesitated. "Yes." She forced a smile and tucked a dark red tendril behind her ear. "Thanks."

"Kit," Brianna said, walking through the front door, her black dress swimming on her small frame, "your man's outside, on the phone. He wanted me to tell you he'll be in soon. Or as soon as he can. Something like that."

"Oh." Kit looked somewhat relieved. "Okay."

"Speaking of men . . ." Brianna's voice trailed off. "Do either of you know who the guy is outside, talking to Meg?"

"Where?" Sarah asked.

"There," Brianna answered, drawing Sarah toward the open front door.

Kit followed and glanced toward the far end of the porch, where Meg stood talking to a tall, good-looking man in black trousers and a white dress shirt.

"Who *is* that?" Brianna demanded.

"Chad," Kit said.

Brianna's eyes widened. "*The* Chad?"

"Yep." A smile hovered at Kit's lips. "Cute, huh?"

Way more than cute, Sarah thought, jostling for a better position in the doorway, wanting a closer look. So this was the infamous Chad Hallahan. Dark blond, thick wavy hair, light eyes, a deep tan. Muscles, too.

Kind of like a baseball player.

Hot.

"Gorgeous," Bree said, whistling appreciatively. "He's definitely got the whole Robert Redford thing going, doesn't he?"

"I don't see it," Sarah said.

"Young Redford, from the sixties and seventies."

"I wasn't born until the late seventies," Sarah reminded her.

"I know, but you've seen his films. *The Sting, Butch Cassidy and the Sundance Kid, All the President's Men . . .*" Brianna paused to take a breath.

"The Great Gatsby," Kit added.

"The Natural!" Sarah put in.

Kit smiled. "You would know the baseball one."

"I think I've seen every baseball movie ever made," Sarah admitted.

Kit nodded in Meg and Chad's direction. "So what do you think he's saying to her?"

"He's probably telling her how sorry he is," Bree said. "That he's here for her, that he's always been here for her, and if she should need anything, all she just has to do is call." Her lips twitched. "You know, boring stuff like that."

Kit folded her arms across her chest. "But she's not going to call him. It's over."

Brianna looked disappointed. "You really think so?"

Sarah nodded. "Meg told me just last week it'd been a big mistake, that he wasn't the right one for her."

"She said the same thing to me," Kit added.

Brianna's eyebrows rose. "The lady doth protest too much, methinks."

Sarah tuned Brianna out, focusing instead on Meg and Chad, because it was impossible not to.

Just as it was impossible to ignore Chad's body language.

He stood close to Meg, very close, clearly concerned about her.

Suddenly Meg's shoulders shook and her head bowed. Chad started to reach for her, but then drew back and buried his hands in his pockets, his expression tortured.

He still cared for Meg, Sarah thought.

He might even still love her.

She turned away. "I need a drink."

* * *

S arah made her way to the far end of the dining room where a small bar had been set up. The young male bartender she had seen earlier was gone, replaced by a pretty woman with long brown hair who was opening a bottle of red wine.

Sarah leaned on the counter. She recognized the label. Dark Horse Winery. Glancing at the row of bottles, she saw they all had the Dark Horse label.

"Are you only serving Dark Horse wine?" she asked, watching as the bartender uncorked a Shiraz.

"Yes. The Hallahans donated the wine." The bartender wiped down the open bottle.

"Do you know the Hallahan brothers?" Sarah asked, intrigued.

The woman nodded. "I grew up in Napa. We all went to the same high school. Craig was a couple of years older than me, and Chad was a year behind."

"What year did you graduate?"

"'Ninety-five."

Sarah was surprised. The woman looked young . . . at least, younger than her. "So did I."

"Where are you from?"

"San Francisco."

"A city girl."

"I am." Sarah smiled. "By the way, I'm Sarah, Meg's youngest sister."

The bartender looked intrigued and extended her hand. "I'm Lauren Summer. I've worked with Meg for years. She's always used us to cater her events." Lauren gestured to the open bottles. "Can I pour you something? Red, white, beer?"

"I'd love a glass of white. Whatever you have that's cold."

"It's all cold, and while the Chardonnay is Dark Horse's big seller, I'm partial to their new Sauvignon Blanc."

"I'll try the Sauvignon Blanc, then."

"If you don't like it, I can pour you something else."

"It could be battery acid right now, and I'd probably drink it."

Lauren grinned, and a dimple flashed in her cheek. "You're different from Meg."

"I'm the baby of the family, youngest of five," Sarah answered drily. "I think my parents were worn out by the time I came along. Meg claims I got away with murder."

"Did you?" Lauren asked, handing her a goblet.

"Not murder, but I did get a car at sixteen," Sarah said, lifting the glass to her mouth, hiding her smile. "And no one else did."

Lauren laughed. "I bet your brothers and sisters had something to say about that."

"Oh, plenty, but Mom said they could all come home from college or whatever and drive me around to all my activities and games because she couldn't. She was working."

"Your mom worked?"

Sarah nodded. "She was a nurse, but then went back to school after I was born. Got her master's in hospital administration."

"Impressive lady."

"She was." Sarah's smile faded as she pictured her mom. Her chest squeezed, heart aching. "She just died. Cancer. Passed away just last week."

"Last week?"

"We thought she was in remission."

"I'm so sorry. And two funerals in a week?"

Sarah nodded. "Mom's, we expected. But Jack's . . . that was a total shock."

Lauren made a rough, inarticulate sound. "Car accidents usually are."

Nine

Sarah returned to Tampa on Saturday night and attended the last game against the Yankees at Tropicana Field Sunday with Ella and Brennan, sitting with Alyssa and her kids in the section reserved for wives and girlfriends.

"Seems like you were gone forever," Alyssa said as they settled into their seats for the game.

Sarah nodded, shifting Ella into a more comfortable position on her lap. "Was forever. Twenty days. So glad to be home. But good heavens, the laundry! Boone must have used every single towel in the house."

Alyssa laughed. "That's because men only use them once, and then they leave them on the floor."

"If they did the laundry they'd maybe hang a towel up."

"Or not. I think Jeff would just go out and buy more."

"Men!"

"And to think I'm raising four boys," Alyssa said, leaning forward to do a quick inventory, making sure all four of them were still sitting, each wearing a Tampa Bay shirt of some sort, with Brennan in his jersey and hat, sandwiched between them.

"I love my boy," Sarah answered, noting that Brennan was jabbing his friends with his elbow and hot dog, but the Neeley boys were used to it. Thank God they didn't seem to mind. "But I'm really glad for my girl," she added, kissing the top of Ella's head. "She adds some sugar to all the spice."

Tampa Bay ended the series with a win, sweeping the Yankees at home. Boone had a home run in the bottom of the eighth that helped the team win Sunday's game, and Sarah was so happy to be there in person, to see him round the bases and then step on home plate. It was just like her early days with Boone, back when it had just been the two of them, dating, and then married and newlyweds.

Sarah hummed as she drove the kids home after the game, feeling better than she had in a long time. This was what she needed. Time with her kids, time with Boone, just being a family. She wouldn't think about his leaving Tuesday morning either, for a ten-day road trip, the first of the season. It was only Sunday night. She still had all of tomorrow.

At home, while Brennan and Ella ate their dinner—grilled chicken, broccoli, and fresh fruit cups—Sarah took the marinating steaks from the refrigerator and turned the broiler on. She'd prepared the twice-baked potatoes before she left for the park, and they were ready to be warmed. Boone loved a big steak after a game, and tonight had been a great game, a big game, especially as contract discussions would begin in another month or so. Everyone had thought he'd be finished with ball by now, but if he continued to hit the way he did today, he could easily play another year. Maybe longer.

He definitely made good money playing ball, and it was still exciting to see him at bat. Boone was gorgeous naked, but there was something undeniably thrilling about him in his team uniform. The shape of his quads, his little butt, the bulge of biceps beneath his jersey. He was tall, big, muscular, and he had a huge swing. When he connected with the ball tonight in the eighth inning, he cracked it. You knew just by the sound of it that it'd be a huge hit, and as the fans surged to their feet, Sarah jumped up, too, holding her breath as her eyes became glued to the ball, watching it sail high, out toward center field, and then over the fence.

Gone.

The fans erupted into wild cheering and Sarah applauded with them, feeling like that young bride who'd never missed a game, either at home or away, and who, when Boone traveled, watched every game on TV, or when that wasn't possible, listened on the radio. Boone always called her after each game, too, and back then, they'd talk for hours at night, he in his hotel room, ordering burgers or steaks from room service, and she curled up somewhere comfortable, eager to hear every detail.

She knew all the dirt on the players, too, from who was hitting well to who was hooking up with groupies. Amused by her questions and endless curiosity, Boone told her virtually everything, which turned out to be too much.

She didn't actually want to know that so many players were players. She didn't want to hear her husband excuse the cheaters and liars' behavior, saying it was hard to judge them when they were living in hotel rooms for six months of every year. "How can you defend men who'd knowingly, willingly, hurt their women?"

"You're getting yourself all riled up," he'd say, drawing her onto his lap and kissing her. "I shouldn't have told you anything."

No, he shouldn't have. Because it just made it all that much worse when she found out he was one of them.

"What's wrong, babe?" Boone asked now, entering the kitchen

and dropping a kiss on her head, dressed once again in the jeans and T-shirt he'd worn to the park earlier that afternoon.

She flashed him a smile as she gave the sautéing mushrooms a stir, hiding her conflicted feelings. Talking about the affair never helped. Boone would just get quiet, and then she'd shut down, and then the tension would be back as well as the isolation. And she didn't want that tonight, didn't want to feel distant or lonely, not when she loved him so much.

Boone came up behind her, standing close, settling his hands on her hips. He peeked over her shoulder into the small saucepan, sniffing the butter, wine, and garlic. "Smells amazing. I'm starving."

She could feel him, and he was hard. "We'll eat in fifteen minutes or so," she said, sucking in a breath as he rocked against her, making her aware that he wanted her.

"Where are the kids?" he asked, dropping his head to kiss the side of her neck.

Her legs went weak and she caught the edge of the stove for support. "In bed, but hoping to see you." She sounded breathless, and he knew it.

He ran his hand along the outside of her hip, and then over to her belly, his palm flat against her tummy, even as he pressed from behind. "It's good to have you home," he said, moving her long hair away so his lips could travel down her nape, sending shivers of pleasure through her.

"I'm going to burn dinner," she whispered, her mouth drying as he slid his hand up her torso to cup her breast, her nipple tightening, body aching.

"If the kids were asleep I'd take you right here," he said, his teeth scraping her skin, fingers kneading her breast, working her nipple so that she felt maddeningly aroused.

He knew exactly what he was doing, she thought, head spinning, stars dancing before her eyes. He knew exactly how to turn her on, make her wet, make her come. "I can't concentrate when you're doing that, and these are nice steaks, and they're already under the broiler."

"I'll go see the kids, tuck them in," he said, stepping back and giving her butt a last rub. "But later you're all mine. And I'm going to take my time."

They ate a half hour later in the dining room by candlelight. The kids were asleep, and Sarah had dimmed the chandelier after lighting the candles, letting the two tapers' flickering light fill the room.

"Delicious," Boone said, wiping his mouth on his napkin before reaching for his wineglass. "Really good, hon."

Sarah leaned back in her chair, sipped her wine, relaxed, happy, or as happy as she could be knowing he was leaving the day after tomorrow for ten days and that she'd had only a day and a half with him the past twenty. "Thank you, babe."

He sighed, stretched. "I love that you cook. Lots of the younger guys say their wives don't make dinner, or won't, so even when they're home, they order out every night."

Having grown up in New Orleans's Garden District, Boone liked atmosphere, and fine dining, and that included china and crystal and candles even at home for dinner. "It's not necessarily their fault," she said. "Girls now spend more time playing soccer than helping Mom in the kitchen."

"But women need to know how to cook."

"And so do men."

"I just hope it's not a lost art."

"Just like all the men now who can't change a tire?"

"Most guys can change a tire."

"Okay. How many can change the oil in their car?"

"I can."

"I know. But you're the exception."

He grinned. "You're feisty tonight."

"I just don't think women should be expected to know how to

cook when they marry. Most girls today grow up spending more time on the soccer field than helping their mothers in the kitchen"—she held up a hand—"and I'm glad. And before you say I'm wrong, think about it. Do you want Ella to grow up more concerned about how to take care of a man or confident that she can take care of herself?"

"Are they mutually exclusive?"

"No. But a girl of twenty or twenty-four doesn't have to know how to cook. She needs to know how to make a living, support herself, and possibly her family one day." Sarah felt some of her fire die. Because if something happened to Boone, she couldn't support her family the way Meg could support hers. Meg had an impressive résumé and years of experience as a successful publicist. Sarah just had a college degree. Yes, she'd planned to go to law school, but she hadn't gone. And now she was thirty-five.

"Baby, what's going on?" Boone asked, leaving his chair and coming to tug her to her feet. He pulled her into his arms, held her. "You're so wound up about everything."

She relaxed against him, feeling the exhaustion hit. "I think I'm just tired."

"Not surprised. You've had it rough these past few weeks."

"Don't want to do that again, anytime soon."

He rubbed her back. "Let's go to bed."

"The dishes."

"They're just dishes. They can wait. Everything can wait. Need some time with you before I fly out."

That's right. He was leaving Tuesday morning. She swallowed her disappointment. "Let's go to bed." She drew back, looked up into his face. "But no molesting me. I need sleep."

He lifted a long, silky strand of hair from her face, his thumb sweeping over her cheekbone. "But, darlin', you like it when I molest you." His eyes glinted with humor and something else. "Especially when I do it with my tongue."

"*Boone,*" she choked, pushing against his chest, laughing, blushing.

"You do."

She broke free, and, shaking her head, she blew out the candles then switched off the dining room lights. "All I know is that I'm tired."

"I know how to change your mind."

She headed for the stairs of their Mediterranean-style house. "Go for it, bud."

He swatted her butt as he followed her up the terra-cotta tile stairs. "Challenge accepted."

Later, nestling into his arms after some seriously satisfying love-making, Sarah closed her eyes. His big chest was damp against her back, but it felt good. He felt good. "Well done, Mr. Walker."

He settled her more comfortably against him. "My pleasure, Mrs. Walker."

She lightly raked his forearm with her nails. "Great game today."

"It was a fun one."

"You looked good."

"I felt good."

"Nothing hurts?"

"No. I feel healthy, strong."

"Good. Let's keep it that way."

"I couldn't agree more."

Sarah counted the days until Boone's return. Every day they tried to Skype each other, or do FaceTime, so the kids could talk to their dad. But the trip wasn't going well. The team had been on the road eight days and they'd won only two games. Boone wasn't hitting well, but then, none of the players were. Over the weekend, the Red Sox had beaten them up pretty bad, a

12–2 loss on Friday, and a 13–5 loss on Saturday. Sunday had been another loss, too, and now Boone was about to head to the park for the fourth and final game against Boston, and he was short on the phone.

"Need this win," he said curtly. "Can't be swept in a four-game series."

"You won't be."

"Can't believe they outscored us thirty-one–eleven. We were just bleeding out there."

She hesitated. "After tonight's game, you fly out?"

"Yeah. Toronto."

"Three games there, and then you come home?"

"But we have to get through tonight. Want that win tonight."

"Who is on the mound?"

"Shields."

"You guys have confidence in him?"

"Yeah."

"So hit. Back him up."

"Gonna try."

But Boone didn't get a hit that night, and it became a game of two pitchers dueling, with the Rays' James Shields the winning pitcher, shutting out Boston, 1–0.

Having salvaged their self-respect, the Rays headed to Toronto, but lost their first game there, and Boone had some words with the batting coach and got benched for the next two games against the Blue Jays, games the Rays won by a huge margin.

It was almost three in the morning when he arrived home Thursday night, following the final game in Toronto.

Sarah woke up to the sound of him opening their bedroom door and then closing it behind him. He undressed in the dark next to the bed, letting his clothes fall to the ground, and he left them there and drew back the covers on his side of the bed.

As Boone pulled back the covers, Sarah felt a lick of cool air on her spine where her nightgown dipped low on her back, and then the mattress dipped beneath Boone's weight as he settled behind her, lying flat on his back.

"Welcome home," she whispered.

"Terrible trip," he said, reaching out to catch her hair and giving it a tug, indicating he wanted her closer.

She moved into his arms, resting her cheek on his chest. "You're back, though. You'll start hitting again."

"I'm still benched for tomorrow's game."

"Why?"

"Gordon didn't like that I questioned his instruction. But I don't think he's giving the right kind of advice."

Sarah was silent, mulling this over. "Benching your DH for three games does seem a little excessive."

"It is. It's personal."

"Because you and he used to play together?"

"Yeah, and I'm still playing, and he's now bouncing around as a batting coach. But he wasn't a great player, and he's not a great instructor, and I'm not going to hit the way he tells me. I'm going to hit the way I know how to hit. That's what's kept me in the game this long."

"What did he want you to do?"

"Bunt." Boone exhaled hard. "But there was no way we could advance a runner, and it was a complete waste of an at-bat."

"So what did you do?"

"I hit. Got on base."

"That's good."

"But Gordon got his panties in a wad. We had some words."

That did not sound good, she thought. "When do you get to play again?"

"It's up to Gordon."

"Why don't you apologize?"

"I'm not going to apologize. He's wrong, and he knows he's

wrong, and I'm the only one who's not afraid to call it the way it is."

"But they need you in the lineup, Boone. You're their big hitter."

"Not according to Gordon. He says they play better without me. That I'm toxic to the team." He made a rough sound deep in his chest. "*Toxic*. Unbelievable."

"How long can he keep you out?"

"As long as he wants."

"*Boone.*"

He shrugged, his powerful shoulders shifting. "It is what it is."

She sighed, not liking where the conversation was going. If Boone wasn't careful—if he didn't mind his p's and q's and play the game right—this would be his last year of ball. "Baby, do you really want to get into a pissing contest with Gordon? You had your best spring training in years. Don't let him bring you down—"

"It's too late for that. Things were said. I have no respect for him now. Never will again."

She sat up, looked down at him in the dark, trying to see his face. "He was probably angry."

"Sure he was. And so was I. But there are certain things you don't say. And he did. He crossed the line."

Sarah's stomach cramped. "What did he say?"

"Doesn't matter, but I've made it known that I've lost all respect for him—"

"Oh, Boone, no. He's a coach—"

"He's a dick. Always was, and now he's on a total power trip. But let's not talk about him anymore. I won't let him get to me." He reached up, slipped a hand behind her head, and brought her mouth down to his, kissing her lightly, and then with more heat. It wasn't long before he had disposed of her nightgown and had her pinned beneath him.

*   *   *

Tampa Bay lost their first game against the Twins Friday night and Sarah didn't know if it was the loss, or something else, but suddenly Boone was back in the lineup on Saturday, and he came out swinging, knocking the ball out of the park with a two-run homer, and remaining hot Sunday, going three-for-four and driving in three of the team's six runs.

Monday was an off day, and since Boone didn't have to travel on Tuesday, he slept in and then hung around the house. It felt like a holiday, and once the kids were off to school, Sarah sat on the couch next to him for most of the morning, watching *Sports-Center* and then the Syfy channel because they were doing a story on a haunted house in New Orleans's French Quarter.

"What do you think?" she asked him, during one of the commercial breaks. "Do you really think the house is haunted?"

"Wouldn't be surprised. When I was growing up, people were always talking about this or that place being haunted, especially in the French Quarter, and that was back before all this paranormal stuff was popular."

"You've never seen a ghost, though, have you?"

"I wouldn't call it a ghost . . . but I've been places that didn't feel right. Places that have a strange energy."

Her eyes opened wide. "Seriously?"

"Yeah."

"What do you think it was?"

"Ghost? Voodoo? Vampire? Don't know." Boone laughed at her expression and extended his long legs, propping them on the leather ottoman. "Baby, New Orleans is an old city and there's been talk of paranormal activity there for hundreds of years."

"Well, ghosts and voodoo, yes, but vampires?"

"Anne Rice. Remember all her vampire books?"

Sarah wrinkled her nose, remembering now. "You said she lived down the street from you."

"A couple of blocks from us. People were always driving by her house slow, hoping to see her."

"Did you ever meet her?"

"I'd see her around, but I didn't talk to her. My mom knew her, though. Nice lady. But people in general are nice in New Orleans."

"You miss it?"

"I do. It's home. Would love to buy one of those big houses in the Garden District one day. Retire there." He glanced sideways at her. "You're still okay with that?"

"Yes."

"You don't mind living so far from your family?"

She shrugged. "We've always lived away from my family."

"But when I retire it's different. I won't be on a team anymore. It'll just be you, me, and the kids."

"And New Orleans is your home."

"It's not yours."

"No, but wherever you are, that's my home."

Boone looked at her a long moment. "I got lucky with you, babe."

She cracked a smile. "Yes, you did."

But later that afternoon, when Sarah returned from picking the kids up from school, she walked into the bedroom to find Boone reading a text. Seeing her, he immediately closed the phone and slid it into the pocket of his jeans.

"Everything okay?" she asked, thinking he'd put the phone away a little too quickly, wondering if it was her imagination, hoping it was her imagination, but Boone looked . . . guilty.

"Yeah. Why?"

He seemed defensive, too, she thought, so she struggled to sound careless. "When I entered the room you seemed to put away your phone awfully fast."

"I was done reading."

"Felt fast."

"Sorry, babe."

Sarah hated the uncomfortable knot filling her chest. Hated the anxiety and unease. Hated that she always flashed to Stacey from Atlanta. Hating that Stacey from Atlanta still had this power over her . . . them. "Who was the text from?"

"Arnie." Arnie Rosenthal was his agent, and had been his agent since Boone was first drafted as a college senior, out of LSU.

But Boone could tell that she didn't believe him. He sighed. "Want to read it?" he asked, fishing for his phone.

She shook her head, reminding herself that Stacey wasn't part of their lives. And neither she, nor her ghost, belonged in their lives either, and so she attempted to defuse the tension with a joke. "Are you being traded?"

Boone didn't smile. "Not yet."

Her smile faded as her feeble attempt at humor was replaced with shock. "Is it a possibility?"

"Hopefully not," he said, walking out.

The next three days Tampa Bay played at home, and while Sarah really wanted to go to the games, she couldn't find a sitter and knew better than to take the kids again, especially on a school night, so she followed the team from home. It was a good series for the Rays, as they swept the Angels, 5–0, 3–2, and 4–3, and with Boone hitting well, he headed off Friday morning for the three-day stand in Texas, feeling strong.

But when he called late Saturday night after a loss, he was really upset. "I think I've messed up my shoulder."

Boone never complained about pain, so if he said he was hurt, it was serious. She also knew an injury at thirty-nine could be devastating.

"How?" she asked, knowing they'd lost the game tonight, 7–2, and that Boone had struck out twice, and then, in his final at-bat he'd been walked, then thrown out trying to return to first base after taking too big a lead on a fly ball.

"I dove toward first. Overshot the bag, and felt something pop."

"Is it dislocated?"

"No. But it's not right. Now my arm's weak. Can't grip anything really well."

"Have you talked to the trainer?"

"Yeah, but Gordon's having a hissy fit. Said I deserved to get hurt if I was going to do a stupid move like sliding back to first."

"Will you be able to play tomorrow?"

"Not sure."

Sarah chewed on the inside of her cheek, remembering the injuries Boone had over the years. The knee injuries. The torn rotator cuff. The stress fracture . . . "You don't think it's the torn-rotator-cuff thing again, do you?"

Boone was silent so long that it made Sarah's insides hurt.

"I'm hoping not," he said at length. "We'll know for sure when I get home. Monday morning they've already ordered the imaging tests."

"Oh, Boone."

"Don't say it."

She swallowed hard. "I'm going to be positive," she said.

"Good girl. It might be nothing. Just a strain or a bruise."

"That's right."

He hesitated. "Kids okay?"

"They're good. Sleeping."

"What are you doing?"

"Waiting up to talk to you, and then I'm calling it a night."

"Well, go to bed. Get some sleep. I'll be home late tomorrow night."

"Love you, Boone."

"Love you, too, babe."

Sunday night Boone arrived home close to two in the morning and Sarah woke as he entered the room and undressed in their adjacent bathroom. She'd been dreaming when he'd arrived and it'd been a bad dream, one of those dreams where she woke frantic—panicked—and it was a relief to hear him in the bathroom, using the toilet, brushing his teeth, knowing that it was just a dream. Boone was okay, she told herself, heart still racing. They were okay. All was good.

She waited until he was in bed, settled under the covers and comfortable, before moving toward him. "Hi," she said, putting her head on his chest and stretching out next to him.

"Hey." He stroked her hair. "Sorry to wake you."

"I'm glad. I like knowing you're home. Makes me feel good."

He smoothed her hair again, then dropped a kiss on top of her head. "Makes me feel good coming home to you."

"Yeah?"

"Yeah."

She smiled in the dark, and yet her eyes burned. "I was having a weird dream just now."

"Weird, how?"

"You were missing. I don't know if you died or you'd just disappeared, but I was looking for you everywhere. I kept running everywhere, calling for you, looking for you. I was searching and searching—"

"And here I am."

She blinked and gulped air. "I can't imagine life without you."

"That's good, because I'm not going anywhere."

But she could still remember her panic in her dream, and she flashed to Meg and the kids, and how chaotic and emotional it'd been at the house in Santa Rosa the day Sarah flew out, following Jack's funeral. She didn't ever want to be in Meg's shoes. Didn't ever want to have to cope with what Meg was going through. "I wouldn't want to raise Ella and Brennan without you," she whispered, pressing closer to him. "I couldn't do it on my own."

His hand moved down to her shoulder, and he held her against him. "You could if you had to, but you don't have to. I'm here."

"What if something happened?"

"Nothing's going to happen."

"How can you be so sure?"

He didn't immediately answer, just held her, his hand warm, his body warmer. "There's no point going through life negative. You've got to be positive. Imagine me approaching the plate each time, thinking I'm going to strike out. If that's how I really thought, I'd never hit the ball."

"You can't compare life to baseball."

"Sure you can. It's all about attitude. Training. Confidence."

She smiled wryly. "If that's the case, piece of cake." Then she fell silent, and in the quiet of their room, she listened to the thudding of Boone's heart.

Buh-bum, buh-bum, buh-bum.

So steady. So strong.

"Boone?"

"Yeah, babe?"

"Your shoulder's going to be fine. You're going to be back in the lineup in just a few days. You're going to have one of the best seasons you've had in years."

She felt him smile. "You think so, Coach?" he drawled, pressing another kiss to the top of her head.

"Yeah, Walker. I do."

But when Boone left for the park the next morning to meet with the trainer and the team doctor, Sarah was nervous. Like most professional sports teams, Tampa Bay had their own imaging equipment, an X-ray for breaks and an ultrasound to detect muscle and rotator cuff tears as well as to check for tendon inflammation. Which meant Boone would know sooner than later how serious his injury was.

And if it was serious, would the team put him on the disabled list, and if so, for how many days?

The disabled list was a bad place for an athlete. It immediately devaluated a player, as it signaled to the rest of the world that he was weak. Broken.

Please don't let Boone be seriously hurt, she prayed. *In fact, please don't let Boone be hurt at all.*

Let it just be tender. A little bruise. Nothing much. And get him back in the lineup tonight or tomorrow.

Boone didn't end up playing for five days. But it wasn't his shoulder keeping him out of the game, it was Gordon, the hitting instructor, who decided that Boone didn't need to be in the lineup. He and Boone were still in the middle of a pissing contest, and with Boone getting banged up in that "stupid play at first," he thought that Boone could use some time on the bench. Some time to sit and think about his commitment to baseball, as well as his role on the team.

After eighteen years playing professional baseball, sixteen of them in the big leagues, Boone didn't need to think about his role on a team or his commitment to his sport. He trained in the off-season, was one of the first players at the park during spring training, and he pushed hard all season long. Baseball was his career. His identity. And for the past eighteen years, his life.

And putting Boone on the bench was probably the worst thing Adam Gordon could do to him.

Sarah suspected Adam knew it, too.

By the time Boone was back in the lineup, he was wound up so tight he couldn't hit. The power plays with Gordon, who'd once been Boone's teammate in Houston but never his friend, had messed with his head. In Houston, Gordon and Boone had tolerated each other, and that was about it. Now it became a war, and as Boone struggled at bat against the Mariners in their four-game series at home, Sarah wondered what would happen once the Rays hit the road after their upcoming series with the A's.

Sarah could feel his rage and frustration, but Boone wouldn't talk about his feelings. She knew from the past that when he struggled at the plate, he'd blow off steam in other ways. Going out with the guys. Staying out late. Drinking more than he should. Talking to women he didn't need to know.

The last was a real concern. Because sober, Boone was pretty much a family man, but put a couple of drinks in him and he loosened up, becoming friendlier, more open. More open to advances.

And now he was going out again, hanging out with the guys, doing whatever it was macho guys did to chill out.

Strip clubs. Titty bars. Nightclubs.

"What if I got a sitter," Sarah said, trying to suppress the wave of worry. He loved her. He did. He wasn't going to hook up with anyone tonight. He wasn't going out to meet up with someone he'd met last night. "You and I could go to Bern's, have a great steak, maybe hit the Fox Jazz Café after."

"Let's do that when I come back from next week's road trip. Tonight I've already made plans to hang with the guys."

"But you'll be with the guys all week on the road."

"I know, but it's Danny's birthday, everyone's going out."

"Doesn't Danny have a wife to celebrate with?"

"Sarah."

She hated that he made her feel like she was being a ball and chain. She wasn't a ball and chain. She was so supportive of him. Had given up her career and family to follow him. He and the kids were her priority. The focus of her life.

She exhaled slowly. "I just feel like I don't get enough time with you."

"It's always like this during the season."

"But you've been so down lately. It's kind of hard to reach you."

"I'm here."

"But disconnected."

"I've got a lot on my mind, babe."

She nodded. She got that. She did. But it didn't make it any easier when Boone pulled away, retreating inside himself, distancing himself. It just made it even harder to feel safe. Loved.

"We never did do anything for your birthday," she said.

"You gave me presents and cards," he answered.

"But we were supposed to do something fun together. Something special."

"We'll do it when I'm back. Make reservations somewhere. Get tickets. Whatever you want to do. You and me, babe."

"We'll make it a joint Boone birthday and Mother's Day treat," she said.

He frowned, his brow furrowing and faint creases fanning from his eyes. "I'm gone for Mother's Day again this year?"

She nodded, refusing to feel sad, or empty. She didn't want to feel anything remotely sad. Sad wasn't good. Sad lined up way too close to depression.

"Damn," he muttered, rubbing his jaw.

She watched him, thinking she loved his square jaw and strong chin. Loved the way his cheekbones were set high and his forehead was broad. He was handsome. Handsome, tough, sexy, and hers.

Her man. Her gorgeous man.

And yet she shared him with a team owner, managers, coaches, and the twenty-four players on the roster.

As well as the fans.

"It's all right, hon," she said. "It's part of the job. I know. And at least we have Halloween, Thanksgiving, and Christmas with you home. You could be playing football or basketball and I'd be carving the turkey all by myself."

He smiled reluctantly. "Funny."

"Yeah," she said, holding her smile, not letting him see how much she hurt just then, and how much she'd been hurting lately.

It wasn't until he was out the door that her smile slipped.

Turning away from the door, she reached up to wipe her eyes.

She wasn't a crier. Didn't like weeping about silly things. But good God, she felt empty, and lonely, and sad.

The sad part was grief. The sad was from missing her mom. Her mom had always been there for her, an adviser, a cheerleader, her best friend. It was her mom who'd helped her weather the ups and downs of marriage, as well as learn to adapt to the unpredictable life of a professional baseball player.

But now Mom was gone and life was getting unpredictable again, and Sarah felt as if she was falling, flailing. She needed Mom right now. She needed someone strong and focused and fierce in her corner.

Boone didn't arrive home until close to three. He took a shower before he came to bed, waking her, and she lay in the dark, staring at the clock, wondering why he was showering now, wondering what he was trying to rinse off.

Don't think that way, she told herself. *Don't go getting crazy . . .*

As Boone turned off the bathroom light and headed for bed, Sarah heard a car door slamming in the driveway next door, and then listened to the *ping ping* as Jeff Neeley locked the car and set the alarm.

So Jeff was home now, too.

Must have been quite the party.

Alyssa would probably be furious. Like Sarah, Alyssa didn't like when her husband stayed out late.

"You awake, babe?" Boone asked, his deep voice unusually rough.

He'd probably been drinking some hard liquor and smoking cigars.

"Yes," she whispered, trying to let go of the anger inside her. He was home. He was safe. She should be grateful for small mercies. But she wasn't. She was mad that he needed to go out two nights in a row and drink and hang out with guys who liked nothing more than "tapping that."

"Did you have a good night?" he asked, reaching out for her and drawing her toward him.

Usually she wanted to be close. Tonight she didn't. Tonight she wanted to punch him. Punish him. He'd been out at a club. He'd been out looking at chicks. And hopefully that's all he'd been doing. Just looking.

"You mad at me, babe?" he asked when she took too long to answer.

"No," she fibbed, because it was three fifteen for God's sake, too late to start a fight. "Just sleepy."

"Sorry, baby." He settled her against him, his chest now a pillow as his legs slipped between hers. "Go back to sleep."

She wanted to. She tried to. But she couldn't relax, not when every muscle in her body hummed with tension.

Boone, though, had no such problem. Within moments, his breathing slowed, deepening. He was almost asleep.

Sarah ground her teeth together, her back molars tight. She couldn't do this. Couldn't do four months of him doing what he wanted, when he wanted, because in his testosterone-fueled world, it was okay.

She eased herself away from his arms, slipping her leg free of his to move all the way over onto her side of the bed. For nearly an hour she argued with herself, argued with Boone, argued with those who said leopards didn't change their spots. Once a cheater, always a cheater, and yet for the past three years Boone had been so focused and committed.

But he didn't feel that way to her now.

She felt scared and open. Vulnerable. Honest to God, she didn't want to be the fool who was head over heels in love with a man who couldn't keep his dick in his pants.

* * *

Sarah was woken by an arm wrapping around her and Boone's deep, rough voice in her ear. "It's okay, baby. Everything's fine."

She opened her eyes and looked up at him.

"You were having a bad dream," he said.

She nodded.

"What were you dreaming?" he asked.

She tried to remember but couldn't recall specifics. Only sadness. Terrible sadness. And it had to do with Boone.

"I think you left me," she whispered.

"I'd never leave you, babe."

Her eyes burned and she held her breath, the air bottled in her lungs. Okay, he'd never leave her, but did that mean he was faithful?

He wrapped his arms all the way around her, holding her secure, and she tried to relax, wanting to be comforted but unable to silence the voices in her head.

What if . . .

What if he was hooking up on the side?

What if it wasn't a casual hookup, but something serious, someone he cared about?

What would she do if she found out? She'd leave him. She'd have to leave him. She couldn't remain with someone she couldn't trust.

And yet as Boone held her, his body so warm and hard against her, she felt some of the panic and fear ease. He had a way of calming her, comforting her, just by touching her. Why his body did that she didn't know. But it had from the beginning.

Even after all these years, she loved how she felt in his arms. She loved how he smelled and tasted. Loved the way his body took hers, filling her, making her feel so much.

He rolled over onto his back, bringing her cheek onto his chest, her hip pressed to his. His fingers tangled in her long hair, separating strands and then pressing them close to the dip in her back. "What's on your mind?" he asked.

"Everything."

"Break it down for me, hon."

She exhaled and then drew a breath for courage. "We're good, Boone, aren't we?"

"Yes, babe, we are." His fingers stilled for a moment. "Why?"

She nodded, closed her eyes, waiting for the relief, but relief didn't come. Maybe there was just too much going on lately, too much change, too much grief. Maybe this wasn't a Boone-and-Sarah thing, as much as a Sarah-being-overwhelmed thing. "I'm just so . . . wound up," she said. "So worried about everyone and everything."

"Tell me."

"You already know . . . just seems like there is heartache and heartbreak everywhere. Meg and the kids, losing Jack. Kit and her strange biker boyfriend. Cass, who really wants a baby and Tommy won't even discuss it with her anymore. And then there's Dad . . . having to go it alone . . . and Mom . . . I miss her so much."

"That *is* a lot. But I think most of that will sort itself out. It usually does."

She nodded, and yet her chest ached and her eyes burned. "I just feel like I should be there . . . helping."

His hand swept lower across her hip and butt. "And what would you do if you were there?"

She frowned in the dark, trying to imagine herself in San Francisco, in the middle of it all. "I don't know. But at least I'd be there, close to everyone. I'd know what people need, too. I'd know what needs to be done. Like visit with Dad, keep him company. Or hang out with Meg and make dinner for her, and take the kids somewhere, doing something fun with them." She drew a quick breath. "I'd tell Cass not to give up on the baby thing—"

"Oh, I don't know if I'd get into the middle of that one, babe. That's between Tommy and Cassidy."

"She's always wanted to be a mom."

"Tommy will be furious if you interfere."

Sarah shrugged. "I just don't think he understands what he's doing to Cass, shutting the door on becoming parents."

His fingertips traced her spine, lingering in the hollow just above her hips. "I'd still be careful there."

"And there's Kit."

"Kit's an angel."

"Dating the devil."

Boone laughed, a deep rumble in his chest. "He's not that bad."

"Yes, he is." Sarah pushed up to gaze down into his face, unable to make out more than just a glint of eyes and teeth. "How can she be so desperate? She doesn't need a man that bad. Jude is a loser. Makes me sick that she's settling for him."

"It won't last," Boone said, pulling her back down and shifting her weight on top of him.

She hitched a breath as he parted her legs, sliding her thighs onto either side of his hips. "You don't think so?"

"No. Kit wants a family. That's why she broke up with Richard. She wanted more, not less."

"None of us liked Richard, and yet now he looks like a prince next to Jude."

"Baby, Jude's just a rebound. He won't last. I'm sure of it." Boone's palm had been making slow, light circles on the curve of her butt cheek and then slipped to that sensitive line just under the cheek where her glutes met her hamstring and she shivered. He traced the line again and the air caught in her throat as everything inside her turned on.

Stretching up, Sarah claimed Boone's mouth, kissing him slowly, letting the bubble of desire warm and grow, until her skin tingled and her breasts ached, nipples taut and sensitive against his hard chest.

She blinked, finding it nearly impossible to concentrate on the conversation with Boone's hands in precarious places. "You really think so?"

"Mmm-hmm."

"I don't have to worry?" she murmured, senses swimming.

"No." His lips covered hers, even as his hand slipped between her thighs and Sarah arched as he found the places she most wanted touched.

He kissed her sighs right out of her mouth. Boone was a man who took his time, and he most definitely took his time now.

Much later, pleasured, satiated, she yawned, ready to sleep. "Thanks, babe," she said, so drowsy she wasn't sure she could keep her eyes open another minute.

"Love you, Sarah."

"I hope you do."

He was silent and she was thinking he'd fallen asleep. But then he broke the quiet, saying, "Why don't you go see Meg and your dad this weekend?"

She opened her eyes. "This weekend?"

"It's Mother's Day weekend. Why don't you take the kids and go?"

"They've got school, Boone, and it's a long flight."

"So let's find someone to stay with them, and you go for the weekend."

"And leave the kids for Mother's Day?"

"If you don't make a big fuss about it, we'll just tell them we're celebrating when I'm back."

She said nothing, weighing the possibility in her mind, thinking it was a lot of money and a lot of flying for just a couple of days.

"If you don't want to go, don't," he said as the silence stretched. "But if you're tempted, do go. After everything you've told me, I think your family needs you more for Mother's Day this year than our kids."

Ten

Sarah flew to San Francisco Friday morning. It was five weeks to the day since Jack's funeral, and yet now that she was back in the Bay Area, with the bright blue sky dotted with wispy white clouds, she felt as though she'd never left.

Brianna borrowed Mom's car to pick her up from the airport, and she filled Sarah in on the way back to Dad's house.

"Nothing's really changed," Bree said, accelerating hard to pass a car and then slamming on the brakes to get the car tailing her to back off.

Sarah tensed, having forgotten what a madwoman Brianna was behind the wheel. "No?"

Bree shook her head. "I'm still staying with Dad. He's still determined to be positive and upbeat, which means he's frenetically busy. Kit and Jude are still dating, much to Dad's disgust—"

"Dad doesn't like Jude either?" Sarah interrupted.

"Can't stand him. And I don't know if it's all the ink, or the bike, or the black leather, but he's not a fan."

"Kit has to end this."

Brianna grimaced, thin fingers tapping the steering wheel. "I don't see that happening anytime soon. She's really into Jude." She shot Sarah a quick look. "I keep waiting to hear that they've run away to Vegas together."

"Stop!"

Brianna shrugged, shot her sister a rueful glance. "You know they're living together."

"*What?*"

"He moved in with Kit."

Sarah's eyes bugged, shocked and disgusted. Kit deserved so much better. She did. "But Kit said he has his own place, a little house in San Leandro, a couple of miles from her school."

"He still owns it. He just doesn't sleep there anymore."

"Oh no." Sarah slumped in her seat, depressed by the news. "Tell me something else. Please. Can't handle thinking about Kit ruining her life with Loserville."

"Hmm, let's see. What else can I tell you? Tommy and Cass are not doing well. Cass can hardly be in the same room with him now, because Tommy has shut her down so completely."

"What does that mean?"

"Cass isn't even allowed to bring up the topic of babies or kids. It's apparently off-limits—"

"That's ridiculous. There can't be things you don't discuss in a marriage."

"I agree with you on that one, but Tommy is doing the ultimate power play. It's his way or the highway, and Cass is considering leaving."

"No!"

Bree shrugged. "It's what she told Dad last weekend."

Sarah's insides suddenly hurt. "She told Dad she was thinking of leaving Tommy?"

Bree nodded.

Sarah couldn't believe it. "How do you know?"

"They were over for a barbecue last weekend. It was great

weather, really warm, felt like summer, so Dad thought it'd be nice to grill some steaks and have family over. Only it wasn't a nice barbecue. Meg didn't come. Kit and Jude were there but Jude had to leave early for something and Kit ended up going, too. And that's when it became apparent that Cass and Tommy weren't speaking to each other."

"At all?"

Brianna shook her head. "Dad pulled each of them aside, independently, of course, and tried to talk to them about finding a middle ground, but Cass said she's over it, and Tommy thinks that with enough time, Cass will come around."

"And this was just last weekend?"

"Yeah."

"Wow." Sarah sucked the inside of her lip against her teeth, picturing Tommy and Cass, remembering how solid they'd once been. The whole infertility thing had really done a number on their marriage. "He could lose Cass," she said softly.

"Dad said as much to Tommy. And he didn't say it nicely. He pretty much reamed Tommy out, but it just got Tommy's back up. The more everyone tries to talk to him about the baby thing, the more adamant he is that it's not going to happen."

Sarah tipped her head back against the seat, suddenly wondering if she should have stayed in Tampa. It sounded like this weekend was going to be endless drama.

"And Meg? What about her? Is she okay . . . considering the circumstances?"

"Mags is Mags—" Brianna paused as she exited the 101, merging briefly onto the 280, before taking Monterey Boulevard to reach their house in the Sunset district. "She's just doing her thing."

"I've only talked to her once in the past five weeks," Sarah said.

"I don't think anyone's talked to her. Or seen much of her. She's not wanting a lot of company, although, of course, Dad sees her at JJ's games."

"He's going to them, then?"

"Hasn't missed one. He's always in his car, heading north."

"That's good."

Brianna shrugged. "I think he could use more downtime—" She broke off as she slammed on her brakes and shoved her hand out the open window to flip off the driver who'd just cut her off. "Dickhead," she muttered, giving him the bird a second time. "Drivers here are so rude."

Sarah choked back shocked laughter. "They are, aren't they?"

But Brianna heard the amusement in her sister's voice. "You think I'm rude, too?"

Fighting the urge to smile, Sarah shrugged. "I wouldn't call flipping someone off nice."

"Whatever."

Still trying not to smile, Sarah looked out her window at the small houses and buildings bordering Monterey. Soon they'd be in Monterey Heights, and then St. Francis Woods. She loved this area with the charming stucco Spanish-style houses built during the twenties and thirties, but her favorite Spanish Colonial Revival house was on Santa Paula. The 1928 mansion was reportedly ten thousand square feet, and it filled an entire corner lot. Such a cool place. San Francisco had so much history.

Sarah loved this city. She'd never planned on leaving it, but then, she'd never planned on meeting Boone.

If she hadn't married him and moved away, she'd probably live in St. Francis Woods now, even though the elegant neighborhood seemed to permanently sit in a pocket of fog. But wasn't that San Francisco's charm? St. Francis Woods could be totally gray and soupy, while on the other side of the hill, the Noe Valley basked in the sun.

"So it's just going to be us for Mother's Day with Dad, then?" Sarah asked, turning to look at Brianna as she braked at a traffic light.

"No. It's the whole family. All of us kids. Meg and her crew, Kit and Jude, Tommy, Cass, you, me."

Sarah rubbed at her temple. "So even though no one's getting along we're all still getting together?"

"Absolutely."

"Oh God."

Brianna grinned. "And best of all, we're cooking!"

"Who is cooking?"

"We, us, the girls."

Sarah closed her eyes, counted to five, and then to ten. "Why can't we just go out to eat?"

"Because Dad wanted brunch at the house. Wants to see us all around the table. Thinks it's a good way to honor Mom."

Sarah understood that. "So it's brunch?"

"Yep."

"What are we making?"

"Kit and Cass put together the menu and have assigned something to everyone." She glanced at Sarah, lips pursing. "I have a big job."

Sarah's eyebrows arched. That was interesting. Brianna was a terrible cook. "What is it?"

"Orange juice."

Sarah choked back laughter. Clearly, no one trusted Brianna in the kitchen.

Saturday morning, Sarah wandered restlessly around the house, climbing upstairs to what used to be Tommy's room and was now a playroom for the grandkids. She opened the doors to the deck to let the sunshine in, needing light and warmth.

The house felt so different without Mom. It was empty, hollow, like a Hollywood set . . . the facade of a house without real people inside.

How did Dad stand it?

Sarah stepped outside, crossing the deck to lean on the railing and lift her face to the sun. She'd gotten here just yesterday, but she missed her kids, missed Boone, and was already wanting to go home.

Where are you, Mom? Are you there, Mom? Can you hear me?

"There you are," a voice said from the doorway.

Sarah opened her eyes, glanced over her shoulder at Bree, on the threshold, looking lost in her shapeless gray sweatpants and burgundy T-shirt emblazoned with the word ANARCHY in antique gold. "Is someone looking for me?"

"Me," Brianna answered, stepping outside and stretching. "Beautiful day."

"It is," Sarah agreed, watching Bree cross to one of the pine Adirondack chairs and sit down, curling her legs up under her. "Where have you been all morning?"

"Sleeping."

"But you went to bed so early."

Bree shrugged. "I like sleeping."

Sarah watched as her sister tipped her head back, eyes closing, letting the sunshine play on her face. She looked relaxed, but also small and pale and shockingly fragile.

She was just a ghost of her former self.

Sarah knew then, definitively, that something was wrong with Brianna. Brianna was sick.

"How about you?" she asked, sitting down in the chair next to Brianna's. "Are you okay?"

"I'm good."

Sarah didn't believe it. But she wasn't going to push Brianna. Between the Kit and Jude stuff and the Tommy and Cass stuff, there was just way too much tension. She didn't want to add to it. In fact, all she wanted was to know that someone was good. "You said that Meg has been keeping to herself?" she asked, looking at Bree. "You think she's okay . . . or not?"

Brianna sighed. "I'd have to go with not okay. She's really torn up about Jack."

"She loved him."

"She wasn't happy with him, though. She was staying out of a sense of duty. Everybody knew it, too."

"But that's Meg. Meg is, always has been, so very responsible."

"And being so wedded to responsibility was killing her." Brianna tipped her head back, looked up at the blue sky with the wispy clouds. "I think she loved Chad."

"She didn't."

"I think she did. But she wasn't going to admit it. Not to us. Maybe not even to herself, because it was the wrong thing to do . . . to love someone who wasn't your husband. To love someone so physically, passionately. Meg is all about control, but Chad made her lose control, so guilt and fear and shame surrounded her feelings, tainting the relationship. So if she renounced Chad, and her feelings, then she could forgive herself."

Sarah needed a moment to take this all in, and she nodded, thinking about it, thinking Brianna might have actually nailed it. "I think you might be right."

"I know I'm right."

Sarah fought the urge to smile. "What makes you so sure? You've detested her most of her life."

Brianna's jaw tightened, and her eyes suddenly watered. She looked away from Sarah. "I don't detest her." Her voice cracked. "Never have. How could I hate Meg? She's a good girl. A good person." She reached up and quickly brushed away a tear. "I just wish I'd been different. I wish I'd been less of a pothead and crazy-ass wild child. I've been so stupid in my life. Have made so many mistakes—"

"Everybody does," Sarah said, sitting forward and touching Brianna's leg, a leg that felt like nothing. Too thin, Bree was just too thin.

"But I've done it for years. Continued for years. Taking too many chances, taking risks, not being smart, not caring . . ." Brianna wiped away another tear. "Please ignore me. Can't believe I'm crying in front of you."

Sarah's chest squeezed tight. "I don't care."

"I do." Brianna sat up taller, stretching her legs out in front of her. "And we're not talking about me, we're talking about Meg. Meg and her guilt. Meg and her shame. We have to help her get rid of it, or she'll never be able to be with Chad—"

"But she'll never be with Chad again," Sarah interrupted. "She won't date him again. She can't. There's way too much water under the bridge."

"Why?"

"Kit told me that people in Santa Rosa and Napa talked about Meg last summer. People were really harsh. Quite a few people shunned her, saying terrible things about her, and it really hurt her."

"So? Why does she care what people think about her? Sticks and stones may break your bones—"

"Yes, but this is Meg. And Meg does care. And she cares about appearances."

"That's stupid. And shallow."

"Not that shallow when you realize she does it mainly to protect the kids."

"The kids?"

Sarah nodded. "Meg's a mom. It's different when you're a mom. Different when you have kids. You've got to do what's right for them, and getting back together with Chad wouldn't be good for the kids. It'd just be opening old wounds."

"But Meg deserves happiness."

"She does. I completely agree with you there. But unfortunately, she won't find it with Chad."

"Well, I'm going to root for Chad. I'm a romantic. I like happy endings."

Sarah blinked, surprised. "You're a romantic?"

"Die-hard." Brianna smiled crookedly. "You didn't know?"

Sarah shook her head. "No." She stared at her sister, seeing her with all new eyes. "Always?"

Brianna grinned. "Yes. But I was scared of falling in love. Scared of commitment. Scared that someone might love me and want me. Scared of finding real love and then being rejected for not being worthy." Her grin faded, leaving her pale face open, her expression uncertain. Suddenly she looked like a girl. Young, shy, vulnerable. "You had no idea that crazy Bree was such a scaredy-cat, did you?"

Sarah stared at Brianna's delicate profile—the small nose, the long eyelashes, the full, sensual mouth beneath a firm chin. She was beautiful. And real. And ill.

"Is it serious, Bree?" Sarah asked quietly, gently, but even then the words felt raspy and sharp in her mouth, making it hurt to speak.

Brianna turned to look at her. "What?"

Sarah held her gaze. "Did you at least tell Mom what was going on with you, before she died?"

For a moment her sister didn't speak, and Sarah wasn't sure she would. But then Brianna's lips moved, and she forced out a word. "Yes."

"You told Mom what was wrong?"

"Yes."

"It's . . . serious. Isn't it?"

Brianna's thin chest rose and fell. Her mouth worked. Then she shrugged, almost carelessly. "It's . . . no. It's . . . fine."

Sarah didn't believe her. "Are we going to lose you, too, Bree?"

"I sure as hell hope not."

That wasn't the same thing as no, was it? Sarah balled her hands in her lap to hide that they were shaking. "Does Dad know?"

Brianna gave her head the tiniest shake. "No."

"Shouldn't he?"

For a moment Brianna said nothing, then she sighed. "I was going to tell him. Mom made me promise that I'd tell him."

"Well?"

Her shoulder shifted. "But now Jack's died and Meg's a little bit crazy and Tommy and Cass—"

"So?"

Brianna shrugged again. "I just . . . I can't."

"But if it's serious, Bree . . ."

"It's not. Not enough to worry him." Her voice hardened. Her gaze met Sarah's and held. "Look at Dad. He doesn't sleep. He doesn't eat. He's running himself ragged. It just doesn't seem right, or fair, to lay this on him now. There's only so much a person can take."

Brianna had made a good point. And yet Sarah knew that Dad was all about being a dad, and he took his role as a parent seriously. "But your health—"

"Is improving."

"Is that bullshit, or are you telling me the truth?"

Brianna cracked a smile. "It's the truth."

"How do I know?"

Brianna held out an arm. "Look at me. Don't I look better?"

"No. You look like a skeleton."

"Hey! I resemble that," Bree joked, but a shadow darkened her eyes and her chin wobbled. "And okay, I know I'm still really thin, but I'm getting better. I've got a doctor here, an amazing doctor. A pioneer in the field, and one of the top specialists in the country. He wasn't taking new patients but Mom made a call—"

"Do you have AIDS?"

"No! God, no. It's just hep C."

Sarah stared blankly at her.

Brianna gestured impatiently. "Hepatitis C. No biggie."

Sarah shook her head. "Hepatitis C is serious, and it's chronic, and it can cause liver failure, so don't act all nonchalant with me!"

"Okay, fine. I've got a fairly serious case, but I'm getting help now and I should be as good as new soon."

"Then why do you look like you're still at death's door?"

"Because . . . it's . . . a serious case . . . but I've got the right doctors now, I've got a good team—"

"You just said a moment ago it wasn't serious. Now you say it's a serious case. What is it?"

"Serious. Pretty damn bad. Happy now? Is that what you want to hear?"

"I want the truth."

"Great. The truth is, I'm sick. The truth is, I might need a new liver. But I also might not. Happy?"

"No! No. And you know what?"

"What?"

"You should have come home sooner. You should have gotten your ass back here the moment you knew you were sick. Jesus, Bree, we live in San Francisco. Some of the top medical research is done right here, just around the corner from our house at UCSF—"

"I know. I'm being seen there now."

"But why did you wait? Why wait until it might be too late? Liver failure? Really?"

Brianna lifted her chin. "It hasn't happened yet."

"*Yet*. But it could. You could be on dialysis forever, or needing a donor liver. And those give out. They don't always work—"

"Thanks for the optimistic thoughts, Sarah."

"I have a right to be angry! I've just lost Mom, and Jack's gone, and now I find out you're seriously sick."

"Sick, but not dead, and that's an important distinction, sis."

"Maybe. But I know you. I'm looking at you. You're . . . you're . . ." Sarah shook her head, her throat aching, her chest so tight it was hard to breathe. "You're a ghost, Brianna. And it's not right. You are you. You've always been bigger than life, so full of life. My entire life I've looked up to you for being adventurous and fierce and alive. *Alive*." She knocked back tears. She was furious. Beyond furious. And the words were tumbling out of her mouth, one after the other. "How could you be so careless? And selfish? We love you, Brianna. We need you—"

"What's going on out here?" Dad's big, booming voice cut Sarah short.

Sarah looked away, bit into her lip, arms crossing her chest to hide her shaking.

Brianna didn't speak.

And Sarah couldn't.

"Girls?" Dad prompted impatiently, and his no-nonsense tone made Sarah feel like a child again. She glanced at Brianna, and then at her father.

"Nothing's going on," Sarah said tightly as Brianna extracted her hand from hers.

"I heard enough to know something's wrong," he answered, walking toward them, hands in his pockets, expression somber, watchful.

Brianna's lips compressed. Sarah tapped her foot, anxious, restless, feeling trapped. Everyone had known since late March that Brianna wasn't well. It was all they'd talked about when she first arrived from the Congo, but with Mom's death, and then Jack's accident, they'd stopped discussing her, stopped worrying about her.

They shouldn't have.

But at the same time this was Brianna's fault. She could have gotten help earlier. She could have taken care of herself. For God's sake, she was an infectious disease nurse. She treated critically ill patients in Africa. Why didn't she treat herself?

Dad stopped before them, standing above them, blocking the brightness of the sun. "Well?" he prompted.

"It's nothing, Dad," Sarah said. "Just a sister thing."

"You called her selfish," he said. "And careless," he added. "Those are strong words."

A lump filled Sarah's throat. It hurt, swallowing around it. "I'm tired of her living in Africa." She jerked her chin up, looked at her father and then at Brianna. "I'm tired of her living halfway around the world and only seeing us once every couple of years. I think it's selfish. We miss her." She got to her feet, stepped around her dad, and gave Brianna another long, hard look. "I miss her."

And then she headed back into the house and down a flight of stairs to the alcove bedroom that had always been hers. Meg, Kit, and Brianna had shared a large bedroom, but when Sarah was born, her father converted a closet and a storage area under the stairs into a cozy nursery, cutting a window into the storage space to bring in natural light.

The nursery was just supposed to be a temporary room. It was tiny and filled with odd angles from being tucked under the stairs and into the eaves, but Sarah loved her room with its slanted ceiling and little window nook and refused to move up into the "big girls" room when she'd outgrown her toddler bed.

Mom hadn't been happy at first, as she'd looked forward to turning the nursery into an office for herself, but Dad convinced her that Sarah, being so much younger than the other kids, needed her own space.

Now Sarah flopped onto her bed and stared numbly up at the floral wallpaper on the angled ceiling, unable to process what Brianna had just said, because no, hepatitis C wasn't a death sentence, but you couldn't let it ravage your body for months, much less years, and Sarah wondered just how long Brianna had been sick. Her gut told her it had been a long, long time.

A knock sounded on her door, and the bedroom door opened. "Can I come in?"

It was her dad.

Sarah sat up. "Yes."

He entered and closed the door behind him, ducking his head to avoid hitting it on a sharply angle.

"I forgot how small the Dollhouse is," he said, stooping as he approached her bed.

She smiled faintly at his use of her bedroom's nickname. Tommy had called her room the Dollhouse years ago, citing its Lilliputian dimensions and quirky charm. "It's cozy."

"You don't have to stay here. There's plenty of space in the girls' room."

"I like it here. It's my room."

He looked around, taking in the peach-and-yellow wallpaper and the dotted curtain. "You know we were going to demo this room, and add the space to our master bath when we did that big remodel."

"I know. I'm glad it didn't happen."

"Your mom wanted a big Jacuzzi."

That hurt. Sarah felt bruised. "She deserved one."

"She was a good girl, your mom."

It took her a second to respond. "Yes. She was."

He gave her a sharp look. "You miss her."

"I do."

"You two were constantly on the phone. Had to up our Verizon plan's minutes twice because of all your talking and texting."

Sarah struggled to hold back the tears. "I think about her all the time. I still reach for the phone to call her, or I think, 'I've got to tell Mom this . . .'" She looked up at her dad, emotions tangled and bittersweet. "It's just so hard. I want to hear her voice. I want her advice. I want to know how you are, and what you guys are doing. And Mom would tell me all that, and more. She was so good at staying in touch, keeping me informed. It didn't feel like I lived on the other side of the country. Mom made me feel close."

He folded his arms across his big chest. "I'm not very good at that, am I?"

"You're a guy. You've never liked talking on the phone."

He nodded and ran a hand through his thick hair, which he still kept short, even though he'd retired from the department earlier in the year. "I should call you more. Check in more often. Make sure we do that keep-in-touch thing your mom was so good at."

"You don't have to."

"I want to. So how often should I do this? Daily—"

"Daddy, get real."

He shrugged. "Weekly?"

"Weekly is good. But honestly, I'm okay, it shouldn't be a chore."

"It's not a chore. You're my youngest. My baby."

"That makes me a thirty-five-year-old baby, Dad."

"You could be one hundred and you'll still be my baby. My little girl."

Sarah unfolded her long limbs and left the bed to hug her dad. "I love you, too, Dad."

His big arms wrapped around her, gave her a quick squeeze. "We've always been so proud of you, your mom and I. You really were a ray of sunshine. Never gave us a moment's worry."

"That's because you guys didn't know all the bad stuff I used to do."

He drew back, looked into her eyes. "What bad stuff?"

She laughed, held her hands up. "Just kidding, Dad."

"But I mean it when I say you made us happy. We lucked out with you." He gave her another intent look. "You were easy. Sometimes I worried that we didn't fuss over you enough."

"I didn't need fussing over."

"I know. But sometimes . . . others . . . did."

Sarah understood where this was going now. "Everyone's different. People have different needs."

He was quiet a moment, choosing his words. "You might have been too young to remember, but your sister Brianna . . . she and I butted heads when she was growing up. She was stubborn, and she had her own ideas about things. I didn't approve of choices she made. It wasn't easy with her. Not like you."

Uncomfortable with the turn the conversation had taken, and aware that at any moment Brianna could walk in, Sarah opened her mouth to protest but her dad continued on.

"That's not to say I didn't love her." His voice deepened. "But I worried about her, and I don't like worrying. I don't like lying awake at night, wondering where my little girl is or if she's okay. So it was easier pushing her away, putting up a wall, telling myself she was out of control. Out of my control."

He paused, looked down at the ground, jaw tight.

Seconds ticked by. Sarah didn't try to fill the silence. She knew her dad. He wasn't finished speaking.

"She's had challenges, obstacles, along the way, but she's a good girl, and your mom always worried about her. Worried that Brianna didn't have anyone. Worried that Brianna lived so far away." He suddenly looked up, into Sarah's eyes, his blue gaze burning, intense. "The last thing your mom said to me was to take care of Brianna—" His voice broke. He swallowed, and his strong jaw clenched, and a small muscle worked near his ear. ". . . that Brianna needed me, because more than ever before, our little Bree-girl needed love."

Sarah's heart turned over. She studied his face, seeing the small tear that clung to his lower lashes.

"Do you know what's wrong with Brianna?" he asked, voice husky. "Do you know what's making her sick?"

Sarah nodded.

"What's wrong?" he asked. "Is it terminal?"

"Shouldn't be. But she can't go back to the Congo. She has to stay here. Get well. Her doctors are close. Mom found her good people at UCSF, and now all she needs to do is get treatment and get better."

"So why did you say she was careless and selfish?"

Sarah lifted her chin. "I was angry."

"Figured that much out."

"I just—" She glanced sideways at him. "Brianna just doesn't take care of herself. She's just so . . . self-destructive. And it makes me mad."

His brows pulled, his expression changing, and for a moment he looked stricken, and unbearably sad. "Right. So that's how it is."

Sarah's phone rang but she didn't move to answer it.

"You can get that," he said.

She shook her head. "It can go to voice mail."

Her dad just looked at her an endless moment, and then reached out to pat her cheek. "Our golden girl. Sweet Sarah." He turned and walked out.

Sarah watched him go, her heart aching, a lump in her throat. He'd looked so lonely for a moment. Lonely and alone.

Her phone rang again. She glanced around, found it on the foot of her bed, and picked it up.

Boone.

"Hey, baby," she said thickly, answering.

"You okay?" he asked.

"Yeah." She wiped her eyes, missing Mom, wishing Mom were here because Mom would know what to do. Mom would know what to say. Mom would know how to comfort Dad and love Bree. But then, Mom would know how to love them all. She'd know the right words to bring them together, making them strong, making them a united family.

A family of hope.

A family of love.

Sarah knocked away another tear. "Aren't you supposed to be playing right now? Don't you have a game?"

"No."

She folded her legs and sat cross-legged on the bed. "Rain-out?"

"Sort of."

"Sort of?"

"I've been released."

Sarah jerked, as if slapped. "What?"

"Tampa Bay let me go."

"Oh my God."

"At my request."

"Boone!"

"It's okay. It's good. This is a good thing. I can't spend the rest of the season sitting on a bench."

"But, Boone—"

"It's fine, babe. It is. Arnie has said there are some teams interested in me. He's hoping to get me picked up somewhere soon."

"And if not?"

"Then I guess we pack our things and move to New Orleans."

Eleven

Lauren was at work on Friday when she got the call that Lisa had gone into labor. She had prepared her staff for the news, warning them that when the contractions began, she would be jumping into her car and racing to Napa join her.

So when Matthieu called, Lauren practically ran from the restaurant, an overnight bag already packed and waiting in the trunk of the car, and drove north fast, arriving at Queen of the Valley Medical Center in sixty-five minutes. She parked and rushed up to the maternity ward only to discover that her sister was in the process of being sent home.

"False labor," Lisa said, looking miserable and disappointed in the wheelchair she'd been provided. Her hands and ankles were swollen, her face puffy, her belly huge. "But it didn't feel false."

Lauren bent down to give her a swift hug. "It's okay. It happens. And watch, you'll get home, get comfortable, get all engrossed in a show, and then wham, the real contractions will begin."

"I'm ready," Lisa groaned. "I feel like I'm about to pop. I don't even walk anymore. I just waddle." She caught Lauren's hand. "So sorry I dragged you all this way for nothing. Will you still come up for the real thing?"

"I'm staying the night," Lauren answered, squeezing her sister's fingers.

"You are?"

"Because I think you're having that baby tonight."

Lisa brightened. "You do?"

"Yep. Just call it a woman's intuition, but I believe your little one is coming sooner than you think."

Lauren stopped by the Bakery & Café after leaving the hospital and greeted the staff she'd known forever, smiling politely at the new faces that had been hired since she'd left.

It was a beautiful day, warm and sunny, and even though it was almost two, the restaurant was packed with a late lunch crowd.

Nice, she thought, walking among the tables and checking on meals and the service and saying hello to the Napa residents she recognized, many of them people who'd been customers in the original location.

Lauren ended up lingering for nearly two hours, even filling in at the hostess stand so the young hostess, who was attending college part-time, could leave early in order to write a paper that was due the next day.

Lauren had never spent a lot of time out front in this new spot. She'd always been more comfortable in the back, in the kitchen, baking or handling things behind the scenes, so it was interesting to be working in the sun-drenched restaurant with the marble floor, its black, white, and red color scheme softened by an abundance of topiaries and potted citrus trees.

It was pretty. Inviting. With a distinctive European flair.

It suited Napa, with its focus on good food and wine.

She understood why the business was flourishing. It wasn't just that the location—the lobby of a historic bank building—was unique, or the food superb, or the service personal and first rate. Although it was all of that, too, there was more to the restaurant's success. Summer Bakery & Café was succeeding because Lisa had been pouring her heart and soul into it.

She hadn't just been showing up, putting in the hours. She'd been vigilant about maintaining high standards, and you could feel her love and devotion in all of the details.

The restaurant's interior and exterior were spotless. There was a lightness and freshness to the halls, the bathrooms, even the back entrance. The restaurant, now a year old, still gleamed and sparkled as if brand new.

No wonder Lisa was tired. This was a big restaurant. They had three times as many tables here as they did at Grandma's house, and now they were expanding, adding a patio service for summer.

Amazing.

Lauren stayed until four when Kip, the evening manager arrived; she talked to him for a bit, getting his point of view, very happy to hear that he was so happy with how everything was going, and then said good-bye and headed home.

She drove past Grandma's house, slowing down to get a look at the charming yellow Victorian with glossy white trim. All the bakery signs were gone now, the big front porch just a porch again. The house was back to being a home.

Her home. Her and Blake's home. They'd lived there for a little over twelve years, from the time he was three and a half until he was seventeen. But she hadn't been inside the house for months. Not since September when she moved to Alameda.

One day she'd go inside again. She'd walk around, maybe sit on her couch or sleep in her bed. But that time wasn't now. Better to avoid the house than see Blake's room, still full of all his things. Things he'd never want or need again.

Lauren didn't go into her house, but she did stop at one of the little gift stores farther down on First, running in to see if there was anything pretty for her mom for Mother's Day, and fell in love with a hand-blown vase made by a local glassblower. The vase was tall and narrow with yellow, orange, and pink starbursts inside the thick, bubbled glass. It would look beautiful holding Mom's roses and dahlias.

As the girl behind the counter wrapped it for her, Lauren picked out a card and wrote a note for her mom. *Thank you for always being there for me, Mom. I have always appreciated everything you've done for me. I know I wouldn't have been able to do anything if it hadn't been for you. Happy Mother's Day, Mom. Love you always, Lauren.*

With the gift inside a shopping bag, Lauren stepped back outside and was walking to her car when an older woman walking her dog stopped her. "Lauren! My goodness, dear, it's good to see you. How are you?"

It was Diane Dieter, a woman who'd been her neighbor when Lauren had lived here on First Street in Grandma's house. Lauren shifted the shopping bag to her other hand to hug her old neighbor. "Mrs. Dieter! How are you?"

"I'm so glad to see you. I think about you all the time." Her expression changed, delight giving away to concern. "Are you okay?"

Lauren forced a smile, knowing exactly what Diane was asking. "Yes."

"It's almost a year, isn't it?"

For a moment Lauren couldn't breathe, the air trapped in her throat. Her eyes stung, prickling, and then she nodded once. "It'll be eleven months tomorrow."

"Such a shame. We miss him. And you. Neighborhood's too quiet without you two."

"Everything looks good around here, though," Lauren said,

determined to shift the conversation away from Blake. "Nothing's for sale either."

"Neighborhood's holding its value," Diane agreed. "Although I heard talk that you'll soon be selling."

"Selling Grandma's house? No. Not even considering it. Who told you that?"

Diane gestured vaguely behind her. "Someone . . . somewhere."

"Well, it's not true. I couldn't sell Grandma's. That's home." And suddenly her eyes stung and burned, and she thought she would cry right then and there on the sidewalk in front of the boutique. She lifted her shopping bag. "I better go. Mom's waiting for me."

"Okay. You go. Give your mom by best. And Happy Mother's Day, Lauren."

It was still light when Lauren reached her parents' house and her dad was out on the tractor, working. She set the present and card on the kitchen counter. "For you, Mom, for Mother's Day."

"Thank you. How sweet of you," her mom said, pouring two glasses of iced tea. "Are you going to be here Sunday for Mother's Day?"

"I guess that depends on Lisa," Lauren answered, following her mom back outside.

"Could be days before she has that baby," Candy warned, taking a rocker and sighing with pleasure that she was finally off her feet. "This is nice."

"I don't think it'll be days," Lauren answered, trying to sit but unable to get comfortable, and so she got up again and walked the length of the rustic wooden porch. Their house was simple, but her dad liked his Western touches—big porch, rock-lined driveway, the old fire pit replaced by an outdoor rock fireplace. "I think it's going to be soon."

"First babies can take days." Candy sipped her iced tea and

watched Lauren pace. "But I can't watch you do this. You're exhausting me. Stop pacing this porch like a caged tiger."

Lauren glanced at her mom, smiled ruefully. "Sorry. I feel a bit like one. I just keep thinking that the phone will ring any minute and it'll be Lisa, and I just want to be ready."

"You'll be ready. You'll jump into the car and fly down the mountain, and knowing the way you drive, you'll be there before she even gets to the hospital. And they just live a mile away."

"I don't drive that fast."

"You drive really fast. I've had to follow you before, remember?" She patted the chair next to her. "Now come, sit. Tell me about the café. You've made a lot of changes lately. How's it going? Are you getting the results you wanted?"

"Is this a ploy to distract me, or do you really want to know?"

"Both. But I am interested in what you're doing. I think it's intriguing."

"Intriguing?"

"And brave." Candy was still smiling but her expression had grown more guarded. "Sinking so much of your own money into someone else's business."

Lauren leaned against the porch's wooden railing. "Lisa told you."

"She misses you at the bakery and café."

"I didn't want to move. I liked Grandma's house. I liked being on First Street."

"You'd outgrown your location."

"I didn't think so."

"The new location seems to be making quite a bit more money for you."

Lauren's shoulders lifted, fell. "It *is* beautiful. I spent some time there this afternoon and I was impressed. Lisa is doing a great job, but I've got to be honest, Mom. It doesn't feel like our place. It's not me. It in no way reflects me. It feels like Lisa and Matthieu."

Her mother folded her hands in her lap. "You're jealous of their relationship."

"What?"

"You've never approved of him."

"That's not true. I like him. I was just skeptical in the beginning. You have to admit he's excessively charming."

"He's a sweetheart."

"Oui, oui, madame," she said, imitating her brother-in-law, but it wasn't meant to sound mean-spirited. She liked Matthieu a lot. In fact, she had a huge soft spot for him, but he was French and affluent and sophisticated and she wasn't any of those things. Nor did she want to be any of those things. She was really a beef-brisket-and-apple-pie kind of girl. And she was proud of it. "But no, seriously, Mom, I'm not jealous. I'm thrilled Lisa is happy. She deserves to be happy, and she and Matthieu have done a fantastic job with the restaurant. But I don't belong there. The restaurant has become Lisa and Matthieu's."

"Because you left Lisa with it."

Lauren shot her mom a quick look. "Because you know why."

"So what are you going to do? Dump the restaurant on Lisa, even though she's going to be home with a new baby?"

"Maybe it's time we sold, then."

"Maybe," her mom agreed calmly. "So when are you going to tell her?"

"I don't know."

"It'd be kinder if you told her sooner rather than later."

"What if I don't know what I want, though? What if I have no idea what's right? What if I haven't a clue what I need?" Lauren shook her head, angry and frustrated. It wasn't as if she'd asked for all this change. It wasn't as if she'd wanted it either. Change had been forced upon her and she was just doing her best to survive. "Blake hasn't even been gone for a year. It's just eleven months since he died. And yet everyone wants me to act like nothing's happened—"

"That's not true, Lauren. We understand you're grieving. We're grieving. Your dad and I miss him every single day."

"Then you understand why I can't make a decision about the restaurant. I can't make a decision to save my life—"

"You said it, honey, I didn't."

Lauren glared at her. "What does that mean?"

"You just admitted that you can't make a decision to save your life, and yet here you are, investing your own money into this other woman's restaurant. I don't think it's wise, and your dad's gotten himself worked up over it. He says this Mimi woman is taking advantage of you."

"No one is taking advantage of me."

"Does this Mimi know you just lost your son? Does she understand you're not yourself?"

"Mom!"

"We're worried about you, Lauren."

"Well, don't be. I'm sad, not crazy."

"You'd be less sad here, with us—"

"That's not true. Alameda's good for me. I'm enjoying doing new things, meeting new people."

Her mom gave her a long, speculative look. "Will you tell me the truth, if I ask you something?"

"Of course."

"Do you have . . . feelings . . . for this woman?"

Lauren blinked, stunned. "Uh . . . *what*?"

"It's all right if you're gay—"

"Mom!" Lauren didn't know whether she should laugh or cry. "I'm not gay. I have gay friends, yes, but I'm not gay."

"You haven't dated . . . ever."

"That's not true. I had a boyfriend in high school, we made a baby, and I . . . chose not to date as a single mother."

"It's okay if you are gay, Lauren."

Lauren choked on a gurgle of laughter. "I know it's okay. I

think gay women are beautiful. I think they're wonderful. But I'm not interested in having sex with a woman."

"Are you interested in having sex with a man?"

Shaking her head in disbelief, Lauren looked away, gazing out past the gravel driveway to the front paddock and the pasture with the gnarled oak tree in the center, to the rolling hills beyond. "Where is Dad? Did he put you up to this?"

Her mom's silence was telling and Lauren made a soft exasperated sound. "Tell Dad that I'm sorry to disappoint him, but I am heterosexual."

"You like men."

"Is that a statement or a question, Mom?"

Candy sighed and gripped the arms of her chair. "Lisa just thought that maybe . . ."

"Yes?" Lauren prompted, turning around.

Her mom sighed again. "Lisa thought that perhaps that . . . John . . . turned you off men."

Lauren laughed, blushed, shook her head. "No, Mom," she said, her voice dropping, deepening with amusement. "You can sleep at night. He didn't."

Audrey Lauren Roussel was born at 11:59 P.M. on Saturday, May 12, arriving into the world with a lusty cry and kicking legs.

She was perfect. She was also beautiful, weighing in at just under eight pounds, her skin a dusky pink and cream, and she had a thatch of dark brown hair and huge brown eyes.

Lauren hadn't been sure how she'd feel when she first held her new niece, but the moment Matthieu put the swaddled infant into her arms, she felt nothing but joy. And the fiercest rush of love. Unconditional love. She'd do anything for this baby. Anything.

She dipped her head and kissed the top of Audrey's soft, sweet head. What a gift she was . . . what a blessing for this family . . .

Lifting her head, Lauren looked over at her sister and was startled to discover Lisa crying.

"What's wrong?" she asked, moving carefully closer to the bed with the newborn in her arms.

"Just so happy you're here. So happy to see you holding her."

"I wouldn't have missed this for the world," Lauren said, and it was true. Witnessing Audrey's birth had been nothing but healing and good.

"You'll be her godmother?" Matthieu asked, stepping toward them, unable to stay away.

Lauren gazed down at the baby and discovered that Audrey was looking up at her, her dark eyes unfocused, and yet there was an intensity in them, a fierce concentration. Lauren kissed her again, in love. "Absolutely."

Sunday morning in San Francisco, Sarah had left her phone charging in the kitchen during their homemade brunch, missing the call from Boone.

She'd been waiting impatiently for his call all morning and only discovered the missed call when she was clearing dishes from the table just after noon.

Disappointed, she immediately unplugged the phone and headed for the living room, where it was quiet, to call him back, wondering if he had news. Hoping he had news. Hoping a team— a good team—wanted to pick up his contract.

But Boone didn't answer when she returned his call and so she left him a message, asking him to call her back as soon as he could.

Hanging up, Sarah dropped onto the couch and tipped her head back, staring at the ceiling, wondering why he had called, hoping it was good news, hoping that he hadn't played his last game in Major League Baseball. Because his career might make her crazy, but it was also his career, and while she had a love/hate relationship with baseball, she loved that he did something he loved. She loved that he was passionate about his work. She loved that he did something few could do.

Maybe it's why she'd stayed with him when she found out about his affair. She hated the affair but loved him. She also understood that he wasn't like your average Joe. He lived in the spotlight. He was paid big money to perform on demand. He was expected to be larger than life. And he had been.

Her phone vibrated in her hands with a text. She grabbed it and read the message. It was from Boone. *On phone with Arnie. Will call as soon as I'm done.*

Sarah exhaled. Had to be news . . . had to be good news . . . but what was good news?

Jumping up, she paced the length of the living room and turned around, paced back the other direction, stopping in front of the mantel, which was bare today except for a pair of glass hurricanes and a framed photo of Mom, in gorgeous color.

In the picture, Mom was looking over her shoulder, laughing at the camera, her thick dark hair short and sassy, her brown eyes flecked with bronze, picking up the gold of her shimmering dress.

Sarah reached out, touched Mom's face through the glass. So pretty.

"I love that picture of Mom," Tommy said from the doorway. He was wearing one of the expensive Tommy Bahama polo shirts Cass liked to give him, and yet he looked uncomfortable, as if he'd been squeezed into a straitjacket instead of the softest weathered cotton fabric.

Sarah smiled unsteadily. "She's so beautiful here."

"She was always beautiful," he said, moving toward her.

"But in this picture, she looks like a movie star."

He stood now before the mantel and studied the photo. "I just like that she looks so happy."

Sarah glanced at her brother and then at the picture. "Definitely happy."

Tommy hesitated, his brow creasing, his jaw jutting. "She was . . . most of the time, wasn't she?"

Sarah saw his frown and felt his restlessness. He'd been tense all day, drumming his fingers on the table during the meal or leaning back in his chair and sighing, staring at the ceiling as if he couldn't wait to get away. "I think Mom always tried to focus on the positives," she said.

"She never pressured Dad."

"But she was also no pushover. If there was something she wanted, she spoke up."

"But she let Dad be Dad. She respected Dad as a man."

"Absolutely."

He made a rough, raw sound in the back of his throat. "She was a real woman."

All of a sudden Sarah knew what they were talking about. They weren't discussing Mom. They were discussing Cass. Tommy was mad at his wife. They all knew. He'd been a dick to her for much of the day. "Mom wasn't always happy, Tommy. And Mom loved Dad, but she didn't let him do whatever he wanted. They had a marriage. A partnership. He'd give on some things, and she'd give on others—"

"But if Dad put his foot down, Mom backed off."

Sarah arched a brow. "Depended what it was about. If Mom felt strongly, she didn't accept the whole putting-your-foot-down thing."

"Yes, she did."

"Nope. We were there, Tommy, when Mom almost left Dad. It had to do with Brianna and how Dad was handling her. And Dad wouldn't discuss it with Mom anymore, so Mom packed. She was leaving Dad. And she was serious."

"I don't remember."

"Then you've blocked it out, because you were there, we were all there, and I was only eleven, but I remember being at the top of the stairs and crying my eyes out and Kit and Meg were holding me, wouldn't let me go down."

Tommy looked away, brow lowering. He remembered. She knew from his expression he remembered. "That was different," he said gruffly.

"Was it?"

"Yes."

"Why?"

He shrugged, impatient. "I don't know, but it had to have been serious."

"And you don't think Cass being unhappy is serious?"

"No, it's serious."

"You guys are at odds. We can all tell, all feel it, but it doesn't have to be this way—"

"Tell that to her!"

Sarah tucked a strand of hair behind her ear, thinking she needed to take a different tack. "You and Cass will get through this, Tommy. It's a rough patch, but if you stick together—"

"I can't force Cass to stay, Sarah."

"You can go to counseling."

"Tried that. It didn't work."

"How many times did you go?"

"Enough to know I'm not going to sit there and be lectured by some lady I don't know about how I need to be sensitive to my wife's needs. I'm not insensitive to Cass's feelings. I'm fully aware that my wife is grieving. Hell, I'm grieving, but what are we going to do? Fixate on something that's not going to happen? Obsess about all the things outside our control, or move forward and enjoy what we have together?"

Sarah heard the rawness in his voice. He was in pain. He absolutely doted on Cassidy, and how could he not? She was the sweetest, most gorgeous, loving girl in the whole world. Cass had been raised with an alcoholic mom in a rough part of San Jose, and from the moment she'd met handsome, swaggering Tommy Brennan Jr. she'd been smitten. He was her hero. Her one and only true love. Tommy and Cass were married less than a year after meeting and it was the best decision Tommy had ever made. Everyone in the family loved Cass. Everyone wanted to see her and Tommy happy. "You still love her?"

He glared at her, his expression fierce. "How can you even ask that? I'd do anything for her. Give my life for her—"

"But she needs to feel it, not just know it. Women need words. They need language—"

"And I've talked, but I'm talked out. I've got nothing else to say."

"Then that's the problem."

"I'm *not* the problem!"

"You are if you can't see that Cass needs more from you, not less."

He rolled his eyes. "What about me? What about what I need?"

"You said you loved her."

"I do. But—"

"Then don't get all macho. Don't get into a pissing contest with your wife. She grew up an only child. It's been her dream her entire life to have kids, be a mom, and now she's lost babies. Plural. Of course she's devastated. You even said she's grieving, which means she needs to keep talking, and she needs you to keep listening."

"I'm done with the baby thing. It's taken over our life and I just want our life back. I want our marriage back—"

"So that's what you're grieving."

"What?"

"You're grieving your marriage, and she's grieving the babies."

He just looked at her.

Sarah reached out to him but he stepped back to avoid her touch. Sarah refused to dwell on it. "You want your marriage back, the same marriage you had before . . . but it's not the same marriage. It won't ever be the same as before. You two have been through too much. Have hurt too much. You've changed. Both of you."

He barked a laugh. "And that's supposed to make me feel better?"

"Maybe it'll be better than before."

"Maybe?"

"If you guys pull it together."

Cass suddenly stuck her head around the corner, long blond ringlets tumbling over her shoulders. "Hey." Her smile was tentative and failed to reach her eyes. "Dad said we're going to have cake soon."

Tommy nodded curtly.

Cass's faint smile faded, revealing hurt and pain.

Sarah's chest squeezed, and though she hated to be disloyal, Tommy was acting like a first-rate jerk.

Slipping her phone into her pocket, she smiled encouragingly at Cass, but her sister-in-law had already averted her gaze and was biting into her lip to keep from bursting into tears.

Jerk, Sarah silently repeated, wondering why men couldn't give women the one thing they sometimes needed most—tenderness.

The three of them headed for the dining room, Tommy and Cass walking on either side of her, making Sarah painfully aware that the two of them were not together. Not anywhere close together.

She spotted Meg and the kids already in the dining room with Dad. Tommy was looking the other way, and he paused before entering the room, focused on the family room. Sarah followed his gaze. Jude and Kit were sitting on the sofa, Kit on Jude's lap. They were kissing.

"Christ," Tommy muttered.

He hadn't sworn particularly loudly, but Kit had what they all jokingly called supersonic hearing, probably due to the fact that she was a teacher.

Kit jerked her head up, looked right at her brother. "What was that?"

"You shouldn't do that here," Tommy growled. "It's not right."

"You kiss Cass all the time," Kit said, still sitting on Jude's lap.

"Not like that," Tommy retorted.

"Like how?"

"Like that," Tommy growled. "If you're going to get raunchy, get a room."

One of Jude's black eyebrows lifted, but he held his tongue.

Kit jumped up, defiant. "Which room would you suggest, Tommy? Yours? The girls'? Mom and Dad's?"

"Knock it off," he snapped.

"You knock it off," Kit said hotly, smoothing the skirt of her fitted, blue sheath dress, which made the most of her curves. And Kit had curves. She was the most voluptuous Brennan girl. "I remember when you and Cass used to make out all over the house."

"That was different," Tommy said.

Kit moved toward him, the light of battle in her blue eyes. "Oh, really? How?"

"Babe," Jude said, reluctantly swinging his long, leather-clad legs off the coffee table and getting to his feet. "Let it go."

But Kit ignored him, her attention fixed on Tommy. "I get that you're not happy, Tommy, and I'm sorry about it. But I *am* happy, and I have a right to be happy without you"—and her gaze swung to include Sarah—"judging me, and criticizing me, and making me feel as if I don't belong in this family anymore simply because I'm dating someone you don't approve of."

"Oh, Kit, no one feels that way," Cass protested nervously.

"Don't say that," Tommy said, contradicting his wife. "Kit's right. No one approves of Jude and I'm not afraid to say so. I don't like him." He looked past Kit to Jude. "Sorry, Knight, but it's how I feel. You might be a perfectly nice guy—which I actually, seriously doubt—but you're not good enough for Kit. Not by a long shot."

Kit made a choking sound. *"Tommy!"*

He shrugged, still pissed off from his conversation with Sarah. "It's the truth. I'm not going to lie and pretend otherwise."

"You don't have to pretend anything," Kit snapped. "Just be polite. Have some manners."

"Apparently I don't have any. But then, ask Sarah. I'm an extremely insensitive man." He glanced at Cass. "I'm leaving. Are you coming with me, or are you going to catch a ride home with Kit and her goon?"

"Tommy!" Kit exploded.

Cassidy paled, blue eyes widening. "We can't walk out now. Your dad has a cake for your mom—"

"Who happens to be dead."

"Tommy," Kit and Sarah said in unison.

"This is Mother's Day," Cass choked, mortified. Cass might have married into this family, but she'd loved Mom dearly. Mom had been more of a mother to her than her own mother and Cass had turned to her often for advice.

But Tommy was beyond caring. He shrugged and drew his keys from his pocket. "Last chance. Going home with me, Cass?"

She didn't answer, too shocked to speak, and he shrugged again, too angry to compromise. "Whatever," he said, his big shoulders rolling. "Tell Dad I'll call him later."

Tommy didn't get far. Dad was out the door, hurrying after him, before Tommy had even started his car.

Everyone else just stood around the dining table looking at the cake that had yet to be cut.

"Why is Uncle Tommy so mad?" Gabi asked, glancing from her mom to her aunt Cass.

Cass's lower lip quivered. Kit moved toward her and wrapped an arm around her, comforting her. "It's okay," she soothed. "Dad will calm him down. They'll be back and everything will be okay."

"I just don't get it," Gabi said.

"Uncle Tommy's just having an off day," Meg murmured, filling the silence.

"But why?" Gabi persisted.

"Because people sometimes do," JJ said sharply, irritated, shoving his hands deep into the pockets of his cords. "It happens, okay?"

Gabi made a face. Tessa sighed. Meg looked away from all of them, pale and hollow-eyed.

"I'm going to sit," Brianna said, pulling out her chair.

Sarah wanted to sit as well but didn't think she could stay put, not when Dad and Tommy were having it out in front of the house.

Hopefully they wouldn't come to blows. They had before. More than once. Dad was a Leo and had his pride, and Tommy—a Taurus—didn't get really angry often, but when he did, watch out.

"But is Uncle Tommy mad at Aunt Cass or at Aunt Kit?" Gabi continued, dragging her chair away from the table and sitting down, mulling over the interesting family dynamics. "Because I heard him yelling at both of them today."

"Stop it, Gabi," Tessa whispered, sitting down, too.

"I just want to know," Gabi answered, chin propped in her hands. "What's wrong with that?"

"Because you're making Aunt Cass feel bad," Tessa said tersely, giving Cass an apologetic glance.

"It's okay," Cass murmured, even as two big blotches stained her cheeks.

Gabi smiled victoriously. "See?"

JJ shook his head.

Tessa covered her face with her hands. "I want to go home."

Sarah glanced at Meg, who was looking paler and more brittle by the moment. This was not the Mother's Day any of them wanted. "Maybe you guys should go home," she said. "Maybe it would be better. You could spend some time together as a family."

Meg's lips compressed. "Can't do that to Dad."

"Meg's right," Kit said. "He really wanted us all here today, to remember Mom."

"But we're not remembering Mom," Brianna said flatly. "We're just bickering nonstop—"

The front door swung open and everyone fell silent. Dad entered the house. Alone. He carefully shut the door behind him and headed to the dining room, where they were all waiting.

"Tommy's gone on home," Dad said gruffly.

No one spoke. Everyone felt awkward. Cass practically hung her head in shame.

"Grandpa, are you okay?" Tessa asked nervously as Dad sank into his chair at the foot of the table.

"Yes," he answered, forearms resting on the table, his forehead deeply lined. "Why?"

"Because you look . . . sad," Tessa said, her voice dropping to a whisper.

Dad held his granddaughter's gaze. "I miss your grandma," he said bluntly. "And I feel like I'm letting her down. She wouldn't tolerate this kind of nonsense. Not from any of you."

Everyone looked in different directions, the sense of unease growing.

"Grandpa, no offense," Gabi said, speaking up to break the weighty silence. "But everybody did fight around Grandma."

"Gabriela!" Meg choked, mortified.

Gabi shrugged and reached for her water glass. "They did,"

she insisted, her gaze sweeping around the table. "But Grandma just didn't let it freak her out so much."

For a moment Sarah wasn't sure if her dad was going to laugh or cry, and then he held his arms out to Gabi. "Come here," he said.

Without hesitating, Gabriela slipped from her chair and into his arms. Dad tucked her onto his lap, his chin just grazing the top of her head. "Spoken like a true Brennan." He smiled ruefully at everyone else. "Well said."

Gabi leaned in, gave him a big squeeze. "So that means we can have cake now, Grandpa?"

His smile turned wry. He had a sense of humor. Had to have one. He'd been raised in a big family, and he himself had raised a big family. "You ready for cake, Gabriela?"

"I am."

He nodded and set Gabi down on her feet. "Me, too."

It was almost as if everyone exhaled all at once. You could feel the tension leave the room. Smiling, Kit headed for the kitchen to get the coffee. Meg stood up to cut the cake. Cass handed Meg the cake plates. And Sarah's phone buzzed with an incoming text.

She glanced down at the phone still clutched in her hands.

I've just accepted an offer from the A's. Happy Mother's Day, babe. We're moving to the Bay Area.

"Oh my God," Sarah whispered, reading the message a second time.

"What's wrong?" Dad asked, instantly silencing the room.

"It's Boone," she said.

"Is he okay? Has there been an accident?"

Kit immediately appeared in the doorway. Everyone else stopped, focused on Sarah.

Sarah shook her head. "No. He's . . . he's fine." She looked down the table at her father. "He . . . uh . . . was released by Tampa Bay."

"Oh, Sarah, no!" Cass exclaimed.

"That's terrible," JJ exclaimed.

"No, no, it's okay." Sarah mustered a smile. "He just texted me to say that he's signed with the Oakland Λ's." She kept smiling to hide her shock and apprehension. "I'm moving home."

Twelve

Sarah flew back to Tampa late Sunday night, unable to process the fact that she was returning to put her and Boone's house on the market.

She was returning to move.

Crazy. Crazy how fast things changed.

She'd been married to a professional baseball player for a long time. She knew trades happened. Knew players got cut from the team and injured. Change was part of the business as teams worked hard to stay competitive, but Tampa had become her home. She'd been happy there. The kids had friends. *She* had friends.

And now it was time to pack up and leave.

Arriving back home, Sarah struggled to wrap her head around the news. She walked around the house, taking in the high ceilings and big heavy beams, the beautiful tiled floor, the stucco walls. It was a Spanish-inspired house, on a cul-de-sac of similar homes, but they were all spacious and luxurious with big yards and large, colorful play structures for kids in the back.

Strange to think that Boone would never return here. He'd never sleep in this house again, or eat dinner at the table, or bump up against her in the kitchen, his lips on her nape, his hand against her breast. And just knowing that Boone was done, gone, changed the place for her.

Although she arrived home late, Sarah was up early to get the kids off to school. She made her coffee extra strong and broke the news that they were moving as she drove the kids to school.

Ella cried.

Brennan appeared indifferent. "That's fine," he said, shrugging. "I don't have many friends here anyway."

"What about the Neeleys?" Sarah asked, referring to Alyssa and Jeff's boys. "I thought you were friends with them?"

"That's different," he answered. "I do like them."

Back home, Sarah put in a call to the realtor who had sold them the house four years before. He promised to get the house in the system by the end of the day.

"Are you ready to start showing?" the realtor asked.

"We will be."

They discussed the price, the market, and Sarah and Boone's expectations. Sarah didn't need to talk to Boone. She was accustomed to handling real estate decisions and managing their moves. "Price aggressively," she said. "School is over just three weeks from now, and once the kids are out, I'll want to get us out of here to join Boone on the West Coast."

Sarah texted Boone after hanging up with the agent. *House will be in the system by closing today. Open house scheduled for Saturday and Sunday. How are things going for you?*

He didn't answer. She kept checking her phone, trying not to be frustrated. Here she was, trying to handle stuff here. The least he could do was check in.

Then she looked up the A's schedule, saw that Oakland was

down in Southern California to play the Angels, and drew a deep breath, understanding.

It was only seven thirty there. Boone was still in bed, sleeping.

Sarah studied the schedule, becoming familiar with it. Boone was in California today and tomorrow, then had two games in Texas, before returning to Oakland late Thursday night for the weekend's Bay Bridge series against the Giants, so called because the two baseball teams traveled across the Oakland Bay Bridge to play each other. And while the series was competitive, drew big crowds, and got lots of media attention, it was a friendly rivalry, unlike the Yankees and Red Sox, which tended to be more intense and sometimes downright hostile.

Sarah had grown up attending the Bay Bridge series with her dad and brother. She'd played sports her entire life, loved watching sports, had dated athletes in high school, but she hadn't ever imagined marrying one.

Hadn't wanted to marry one.

And then along came Boone and nothing had ever been the same.

Sarah was deep in the middle of cleaning and decluttering the kids' rooms when Alyssa came over.

"They've just put a For Sale sign up outside your house," Alyssa said, stepping around the cardboard boxes Sarah had dragged from the garage. "It's true, then? You're leaving."

"The Rays let Boone go."

"I'm shocked. And sad."

"It's caught me off guard," Sarah admitted, crouching next to a box to tape the top closed. "I had no idea it would come to this."

Alyssa watched her start filling another box. "Jeff said Boone wanted out."

Sarah dropped the armful of stuffed animals into the box and glanced up at Alyssa, wondering what else she might have heard from Jeff. "Boone wasn't happy."

"I know. And the coaches are wrong. They should have been playing him more. He's having a great year."

Sarah smiled gratefully. That was a nice thing to say, but then, Alyssa had always been really loyal. "I'm going to miss you."

"When do you leave?"

"Not for a couple of weeks. Going to wait until school's out."

"What about Boone? Will he stay with your family, or . . . ?"

"The A's have booked him a suite at one of those corporate hotels that have kitchens and living rooms. He'll be there until we arrive and I can get us a rental house someplace."

"Not going to buy?"

"No. I doubt we'll be in Oakland long. We'll probably finish the season there and then . . . who knows? It's anybody's guess." Sarah attempted to tear off a strip of tape but dropped the roll and it wobbled over to Alyssa. "I'm kind of hoping he's going to retire, but it'll be a huge adjustment for him. He's always played ball. He's always had the game to focus on."

Alyssa picked up the tape and handed it back. "I hate the off-season for that reason. Jeff's a bear when he's not playing. Grouchy, grumpy, and lazy. I like him playing ball. Gets him out of the house. Keeps him busy."

"There is that." Sarah stacked the second box on top of the first. She brushed off her hands, glanced into Ella's closet, which was now nearly empty. "Wow. Can't believe this is happening. I had no idea when I headed to San Francisco a few days ago that we'd soon be moving there."

"You have to be happy that you're moving home."

"I think so." Sarah caught sight of Alyssa's puzzled expression. "Things are kind of crazy there right now. Lots of drama."

"Everybody's still grieving. They will for a while."

"I know. And I am looking forward to seeing more of my dad. It'll be good for my kids, too. They love their grandpa."

Alyssa's eyes watered. "I'm happy for you, but sad for me. I'm really going to miss you."

"No! Don't!" Sarah's eyes suddenly burned, too, and she moved forward to give Alyssa a huge hug. "Don't be sad, not yet. I'm not going anywhere for a while. I'll be here at least three more weeks—"

"Three weeks! That's nothing."

"We will just have to make a plan to get you, and the kids, out to see us in California soon."

The morning rush at Mama's Café was over and the lunch crowd hadn't yet begun to trickle in. Lauren took advantage of the quiet moment to talk to the cook about the lunch specials and how things should be prepared, as well as the presentation. She hadn't been happy at all with the way breakfast had gone. Even if they were slammed, they couldn't do sloppy, and never ugly. Food had to look good and taste good, as first impressions mattered.

Emerging from the kitchen, she glanced at the glass cabinet displaying the day's homemade desserts. They had five pies and three cakes. She'd made every one this morning, and even though it wasn't even noon yet, the cherry pie was already half gone, the lemon meringue was short two slices, and the entire hummingbird cake had disappeared. Lauren suspected it'd been bought earlier, but she hadn't seen it go and she approached Phyllis, one of the waitresses who opened the café with her every morning, who was at the cash register.

"Where did the hummingbird cake go?" Lauren asked as Phyllis bent over her notepad, totaling a bill.

"Sold it," Phyllis said, glancing up at her before looking down again, double-checking her math. "Someone came in and bought it for her bridge party."

"How much did you charge?"

"Thirty dollars."

"She didn't balk?"

"Nope." Phyllis tucked the notepad back into her apron. "And that's still less than what we'd make if we sold it by the slice."

"The cakes are doing well," Lauren said as the café door opened. A young couple entered, hand in hand. They were long-haired, scruffy, but happy-looking. Bette appeared, two menus in hand, and seated them.

"Very well," Phyllis agreed. "Yesterday a lady came in, right after we opened, and bought the candy bar cake for her husband's birthday. She said she came early to be sure she got the cake but thought maybe we should consider doing special-order cakes."

"I don't know how Mimi would feel about it."

Phyllis gave her a pointed look. "I think we both know that Mimi doesn't care what you do as long as she keeps making money."

"True."

"The bakery items do really well. Have you seen the pies? Some of them are already half gone."

"I saw."

"We're developing a reputation."

Lauren grimaced. "As long as it's a good one."

"Of course it's a good one! Why would you say that?"

Lauren brushed her hand across the counter, seeing a sheen on it, and made sure it wasn't sticky. It wasn't. "Normally I only hear the bad stuff."

"That's because you always want to be told about the bad stuff." Phyllis gestured to Bette that she saw the young couple Bette had seated in Phyllis's section. "Which reminds me, some-one sent back the grillades and grits earlier."

Lauren frowned. That wasn't good. The grillades and grits were new items on the menu, and hadn't been ordered very many times yet. "Was there something wrong with it?"

Phyllis shrugged. "He didn't say anything bad about it, just took a bite and then didn't want it anymore."

"Did you offer something else?"

"I did, but he said he was fine with the biscuits."

That really wasn't good. Lauren's frown deepened. "You refunded him the grillades?"

"He told me not to. But he's still here. Should I?"

"Where is he?"

Phyllis pointed to a table by the window. "That's him. Spartacus. Over there."

"Spartacus?" Lauren repeated, amused.

Phyllis's gray head bobbed, her brown eyes dancing. "That's what Bette called him. He's the big guy in the booth in the back. The one who looks like a superhero."

Lauren hadn't seen him, at least not until now. And now that she'd seen him, she couldn't believe she'd missed him.

He was big—at least six three—and built. Broad shoulders, thick biceps, wide rib cage. Nice face, too, not that she was looking. Lauren hadn't dated since before Blake died. Didn't think she ever would again.

"I was just about to give him his bill," Phyllis added. "Do you want me to take off the grillades and grits?"

"They're fourteen dollars, aren't they?"

Phyllis nodded.

Lauren sighed and held her hand out for the bill. "Let me go talk about it to him. Find out what was wrong."

Sighing inwardly, she headed for the corner booth where the customer was sitting.

He looked up at her as she approached. His gaze met hers, held.

Lauren blinked, taken aback, suddenly understanding why Bette had nicknamed him Spartacus.

He was intense.

And intensely good-looking.

"Hi, I'm Lauren Summer. I'm the manager," she said crisply,

annoyed that she suddenly felt self-conscious and warm. "I understand you weren't happy with the grillades?"

"It was fine," he drawled, reaching into his back pocket for his wallet, his soft knit shirt growing tighter, hugging the thick plane of his chest. "And the biscuits were great."

He was solid. Built. Lauren hated that she noticed. "What was wrong with the grillades?"

"They were fine. It's not a big deal—"

"Fine isn't good," Lauren interrupted as he opened his wallet and drew out two twenties. "Fine is just fine. Fine means possibly passable. Which isn't good enough for me. I want our food to be excellent."

He looked up, smiled, creases fanning from his eyes. "The biscuits were."

"Biscuits are easy," she retorted impatiently.

"Actually, they're not as easy as people think." He dropped the twenties on the table, and slid out, and stood, towering over her. "And your biscuits were *really* good. Next time I'll just have biscuits and gravy and I'll be a happy man."

She didn't know why her heart did a funny double beat. He had an accent, not French like Matthieu's but Southern, and it made an impression. Flustered, she glanced down at his bill, deciphered Phyllis's scrawl. "You didn't try our gravy. So you might not like it either."

The corner of his mouth lifted. "Then I guess I'll find out next time, won't I?" He slipped his wallet back into his pocket before walking out, leaving Lauren standing there, staring, jaw open.

He came in again the next day, at approximately the same time. This time Bette seated him in her section, wanting to wait on Spartacus herself.

Lauren stayed in her section, successfully avoiding him, but she did make note of what he ordered—sweet-potato pecan waffles, scrambled eggs, spicy sausage, grits—and if he ate it.

He did. All of it.

After he paid his bill, Bette headed straight for Lauren. "He told me to tell you that it was fine," she said.

Lauren wasn't sure if she should be amused or insulted. "Fine?" she repeated.

Bette nodded. "But he did say if you're wanting to improve, the waffles would be a smidge better if you toasted the pecans a little more."

"He said that?"

Bette waved a twenty under Lauren's nose and grinned. "Yes, and he left me this for a tip."

"Well, I guess you can retire now," Lauren said, remembering that he'd dropped the two twenties yesterday before she'd even given him the bill, even as she replayed his comments over in her head.

Everything was fine . . .

But if you're wanting to improve . . .

Was he serious or teasing?

"If he comes back, I'm waiting on him tomorrow," Phyllis said, joining them. "Not because I want the tip, but because he's just easy on the eyes."

"He *is* a handsome one," Bette agreed. "And he seems familiar. I keep thinking he's a professional athlete. Quarterback or wide receiver."

Phyllis thought it over. "Now that you mention it, he does look familiar, but he's not with the 49ers. I know my Niners."

"Could be baseball," Bette said. "He's got those nice legs."

"A great butt."

Lauren groaned. "Enough!"

"Don't act like you didn't notice." Phyllis wagged her finger at her. "We all saw you yesterday, staring."

"I wasn't staring!" Lauren protested.

Phyllis and Bette exchanged glances.

"You were, too," Bette said, slipping her tip money into her pocket. "And it's perfectly okay, because he's a fine-looking man and you're a pretty woman—"

"I'm not interested in dating a customer," Lauren interrupted, perfectly aware that Phyllis and Bette might be flirtatious, but at sixty-two and fifty-seven respectively, they were experienced, mature, hardworking waitresses who talked a good game but never took it too far. "So if you two want to fight over him—even though you, Phyllis, are married, and you, Bette, have a boyfriend—be my guest."

He did come back for a third morning in a row, but he seated himself at the counter instead of waiting for a booth.

The counter was Lauren's, and she could have sworn by his expression that he knew it.

"Coffee?" she asked, greeting him and sliding the menu toward him.

"Juice," he said, and didn't bother with the menu, pushing it back. "What's your special today?"

Her hands went to her hips. "You didn't like the waffles yesterday."

"I did."

"No, you told Bette to tell me they were fine." Her eyes held his, her expression reproving. "And we already established that fine is not fine, and then you added that the waffles could be improved if we toasted the pecans more."

He smiled. "Just a smidge more."

She considered him a long moment. "You were right." Lauren reached for his menu, tapped it on the counter. "I tried the pecans. They definitely needed to be toasted more."

"Just a smidge." The edges of his lips curved up again. He wasn't a kid. He was a man, had to be mid to late thirties, and when he smiled, creases formed at his eyes and mouth, making him even more beautiful.

Amazing how just that tiny smile could make her pulse quicken. And Lauren considered herself impervious to men, which made this one man doubly dangerous. "You know your food," she said.

"I know Southern food," he corrected.

"You're from Louisiana?"

"New Orleans."

She noticed he said it more like "Naw'lens." "Our special is eggs Sardou."

"Can I get it with a side of grits?"

Something in her shifted yet again, and she felt a sharp dart of pain in her chest, near her heart. "Absolutely."

I t was on the fourth morning that Lauren found out who he was. It was early still, not even six A.M., but Phyllis had the sports section from the *Oakland Tribune*, and she put it on the counter and spread it open.

"I was right," she said, pointing to an article. "He is a baseball player. He's new with the A's."

"What's his name?" Bob, the cook, called, from the kitchen.

"Boone Walker," Phyllis answered. "He's a DH. Designated hitter—"

"I know what a DH is," Bob retorted loudly.

Phyllis ignored him, tapping the black-and-white photo and caption. "Only been with the team a week and he's already making the headlines."

Lauren glanced over Phyllis's shoulder to read the headline: VETERAN BOONE WALKER'S BAT MAKES BIG IMPRESSION. "Nice," she said.

"I told you," Bette said, moving in closer to get a better look. "I knew he was a professional athlete."

"You said football. I said baseball." Phyllis nodded for emphasis. "I knew it from those legs."

"But neither of you knows anything about him," Bob said. "I do. I've got some of his cards. He used to be with Houston. Before that, he spent four years with the Reds and a year in Seattle."

"That's a lot of moves," Lauren said.

"That's because teams were fighting over him," Bob added, looking under the warmer. "He used to really hit the ball—"

"Sounds like he can still really hit the ball," Phyllis interjected.

Bob didn't like being interrupted and glared at Phyllis. "But he's old now. Not making what he used to, and Walker was one of those guys who, back in the early nineties, was earning four or five million a year. That's good money."

The door opened and customers walked in, effectively curtailing the conversation. But four hours later, when Boone Walker entered the café, the staff all paused, looked at him, aware now of just who he was.

"Morning," Boone said, taking a seat at the counter.

"Morning," Lauren answered, hating that she suddenly felt nervous. It shouldn't matter that he was with the A's and a baseball player.

But it did. She didn't like baseball, didn't like the players, didn't like anything to do with the sport.

Blake had played baseball, but it hadn't been by her choice. She'd never suggested it to him; in fact, she'd done everything in her power to keep him away from the game, signing him up for soccer and swimming, but when he'd heard that friends in his preschool class were playing T-ball, he'd insisted he play, too.

Blake was a natural, too. There wasn't a sport he couldn't play, and by the time he reached high school, he was getting some serious looks from scouts.

Those who were in the know said Blake had a chance to make it in professional baseball.

Those who were in the know said he had God-given talent.

He did. But he'd also inherited some of that talent from his dad, the Yankees' ace pitcher, John Meeks.

"Coffee?" she asked, holding up a fresh pot.

"Please." He watched her fill a mug. "You serve good coffee here. I like that it's nice and strong."

"That's how coffee is supposed to be," she answered, setting the cup down in front of him and then handing him a menu. "Have a couple of specials today. *Pain perdu,* and then one of my personal favorites, breakfast pork chops and eggs. The pork chops aren't fancy, but they've got great flavor, and we don't overcook them."

"Sold."

"Hash browns or country-fried?"

"Country-fried. And a little crispy, if you can—"

"That was a great game last night, Mr. Walker," Phyllis said, leaning across the counter to get his attention.

Boone looked surprised. "Thank you."

"How are you enjoying playing for the A's?" she added.

"It's good. Things are going well."

"You're still new here, I know, but if there's anything I can do, just let me know."

Bette pressed in close to Phyllis and beamed at Boone. "Welcome to Oakland."

A bit bemused, Boone glanced from Phyllis to Bette and then to Lauren. "Thank you."

"How are you settling in?" Bette asked.

"Good. Still new here, but it's going well."

"I'd say, if last night's game is anything to go by." Bette beamed. "Quite the hitter, aren't you?"

"I try," Boone answered.

"And you just keep trying," Bette said firmly, before Phyllis tugged her away.

Boone looked at Lauren. She smiled faintly, shrugged. "You were written up in the morning's paper."

"I was?"

"We've got the article here somewhere. Want to see it?"

He shook his head. "That's all right."

"It was a nice write-up," she said.

"All right, if you can find it easily, but otherwise don't bother. It's not a big deal."

A little later, as she served him his breakfast, Lauren slid the folded-up sports section next to his plate and left him to his meal. Checking on him, she found him engrossed in the paper and his meal, and she couldn't help smiling. With his head bent and his fork hovering midair, he looked so focused and earnest. The all-American boy reading the sports pages.

Still smiling, she moved on, aware that she might have developed a small, teeny tiny crush on handsome Boone Walker.

She knew when he was done and ready for the bill. Lauren placed the paper facedown in front of him. "Have a good day," she said.

"How can I not?" he answered. "It's beautiful out."

"It is," she agreed, glancing out the big plate-glass window at the bright, clear sky. "Feels like summer."

"I like that your summers here don't have all the humidity we get in the South."

"The Bay Area is pretty nice, climate-wise."

"I know. My wife's lucky. She was raised here."

His wife. He had a wife.

Lauren felt a strange pang of emotion—part disappointment, part regret. It was stupid, though, to feel anything. She didn't know him. He was just a customer. Had only been in a handful of times.

"She must be happy being back here, then," she said, struggling to find something to say.

"She will be. She's not here yet. Still with the kids in Tampa for another week or two."

"You have kids?"

"Two. Boy and girl. Eight and five."

She heard the pride in his voice and her heart contracted again. "It'll be nice when you're all together again," she said, adjusting the pots of jam and jelly. She'd begun making them on the weekends. Since she didn't seem to have anything else to do with her free time. Her own fault, but still. "Must be hard living apart."

He shrugged. "Don't like it, but we've been doing it so long, almost don't know any other way."

"Your wife doesn't mind being apart?"

"Oh no, she hates it, but it's part of the game. Fortunately, she'll be here in a couple of weeks. Once my kids are out of school. Bad thing is, she arrives just as we leave, but on the plus side, we'll be together for Father's Day. Haven't been with them for Father's Day in years."

Thirteen

It'd been two weeks since Sarah had seen Boone and she was beginning to go a little crazy.

They were talking on the phone a couple of times every day and Skyping once a day, but trying to keep the house clean and ready to show at a moment's notice wasn't fun. It didn't help that Brennan had been getting in trouble at school. Sarah was just grateful that the term was almost over.

Last night had been what turned out to be Brennan's team's final Little League game of the season. The team had hoped to make the playoffs, but they'd lost. Some of the kids—and one of the moms—blamed Brennan for the loss, saying that he had distracted the team with all his acting up.

Sarah knew that her son *had* been rowdy. He'd found it hard to sit still in the dugout, and he deserved to be benched for a while. But not for the entire game.

She had been upset, sitting in the stands with the parents, watching Brennan, isolated from his team at the far end in the dugout. He'd sulked at one point, and then gotten angry, kicking his foot against the chain-link fence. At first the coaches had ignored him, but eventually one walked over, told him to knock it off and be quiet.

Brennan complied.

But he also put his head down and cried.

It hurt to watch. Sarah understood some of his feelings. She'd been an active little girl and needed exercise. Her parents had put her in sports when she was four just to help channel some of her endless energy. She'd been a natural athlete—coordinated and competitive—but she'd also been disciplined. That's where Brennan struggled.

But that didn't mean he didn't have a good heart.

Unfortunately, no one else seemed to know that.

Last night she didn't have a chance to talk to Boone about their son's final game, as Boone was in Minneapolis, playing in the second game of a three-day series against the Twins. He was already at the park by the time Brennan's game was over, and then Sarah, worn out from the long, emotional day, was asleep when Boone's game had ended.

But when he called that morning from his hotel room, she couldn't contain her frustration. "I understand benching him for an inning, but for most of the game, when they're trying to make the playoffs? It crushed him." She drew a deep breath, still feeling bruised from the night before. "And then when he cried, people made fun of him—"

"He shouldn't cry. He's too big for that now," Boone said.

"He's just eight."

"Almost nine, and he's got to learn. Self-control is really important, especially if he wants to continue playing sports."

"I don't know if he does. Last night when we got home, he said he was done."

"He's just upset right now. He'll calm down, forget this."

Sarah hesitated, trying to find the right words to keep Boone from getting defensive. "I think we have a problem. I think Brennan might have a problem. He really does struggle with control—"

"Kids do."

"—but none of the kids on the team seem to struggle as much as our son." She waited to see if Boone would say anything, and when he didn't, she continued. "I've been watching him at practices this week, watching him on the playground at school when I'm there for yard duty, and he's beginning to have a hard time fitting in. I don't know if kids . . . like him . . . as much as they used to."

"He has lots of friends."

"I—don't think he really does. I think his friends are starting to find him annoying. What I see is them yelling at Brennan or telling him to knock it off."

Boone remained silent.

Sarah chewed nervously on her lip. "You know the school has suggested that Brennan might be ADHD—"

"He's not hyperactive. I'm not putting him on Ritalin."

"There are different medicines. It's not always Ritalin."

"I'm not going to medicate my kid. He's a boy—"

"Who can't sit still, follow directions, control his impulses, or make friends!" she burst out before biting down, tears not far off. She hated parenting with Boone long distance, hated that he was gone so much that he didn't see what she saw. "I'm not a fan of medication either, but as his mom, as his mom who loves him, I'm telling you I'm concerned. I'm genuinely concerned we're not doing enough for him."

"I'm not going to put him on medication. I grew up with kids on Ritalin and it turned them into zombies. Won't do that to Brennan. He's a bright, active boy—a healthy, normal boy—and schools need to figure out how to teach normal, healthy boys instead of punishing them for not being girls."

Sarah rubbed the tight muscles at her neck. "Is that what I should tell the school the next time they call?"

"Brennan will be starting a new school in the fall—"

"And you don't think this problem will follow him?"

"No. He's going to have a fresh start, and I'll be there to make sure he settles down and pays attention."

She wanted to say that Boone had been there last fall, and the year before. She wanted to say that having Boone there, or not there, didn't change a thing. Brennan had a problem, but if Boone refused to see it, there wasn't much she could do at this point.

"It's going to be okay," Boone said.

Sarah sighed inwardly, wishing she could believe him.

"He's a boy," Boone added. "I know what I'm taking about."

"Okay," she said, grudgingly conceding, but not convinced.

Boone knew it, too. "One day soon I won't be playing ball, and I will be there every day, helping with practices, helping coach his team. And when I'm his coach, I'll know how to talk to him, keep him focused and motivated."

"That'll be good," she said. "Good for all of us."

"Yeah," he agreed, but it was a halfhearted answer on his part and Sarah knew why.

Boone didn't want his career to come to an end. She understood that. He'd miss baseball. But they—his family—needed more of him. They needed more of him as a father, a husband, as an active, responsible, engaged adult.

"So have you had breakfast?" Sarah asked, changing the subject. "When do you head to the ballpark?"

"Still have a couple of hours before we have to be at the park, so I'll maybe go check out the restaurant downstairs. There's also a coffee shop across the street."

"Where did you eat last night?"

"In the restaurant downstairs, but it was a zoo. I guess lots of fans know the A's always stay here. Girls everywhere."

Sarah swallowed hard. If Boone was telling her it was a zoo, with girls everywhere, then it must have been pretty crazy, as he had learned to keep the worst of it from her, knowing she worried, knowing she tended to get insecure.

She hated feeling insecure, though. Hated worrying about him, hated wondering, if he didn't call promptly every morning, if he was sleeping alone or with someone else.

The problem with insecurity is that once the first doubts crept in, they multiplied quickly.

Better not to let him know she was worried. Better to remain confident. Confidence was sexy. Confidence was appealing.

Insecure and clingy was not.

"You played well last night, though?" she asked, determined to keep the conversation moving forward.

"Went one for three. Shoulder's a little sore. Might try to get it iced before the game."

"That's a good idea."

"How are the kids?"

"Good. We're all good. Well, except for Brennan, who is still upset about last night's game."

"Want me talk to him?"

"Sure. That'd be good. Maybe you could call him when he's home from school."

"I'll probably be at the park by then. I will try to call tonight. If the game doesn't go too late."

"Sounds good."

"Sarah?"

"Yes?"

"You sound sad, babe."

And just like that, her eyes burned and her throat felt raw, her chest aching with emotion. She was sad. And overwhelmed. As well as lonely, stressed, scared, nervous, angry, exhausted. "I miss you," she whispered.

"I know."

"And I'm going to miss Tampa when we move."

"I thought you hated living in Florida."

"I don't hate Florida. I just hated being so far away from everyone."

"And now you're going to be moving home."

"Oakland isn't home—"

"You know what I mean. We'll be close, and we don't have to live on the East Bay. We can check out San Francisco. Find something in that neighborhood you like so much . . . what's it called? St. Francis Woods?"

"That'd be too far from the Coliseum. You don't want to do that much driving."

"It's what? Fifteen minutes across the bridge, no traffic? Thirty with?"

"Can be an hour."

"So? What else do I have to do?"

She smiled wistfully. "Be with me."

"And I will be. Soon. It's just another week or so."

"But then you'll be going on the road."

"Sarah."

She closed her eyes, hearing the weary note in his voice. He was starting to get exasperated. She didn't want to annoy him, not now, not with so much distance between them.

Scrambling to think of something positive to share, Sarah seized on a new subject. "We might have an interested buyer. Someone came back today for the second time. Apparently he wants to bring his wife to the house this weekend."

"That's great."

"I think so." She forced a smile into her voice. "Before you know it, the kids and I will be in California, and everything will be fine."

"That's right."

She exhaled slowly, telling herself to keep it together, remembering that once upon a time she'd been a fierce competitor, and tough. She'd poured herself into her sports, balancing athletics and academics, along with all the community service her private high school demanded. And while she'd dated in high school, and had attended every dance, she'd never wanted to have a serious boyfriend. She'd been too independent then, too focused on her goals. There was a reason she'd been offered full-ride scholarships to four different Division I schools, before she had chosen to go to UCLA and play volleyball for the school. She was smart. She was gifted. And she worked hard. "You love me?" she murmured.

"Honey, you know I do. With all my heart."

It was the Saturday of the Memorial Day weekend, and once the morning rush at the café ended, Lauren hopped into her car to head up to Napa for the night.

It'd been a relatively quiet few days at the café. The A's were on the road, and she wouldn't admit it to anyone, but she was lonely. She was missing Boone.

She wasn't ready to miss him. She barely knew him. But she definitely felt butterflies when he was around.

To take her mind off him, she decided to go see her new niece. She couldn't wait to hold the baby again, and it'd be good to hang out with Lisa and catch up. It'd been a long time since they just talked.

Lisa had said she could make a light lunch, but Lauren had told her she'd already made something at the café and was bringing the chicken, beet, and citrus salad with her.

They ate lunch outside on the stone terrace flanking the family room with the view of the adjacent vineyard; Audrey, in her pink fleecy onesie, was sleeping in a bassinette next to the wrought-iron table.

Now and then Lisa would put a hand into the bassinette and lightly touch the baby, checking on her.

Lauren smiled as she watched her sister with her daughter. Lisa was really enjoying being a mother. She and Matthieu had tried for years to get pregnant before turning to fertility specialists. Her doctor prescribed a medicine to help stimulate egg production and recommended that Lisa take up yoga, meditation, and add twice-weekly acupuncture to her schedule. She did all of the above and had been thrilled to finally be pregnant.

Lauren looked away from her sister and the baby to the view of the hills and grapes. Matthieu seemed to be getting a lot more serious about his wine now. He'd said it would just be a hobby when he'd bought the neighbor's property and taken over their small vineyard, but apparently he was eyeing another property to the east, claiming it'd be a good investment.

"Matthieu likes to acquire things," Lauren said now, thinking of the 1899 bank he owned in downtown Napa that housed their restaurant and the old newspaper building he was currently renovating.

Lisa shrugged. "If he has the money, why can't he?"

True, Lauren thought, silenced.

And maybe Mom was right. Maybe she was a little bit jealous of Lisa and Matthieu. Maybe she was just a little bit jealous that Lisa had so much and she herself had so little . . .

But it was a horrible thing to think, and selfish. Lisa deserved every happiness. Lisa wasn't just her big sister, she was also her best friend. Growing up, they'd been inseparable, and then as twentysomethings, they lived together in Grandma's house, worked together at their bakery café, and stayed up late talking after work was done and Blake was in bed.

Lauren had never needed many friends. She had her parents. She had her sister. She had her son.

Then Lisa met Matthieu, and before Lauren knew it was even serious, he proposed. He and Lisa went house hunting. Got married. Traded up their house for a slightly bigger one in a much better neighborhood. They traded up one more time a few years back, landing them here, which gave them the space to remodel the existing house into a seven-thousand-square-foot mansion with copper turrets just like a real French château.

It was hard keeping up with the Roussels.

Audrey woke up and made a little bleating sound. Quickly, the bleating became a hard cry.

Lisa picked the baby up, inspected her unhappy face. "Hungry, aren't you, sweetheart? You slept a long, long time," she crooned, lifting a lapel on her blouse so Audrey could nurse.

Audrey had no problem latching up and soon settled down. Lisa patted the baby's back, content to just sit on the terrace and soak up the dappled sunlight. "It's so nice to have you here," she said, smiling across the table at Lauren. "I was so glad to hear you were coming up to see us. I really have missed you."

"I've missed you, too." And Lauren had. She was only now beginning to understand how alone and lonely she'd been this past year. But moving to Alameda had been a good decision. The change of scenery, the work, the long hours . . . it'd kept her busy and had forced her to function, even as she struggled to come to terms with what had happened.

Lauren knew she still had a long way to go in terms of dealing with Blake and his death, but she wasn't quite as raw as she'd been last Thanksgiving. Yes, the pain was there, a constant throbbing, but it didn't consume her morning, noon, and night. It really only hurt bad at night. As that was when she was alone, in the dark, with nothing but her thoughts.

"Have any idea when you're going to come back?" Lisa asked, tone casual, but Lauren knew from her sister's expression that there was nothing casual behind the question.

Lauren started to answer, then stopped. Should she tell Lisa now that she wasn't sure she was coming back? Should she wait until she'd bought Mama's Café from Mimi? Until she was sure Mimi would sell to her?

"Mom said you might not return anytime soon," Lisa added after a moment. "She said you might be done. Is that true?"

Lauren made a face. "That was nice of Mom."

"She knows I'm torn about returning to work. I'm supposed to go back soon, but I don't want to leave Audrey."

"Then don't." Lauren was firm. "If you don't have to work, and you can afford to stay home with her, and you want to stay home, stay."

"And the restaurant?"

"It's just a restaurant. Sell it."

"We are making money."

"That's got to be appealing to a buyer."

Lisa glanced down at Audrey. "We've had offers."

"Recently?"

"Last month."

"Was it a bad offer?"

"No. It was a very generous offer."

"So why didn't you accept it?"

"I couldn't." Lisa looked at Lauren, expression stricken. "Because if we sell the restaurant, you have nothing to come home to."

"Oh, Lisa," Lauren whispered. For a moment she couldn't speak. "I don't come home because of the restaurant, I come home because of you! And now there's Audrey. And Mom and Dad, who are over the moon being grandparents again."

Lisa wrinkled her nose. "You didn't mention Matthieu. Do you still dislike him that much?"

"Lisa, I love your Matthieu. I think he's awesome. Gorgeous and sweet and sexy and awesome—"

"Okay, well, maybe that's enough."

Lauren grinned and dragged a handful of glossy brown hair back from her face, relishing the smell of fertile, sunbaked soil and Lisa's white roses and lavender that bordered the garden.

Suddenly the conversation she'd had with their mother two weeks ago came back to her and she turned to Lisa. "Speaking of men. Did you tell Mom I'm gay?"

"No!" Lisa spluttered, then snorted. Audrey lifted her tiny head and looked up at her mother, eyes barely able to focus, and Lisa, still giggling, touched the baby's cheek, encouraging her to latch back on. "Did Mom say I did?"

"Not exactly. But she and Dad seem to think I am."

"That's hilarious."

"It's not hilarious. And I'm not gay. I'm just not interested in dating anyone."

"No one?"

"No."

"There is absolutely not one man that's caught your eye since you've moved to Alameda?" Lisa demanded.

"Well . . . okay, there is this one guy."

"And?"

"And nothing. Because he's married."

"Oh, Lauren. *No.*"

Lauren grimaced. Married women obviously didn't want to hear that single women had crushes on married men. "I wouldn't go out with him. I just meant that he's a dude, and he's appealing, so there's hope . . . you know?"

But Lisa wasn't buying it. "For you to mention a man . . . that's significant."

"You asked!"

"So how do you know him? Does he live in your apartment building? What does he do? Does he know you're interested?"

"Oh my God, Lisa. I'm not interested. And even if he were single, I wouldn't go out with him."

"Why not?"

"He's too . . . good-looking."

"I didn't know there was such a thing."

"Well, there is. And I don't want to get involved with someone who is that handsome. That's just asking for trouble."

"Is he really that attractive?"

Lauren nodded. "And he's tall. Built. Serious muscles. The girls at work call him Spartacus."

"The girls? I thought all your waitresses were senior citizens."

Lauren laughed. "Most of them are, but we do have a few younger ones, and young and old have nicknamed him Spartacus due to him being gorgeous and looking like a gladiator."

Lisa fanned herself. "Keep going."

Lauren rolled her eyes. "See? That's why I wouldn't date him even if he were single. But since he's not, I can be his friend and enjoy his company. And I do. I feel good around him. Safe."

"Aha!" Lisa cried, and again Audrey looked up, confused.

Unable to resist, Lauren leaned forward and gently stroked the back of the baby's head. Her head was warm, her dark hair silky. Lauren's heart turned over. So amazing, the miracle of life.

"You don't have to act flirtatious around him to get into trouble," Lisa said after a moment. "Just caring for him is dangerous."

"How?"

"Don't be stupid."

"Don't be rude!" Lauren retorted.

"You're too pretty," Lisa said bluntly.

"I'm not."

"You are. But you avoid the mirror, so you don't know how you look, but you're beautiful, inside and out, and I'm telling you this straight up so you will realize that not many women— make that not *any* woman—is going to want you hanging around her man."

Lauren's insides churned. She fussed with a button on her thin knit sweater. She didn't want to hurt any woman. She certainly didn't want to hurt a marriage.

"So what do I do? Tell him he can't come to the café anymore?"

"Yes. Or you put him in someone else's section and you keep him at arm's length. Limit chitchat. Don't smile too much. Don't be too warm. Don't act happy to see him." Lisa's gaze rested on Lauren's face and she registered the flicker of emotion that crossed Lauren's features. "Have you really fallen that hard for him, Lu-Lu?" she said, reverting to the name she'd given Lauren when she was just a baby.

Lauren tugged on the small button. "Haven't fallen. Possibly falling."

"Then stop falling right now." Lisa's voice was stern, and it put a lump in Lauren's throat.

Lisa put the baby on her shoulder and began patting her back. "There's a pattern here. You see it, right? And you nailed it when you said you went for safe. You really do."

Lauren bit down.

"You go for guys who can't hurt you," Lisa continued. "Guys already committed elsewhere. Damien—gay. Which made him safe. This guy at your work, married, which makes him safe. So why like a hot guy who is single when you can fall for a married man who can't pursue you, or reject you, because he's already got a woman?"

"That's silly. I don't think that way—"

"Oh, you do, absolutely you do, and have since John smashed your heart when you were seventeen. But honestly, Lauren, he wasn't worth it. He wasn't. The asshole took your virginity in a friggin' shed!"

Lauren's eyes bugged open. "You read my diary!"

"Of course I read your diary. I've read every word you ever wrote."

Lauren spluttered indignantly. "That's wrong."

"Okay, it was. Sorry about that. But the point is, he was an asshole when he first had sex with you, and an asshole when he and his richy-rich folks insisted you terminate the pregnancy, and an asshole when he never acknowledged Blake's birth, or death, so we know what we're dealing with. An asshole.

"And we know this, definitively," Lisa continued, nowhere close to being done talking. "He's on his second marriage—his first wife has nothing nice to say about him. I read the interview with her in *Redbook* magazine a couple of months back—and you are lucky, Lauren Summer, *lucky* to be free of him. John wouldn't have added a damn thing to your life. In fact, from what his ex-wife said in the interview, he would have just sucked you dry, the way he sucked her soul and spirit from her. So move on. Not all men are like John. There are really nice ones out there. I know. I married one. Matthieu is wonderful—" She broke off as Audrey burped. Lisa smiled, pleased, before concluding, ". . . but not perfect. We have our fights. Our problems. But I like him. A lot."

"That's good. Because you married him."

"I did. And I want you to have what I have, but you can't, you won't, not if you don't put yourself out there. You're going to have to take some risks. Open yourself up to hurt, and rejection. Give up the need for safe."

"Don't think I can."

"Yes, you can. You're strong, Lauren, so much stronger than you think."

Lauren heard what her sister was saying but she couldn't go there, not yet, and so she shook her head.

Maybe one day she could date.

Maybe one day she could feel pretty and sexy.

But it wasn't now. Wasn't yet.

"Don't shake your head. Don't do that. You're thirty-five, Lauren. Don't you want to have more? A husband . . . a family—"

"I had a family."

Lisa's eyes clouded. "No one can ever replace Blake. No one will ever replace him. Not in your heart. Or mine. Or Mom and Dad's. We all loved him. He was everyone's boy." Her voice cracked and she drew a slow, deep breath. "But that boy wasn't a sponge. He didn't just take love. He gave it back. One hundred percent. And Lord, Lauren, he loved you. You say he was the sun, but you were his sun and moon and he wasn't even going to go away to go to college because he couldn't bear leaving you alone."

Lauren bowed her head, unable to breathe, unable to think, unable to see.

It hurt. Badly. And she wanted her boy. She wanted him back. She'd give anything to have him back, and yet she knew that was impossible. But it didn't stop her from dreaming. Didn't stop her from needing, craving, aching.

They said a mother's love was endless, bottomless, and it was true. Even with Blake gone, the love went on and on. Just as it always would. The love made him real, and it was all she had left of him.

This deep ache.

This pain.

This burn.

"I just wish I could talk to him, see him," Lauren whispered, arms bundled tightly over her chest. "Make sure he's okay."

"He's okay," Lisa answered huskily.

Lauren lifted her head. Audrey had also stopped nursing and was listening intently.

"How do you know?" Lauren asked.

"He's on the other side. With Grandma and Grandpa, and you know they're taking care of him. You know how they loved him when he was a baby, always fighting Mom and Dad for a chance to take care of him."

Lauren swallowed hard and smiled through her tears. "Everybody loved him."

"Everybody. And he's still loved, and I bet all he wants is for you to be loved. It's what he always wanted for you. To have someone to take care of you after he was gone."

Lauren's lower lip trembled and she bit into it. "But I didn't need anyone else. I had Blake."

"Children don't stay with us forever. They grow up, they move out, they sometimes move far away. Come on, Lauren, baby, can't you see it . . . can't you understand that Blake was never meant to be your everything? Yes, you loved him, yes, you adored him, but he wasn't you. He was just part of you, and the rest of you now has to go on."

Fourteen

Monday morning came way too early.

Lauren turned off her alarm three times before finally throwing back the covers and dragging herself to the shower. Four A.M. was too early, she groused. Four was insane.

In the shower she washed her hair and rinsed it in cold water, needing the chilly temperature to wake her up and shake off her lethargic mood.

Four cakes today, she told herself, drying her hair. Four cakes, five pies, and if she found the time, bread pudding. She hadn't made bread pudding for Mama's yet, but it was a natural. A rich bread pudding laced with golden raisins and topped with a warm praline bourbon sauce.

But riding her bike to work, Lauren knew why she was making bread pudding. It was for Boone. The A's were supposed to be back in town today.

Lisa would be so disgusted.

Lauren put Lisa out of her mind.

Phyllis was already at the café when she arrived. "Five minutes late," the waitress chided, but she was smiling. She'd begun to come in a half hour early to help Lauren with the baking. Turned out she had a gift for piecrust and cream fillings. "First time this year. What did you do last night? Have a date?"

Lauren unlocked the restaurant and held the door open for Phyllis. "No. But I was in Napa for the weekend."

"How's that baby?" Phyllis asked, rolling up her sleeves in the kitchen and preparing to get to work.

"Gorgeous. Giving me massive baby cravings."

Phyllis shot her a swift glance. "You like kids?"

Lauren pictured seventeen-year-old Blake stretched out on the sofa watching TV, all lanky and long, his limbs hanging off the faded cushions, his hand buried in a cereal box. *Come watch this, Mom, it's funny.* Of course the segment was never funny, just gross. Boys.

Lauren took a quick breath. "I do."

Phyllis was already measuring out flour and salt and preparing to cut in the butter. "You want them someday?"

"If it works out," Lauren answered.

"Never married?"

Lauren flipped open her cookbook to her favorite cake recipes, recipes she'd tinkered with and doctored over the years until they were perfect, and perfectly her. "No."

Six hours later she was in middle of bussing a table when she knew he was there.

Boone was back. She could tell, without even turning around, feeling the sizzle of energy he brought with him, an energy that surrounded him, illuminating him, making him bigger, stronger, more physical. More real. More potent.

He took his usual spot, right in the middle of the counter, and spread the newspaper out on either side of him, discouraging folks from taking the seat next to him.

"You're back," she said, smiling as she greeted him, aware that her hands were suddenly damp and her heart was beating a little faster than it should. He wasn't the one for her . . . he wasn't.

"Flew in late last night."

"Phyllis said you were in Minneapolis."

He nodded. "Started there, and then we played the Royals."

"How did you guys do?"

He shrugged tiredly. "Good enough."

"You look like you need a break. When do you get a day off?"

"Just had a day off, but it was a travel day, so it wasn't all that relaxing."

"Why didn't you sleep in today, then?"

"I'm in a different time zone. But tomorrow it'll be better. The first day home is always the hardest."

She nodded, sympathetic. She didn't travel, but she struggled with insomnia and knew firsthand how hard it was to function when you were sleep-deprived. "Let me get you some coffee, then."

She took his order, left him to his paper, but kept an eye on his coffee as she took care of her other customers.

The door opened at one point, flooding the café with sunshine. Lauren paused and glanced out the open door at the cloudless blue sky. Beautiful day. But then, Napa had been beautiful all weekend—those golds and greens of the wine country were so inviting.

When Boone's order came up, she brought him his meal, plus a small dish of her bread pudding with the bourbon sauce. "I want your opinion about the bread pudding," she said. "That is, if you like bread pudding."

"I love bread pudding. It's one of my mom's specialties."

"Well, I can't wait to hear what you think."

He tried it right there and then, taking a big bite with his spoon. He chewed thoughtfully, swallowed, took another bite. "It's good," he said with a nod. "Really good."

She leaned in, hearing an unspoken *but* in there somewhere. "So what's wrong with it?"

He shook his head. "Nothing."

"No, there's something. I hear it in your voice."

"There *is* something, but it's just my opinion. I don't think you need the bourbon sauce. And I like bourbon sauce, and this is a good bourbon sauce, but the bread pudding is flavorful on its own, and I think in this case, the sauce overwhelms everything else."

"I'll keep that in mind."

"So are you going to add the bread pudding to the menu?"

"Only if you think I should."

"I think you must."

She smiled, refilled his coffee, and moved on to take care of her tables, but she hummed as she worked, happy.

He really liked her bread pudding. Her day was a success.

It wasn't until he looked ready to go that she returned to the counter and presented him his check.

"Do you ever get back to New Orleans?" she asked, glancing around to make sure no one needed her. But things had slowed down. Tables were emptying out and there were no customers waiting to be seated.

"Haven't in a while, but I'll be moving back when I retire."

"You have family there?"

"My mom."

"She must be happy that you'll be going back."

"She is."

"Does she ever come watch you play?"

"She's not a big fan of baseball. Mom hoped I'd go to med school. Wanted me to be a doctor like my dad. But I wasn't interested in medical school. Have never wanted to do anything but play ball."

"So what will you do when you retire?"

"I don't know. Haven't thought that far."

"What do most players do when they retire?"

"Depends on the player's age, and experience. Some guys have to get a job right away, others enjoy retirement. I know a lot of guys who sell cars, or start a business. Some of the smarter ones are able to live off their investments."

"Can't imagine being able to retire in your thirties, or even forties," she said. "My dad's seventy this year and he still works every day."

"What's he do?"

"He's a rancher in Napa."

"Is that where you're from?"

She nodded. "Born and raised. Used to have a restaurant in downtown Napa with my sister, but then I came here in September to manage the café."

"Why did you leave Napa?"

"Thought it was time for a change."

"Change is good," he agreed.

"Change is great." She headed to the register to get him change but Boone didn't wait for her to return, meeting her at the register instead.

"I don't know what your schedule is," he said, taking the cash she gave him, having already left her tip on the counter. "But if you're out of here early enough, why don't you come to the game tonight? I can put you and a friend on the pass list."

Lauren looked to the window and the bright swath of sunlit sky. She never went anywhere after work. Just the café and her apartment, back and forth, back and forth. "Does sound fun," she said.

"Then come. What's your last name? I'll have it on the list. Just check in at will-call, they'll give you tickets."

"I don't know who I'd take."

"You don't have a boyfriend?"

Lauren flushed, suddenly self-conscious. "No."

"How about bring Phyllis, or Bette, or that new girl . . . what's her name?"

"Karen. And maybe one of them will come, or maybe I can find a friend. Do I need to give you a name now?"

"No. The tickets will be in your name. Just show up, and if you get to the park early enough, come down to the field and say hi."

She wrinkled her nose. "That wouldn't be awkward?"

"Awkward how?"

"You don't think people will talk?"

He frowned. "Why?" His frown deepened and then his expression changed as he understood what she was saying. "I'm not hitting on you, Lauren. I'm just offering you tickets to a game."

"I . . . didn't mean it . . . that way," she stammered. *Or had she?*

From behind the grill, Bob called to her. "Order up, boss."

"Better go grab that," she murmured, uncomfortable and confused, and desperate to escape,

But Boone put a hand out, stopping her. "Have I led you on somehow? Said something wrong—"

"Oh God, no!" Lauren shoved her hand behind her back, mortified, and terrifyingly close to tears. She never cried at work, and wasn't going to cry now. "*No.* I was just thinking about your wife, wanting to be respectful."

Boone's gaze searched hers. "I love my wife."

Her throat ached, and her chest squeezed tight. She didn't understand men. She'd never dated a lot. Had Blake in high school and then just a few dates here and there before meeting Damien four years ago. She'd liked Damien, a lot, and he had adored her, and Blake. She'd thought that maybe she'd found someone special, someone gentle and kind, someone who didn't push her physically because he cared about *her,* respected *her*—

And he did.

But that was because he liked her. Loved her as a person. But it was purely platonic. They were close, maybe fast becoming best friends, but it wasn't a romance. He was gay. But she knew that, right?

She hadn't. And Lauren had felt stupid, so very, very stupid, when he told her.

She felt just as stupid now.

"Let's just forget the game," she whispered, embarrassed. "Maybe another time."

But Boone shook his head. "No, I still want you to come tonight. It'd be good for you to get out. From what Phyllis says, you don't get out much—"

"I'm fine."

He gave her a sharp look. "And we both know that fine isn't fine."

Lauren suddenly smiled a lopsided smile. "I hate it when people use my words against me."

"You'll have fun tonight. I'll introduce you to some of the players, and you'll sit with the families and friends—"

"Uh, families?"

"And friends. There's some kind of giveaway, too. But remember, come down to the field during batting practice and warm-ups and say hello so I know you got in okay."

He tipped his head at her and then headed out, pushing open the café door to step into the dazzling California sun.

Lauren watched him go, heart thumping, feeling emotions she hadn't felt in years, feeling emotions she shouldn't feel for him.

He wasn't hers.

He would never be hers.

He wasn't a man she could fall for.

The new waitress, Karen, went with Lauren to the game. Lauren had been unsure about actually going, but Karen—a diehard A's fan—knew everything about the Coliseum, from what to wear (a jersey and shorts, or a jersey and jeans), to how to get there, to which parking lot was best.

Lauren didn't have a jersey and instead wore a white T-shirt to avoid clashing with the team's colors. Reaching the stadium, they parked and Karen hurried her to the will-call booth, then steered her to the right entrance and on down to the lower seats next to the field to get as close to the players during warm-ups as possible.

They were just like Blake and his friends, Lauren thought, watching players lob the ball back and forth as others took practice cuts, while still others did easy sprints in the outfield . . . only she and Karen were big kids.

Big kids, she thought, gradually becoming aware that she was just one of many crowding the fence. Kids clinging to the fence were cute. The women in tight T-shirts and skimpy dresses weren't. Lauren drew back, self-conscious, not wanting to be one of the overzealous females trying to draw attention to herself.

Karen didn't have any qualms about making a fool of herself. She whistled loudly when Boone headed into the cage for batting practice. He looked up, she lifted her hands, gave him the Shaka, and whistled again when he nodded acknowledgment.

"He saw me!" Karen crowed happily, climbing the stairs to join Lauren at the next level.

"I saw," Lauren said.

"This is so cool," Karen enthused. "Do you think he can get me some autographs?"

"I don't know."

"I'll go ask." She dashed back down the stairs, pushing up to the fence. Boone was still in the cage, swinging, but as he finished he stepped out, adjusted his batting glove, and looked up into the stands.

Karen shouted something down to him, he nodded, he asked something, and Karen pointed behind her, to where Lauren stood.

Boone looked up, spotted Lauren on the landing, and gestured for her to come down. She shook her head. He rolled his eyes, gestured again, and Lauren reluctantly headed down, watching the kids swarm Boone, baseballs and programs and Sharpies in hand.

Boone was signing autographs as Lauren reached the fence. "Is it always like this?"

"This is nothing," he said, handing a ball back to a little girl, then tapping her lightly on the brim of her hat. "You should see it in New York, or Philadelphia. Fans are rabid there. This is pretty tame." He looked up at Lauren. "Haven't you been to a professional baseball game before?"

Lauren shook her head. "No."

"No? Never?"

She shook her head again, stepping aside to let two teenage girls pass.

"But you know the game, right?" he asked, signing a program and then another quick scrawl on someone's miniature souvenir bat. "You've seen it played?"

"Yes."

Someone on the field shouted something to Boone and he glanced over, nodded, and signed one more autograph before stepping back. He lifted his hands, indicating he was done. "Got to go," he said, and then smiled good-naturedly at the resulting groans and boos.

"Good luck!" Lauren called to him.

He winked at her and jogged out onto the field, and as he jogged away, his uniform pants clinging to his powerful legs, Lauren's insides did a funny little flip.

God, he had a body. And a killer smile. And he was nice, so nice . . . and she was pathetic, so pathetic.

Pathetic, she repeated, following Karen up to their seats. Everything about her crush was juvenile and pathetic, but she couldn't help liking him. Couldn't help liking everything about him—his build, his face, his age, his maturity, his swing, his love for his wife.

He was an incredibly beautiful man, she thought, reaching her and Karen's row and stepping over feet as they headed for the seats, yet his love for his wife was probably the thing she found most appealing about him.

Which was also the thing that made him so completely off-limits.

But God knew, Lauren silently added, sitting down, she had to have a thing for unrequited love. First, John in high school, then Damien, her former neighbor and a best friend, and now Boone. Boone Walker.

Opening her program, she leafed through the pages until she came to his bio, reading it once, and then a second time, and then putting it away, feeling rather sick inside.

He's not free. He won't ever be free. Which meant she couldn't do this, couldn't fixate on him, couldn't allow herself to become any more attached. The last thing she needed was to have her heart broken again.

It was a full moon, and the weather perfect for a game. Lauren had to put on her coat by the third inning, but she was never cold. How could she be cold jumping up and down, cheering with the other twenty thousand fans? And she was jumping up and down a lot as the A's crushed the Rangers, 12–1, the A's big bats swinging.

Boone literally knocked the ball out of the park, and Lauren high-fived with Karen and others who felt like friends by the end of the night from cheering and high-fiving so much.

It was a truly fun night, and Lauren surprised herself by enjoying everything about the game at the Coliseum. She loved the outrageously expensive hot dogs and popcorn, and the even more expensive beer. She bought a souvenir pennant and a hideous green-and-gold pen. And while it did take forever to get out of the park, she was really glad she'd agreed to come.

It'd been a long time since she did something fun.

Too long.

And yet it was also strange that on her first night out she would go to a baseball game. Because just like Boone, this was what John did every night, except John was a pitcher, one of the Yankees' finest.

In bed, Lauren stared at the wall, the full moon bathing her room in bright white light, and for the first time in a long time she was able to visualize John.

She could see him in his Yankees uniform, sitting with the other players in the dugout. She could see him running onto the field to take the mound. Could see him wind up and throw the ball. And he'd be beautiful, too. And the girls would all love him. The fans would love him. Because John Meeks was a star.

D id you have fun last night?" Boone asked, taking his favorite seat at the counter.

"I did," Lauren said, bringing him his coffee. "You put on quite a show, with that second home run in the ninth. Had the fans going crazy."

"I got the right pitch at the right time."

Bette walked past, tapped the chair next to Boone with a menu. "You like playing the hero card, don't you?"

"Now, I don't know about that," he answered, but he was smiling. He was enjoying himself, enjoying the attention. "Everybody was hitting last night."

"That may be so," Phyllis said, jumping in on the conversation. "But your two home runs put a lot of those runs on the board."

Boone shook his head. "I just did what I'm paid to do. Hit the ball."

"And how you hit it. Clear out of the park." Bette sighed, dreamy, reliving the moment. "Now, that's baseball."

Boone grinned. "Good thing I didn't strike out in the ninth last night, would hate to think what my reception would have been like this morning."

Phyllis waved her hand at him. "Aw, sugar, don't you fret, you would have been fine. Some of us don't care if you play baseball. We just like looking at you 'cause you're handsome." She gave him a naughty smile and a come-hither glance before sashaying away.

"Everyone loves you," Lauren said, struggling not to giggle. "Young ones . . . old ones . . . but something tells me the old ones are the worst."

"The old ones certainly aren't shy about their feelings," he agreed. "But they're often pretty dang funny, and usually very sweet. It's the young ones you have to worry about. They throw themselves at you, and they don't want chitchat or an autograph. They're pretty hard-core."

After last night's game, Lauren could see what he meant, and she thought of Boone's wife, at home with the kids.

It couldn't be easy being married to a professional athlete. You'd have to be strong, and confident about your marriage. Good thing Boone was a devoted husband.

Later, when Boone reached for his wallet, Lauren refused. "Today's on me," she said. "My treat for taking care of us last night."

"Want to go again tonight?" he asked, sliding from his seat and rising. "It's going to be another beautiful night and another good game. I can put you girls on the list again."

"Karen has to work, and I've got to place orders and do payroll."

"You can come late. I'll make sure they put you in the family section. The wives and girlfriends are all really nice—"

"I appreciate that, but let's leave that section to the wives and girlfriends. They might tolerate outsiders, but I'm sure they don't really want strange women there."

He slid a folded ten-dollar bill beneath the edge of his plate. "Chris wants you there, though."

"Who?"

"Chris Steir." He saw her blank look. "Bats right before me. Center field. Number seven. Girls think he's pretty good-looking."

Lauren wrinkled her nose. "Yuck. No thank you."

Boone's deep laugh rumbled in his chest. "What do you mean, yuck? No thank you?"

"I'm not into that scene. It's not for me."

"What scene?"

"Baseball groupie . . . being one of those girls who chases players." She saw his expression and hurriedly added, "You're a friend, and I like you, but I'm sorry. I couldn't ever date a baseball player."

"Why don't you like baseball players?"

"I think they're arrogant and spoiled and self-centered—"

"How do you really feel, Lauren?"

She laughed and blushed. "You did ask."

"I did, and yes, there are players who can be total dicks, but there are nice men in this world, and nice baseball players."

"Perhaps."

"So . . . you might come tonight?"

"No."

"Chris is going to be crushed."

"Yeah, I bet."

"He wants to meet you."

She rolled her eyes. "Sure he does."

"I'm serious." Boone reached into his pocket and fished out a folded piece of paper. "He wanted me to give this to you."

Lauren took the slip of paper and opened it. *Call me,* it said. And underneath the scrawl was a phone number and the name Chris.

Lauren looked up at Boone, eyebrows arching higher, incredulous. "This is a joke."

"No."

"He wants *me* to call *him*?"

"He likes you."

"He doesn't even *know* me." She wrinkled her nose. "And where's my name, hmm?" She waved the slip of paper. "This could be for anyone. He could have a hundred of these all photocopied and ready to go. One for you, little lady, and one for you!"

Boone laughed. "Chris isn't like that."

"How do you know? You've only been with the team what . . . two weeks? Three?"

"Three."

"Well, I've never met him, but I can tell you, he's not for me." Lauren crumpled the paper and dropped it in Boone's water glass.

Boone grinned. "Should I let him know that you weren't impressed?"

"Tell him—politely—no thank you."

"He really is a good guy—"

"No. Not even remotely interested. But I do hope you'll have a great game."

Sarah woke up to the sound of rain. She'd gone to bed to the same sound. It'd been raining off and on for three days now, but when it rained, it really came down, a hard, warm downpour that heralded the start of the hurricane season.

She put on a robe over her pajama shorts and tank top and headed downstairs to make coffee.

She'd gone to bed blue and woke up frustrated. Still no word from Boone.

What was he doing in California? Why did she hear from him so infrequently these days? It seemed like the only time he had time to talk was when he was on the road, which didn't make sense. He should have just as much time in Oakland.

Last night he'd had an amazing game, too. She knew because every one of her Bay Area friends from high school had texted her.

He's amazing!

What a game.

You must be so proud of Boone!!!

Sarah had to get on ESPN.com to see what all the fuss was about. And her friends had been right. Boone had been a rock star the night before, belting out two big home runs in the game at the Coliseum, putting five runs on the board, helping crush the Rangers.

This morning they were still talking about him on *SportsCenter*. Sarah listened as she made breakfast for the kids.

If he keeps this up, he could easily play another couple of years.

Walker certainly is hitting the ball well right now. I think going to Oakland was exactly what he needed.

Sarah woke the kids up and fed them, keeping an eye on the storm outside. The wind was shredding the palm trees in the yard. She was glad this was the last week of school, glad they were flying out Friday afternoon, but seriously irritated with the storm for killing all the momentum on selling the house. No one wanted to look at houses when they had to wade through rivers of water to reach them.

A half hour later, after dropping the kids off at school and watching as they sloshed across soggy grass for the building, Sarah headed home to clean on the off chance someone would call and want to come by today. Windexing done, vacuuming done, dusting done, she stared across the gigantic living room with the high ceiling and big dark beams. A beautiful Spanish/Tuscan–inspired house. *So come on buyers, buy.*

But standing there in her big, lovely house—a house Boone paid for, just as Boone paid for everything else—Sarah felt empty.

She had everything she ever wanted and it meant nothing. Because she didn't have Boone. Not with her.

And she wanted a husband who would be with her. Sleeping with her. Eating with her. Going on walks and to the store and to a movie and whatever else they wanted to do.

Her phone finally rang. *Boone. Thank God.*

"Morning, hon," he said, his voice scratchy with sleep.

"Just waking up?" she asked, dropping onto the couch and curling her legs under her.

"Yeah. Still in bed." He yawned. "How is it there? What are you doing?"

"Raining like crazy. Super stormy weather. And I'm just cleaning house. Again."

He said nothing, and that made something inside her twist, churn. "I hate selling houses," she said, anger rushing through her. "But I do it every time we move, 'cause that's my job."

"You do it well. We've never lost money on a house, thanks to you."

She should own the compliment, she should, but she couldn't, not when the anger was bubbling and festering inside of her. She needed to get it out. Needed to feel calm again. Good again. "You have no idea what it's like, cleaning and cleaning, hoping someone will come by. And then when you get an appointment, you clean even more and leave everything just so—pillows plump, candles lit, fresh flowers on the counter. You want it to look like a dream house, a model house, and so you throw the kids in the car and do one more quick Windex on the windows and doors . . . and you drive around and around, hoping for good news, hoping they'll love it, and then you find out the buyers were only there a few minutes. They walked in, walked out, really had no interest in seeing the house but were there, just killing time—" Sarah broke off, a lump filling her throat from spilling all her bitterness.

She sounded like a bitch.

That was probably because she felt like one, too.

"You'll be here end of the week," Boone said quietly, no emotion in his voice. "Even if the house doesn't sell—"

"But I want it to sell. I haven't spent weeks cleaning and showing the house not to have it sell. I don't do anything anymore but keep the house pristine."

"A couple of months from now this will be just a memory. Try not to let it stress you out so much."

Sarah closed her eyes, pressed a hand to her forehead. "I miss you."

"I miss you, too."

But he didn't sound as if he missed her. He sounded frustrated and irritated that he was even having to listen to her. "I'm sorry I'm upset," she whispered, pressing two fingers against her temple, feeling dangerously close to crying. God, she was a mess. An absolute wreck.

"It's fine."

"At least we'll see you soon. Just three days now."

Boone hesitated. "Not three days, babe."

"Yes. We fly out Friday—"

"Sarah, we're not home Friday. The team's on the road."

"What?"

"We talked about this. Remember?"

"No, we didn't. We never talked about this. I would know if we did—"

"Babe, I told you. I said I felt terrible that we were going to be leaving the day you guys fly in."

"No, Boone. No. You never mentioned it. Not once—"

"I'm sorry, then. But I figured you had to know. You have the schedule. I'm sure you knew—"

"I didn't."

"—we will have just left that morning for Phoenix."

Sarah didn't speak for the longest time, tears clouding her vision, a lump clogging her throat. "How long are you going to be gone?"

"We'll be back late on the fourteenth."

Sarah closed her eyes, pressed her forehead to her bent knee. Ten more days. Ten more days before she'd see her guy.

"The kids miss you," she said.

"And I miss my family."

Bullshit, she thought, squeezing her eyes shut. He didn't miss them. He probably didn't miss them at all because he probably had a whole other family when he was on the road like this. A wife and kids. A girlfriend. He might even travel with his girlfriend for all Sarah knew.

"*Sarah.*"

She shook her head, back and forth, back and forth, grinding her forehead against her knee. "I'm just . . . lonely," she whispered when she trusted herself to speak.

"It's only ten days, hon."

Only ten. Piece of cake. "I'm . . . not . . . doing well, Boone," she said huskily, struggling to keep her voice from breaking.

"This is a tough time, but you're doing fine. You're strong."

He didn't know. Because she didn't tell him. She didn't like telling him the truth, because she didn't like thinking about it in the first place.

Her fears. Her worries. Her pain.

No, better to be positive. Better to focus on the good, and the healthy, and the happy. It was her job to keep them together, as a couple, and as a family. If she lost confidence in him—in them—they'd never make it. Never. "I just wish . . . I just wish . . . I could see you."

He didn't answer.

She continued: "I want to see you when we get there. I want you to pick us up from the airport. I want you to be . . ." *there,* she silently added.

For me.

"Time will pass quickly," he added firmly, adopting the authoritative tone he'd take with whining kids. "And you've got a lot to do when you get to California. You've got to find us a place, and get us settled, and then all the bad stuff will be over, behind us."

She said nothing, resenting that she had to find a place, and she had to get them settled, and then, and only then, would the bad stuff be over.

Personally, she'd rather go out and play ball. And sign autographs. And head out to have drinks in some hot nightclub with the guys.

"Right," she said grimly.

"There's light at the end of the tunnel. I'll be home with you for Father's Day. I'll be off the next day. We'll be able to hang out and relax—see your family, and your dad."

Great. She couldn't wait for that off day. "And when is that?" she asked, checking her sarcasm.

"The eighteenth, I think."

The eighteenth. Sarah balled her hands into fists. Just two weeks from now. No problem. She'd wait.

But then, she really didn't have a choice, did she?

Fifteen

Wednesday, June 6, was another spectacular morning in Alameda, and business was good at the café, so good that customers were on a twenty-minute wait list for a table.

Lauren liked a busy morning. It was how it was supposed to be. Only problem was, she, and the other waitstaff, were all moving so fast it was hard to say more than two words to their regulars.

Boone hadn't been in yet, though, and it was getting late enough that Lauren didn't think he'd show. Which wouldn't be a bad thing either.

She lined up her order beneath the warmer, making sure everything was there even as she tried to convince herself that she didn't need to see Boone.

He didn't matter.

He couldn't.

"First Spartacus, and now Thor," Bette said, whistling under her breath as she joined Lauren in front of the grill. "Things are getting exciting at Mama's Café."

"What?" Lauren asked, adjusting the fruit garnish on one plate before letting Bob know she needed another short stack of blueberry pancakes.

"Coming," he answered.

"Thor's here," Bette repeated, still waiting on an order herself.

Lauren frowned, her brows tugging together. "Who? Where?"

Bette nodded at the counter. "There, at the counter. Thor. See him? He asked to be seated in your section. And if that ain't Thor, I don't know who he is."

"Thor," Lauren repeated dumbly, glancing over her shoulder, her gaze sweeping the expanse of dark gold counter.

Then her eyes widened. She'd spotted him.

Immense shoulders. Huge biceps. Thick blond hair caught in a ponytail, a strong tan jaw, high cheekbones beneath blue eyes.

She immediately understood the reference.

She also had a sneaking suspicion she knew who he was. She hoped she was wrong.

"Humph," she said.

"Humph," Bette echoed, mocking her. "Don't act like your eyes didn't bug out just now. 'Cause they sure did."

Ignoring the waitress, Lauren stacked the warm plates on her arm, delivered the order to her table, returned for additional butter and syrup, delivered that, then headed to the counter, where someone had already taken care of getting her big, brawny, blond customer a menu, coffee, and water.

"Good morning," she said, pulling out her notepad. "What can I get for you?"

"What do you recommend?"

She glanced up and her gaze collided with his. He had piercing blue eyes. Blue, blue eyes. She looked swiftly away. "Everything's good. Just depends on what you're in the mood for."

"I'm hungry. Want serious food."

He had a very deep voice, which matched his deep chest, and his arms. And suddenly she flashed to Monday night's game, remembering that he batted before Boone. She recalled how he'd hit a double just before Boone's first home run, which had put all the fans on their feet. She'd been one of them. "I'd recommend our steak and eggs, then," she said, fixing her gaze on his strong chin. "I'm also partial to our corned beef hash. It's homemade and you can get two or three eggs with that, prepared any way you'd like them, and a side of toast, biscuits, or a short stack of pancakes."

"It all sounds good."

"It is."

"So order for me."

Startled, she opened her eyes wide. She looked up into his eyes. "What?"

"Surprise me. Bring me something you think I'll like."

Heat rushed through her, warming her, making her face feel hot. "But I don't know you, and wouldn't presume to know what you'd like."

"But you know good food."

"Everybody has different tastes."

"Boone said I can't go wrong here—well, except for something called grillades—but other than that, he said it's all really good." His blue gaze held hers. "Why didn't you call me?"

"I don't know you," she reiterated, chin lifting a notch, hoping she sounded calm and controlled, because on the inside her heart was thumping like mad.

"I'm Chris." He smiled at her, eyes crinkling, his eyes cornflower blue.

"Chris Steir, number seven, center field," she answered, thinking he was definitely handsome, if you liked rugged, blond men who resembled superheroes. Which she didn't, she mentally added. She'd always had a soft spot for brunettes. Brunettes with blue eyes. "Let me get your order in."

She wrote his order up, standing in front of the grill, scribbling down the steak and eggs with country-style potatoes and a side of buttermilk pancakes. She had no idea if he would like any of it, but it didn't matter. He'd told her to order what she thought was good, and she preferred simple home-style food that tasted good. So this was what he was getting.

With his order in, she refilled his coffee, careful to avoid eye contact, and it wasn't until she served him his breakfast that she spoke to him again. "What else can I get you?" she asked, hands on her hips, tone brisk. "Ketchup, hot sauce, steak sauce?"

"Your phone number?"

Her head jerked up, her eyes met his. He was smiling at her, but she didn't smile back. "I don't know why you want my number."

"I want to take you out."

"Why?"

"Because."

"Because?" One of her eyebrows lifted. "That's your answer?"

His smile was crooked and his eyes laughed at her. "Yes."

"That's terrible."

"Doesn't work for you?" he asked, reaching for his knife and fork and cutting into the steak. It was dark pink and juicy, and he looked up at her and nodded approvingly. "Just how I like it."

"Medium?"

"No, feisty." He winked at her. "And I will take some hot sauce, if you have Tapatio."

She didn't budge, just stood there, staring at him, telling herself she despised men like him. Arrogant. Overly confident.

He arched an eyebrow. "Or Tabasco. That works, too."

"Do women fall for this? Mr. I'm-So-Sexy-You-Can't-Refuse-Me?" she demanded tartly, reaching under the counter for bottles of A.1., Tabasco, and ketchup, and practically slamming them down at his elbow.

His blue gaze warmed as it rested on her flushed face. "Does it bother you that I find you beautiful?"

"Yeah. It does."

He laughed, a big, deep laugh, and his white teeth flashed. "Why?" he asked, popping a generous bite of steak into his mouth.

"Because you don't know me."

He chewed, swallowed, his eyes never leaving hers. "But I know what I see. I like what I see."

Just like John Meeks, she thought, drawing a quick, uncomfortable breath. "And I think that's shallow."

He cut another slice off the steak, shrugging, broad shoulders shifting. "Guess I'm shallow." He stabbed the juicy steak, lifted the bite, but then hesitated, his expression turning thoughtful. "Is that *bad*?"

She opened her mouth to say something sharp and reproving, wanting to put him in his place, but then surprised herself by laughing. "*Yes.*" She choked on more smothered laughter. At least she could give him points for being funny. "Most definitely."

Chris grimaced as he chewed, and yet his eyes danced, the brilliant blue depths bright, alive.

So alive.

A shiver raced through her. She felt the tingle from her nape to her breasts and then deep inside. Goose bumps covered her skin. And yet she didn't like it, didn't want to like him, didn't want to feel anything for a person who reminded her of the high school boyfriend who'd fathered her child and then hadn't even bothered to send a sympathy note when his son died.

Chris swallowed, took a sip of his water, blotted his firm mouth with his napkin. "Now I know this is probably going to sound shallow, too, and I'm sorry about that 'cause apparently shallow isn't good, but you're seriously sexy, and I really want to take you out."

Before she could answer, he added, "By the way, can I get a milk?"

Lauren spluttered and, shaking her head, went to get him his milk. She carried it back, a large glass, and it was cold. Hopefully it'd cool him off.

"Thanks, darlin'," he said as she put it in front of him.

"Not your darlin'." She caught Phyllis's eye, nodded, realizing she had a table waiting. "And I've got customers waiting. So you're okay?"

"Come to the game tonight, we'll go out after."

"No."

"Okay, I'll pick you up after the game, we'll go to dinner then."

"No."

"Come on, baby, you want to go out with me."

"No." And yet her lips were twitching. She was amused.

"Why not?"

"Because."

"What kind of answer is that?"

She smiled, rolled her eyes, aware that he'd just thrown her own words back at her. "I don't know you—"

"You kind of do—"

"I really don't—"

"Then we'll bring Boone along. You know him. He can be your chaperon."

Lauren flushed. "That's ridiculous."

"Then what is it?"

"I—" She opened her mouth to speak, but how did she tell him he reminded her too much of an ex? How could she tell him she was rejecting him for being big and brash and confident? She couldn't. "I'm in bed by nine or ten every night."

"What? Seriously?"

She nodded. "I open in the mornings. Come in between four and five to get all the baking done." She gestured to the lighted display case filled with gorgeous pies and cakes. "Those are mine."

His gaze swept the display. "You made those?"

She nodded again.

"How?" he demanded.

She shrugged. "How do you hit a ball?"

He shrugged right back. "Practice."

"There you go." And then she walked away to take care of her other customers.

But she'd walked away smiling.

The rain had finally, thankfully, stopped in Tampa. The weekend was supposed to be beautiful, too, which didn't really impact Sarah as she'd be gone tomorrow afternoon, on a flight as soon as the kids were out of school.

With tonight being their last night in Florida, she invited Alyssa and the kids to come over, since Jeff was on the road with the Rays.

While the kids ate pizza in front of the TV, Alyssa and Sarah hung out in the kitchen, sharing a bottle of wine, nibbling on cheese and crackers and chocolate peanut butter cups from Trader Joe's.

"My roof has a leak," Alyssa said forlornly as Sarah popped a cracker covered with Brie into her mouth. "And of course Jeff is gone."

Sarah swallowed and wiped her fingers on a cocktail napkin. "It wouldn't leak if he were home."

"It's Murphy's Law that things only break when the men are on the road."

"But we like taking care of everything," Sarah reminded her, lifting her wineglass. "It's fulfilling."

"So is raising four boys on your own." Alyssa clinked her glass against Sarah's. "To the good life."

"The good life," Sarah echoed before drinking.

Alyssa set her glass down abruptly. "Are you sure you have to go tomorrow? I'm going to hate it when you're gone! You're my closest friend here. The other wives are sweet, but they're not you."

"Grouchy and short-tempered?" Sarah retorted, taking another long sip from her glass.

"No. Funny and honest. You *are* honest. It's tough being married to a baseball player. Tough being a good wife when a thousand other women want your man."

"Women have just got to leave married men alone."

Alyssa did another clink with her glass. "So . . . how's your sister?"

Sarah glanced at Alyssa over the rim of her wineglass. "Which one?"

"The one who just lost her husband."

"Meg." Sarah gave Alyssa another searching glance, wondering if it was coincidence that they were discussing extramarital affairs and Alyssa was asking about Meg. "And she's okay, I think. She isn't talking much to anyone, just focusing on her kids."

"And the other . . . three?"

"Two. Brianna and Kit, they're the fraternal twins, but there's also Cass, my sister-in-law."

"And you like her?"

"I like them all. I've always gotten along with all of them."

"Until Meg had the affair last year."

So Alyssa *was* referring to Meg's affair. Sarah realized now that it was something Alyssa would never forget either, which made her wish she'd never told her friend in the first place. Meg deserved to be remembered for all the good things she'd done in her life, not the one mistake.

A gigantic mistake.

Just like that, Sarah flashed to Boone's affair three years ago.

No, affairs weren't something one forgot.

Eager to think about something else, she grabbed her iPhone from where it was charging on the counter and flipped to her calendar.

"So, when are you guys coming to see us?" she asked, looking up at Alyssa.

"I don't know."

"The Rays will be playing at the Coliseum July thirtieth, thirty-first, and August first. Come out with the kids. Stay with us. We can sightsee or just hang out. It'll be really fun."

Alyssa sighed. "Flying across the country with four boys isn't my idea of fun."

"I know, I hear that, but once you're there, you'll be glad you did it. You can stay for as long as you want, too. We can go up to Napa, do some wine tasting, visit the mud baths in Calistoga."

"With all the kids?"

"No!" Sarah laughed and refilled their glasses. "You and me. It'll be a girl thing."

Alyssa considered the idea. "Maybe." Then she grinned. "But only if I can meet your wicked sister . . . and her sexy vintner boyfriend!"

"They're not together anymore."

"Thank God! That means he's free."

Chris returned to Mama's Café for the second morning in a row, entering the restaurant with swagger, as well as some famous company.

Lauren had been making coffee, and she paused a moment as she spied Boone, and two other players, trailing after Chris. Four baseball players in her café now. Pretty soon she could be feeding the whole team.

Bette was nearly swooning. She led the men to a booth—Phyllis's, since Bette's were all full, talking to them a mile a minute.

Lauren shook her head, smiling, glad she didn't have to wait on the guys today.

Phyllis walked past with four ice waters. "Hello, Oakland A's," she said saucily.

"Enjoy," Lauren muttered, pushing Brew on the machine.

"I will, but I'm not selfish. You can come say hello."

Lauren rolled her eyes. "You're shameless."

"I know. And I enjoy every minute of it!"

Bette approached, and reaching past Lauren, she opened the display case to lift out a peach pie. "I wish I'd had an open table," she groused. "It makes me sick that I had to give those men to Phyllis."

"They're customers, ladies, not treats," Lauren said, amused despite herself.

"Well, I can't help but think that hunky Chris Steir is treat-worthy," Bette said, plating two generous slices of the pie. "I would snap him up and take him home with me. He's delish . . ."

Lauren shook her head. "Bette, you're old enough to be his mom."

"Maybe even his grandma," Bette agreed cheerfully, returning the pie to the display case. "But I don't care. He brings out the cougar in me. Grrr."

Choking back horrified laughter, Lauren gathered the cups of tea and carried them to her table, along with the promise to bring fresh coffee as soon as it was done brewing, and then, turning around, walked smack into Chris.

Lauren gulped as he reached out to steady her. "Sorry," he said. "Didn't know you'd turn that fast."

Lauren glanced past Chris to Boone. He was observing her, curious. There was something intent, and watchful, in his eyes. It made her grow warm, too warm. It made her wonder if he might possibly be attracted to her.

It was a strange thought, a little heady as well as a little disturbing. Flustered, she looked at Chris. "Hi."

"How are you?" he asked.

"Fine."

"Fine?"

"Yeah," she exhaled, feeling breathless and out of sorts.

"I'm sorry," he said, forehead creasing. "How can I help? Is there anything I can do?"

She mirrored his frown. "Excuse me?"

"Boone told me about 'fine.'" Chris sounded concerned as well as apologetic. "Apparently, fine isn't good. Fine is just . . . fine."

Lauren's gaze narrowed and she stared at him hard, annoyed, before she burst out laughing. "You are *so* ridiculous."

He seemed pleased that he'd made her laugh. "How come we're not in your section?"

"Because it's full."

"How come our waitress wouldn't trade with you?"

"Because I didn't ask her to."

"Why not?"

"Because I didn't want you."

Chris crossed his massive arms over his chest, and his biceps flexed, muscles rippling. "Now I don't believe that for one minute."

With his feet planted, he looked enormous and powerful. Lauren wasn't sure if she was impressed or intimidated. "Were you born this cocky?" she asked tartly.

"I've always had a lot of confidence."

"Do you ever think it's misplaced?"

His blue eyes heated, sparking. "Were you born this prickly?"

"I wouldn't be prickly if you didn't get personal."

"It's my fault."

"Absolutely."

He just grinned. "I'm not allowed to like you?"

"Nope."

"Why not? You're not married. Don't have a boyfriend—" He held up a finger when she opened her mouth to protest. "And don't try to pretend you do. Phyllis already told us you don't." He gave her a look. "So, why can't I like you?"

Because he was too much. Too much size. Too much power. Too much personality. Too much energy.

People like him annihilated people like her. Not intentionally, perhaps, but ambition, need, desire, greed—who knew what it was—turned some folks into human bulldozers, leaving destruction in their wake.

She knew. John had been one.

The sound of shattering glass saved her from answering him. "I have to go," she said, racing to the kitchen to discover that the window over the big stainless sink was broken, with shards of glass sparkling on the floor.

"What happened?" Lauren asked.

Bob went to the sink and carefully retrieved a wet baseball from a tub of sudsy water. "I was showing José my windup," he said remorsefully. "The ball got away from me."

Lauren shook her head in disbelief. What had happened here at Mama's Café? Baseball fever had taken over. "You guys clean this up. Don't get cut. I'll call a glass company and get them out today."

She headed back to the front and used one of the old phone books under the register to search for glass and window companies. She phoned two before she found one that could come out early afternoon to replace the window.

As she gave the address and cross street for the café to the glass company, Chris stepped outside to take a call, and she watched him talk on his phone, and as he talked, he paced a little, and she found herself studying his profile.

With his dark blond hair drawn back at his nape, you could see his features clearly. Straight nose, firm, full mouth, high cheekbones, wide brow. He was good-looking, possibly even better-looking than Boone, but he had a raw physicality to him that unsettled her.

But he wasn't out of control. You could tell from the way he moved that he was supremely comfortable with his body, comfortable in his skin. It was obvious just looking at him that he was a professional athlete.

Maybe that's what she didn't like.

Maybe it was the fact that his muscles were so developed and that he exuded confidence, energy.

Sexual energy.

Which definitely wasn't for her.

Boone left his table to come talk to her once she'd hung up the phone.

"Glass company on the way," she said, smiling at him as she put away the phone book.

"Bette told us what happened," Boone said.

"Bob has one impressive windup."

Boone smiled. "You don't seem angry."

"How can I be? Bob has baseball fever. You guys have infected us by coming in to breakfast."

Boone's smile slowly faded. "So, are you going to go out with him?"

"No." Lauren sighed. "What is this? Third grade?"

"I just think you're a sweetheart. You need a nice guy—"

"Sorry. Wasn't raised that way. My dad insisted my sister and I be self-reliant."

"Okay, your dad is right, so let me rephrase that. You deserve a nice guy. Somebody who will be good to you . . . and will spoil you. Surely, that's not a bad thing?"

No, it wasn't a bad thing. All women wanted to be loved and cherished.

She looked past Boone to Chris, who was still on the phone outside. Her chest grew tight. She reached into her apron and felt for her notepad and pen. "I think Chris is funny. He makes me laugh. But—and please don't take this the wrong way—he's not my type. He's . . . just too . . . everything."

"What does that mean?"

Her shoulders twisted. "He's over-the-top. Doesn't have a subtle bone in his body."

"Chris is funny, but he's not a clown. And he's no meathead either. Steir is one of the smartest guys I've ever met."

Lauren rolled her eyes.

"In the off-season he goes to school," Boone added.

"Trying to get his GED?"

He laughed. "Chris is in the middle of getting a graduate degree in mechanical engineering at UC Berkeley."

She was surprised. She glanced back to Chris, who'd ended the call and was now pocketing his phone. "Is he not doing well professionally?"

"Chris is one of the best outfielders in the American League. But he's also a thinker. He's one of those guys who needs to use his brain."

Sixteen

They'd done it. Made it. Sarah had arrived in California with the kids, flying in late Friday night. Her dad had picked them up at the San Francisco airport and they were staying with him this week while Boone was gone.

Brianna was still at the house with Dad, but she'd gotten a job volunteering with a women's shelter and was working all day Saturday, and Dad was playing golf, so Sarah took the kids to the California Academy of Science located in Golden Gate Park.

The building wasn't far from where she'd grown up, and she'd loved the natural history museum and aquarium as a kid, but it was even better now. The park also had a children's playground, also recently renovated, and the stunning 1912 carousel shimmered with fresh paint and color.

But by midafternoon the famous San Francisco summer fog began to roll in, in wisps at first then thickening and cloaking the park's signature eucalyptus trees. Temperatures dropped rapidly, and it wasn't long before Ella and Brennan, Florida kids, had had enough of the slides and swings and begged to return to Grandpa's.

Back at the house, both kids wanted hot baths before watching a movie. With them in their pajamas, Sarah let them settle down to watch the movie so she could make dinner for everyone, having pulled a package of pork chops out of the freezer that morning.

Dad entered the kitchen via the laundry room, which connected to the narrow one-car garage, the Edwardian-era structure better suited to a horse and buggy than the modern-day SUV. He removed his cleats by the door and then padded into the kitchen in his socks.

"Something smells good," he said, sniffing appreciatively, passing the stove to get a look at the browning pork chops. "Making your mom's pork-chop casserole?"

"I am," Sarah answered. She was just about finished peeling the potatoes she would then slice and place in the dish. "Hey, can we open that bottle of wine in the fridge? I wanted a glass but wasn't sure if you were saving it for something."

"I bought it for you," Dad said, retrieving the Chardonnay and then searching one of the drawers for the bottle opener. "But don't drink it all tonight. It's not good for you."

Sarah stopped peeling to look at him. "I don't drink that much, Dad."

"I just care about you." He peeled the foil off the bottle and then eased the cork out. "You're important to me."

She stifled her irritation and rinsed off her final potato. "I appreciate that. But I'm careful. I have to be. I'm pretty much a single parent these days."

"Where is Boone playing tonight? Arizona?"

She nodded. "He called while we were at the museum, but I couldn't get good reception, and then when I called him back a half hour later, he was already at the park. I always forget that Arizona is a different time zone than California."

Late that evening, after the kids were in bed and Sarah still hadn't heard from Boone, she called him. It was almost eleven her time, which meant it was midnight his, and the game had been over for hours.

Trying to be playful, she asked him if he was out having fun with his girlfriends.

Boone hesitated a moment too long. "Yeah," he answered curtly. "Yeah, I am."

Sarah swallowed, realizing belatedly it wasn't the right thing to say to him. He wasn't amused. "I was just kidding," she murmured.

"No, you weren't," he answered. Boone didn't get angry often, but when he did, it wasn't nice. He was angry now.

"I'm sorry."

He didn't respond, and she could feel his anger on the line, and his anger, coupled with the silence, made her feel sick. And disgusted.

Why had she made a joke like that? Feeble, so feeble . . .

"I took the kids to Golden Gate Park today," she said, trying to smooth things over. "We visited the natural science museum and aquarium and then the children's park. It was fun."

"Sounds fun."

"That's where we were when you called. Earlier."

He said nothing. Sarah struggled to keep the conversation moving. "The kids froze when the fog moved in. And I forgot we might need sweatshirts. We ran to the car, teeth chattering."

"You won't forget next time."

"No. But it won't be like this in the East Bay. Summer is summer there. It's just here in the city that it gets so foggy and cold this time of year—"

"Listen," he interrupted. "Next time you call, don't call just to give me shit, okay?"

"I was trying to be funny."

"It's not funny."

Sarah was now on the defensive. "Got it, babe. No need to be so rough."

"I'm rough because I'm tired. I'm rough because I don't talk to you often, but when I do, it's never good. You're never happy. You're never glad to hear my voice—"

"Yes, I am!"

"You don't sound happy, though. You sound angry. Mistrustful. As if I am hooking up with chicks right and left—which I'm not. I won't. I told you that."

Sarah glanced over her shoulder into the family room, where her dad was watching TV. Brennan was on the couch, on his stomach, fast asleep. Ella was already upstairs in the bed, sleeping. "I'm sorry if that's how I make you feel."

"It is," he said curtly.

She bit her lip, chastised. "I'm sorry, and I probably shouldn't have called so late," she added awkwardly, just wanting to end the call now, before it got any worse. "Call me in the morning if you have time before tomorrow's game."

"I had a terrible game tonight," he said abruptly. "Went oh-for-three."

"I'm sorry."

"I played almost as bad last night. I'm just not . . . happy . . . with how I'm playing. Okay?"

"Okay."

"I'm not running around, chasing skirt. I'm in the hotel, eating in front of the TV and trying to figure out how to play better tomorrow."

"Okay."

"Does that make you feel better?"

Sarah swallowed hard. "No."

"Why not?"

"Because I don't like hearing you didn't do well in a game."

"It is what it is," he said impatiently. "And I didn't call you because I didn't want to bring you down. This is my job. But you're my wife, my family. The career will end. But you, babe, I keep forever."

* * *

Sarah slept fitfully that night. She didn't like conflict or tension with Boone, especially when he was on the road and she couldn't be sure things were completely smoothed over.

In the morning she headed downstairs after checking to see that both the kids were still asleep. Dad was in the kitchen, drinking coffee and reading the paper. He'd been up for hours. Brianna was still in bed, though, and Sarah poured herself a cup of coffee before borrowing a section of the paper from her dad.

"The sportswriters are all over the A's today," her dad said, turning pages in the sports section. "Fair-weather fans," he added.

"Boone said it was a lousy game," Sarah said, taking a seat at the table.

He closed the sports section and pushed it toward her. "I better go. Don't like being late."

He'd dressed nice this morning. "Off to Mass, Dad?"

"Would you like to come?"

"No. I better stay with the kids."

"They could come, too."

"They're still sleeping."

"I should have woken you all up, then."

She saw his smile. He was teasing her, fully cognizant that her family didn't attend church. Not like Meg and the kids. Not like Kit. Or Tommy and Cass. "Thank you for thinking of us, but we're all right." She stood up and kissed his cheek. "Do you want breakfast when you come home? I can make something if you'd like."

"Nah. I'm heading to the stadium for a one o'clock Giants game. Uncle Pat got tickets, so we're doing that. What are you guys doing today?"

Sarah shook her head. "I don't know. Kick around, relax. Tomorrow I'm heading out to look at rental houses with my friend Dev from high school. Do you remember him? Dev Phinney? He's now a big real estate agent in the East Bay and he's got a bunch of listings to show me."

"You're not buying, are you?"

"No. Just renting. I don't expect we'll still be here come spring, but you never know."

"So why is Dev taking you around? I wouldn't think he'd normally handle rental properties."

"He doesn't." Sarah smiled. "I think he's just hoping we'll remember he helped us out should we ever want to buy."

Her dad didn't smile back. His expression was stern. "Just make sure he doesn't get any other ideas. You might feel like a single mom with Boone on the road, but you're not."

"*Dad.*"

"I'm just saying."

"And I'm just saying 'relax.' "

"It happens, Sarah."

"Yeah, I know. But I'd never cheat on Boone. I wouldn't. If I weren't happy, I'd tell him. I'd leave first. Trust me on that."

It was two thirty on a Sunday afternoon and Mama's Café was empty save for one woman at a corner booth drinking coffee and eating a slice of cake while working on her computer.

Lauren wandered aimlessly around the restaurant, unusually agitated. It was slow. She was tired. And she was bored.

Why was she working every day?

And why, when she worked, was she putting in these excruciatingly long days? If she owned the café and was making a bigger percentage of the profit, great, but right now she was doing all this work on a salary, with just tiny bonuses every week for good revenue return.

It was time that either Mimi agreed to sell or Lauren scaled back her hours, her commitment, and her personal investment in the place.

It'd been a fantastic challenge when she started in September, taking over running a floundering café that had charm and potential but not much else.

Now the café was doing a steady business, and the mornings and early afternoons were both really strong. Dinners were still unpredictable and the late afternoon tended to be dead slow, but that wouldn't be such a bad thing if Lauren had someone else to babysit the café.

She had no one to blame but herself. She was the one who'd drawn up the schedule. She was the one who'd wanted all the hours, but enough. She'd had enough. It was time to take a break. Time to mix things up. Maybe, just maybe, it was time to start living a little . . . movies, shopping, lunches with friends.

Not that she had friends here. But she did in Napa. She had Lisa. She missed Lisa, too. Missed working with her, shoulder to shoulder in the kitchen, talking and laughing as they made bread, or cakes, or whatever else they were baking.

Was she ready to return to Napa? To Summer Bakery & Café? A wave of nostalgia hit her, nostalgia for the way it'd once been.

The memory of working in Grandma's big kitchen with Lisa teasing her, and she could smell the raw yeast of rising bread and the warm cinnamon wafting from the oven, and for a moment she thought it was time to go back, time—

But if she returned, it wasn't going to be to Grandma's kitchen. She'd return for that big, shiny marble restaurant downtown, the one with walls with nine-foot-tall windows and twenty-foot plaster ceilings . . . all beautiful, but not her.

And Grandma's house wasn't Lisa anymore. No, both sisters had moved on, moved elsewhere.

Lauren's chest felt tight and tender as she checked on her customer with the coffee and computer. The customer put her hand over her cup, not wanting another refill, so Lauren removed the dessert plate, left the bill, and, after dispensing with the dirty dishes, glanced at her phone, knowing she needed to get back to her parents about Wednesday.

They wanted her to come home since it was the one-year anniversary of Blake's death, but she was dreading it.

Her parents wanted to go to the cemetery. Place flowers on Blake's grave. Share memories while they all stood there together. But cemeteries weren't for her, and there were a hundred ways Lauren would rather remember her son than by laying flowers next to a gravestone.

The cake and coffee customer paid and left, and with the café empty, Lauren seized the moment to call home. Her dad was in front of the TV watching the San Francisco Giants game. "Is this a bad time?" she asked, hearing the TV noise in the background.

"The Giants are losing," he said gruffly.

Her dad was a true San Francisco sports teams' fan, which meant he actively disliked the Oakland Athletics and despised the Raiders and wouldn't tolerate any disrespect to his teams, in his house. So no one had ever shown any. But then one day, many years ago, toddler Blake, just three, announced to his grandfather that he didn't like San Francisco. No, he liked Oakland Athletics, and *loved* the Raiders.

Everyone had spluttered with muffled laughter.

Dad got red in the face.

Everyone was sure that in a few weeks Blake would forget all about his favorite teams. But he didn't. He fully embraced all the Oakland teams in preschool and never turned his back on them, collecting all sports memorabilia he could for the A's, the Raiders, and the Golden State Warriors.

And while Dad, who'd been the one to introduce Blake to sports, would huff and puff about disrespectful kids whenever Blake flaunted his black-and-white football jersey, or his favorite green-and-yellow baseball jersey, their sports rivalry and banter actually bonded them. Sports bonded them. And if Blake were alive today, he'd probably be sitting with his grandfather right now, watching the game and making fun of Dad's beloved Giants.

"Want me to call back later?" she asked.

"No. It's fine. I could use the distraction," he said, muting the TV.

Lauren smiled, feeling his pain. "So, Dad, I've got to be honest. I can't come home Wednesday. I can't come home for that kind of an anniversary and do the whole cemetery thing, with flowers and all of it. It doesn't feel right to me. I don't want to remember Blake that way. Maybe one day I can go there, visit, but it's not that time yet."

He heard her out, letting her get all the words spoken before agreeing with her. "I get it. I do. Part of me feels that way, too, but your mom wants to go. She needs to go. Likes to go. And she does, you know, every couple of weeks."

"What does she do there?"

"Prays. Talks to him. Makes sure the gravestone is clean."

Lauren's eyes suddenly felt gritty. "Doesn't it make her . . . sad?"

"Sometimes. But it also gives her a sense of purpose. Makes her feel useful. As if she is still taking care of him."

Lauren hung up the phone and slid it slowly into her pocket. Eyes still stinging, she blinked, clearing her vision.

So that's why Mom went.

Lauren swallowed hard. She finally got it.

Sarah wasn't on vacation. She had a job to do, and that was to find her family a rental house for the next three to six months. Possibly longer if the A's extended Boone's contract.

So on Monday morning, she blew through Dev's list of rentals in three hours and shot down his suggestion of a nice lunch at a popular spot in Walnut Creek. She wasn't interested in chitchat today. She wanted to find the right house, sign the contract, get

the utilities on if they weren't, and then call the moving company
and let them know where the truck could go on Wednesday.

"You're all business, aren't you?" Dev complained good-
naturedly when they'd worked through lunch, and then only hit
Starbucks so Sarah could use the restroom and grab an iced tea
for the road.

Sarah looked at Devlyn; he'd been cute in high school, and he'd
grown into a handsome man, but she wasn't with him today
because she craved his company. She was here, in his car, because
she needed to get things done. "Work is work," she said, "Play is
play. And I don't find looking at houses fun."

"Maybe you just haven't had the right realtor," he teased.

"Perhaps. Because the right realtor would know that the only
thing I want today is to find a house so that when my husband
returns Thursday night, he'll have a couch and TV in the family
room, clothes in his closet, food in the kitchen, and a bed with
sheets that he can sleep in."

She found a house she thought would work, too. It was the last
house Dev showed her, and she knew why he was saving it for
last. It was actually perfect for them—big, private, in an outstanding neighborhood in Orinda, an affluent East Bay
community—and it was ideal for Dev since he was the agent for
the house, and the seller had told him to get it rented or sold
within the month or he was giving the listing to someone else.

"Found a house," Sarah blurted as soon as Boone called her
that night.

"Yeah, I saw your text. Tell me about it."

"It's in Orinda. It's big, plenty of space, an acre, with a work-
out room and a pool."

"Your text said it was expensive."

"But we'd get a great deal on it if we'd be willing to sign a six-
month rental agreement."

"I don't know that I'll still be with Oakland come September."

"I thought about that. But it doesn't mean we'd all have to

move. We could stay in Orinda . . . enroll the kids in school there. It's got a great school system. One of the best in the country."

"Not private?"

"Wouldn't need to go the private route here."

"Tell me more about the house."

"It's been on the market for almost two years. Owners bought high and were willing to sell at a loss, but not in the millions. So, they've pulled it off the market, waiting for prices to come up a bit, and are now trying to rent it out."

"And you like the house?"

"It's . . . big. Mediterranean. But . . ."

"Yes?"

"It's dated."

"How dated?"

"Early 1990s. Faux walls everywhere. Sponge-painted halls, bathroom."

"What colors?"

"Um, your favorites?"

"Uh-huh."

"Peach, rose, and teal green."

"Nice, Sarah."

Sarah laughed so hard her eyes watered, tears running at the corners, and as she laughed, some of the terrible pressure in her chest eased. Things would be okay. They would. She just had to stay positive. Had to keep her focus. Family first. It's what Mom always did and it worked. Just be like Mom and it'd be okay . . .

"I actually had to cover my mouth when I saw the master bathroom to keep from laughing out loud," she said, wiping her eyes. "But it was so, so hideous. Emerald walls with burgundy trim."

"Stop," Boone protested, but he was laughing, too.

"Serious."

"Can we paint it?"

"I don't know. The seller thinks it's pretty sweet."

"I bet. And no one has convinced this brilliant individual that perhaps the color scheme is hurting his ability to sell?"

"The thing is, the house looks great from the street. It's got the curb appeal. Big iron gates. Completely secure yard. And a gated pool."

"Well, that's good," he said gruffly.

"There's room for a dog—"

"No."

"Maybe."

"No."

"The kids really want one."

"In a rental house?"

"I know you weren't raised with dogs, Boone, but I think it'd be good for Brennan. He's . . . struggling . . . I think a dog could be really good for him."

"We'll see."

She knew what that meant, and she let it go for now, but in her mind the topic wasn't closed. Puppies were a lot of work, but they were also full of love. Unconditional love. Maybe a puppy was exactly what they needed.

"So, when do we move in?" Boone asked, changing the subject.

"Hoping to sign the contract and hand over a check tomorrow. Then it's ours. Which is good, because the moving truck comes Wednesday."

"Wish I could be there, babe."

"I know, but Dad and Tommy, Cass and Kit"—she took a breath—"and Jude . . . they'll all be here Wednesday night helping unpack. They've all agreed to return on Thursday, too, and finish helping me get the job done so things will be settled when you get home."

"That's cool."

"I know. It's the first time I've ever had the Brennan bunch to help me unpack. Pretty nice."

"We'll have to take them to dinner—"

"We are."

He laughed. "And when is that?"

"Father's Day. After the game."

"Sounds like fun."

"But they're all coming to the game, Sunday, at the Coliseum." She hesitated. "Can you get tickets for all of us? There will be a lot of us. Thirteen with the kids."

"Not a problem. I'll get everyone on the pass list. And it'll be good to see them all. I look forward to having the family together."

"I know. It's just weird it's not at a funeral."

Boone laughed. "Miss you, babe."

"Miss you, too, Boone."

Lauren didn't work Wednesday morning, having taken herself off the schedule until noon.

She still woke up early Wednesday though, driving to Napa as the sun rose, turning the landscape into silver and gold.

She reached the cemetery just as the groundskeeper unlocked the front gate.

Lauren left her car to enter the quiet cemetery.

She hadn't told anyone she was coming to Napa today.

It was better not to tell anyone.

Better to do this her way.

Walking along the gravel path, Lauren could almost pretend she was in a park, with its manicured lawns and hedges and flower-beds. But then she was moving between tombstones and head-stones and the plastic flowers dotting different graves and it wasn't a park anymore, but something terribly still and sad.

She stopped just before she reached Blake's headstone, sud-denly unable to take another step closer, not sure she could do this. Not sure . . .

And then she was sure.

Sure she needed him.

Sure she missed him.

A year. It'd been a year today since he'd died.

Crouching before his gray headstone, she put her hands flat on the cold granite, covering his name, warming the stone.

Mama's here.

I came.

Miss you, baby. Miss you bad.

She leaned forward, kissed the stone. Kissed it again.

A year, baby. A lifetime since you left. Hope you're okay. Hope you're happy. Hope there's no pain.

Blinking hard, she carefully traced each letter of his name.

JONATHAN BLAKE SUMMER.

I miss you. I miss you so much. You have no idea how much I miss you and your hugs and your stinky shoes and the way you left your clothes all over the place . . .

As she talked to him, Lauren traced his name again and again, as if she could somehow draw him into her, or pass her love through her fingertips and into the stone, reaching him somehow. Because love didn't die. Love didn't end. Love was there in the beginning, and love was there at death. Love was what tied them all together . . .

It wasn't until Lauren was on the way home a half hour later that she realized she'd forgotten to take Blake flowers.

But maybe that was okay.

He didn't need flowers. He had her heart.

A t work on Saturday morning, Lauren wondered when Boone would return to the café. She hadn't seen him in nine days and knew he'd been on the road for six games, but the Athletics were back now, had played at the Coliseum last night, with another game tonight, and Boone always stopped by the café on his way to the stadium.

The fact that neither Boone nor Chris came in yesterday generated conversation among the café kitchen and waitstaff, but now that it looked like neither would be in again today, Lauren couldn't help but wonder if Boone had told Chris what she had said about him.

That he was too much. Over-the-top. That he didn't have a subtle bone in him.

She cringed as she took orders and seated customers, adding names to the wait list. She shouldn't have said what she said about Chris. It didn't make her feel good remembering.

As it was Saturday, the morning rush lingered until early afternoon with customers continuing to line up for the café's special weekend brunch menu. Lauren was doing double duty today, working her own section as well as helping Crystal, the new waitress, cover hers, since Crystal was overwhelmed.

Crystal had been hired on Thursday to replace Karen, because Karen had started to come in late almost daily, and Lauren wouldn't tolerate tardiness on a regular basis. If you were scheduled to work at seven, that meant you were waiting tables at seven, it didn't mean you were walking in the door at seven, or five after seven, or twenty after seven, or twenty-seven after seven. Lauren had talked with Karen about it several times, too, and Karen always apologized and had an excuse. But excuses only went so far, and Lauren was finally forced to let her go. Lauren was sorry, too. She'd enjoyed Karen and found the younger girl quirky and fun, but Lauren took her job seriously. She expected her staff to do the same.

Now Lauren bussed one of Crystal's tables, a popular booth in the corner, before carrying the big gray tub to a cluster of tables where a party of eight had been sitting. Quickly, she cleared the first of the two tables, and then the second, and then dragging the second table away, created space between the tables again. She was just about to lift the heavy, dirty-dish bin when Chris suddenly materialized and picked it up for her.

"Where does this go?" he asked, his dark blond hair loose over his shoulders; his T-shirt was impossibly tight, revealing more muscle than was decent, and the old, soft, faded denim jeans he was wearing hugged his quads and ass.

"Show-off," she muttered.

"What was that?" he drawled, eyebrow quirking, lips curving.

Lauren was pretty damn sure he'd heard what she said, so she smiled sweetly. "I said I've got that."

He laughed, and a dimple flashed in his cheek.

Her pulse jumped and her insides did a weird flip, and her hands suddenly felt damp. She wiped them on the back of her skirt.

She wouldn't admit it to anyone, but she was glad to see him. It'd been boring without him and Boone. She missed the superheroes. They certainly livened up the place.

"I'm not going to let my girl carry this. Show me where to put it. The kitchen?"

"Not your girl," she corrected, before gesturing for him to follow, ignoring the gawking looks from some of the other customers. Customers who clearly knew who hulking Chris Steir was.

"Not yet maybe," he replied, trailing after her into the kitchen, where he greeted Bob and José, who were at the big stove, cooking up eggs and pancakes and keeping a close eye on sizzling bacon and sausage.

"Never," she muttered as Bette passed and made moon eyes at Chris.

Chris laughed softly and stuck close to Lauren on their way back out.

"You need a busboy," he said, stopping in front of the dessert display case, allowing the heavy kitchen door to swing shut behind them. "You're too busy not to have one."

She blew a strand of hair from her eyes. "We weren't always this busy."

"But you are now."

They were, too, Lauren thought, glancing around the café, her gaze moving from the full tables to the crowd by the front door, and another large cluster of people outside, all waiting to get in. "Not sure why," she said.

"The word's out that you serve great food."

"The word's out, huh?" she asked, looking at him, trying to hide her smile. He was cute. Too cute for his own good.

"Yep."

He sounded so sure of himself. "Just where is the word out?"

"Well, on the A's team blog, and some of our Twitter feeds."

"Whose Twitter?"

"Mine." He saw her incredulous expression and crossed his arms over his chest, trying to look humble. "I have quite a big following."

"I bet you do," she said, struggling to hold back laughter.

"I do."

"I know. I'm agreeing with you."

"You're not." His lips pursed. He shook his head. But his eyes were smiling down at her. "You're making fun of me for being on Twitter."

"I just don't know anything about it."

"You should be on it. You could do a tweet each day about your special, or something happening. People would love it. People would love you."

"Uh-huh." She smiled, trying to be kind even though he had no idea what he was talking about. People wouldn't want to hear about the café, or their specials, and they certainly wouldn't want to hear from her. "I'll keep that in mind."

"You're not even listening to me, are you?"

"No." Her lips twitched. "Not really."

"Why not? Everyone else listens."

"I don't know."

"I don't know either. But it's something we need to sort out. Have dinner with me tonight so we can discuss it."

"No."

"*Wow.*" He laughed, hard, and he bent over, still laughing, hands on his knees. "That was a rough no. Nothing apologetic about that one at all."

Lauren blushed, face heating. "Maybe it was a little harsh."

"A little? You're mean. I think I'll go have a seat at the counter and cry."

Lauren's cheeks burned, and her insides felt fizzy. "You're ridiculous."

He stopped laughing and reached out to sweep his thumb across her warm, pink cheek. "Okay, I won't cry. But I will go sit and let you wait on me, hand and foot."

Lauren giggled, and spluttered, "You're beyond hopeless."

"I've heard that," he said, nodding earnestly.

She laughed even harder, her eyes watering at the corners. She wiped beneath her eyes, making sure they were dry. "This won't work. I can't possibly manage this restaurant, take care of my section, train Crystal, and handle you."

"Sure you can. Just take a couple of nice, deep, cleansing breaths, and you'll find your center. In the meantime I'll grab a seat at the counter and I'll eat whatever you bring me. Steak, corned beef hash, omelet. It doesn't matter."

And then he strolled to the one open seat at the counter, his faded denims so soft and worn they looked like a second skin, outlining his butt and hamstrings.

Thirty some minutes later Chris was finishing his breakfast, which he'd ended with a slice of her peach mango cobbler and then a second serving of cobbler.

"That's good," he said, nodding approvingly. "My grandma's from Texas and she made cobblers, good cobblers, but this rivals her best."

"I like cobblers, too," Lauren said, removing the dessert plates and returning with another glass of milk. Chris liked milk. He drank two or three glasses with every meal. "Were you raised in Texas?"

"No. Phoenix. But I went to school in Texas. UT."

"Ah. A desert boy."

"*Boy?*" Chris gave her a look. "I'll have you know I'm a *man,* Ms. Summer."

He was teasing her, trying to be funny, and yet the sexual implication made her blush. "You're thirty," she said, having read his age and all his statistics in the A's program when she attended the game with Karen.

"Is that not a man where you come from?"

She laughed, her cheeks suddenly impossibly hot. "No, it is."

"But you don't take me seriously, though, do you?"

"I, uh—" She glanced up at him, perplexed. "I do."

He gave her a pointed look.

She frowned. "Don't I?"

"No."

"Order up, boss," Bob called from the kitchen.

Lauren shot Chris a quick, troubled glance and went for the plates under the warmer, and yet as she served lunch to her table, and refreshed their drinks, and then the drinks at another table, she kept mulling over what Chris had said. About her not taking him seriously. As if he wasn't a man.

She walked behind the counter, stopping in front of him to fish out his bill. "Maybe it's because you're younger than me."

"By shoot, what? Five years?"

"How did you know?"

"Boone told me." He held her gaze, his expression searching. "I guess you told him."

"Can't believe he remembered."

"Apparently you and his wife are around the same age." Chris's gaze never wavered. "She's here now. With the kids."

"That's good. He's missed her."

"It's good they're here now. They've been going through a rough patch for a while."

"How do you know?"

"He and I share a room on the road."

"Ah."

Chris grabbed a roll of cash from his pocket and counted out three tens, leaving them on the counter. "So when are we going out again?"

She smiled, shook her head. "You're shameless."

"I'm not giving up."

"You should."

"I won't."

"We're not at all compatible."

"How can you say that?" He leaned on the counter, looked into her eyes. "You don't even know my type."

"What *is* your type?"

The edge of his mouth lifted. He stood, towering over her. "You."

And then he was walking out. Make that sauntering out. And drawing every single woman's eyes in the café.

She shivered.

He was certainly hot, handsome, and available. Which is why he terrified her. There wasn't a single safe thing about him.

Apparently her sister, Lisa, knew exactly what she was talking about.

Quickly, Lauren began gathering the rest of Chris's dishes, put them under the counter in a dish tub, and scooped up more dirty dishes from another spot farther down.

"He likes you," Boone said abruptly.

Lauren's head lifted, and she turned toward him, hands filled with dishes. He must have arrived while Chris was still here, and neither of them had noticed. "When did you get here?"

"Five minutes ago."

"Didn't see you come in."

"I know. I'm hurt." But Boone smiled as he said it.

She smiled back. "Let me get the counter cleaned up and I'll get you some coffee."

"Take your time."

But she didn't. Lauren returned with a clean dishrag and wiped the counter down before setting him up with a new place setting. She chatted with him as she put the silverware down, asking about his road trip, and his wife and kids, and what they were doing for Father's Day tomorrow.

It was easy talking with him, she thought, after putting in his order. Easy being around him because she was comfortable with him. Boone Walker was handsome, but nonthreatening. Chris Steir, on the other hand, was very threatening.

Again Lisa's words came back to her. Married, safe. Single, not safe. *Hmm.* The pattern was becoming uncomfortably, overwhelmingly clear.

"My wife's family is attending tomorrow's game," Boone said, adding milk and sugar to his coffee. "Should be fun. First time they've seen me play in an A's uniform. Then after the game we're all going out to eat somewhere. Sarah's sister Meg is making reservations—" He broke off as he saw the look on her face. "You okay?"

Lauren simply stared at him, thoughts spinning in every which direction. Meg. Meg Roberts. Meg had a sister named Sarah. Meg also had a sister whose husband played Major League Baseball. Was it possibly the same Sarah . . . Boone's Sarah . . .

"What's wrong?" Boone reached out, grabbed her wrist. "You feeling faint?"

She shook her head, but truthfully, she *was* feeling a little faint. As well as stricken. Had she . . . had she . . . been lusting after Meg's sister's husband?

Oh God.

"I think . . ." Lauren drew an unsteady breath. "I think I've met your wife."

Boone's hand fell away. "Sarah?"

Lauren nodded. "Yes. Back in April. Does she have a sister named Meg? Meg Roberts?"

"Yes." Boone looked dumbfounded. "Where did you meet Sarah?"

"At Jack's funeral reception. I catered it. With my sister."

"You know Meg and Jack, then?"

"I used to work with Meg a lot when she handled PR for Dark Horse Winery, and we also did some parties for the Robertses. It was surreal returning to their house for the funeral reception."

"I still can't believe Jack's gone. He died just days after my mother-in-law's funeral. Sarah was there at Meg's when it happened."

"I remember your wife from the reception. We talked for a little bit when I was giving the bartender a break. Sarah's beautiful, and funny."

"She is," he agreed.

"Boss, order up!" José shouted from the kitchen.

Lauren carried plates to customers, refilled coffees, and then took care of two different customers at the cash register before grabbing Boone's breakfast from under the warmer.

She placed the steak and eggs in front of him. "Let me know if it's overdone. José's been overcooking the steaks lately."

"Will do," Boone answered, picking up the steak sauce. But then he hesitated. "Steir likes you," he said bluntly. "I think you should give him a chance."

"Has he ever been married?"

"No. But he was with his former girlfriend for three years. They lived together for a couple of those years, and the relationship ended last February."

"Do you know what happened between them?"

Boone shook his head. "I do know she'd like to get back together. She attends games sometimes. Hangs out at the nightclubs some of the players go to, hoping to attract Chris's attention."

"Does it work?"

"Chris doesn't go out much. And when he does, he's not into

hooking up. Not to say he's a choirboy. But as men go, he's pretty decent."

"What? So the rumors aren't true? You ballplayers aren't all easy?"

Boone was supposed to laugh. She'd been outrageous just to make him laugh. But he gave her an odd look and then shook his head. "Nope," he said quietly, wearily, cutting into the steak. "Not that Sarah believes me."

Seventeen

S arah had dinner ready for Boone when he returned from the park. The A's won, 6–4, and Boone had called as he left the Coliseum, letting her know he'd be home in thirty minutes or so.

The kids were both in bed when he walked in, and she'd lit candles all over the house and dimmed the lights, and greeted him in a pink, floaty sundress he'd bought for her a couple of years ago and some gold dangly earrings that made her feel like a harem girl.

"Wow," he said, dropping his duffel bag by the door and glancing around the entry and the sunken living room glowing with candlelight. "What's the special occasion?"

"It's an early Happy Father's Day dinner," she said, smiling, bringing him his favorite drink, Jack Daniel's on the rocks. So okay, it was in a juice glass because most of their dishes were still packed, but Boone wouldn't mind.

She was right. He smiled and kissed her. "Lucky me," he said.

She smiled as he took a long drink from his glass. He swallowed, shook his head, and then he was kissing her again, not the light kiss of a moment ago, but a deep, hungry kiss that tasted of whiskey and desire, a kiss that put fire in her veins and need in her heart.

Reaching up, she clasped his face, holding him closer, kissing him more deeply, giving him everything, just as she always had. Just as she always would—

"Yuck," Brennan said, making a gagging sound as he came down the stairs in his pajamas. "Gross."

Sarah pulled back, blushing, smiling, her gaze briefly meeting Boone's before looking at Brennan. "What are you doing up?"

"Hungry," he said, skinny and wide-eyed. "I need something to eat."

"You already had dinner, and you're supposed to be in bed," Sarah said, moving toward him and lightly swatting his backside, trying to get him back up the stairs. "It's now your dad's and my time."

Brennan danced past her and went to Boone. "Mom said you got a home run."

"I did," Boone said, scooping him up, giving him a hug before putting him back on his feet. "But you're supposed to be in bed."

"Can't I hang out with you?" he asked.

"No," Sarah answered. "It's eleven. You need to sleep—"

"Not tired," Brennan said. "And I'm hungry. Can I have a snack?"

Sarah exchanged glances with Boone. Boone shrugged. "Fine," she said, aware that the sexy moment was gone. "Come on. Let's see what we can find you in the kitchen."

Boone and Brennan followed her into the vast kitchen with its adobe tile floor, bright green ceramic-tiled counters, and white plaster walls. Horrible color scheme and an even worse layout. Boone sipped his whiskey as Sarah searched the still empty pantry for something Brennan could eat.

"Goldfish?" she asked him, holding up the bag of crackers.

Brennan shook his head.

"Granola bar?" she tried.

He shook his head again "Pop-Tarts?" he suggested.

"Not before bed," she answered.

"I'm *hungry*."

"A breakfast bar?"

"Yes," Boone said, answering for Brennan. He crossed behind his son, reached past Sarah, and grabbed the box, pulling out one foil-wrapped bar. "Here. Take this to your room. It's late. Go to bed."

Brennan grimaced at the bar in his hand and glanced over to the stove, where steaks were marinating. "Why can't I have a steak?"

"Because those are for your dad and me," Sarah said, crossing the kitchen to turn the oven broiler on.

"I didn't have steak for dinner," Brennan protested.

"No, you had mac-and-cheese, and turkey wieners. Now take your breakfast bar, give me a kiss, and go back to bed."

Brennan started to protest but caught sight of his dad's face and sighed, his shoulders slumping. "Fine," he said unhappily.

"Good night, Brennan," Boone said.

Brennan sighed again. "Good night." He gave his dad a hug, and then his mom, and head hanging, he headed for the stairs, looking utterly dejected.

Sarah watched him go, lips curving ruefully. "He does a good job making me feel guilty."

"No need to feel guilty," Boone answered, draining his glass and moving toward her, hands settling on her hips. He tipped her back, exposing her neck, and kissed his way from her earlobe to her collarbone as one hand slid under the filmy fabric of her skirt to the inside of her thigh.

Within a few minutes neither of them was even thinking of steak.

* * *

Lauren was at work the next morning, absolutely slammed, the waiting area filled with people and a crowd outside all waiting to get in because it was Father's Day and everyone wanted to treat their dad. Their wait time was running close to an hour and even the counter had been full all day.

Crazy.

But then, around ten, the crowd shifted by the entrance, making way, and there was Chris. It was, she thought, like the parting of the Red Sea.

Not that she was comparing Chris to Moses or anything . . .

"Morning," she said, placing a menu in front of him as he took a seat at the counter that had just been vacated.

"Morning," he answered.

"How did you get a seat that fast?" she asked him, gathering the previous customer's dirty coffee cup and beignet plate and wiping the counter clean.

"Offered a guy twenty bucks."

"No, seriously."

He looked her in the eye. "Seriously."

She held his gaze, searching his blue eyes for the truth. He didn't seem to have a problem with it. He just let her look and look.

"I didn't see you approach him," Lauren said, putting a hand on her hip.

"I didn't have to. I sent that kid—there, see him, in the white T-shirt, with his family by the door?—to ask. And he did."

"The kid did?"

"Yes."

"And the man gave up his seat because you offered him money?"

"He was done. Just lollygagging and licking the powdered sugar from his thumb."

"You can't give my customers money to leave."

"That's a valid point, and you should know, I didn't actually give him any money."

She sighed, slightly relieved. "Okay."

"Just an autograph."

"Chris!"

He smiled. "Half the people here are going to the Coliseum for today's one o'clock game, including the guy at the counter and the boy in the white T-shirt. They all know we won't have a game without me, so everybody's happy to help."

She leaned forward, leveled her gaze with his. "You do know that is the most absurd thing I've heard in years."

Chris smiled into her eyes. "A man's got to do what a man's got to do to win the woman he loves."

"I have never, ever met a bigger flirt in my life."

"I flirt with you because it's fun. And I might say outrageous things, but I do it to make you laugh, but I don't say anything I don't mean. And I fully intend to make you my woman. It's just a matter of time."

"No."

"Come on, darlin'. Work with me."

"Why me? Why not another waitress somewhere else?"

"I'm not interested in a waitress, Lauren. I'm interested in you. I saw you at the ballpark and I just"—his big hands lifted, an expansive gesture—"knew."

"Knew what?"

"That if you were single, you were meant for me."

"That's not love, Chris. That's lust."

The corner of his mouth tugged. "Then I fell in lust with you at first sight."

She glared into his blue, blue eyes. She was not amused and not going to fall for this any longer. She wouldn't smile back, and wouldn't listen to this banter.

He was trying to tease her, trying to make her laugh, and it was how he was trying to win her over. But she wouldn't be won. She wouldn't. The fact was, she didn't even like him. Didn't even like—

Bullshit.

She liked virtually everything about him. Lauren gulped air. Her heart raced. "You don't know anything about me . . . who I really am. I'm not all fun and games."

His jaw flexed, and a small muscle popped in his jaw, back by his ears, as he fought a smile. "Now, that surprises me."

Heat rushed through her. Heat and a funny, dizzying wash of hope. "I've had a lot of things happen . . . things that aren't nice and pretty."

"No one gets through life unscathed."

His deep voice shivered through her, low and male and sexy, making her insides jump and quiver and her skin tingle to life.

If he'd had a less appealing voice, maybe she could do a better job ignoring him . . .

Resisting him . . .

Chris's blue gaze met hers, held, holding so long that she forgot to breathe and her head became light.

"What?" he asked quietly. "What do you want to know? Ask. I'll tell you."

Her eyes searched his face. Strong cheekbones, a broad brow, thick jaw, square chin. A masculine face, but also open. "Boone said you were with your girlfriend for three years and it ended a couple of months ago."

"Yes."

"He also said she'd like to get back together."

"Sounds like Boone's doing a lot of talking."

She shrugged. "Tell me about her."

"She's . . . beautiful. A model." He ignored Lauren's arched eyebrows. "And ambitious. But Holly works hard, and deserves every good thing that comes her way."

Holly was her name . . .

A girlfriend named Holly.

"Are you still in love with her?" Lauren asked, feeling a squeeze in her chest. Why she'd feel anything was beyond her. She didn't like Chris . . . did she?

"No. Not like I did. I mean, I'll always care about her. But we're done. I'm done. Have no desire to get tangled up with her again."

"Things ended badly?"

"We had one of those hot and cold relationships, where it was either really good or bad, and after years of breaking up, getting back together, I just had enough. Not going to do it anymore. And I'm not blaming her. Might have been me."

The entire restaurant might as well have shrunk and disappeared. Lauren could see only Chris. "Why would it be you?" she whispered.

His blue eyes held hers, burning her, burning into her. "Because I started out wanting one thing but then realized I needed something else."

"What was that?"

"Need a best friend, not arm candy."

For a moment there was just silence. Lauren exhaled slowly, dizzy, dazed. Her heart was thumping and a lump the size of her fist filled her throat, making her want to cry.

At that moment she felt completely undone and she didn't even know why.

"Today," Chris said quietly, breaking the silence.

She looked at him blankly.

"Today, after the game. You and me," he added. "It's a one o'clock game, it'll be over early, you won't even be out late."

She swallowed hard and stared at him, lost, thinking she was already lost.

"Unless . . ." His lashes dropped as his gaze rested on her mouth, making her lips tingle and her skin feel far too sensitive.

"Yes?"

"You'd like to come to the game. Watch me play. Then go have dinner with me."

She didn't want to.

Not true.

She did.

But she had to work through this crazy Father's Day rush at the café, and then, once things had calmed down, she'd been toying with the idea of heading home to surprise her dad. It was Father's Day after all. She'd told her mom she'd try to come home if she could pull it off, but Mom wasn't to tell Dad in case Lauren couldn't. Lisa, the optimist, had made a dinner reservation for the five of them at six.

"I've got to work until fairly late this afternoon, so I'll miss the game. I'm sorry."

"And dinner?" Chris's blue gaze held hers, steady, so steady and calm.

He had nerves of steel, she thought. And that crazy confidence. She still didn't know quite what to think of him, but she wanted to know more. Was ready to learn more.

"I have to go home tonight. It's Father's Day."

"Where's home?"

"Napa."

"Nice."

She looked closely into his eyes, not sure what she was looking for. "Want to go with me after the game?"

If she'd surprised him, Chris didn't show it. He nodded once, decisively. "I'd like that. But the game could go extra innings."

"So we'll drive up whenever you're done."

He was studying her just as intently as she studied him. "Should I drive, or do you prefer to?"

"I've been up since four. So if you like driving . . . ?"

"I do. I'll drive. You can chill." He grabbed his phone from the front pocket of his jeans. "Give me your number and address, and I'll text you when I'm on the way."

* * *

Lauren couldn't believe she'd invited Chris home with her. Couldn't believe they were driving home now, and making great time. They were just twenty minutes from Napa and they'd probably miss dinner itself, but it looked as though they'd make it for dessert.

Lauren had texted Lisa the news at six, letting her know they were running late and not to count on them for dinner, but to save two seats for dessert.

Lisa had immediately texted back. *What? Who is coming with you!?! Tell me it's not the married man!!*

It's not, Lauren answered. *Someone new.*

Who??

It's just a first date, Lauren texted back. *Nothing serious.*

Lisa couldn't believe it. *You're bringing a first date home on Father's Day???*

Thought it'd be a good litmus test . . . don't you think?

Ok. Feeling sorry for the poor bastard.

Lauren was in the car when she got the message and giggled. Chris glanced at her, eyebrow lifting. "What?"

"My sister." Still smiling, Lauren slid her phone back into her purse. "She's worried about you."

"Why is that?"

"I've never brought anyone home before."

Chris's brow creased but he didn't look too concerned. "Never, as in . . . lately, or . . . ?"

"Never as in never. I don't date."

"I see."

Lauren looked at him, adding with great relish, "My parents think I'm gay."

His eyebrows lifted. "Are you?"

"No." She glanced down at her fingers, noting she'd torn a nail. She kept them short, but she'd still managed to rip one doing something or other at the café. "My dad doesn't like the A's either." She looked back up at Chris, feeling horribly evil, and unusually mischievous. "Maybe we don't say anything about your career?"

"Will do," he replied. And to his credit, he still sounded completely unruffled. "Anything else I should know?"

The lights of Napa gleamed in the distance. They weren't far now. Would be parking and entering Angèle, one of Lauren's favorite Napa restaurants, in minutes. Lauren rubbed her hands on her legs, suddenly nervous.

What was she doing bringing Chris home with her, unannounced like this, without them even going out to dinner first?

What was she thinking?

Was she trying to humiliate him? Herself? Make a point? And if so . . . to whom?

"Chris," she whispered, stomach starting to churn, panic building. "You asked if there was anything else you should know."

"Yes?" He glanced at her as the GPS changed screens, showing him that he'd be turning soon. They were almost there.

Her belly flipped, and flipped again. "There's actually a lot."

"Okay."

"I probably should have told you before . . ."

"Is your husband going to be there?"

She laughed, just as he'd intended. "Not married. Never have been."

"Okay."

Lauren shifted in her seat, her gaze fixed on Chris. "Never married," she repeated, "but I had a son."

She waited for some reaction. Chris remained silent, but she could tell he was listening.

Lauren pressed on. "Got pregnant in high school. Kept him. Raised him with my family's help." Her fingers curled into her palms. "He would have been a senior this year. Would have graduated last—" She was unable to finish the sentence.

Would have graduated last week.

Would have been something seeing him in his cap and gown.

The school remembered him anyway. Someone in the community had funded a scholarship in his name.

"Would have," Chris said quietly.

She nodded. "He died last June."

"How?"

"Car accident." She swallowed hard. "Two other kids died with him. And the fourth was left paralyzed."

It wasn't dark yet, just the pale gold and lavender of twilight, and she could see Chris's face, his features set, mouth firm.

Her heart ached. Everything in her felt tender and bruised. "I moved to Alameda last September, needing to get away from Napa. But Napa is still home. It'll always be home. But it's hard coming back, so I don't do it often."

"Yet you're coming back tonight," Chris said.

"Trying to step up for my family. Be there for them again . . . as much as I can."

"I bet you were a great mom."

It was the last thing she'd expected him to say, and she blinked, holding back tears. "He was amazing. Really smart. And talented. And sweet." She struggled to keep control. "It's been . . . hard . . . trying to . . . move on . . . without him."

Chris didn't immediately reply. A minute passed before he reached for her hand, lifted it to his lips, and kissed her palm, sending sharp darts of sensation up through her arm.

"You're doing good, darlin'," he said. "Just keep doing what you're doing. One foot in front of the other, and you'll get there."

Lauren's family was seated at a table in the corner of the restaurant by the window overlooking the river. The interior was dim. Candles flickered on tables, reflecting off the glass.

Lisa spotted Lauren before they'd even woven their way

through the crowded floor to the table, and she jumped up, grinning.

"You're here!" she exclaimed, moving toward Lauren and giving her a hug. "Holy shit," she whispered in Lauren's ear, clearly approving of Chris, before turning toward him and introducing herself. "I'm Lisa," she said, smiling up at him, offering her hand. "Lauren's big sister."

"I've heard a lot about you," Chris answered, taking her hand but then leaning down to kiss her cheek. "It's nice to meet you."

Lisa gestured to her husband. "Matthieu, my husband."

"I'm Chris," he replied, shaking Matthieu's hand.

"Rick Summer," Lauren's dad said gruffly. "My wife, Candace."

"Candy," Lauren's mom corrected.

"Chris," Chris repeated, shaking more hands.

The baby let out a wail from her car seat in the corner.

"And that's Audrey," Lisa added, before gesturing to the table. "Now come sit. We're so happy you're here!"

For the next hour, over coffee and dessert, Lisa and Dad peppered Chris with questions.

"So what do you do, Chris?" her father asked, almost immediately.

"I'm finishing school," Chris said easily. "Earning my master's in mechanical engineering."

"Where?" her dad asked, eyes narrowed.

"At Cal," Chris answered, giving the nickname for Berkeley, the first university founded in the University of California system. "My undergraduate degree was from UT Austin."

"Mechanical engineering there, too?"

Chris nodded.

"You're Texan?" Dad persisted, drumming his fingers on the table, expression brooding.

Chris wasn't fazed. "No. Was raised outside Phoenix. My dad's parents are from Texas, though."

Dad looked from Lauren to Chris and back again. "So how long have you two been dating?"

Chris glanced at Lauren, took her hand. "Not long," he said, smiling into her eyes. "But I've been chasing her awhile."

Lauren's face burned, cheeks hot, and shyly she glanced down at their hands. She liked the way her hand felt in his. Liked the way his fingers curved around hers. She felt surprisingly good. Warm. Safe.

"What do you mean, chasing her?" Dad demanded. "She wouldn't go out with you?"

Chris grinned lazily. "Nope. Didn't want to have anything to do with me."

"You should have left her alone, then," Dad muttered.

"Dad!" Lisa and Lauren exclaimed at the same time.

Matthieu glanced away, trying not to laugh. Mom appeared mortified.

But Dad shrugged, unfazed. "What? I'm not allowed to ask?"

Lauren's face still felt too hot. "You're being a little aggressive with the questions, Dad. Don't you think?"

Her dad ignored her. "Chris, do you mind?" he asked.

Chris grinned, shook his head. "Nope."

"See?" Her dad sat back, victorious.

Mom changed the subject then by asking Lauren about business at Mama's Café, which led to a discussion about business at Summer Bakery & Café, which led to further discussion about the future of the Napa restaurant.

It was Lisa who put a stop to all the speculation about the Napa café's future. "This doesn't have to be decided now," she said. "And it's no one's business but Lauren's and mine, and oh, maybe that's because it's our business."

"But your sister isn't even here, helping you out anymore," Dad retorted, clearly in one of his more confrontational moods.

"But once again, that's none of your business, Dad," Lisa said gently but firmly, looking him in the eye. "I went into business with Lauren, not you. Any money you loaned us to start the business was paid back ten years ago, and I have always been totally supportive of Lauren going to Alameda and working at Mama's. If, and when, we're ready to sell, we'll sell. Until then, we won't. So there's no point in continuing this conversation because it's not a group decision, it's a Lauren and Lisa decision."

Dad mumbled grumpily and shuffled his feet. Mom looked at her watch. Then Lisa looked at her iPhone. "We probably should go," she said, sounding regretful. "Audrey's going to need to eat and I'd just as soon nurse her at home."

They were all on their feet then, gathering purses and shawls. Lauren handed her dad a wrapped box. "For you to open at home," she said. "Happy Father's Day," she added, giving him a kiss.

They walked out together, and on the curb her dad shook Chris's hand and then gave Lauren a hug. "Be smart," he said gruffly, holding her close, his beard-roughened cheek grazing hers. "I don't want to see you hurt."

"I understand," she answered, kissing him back.

He still held her. "And just so you don't think you've pulled anything over on me, I know exactly who Chris Steir is." He let her go, brows lifting. "And I still don't like the Athletics."

Lauren laughed, hard. "Good night, Dad."

His stern expression eased. "Good night, sweetheart." He gave Chris a half nod.

Chris held Lauren's hand as they walked the half block to his car. "Your dad reminds me of my dad," he said. "Tough guy."

"Yeah. He's . . . opinionated."

"He's entitled to be."

Chris opened the door for her, and she stepped up into the

passenger seat of his black SUV. It was a new one, a luxury model, Cadillac or something like that, with lots of chrome and all the windows tinted black. "I have to be honest," she said as he climbed in on his side. "This doesn't seem like the kind of car you'd drive."

"No? What kind of car did you think I'd drive?"

"A sports car. Something red, fast."

"Actually, this isn't my car. I borrowed it from Boone for the night."

She turned in her seat, faced him. "This is Boone's car?"

He nodded, smiling shamefacedly. "I have a car—it's a '60 Cadillac, big fins, bullet grille, hardtop, sweetest paint job ever— and I baby the heck out of it."

"You were afraid to drive it to Napa?"

"No. It just wouldn't start when the game was over. And so I told Boone I needed his car and he gave me his keys."

"You left him with a car that wouldn't start?"

"Oh, I didn't give him my keys. My car is still in the team parking lot. Walker went home with his family." He saw her face. "It's okay. His wife was there, and she has a car, and her whole family was there, too. Thirteen or fourteen of them. So he's fine. Trust me."

"What about tomorrow's game?"

"We're off tomorrow. He's good." Chris reached out, caressed a strand of her hair. "We're good."

Lauren watched him start to type an address into the GPS. "Do we have to go back right away?" she asked.

"No. Absolutely not. I just know you get up early every morning—"

"I'm taking tomorrow off."

He sat back. "So where do we go?"

"I'll show you my sister's and my restaurant, it's a block from here, and then I'll take you by our old place."

Chris didn't say much as Lauren walked him around Summer

Bakery & Café, just nodded and nodded again as she pointed out the bakery, the café, walked him back to the huge kitchen. An impressive kitchen. "It's beautiful," he said as she relocked the door and they returned to his car.

"Now I'll show you where we used to be," she said, giving him directions to First Street. "Go slow," she added as they approached the house. "There." She tapped his arm, pointed.

He braked in front of the white Victorian house with the red-brick path and the big front porch. The house was dark except for the pair of porch lights that flanked the front door.

"That's it," she said. "That was where our first restaurant was, in that little Victorian house. It was our grandma's house. She gave it to Lisa and me, and we turned it into a bakery and café, and Lisa and I lived in the back. With Blake."

"How old were you when you and Lisa opened the restaurant?"

"Twenty-two or twenty-three. Blake was four." She frowned, trying to remember. "I'm sure Blake was four. It's all kind of a blur now. So much has happened since then. It was so much work, getting started, but my mom and grandma helped so much. They were always around the first year or two, making sure things were okay. I don't think either of them thought Lisa and I would pull it off. We weren't great cooks back then, but we were young and stubborn."

"I bet you and Lisa have stories."

"So many stories," she agreed.

"She loves you a lot, doesn't she?"

"She's a great sister and still my best friend." Lauren stared out the car window at her old house, remembering the years there and the neighbors on this street. It was a close-knit community, but it'd been too close for her after Blake died. She couldn't handle the sympathy and pity, or even the cautious, kind smiles as people popped into the bakery to pick up a dozen dinner rolls, a loaf of warm cinnamon bread, or to order a special-occasion cake. Grief was a hard thing. It was also something she needed to do alone, away from her family and the community that had always rallied around her.

"Do you want to go inside?" she asked abruptly.

Lauren hadn't been in the house since she moved. Mom went over once a week. Cleaned. Dusted. Watered the plants. Collected the mail. Lisa had told her that just recently. Lauren had been shocked, but it'd also made sense. Mom went to the cemetery to take care of Blake. Mom came to the house to take care of Lauren. It was her way of nurturing. Her way to stay connected.

"I'd love to," he said.

He parked, and they walked up the brick path. Lauren's stomach hurt as she unlocked the front door. He followed her in and she turned on lights. The front of the house still looked like a business. Big, open areas, empty areas where tables used to be. A counter. A bakery display cabinet. An old cash register.

Her stomach knotted again. "Not very fancy," she said apologetically.

"Homey," he said.

She nodded and led the way through the kitchen and into the back, where she and Blake had lived. Lauren rattled off the names of the rooms as she went. "Our tiny kitchen. Cozy family room. Then just the two bedrooms and our bath. Small, isn't it?"

"It's your home."

She nodded, opening her bedroom door, gesturing to the old-fashioned bedroom set. "My bedroom." She looked up into his face. "It was Grandma's furniture. But I kept it. I like it."

"Sweet."

She spotted the framed oval photograph of her holding baby Blake on the dresser. It was taken on her first Mother's Day. She looked like a kid. But then, she had been just a kid.

Lauren backed out of the room, Chris followed, and she moved down the hall to Blake's room. Carefully she pushed the door open. Moonlight fell through the small window onto the twin bed, the covers smooth, pillows plump, his pitcher's glove nestled against the lower pillow.

Gone. Still gone.

It'd been a year now. He wasn't coming back.

She flicked the light switch, swallowed hard as the overhead light revealed the framed jerseys on the wall, and the baseball pennants and the poster Blake had gotten signed at a game his Aunt Lisa had taken him to when he was thirteen.

"He liked the A's," Chris said quietly.

She battled to breathe. "Loved them."

Chris spotted the glove on the bed. "He played?"

She nodded. "A pitcher."

Chris looked at her then, his blue gaze resting intently on her face. "You don't have to do this."

Lauren realized then she'd been holding her breath and she exhaled in a rush, dizzy and terrified, but also relieved. She hadn't lost it yet. Hadn't screamed or fainted or died. No. She was still here, standing calmly. "I don't come to the house. Don't open this door. Maybe I should, though. It makes it more . . . real."

"He was real."

"And then gone. That's the part I can't wrap my head around."

"He liked Catfish Hunter," Chris said, pointing to a poster at the wall.

Lauren smiled crookedly. "Blake's favorite player."

"Good man." Chris craned his head from the doorway, trying to see everything.

"You can go in," Lauren said. "It's okay."

"You're sure?"

"Yes."

She watched him enter and walk slowly around the perimeter, examining the sports memorabilia, both of professional teams and Blake's own trophies and team photos. She saw him linger before a picture of Blake on the mound. It'd been taken by a professional photographer a year ago last April, two months before the accident, and had run in a *San Francisco Chronicle* article about the area's most promising athletes.

It was a good shot of Blake, in full windup. But what she loved about the picture wasn't the pose; it was his expression.

Focused. Fierce. Alive.

And just like that her heart seized, and she looked away, closing her eyes, holding back tears.

Remembering how she'd begged God to give him back. Remembering all the things she'd offered in exchange for one more chance to speak to him. One more chance to hold him. One more chance to tuck him in, tell him good night.

"I don't think I could handle it," Chris said bluntly, breaking the silence. "Not if it'd been my son."

Lauren walked to the bed, touched the thick, quilted bedspread. "I don't know that I *have* handled it. I've run away . . . ignored it . . . denied it . . ."

"You did what you had to do."

"It about killed me. Worst, hardest thing I've ever done. And it's not over yet."

Chris's mouth compressed. "It might not ever be over, darlin'."

She nodded, agreeing with him. At least he didn't sound as if he was condemning her. So many people wanted to rush grief. They wanted the uncomfortable part over. "I honestly didn't think I'd survive the pain. But it's been a year, and I'm still here."

Her fingers brushed across the quilt again, feeling the stitches and seams.

Good night, buddy.

Good night, Mama.

Sleep good, baby boy.

You, too, Mama.

And then the kisses, and the thin arms wrapping around her neck, squeezing tight. He kissed her good night every night until he died. Not on the lips, of course. He stopped doing that in third grade, but on the cheek, or the top of her head once he was six-teen as he took off to join friends somewhere.

Be careful, Blake.

I'm always careful, Mom.

I mean it, Blake.

I know you do, Mom.

I couldn't stand it if anything ever happened—

Easy, Drama Mom. Nothing's going to happen . . .

"Lauren?"

Chris said her name gently, but she jumped even so, having forgotten he was there. She looked at him, eyes wide.

"Do you want to stay here tonight?" he asked.

Lauren glanced around the room, tears filling her eyes at the thought of leaving, but there was no way she could stay. It was still too much. The room felt like Blake and made her want him, need him. She wiped her eyes. "No. Let's go."

They stepped out, and she turned off the light and headed to the front door, but then Lauren held up her hand, asked Chris to wait, and she ran back to Blake's room and grabbed his leather glove from the pillow on his bed.

She returned to Chris, the glove pressed to her chest. "Maybe I'll just take this. You don't think he'd mind if I borrowed it, do you?"

Chris pulled her to him and held her close, the glove between them. He kissed her forehead, and then her cheek, and then the corner of her mouth, before finally kissing her sweetly, gently on the lips. "I don't think he'd mind at all," he whispered. "In fact, he's probably very glad."

Eighteen

Sarah glanced at the calendar as she paid her bills online. Hard to believe they'd been in the East Bay a month now.

June had come and gone. As had the Fourth of July. Boone had been home for the Fourth, with a game at the Coliseum, and then there had been a break for the All-Star Game, which had been held this year at Kauffman Stadium in Kansas City.

Boone hadn't played in an All-Star Game for four years, but Sarah was glad to have him home for those days, and discovering that the house in Capitola was free, they headed as a family to the beach for three nights.

It felt like a real vacation. And they felt like a real family. A normal family. During the day they soaked up the sun, and then at night, sunburned and exhausted from all the playing, everyone slept well.

Sarah had loved watching Boone with the kids on the beach, building sand castles with Ella and jumping waves with Brennan. Sarah lounged on her towel, working on her tan, a wine cooler in the plastic cup beside her.

Boone had teased her about drinking early, but then reaped the benefits when they had torrid sex in the master bedroom while the kids ate peanut butter and jelly sandwiches and colored at the dining room table.

But then, the entire trip to Capitola was filled with quickies and make-out sessions. On Wednesday they had sex so many times that Sarah stopped counting her orgasms after five, aware that she was just being greedy.

But God, it'd felt good to be with him, and love him, and hug him, and play with him. Boone was her best friend and this little break had been exactly what she needed . . . a chance to relax, escape the stress of moving and adjusting to a new city and new team.

Boone had enjoyed the trip to Capitola, too.

"That was fun," he'd said as they drove home Thursday afternoon, holding her hand as he steered with his left, comfortable with the tight curves on Highway 17 in his big black SUV. He didn't drive the mountain pass often but he was a good driver, and he loved this car. Loved his big cars . . .

And just like that, Sarah found herself thinking of that woman he'd hooked up with. He'd had a big SUV then, too. And they'd done it in the car . . .

Sarah had pulled her hand free from Boone's and put it to her mouth, suddenly sick.

Why had she thought of that? She hated remembering! Stupid brain. Stupid thought process. If only she could just take a pill and forget . . . forget all the bad stuff . . .

"Carsick?" Boone had asked, slowing down and moving to the right lane. Ever since they'd had Brennan, Sarah had been motion sensitive. "I can pull over."

"I'm all right," she'd answered, taking a quick breath and sitting taller as the tall evergreens whizzed past them on the side of the road.

"Don't look around. Stare straight ahead," he'd said, shooting her another concerned glance. "We'll be out of this soon."

"It's all right, babe." She'd swallowed, trying to push away the bad memories and reclaim the good. She pictured the beach house and the buttermilk pancakes she'd made that morning. Pictured them eating pizza on the beach last night. Pictured all four of them yesterday working so hard to decorate Ella's sand castle with broken shells, sea glass, and pebbles. She tried to feel the bright, hot sun and smell the tang of salt and hear the cry of seagulls over the crashing waves . . .

It's what Mom had always done. Remember the positives, focus on the positives, and almost always, the positives outweighed the bad.

And in Sarah's case, it was true. She loved her family and she wasn't going to let something that had happened three years ago destroy their happiness now

Sarah tore open an envelope from the electric company, glanced at the bill, pleased to see it was less than what they'd spent in Florida with all their air-conditioning. They used air conditioners here, but not as much, and that might be the only good thing about their rental house.

It was just so ugly on the inside.

She'd known the décor was tired when she'd previewed it, but now, living in it, she found it hard to like it. Virtually every room needed a makeover.

The owners were still hoping the Walkers would buy the place. Not a chance.

Sunday morning, Lauren's alarm went off at four. She opened her eyes with difficulty, not wanting to wake up so early anymore. Not wanting to work her weird hours.

It'd be nice to have a normal job . . . eight to five, or something like that. It'd be nice to be free every evening and hang out with Chris . . .

Not that Chris was free every evening.

Not that Chris was ever free evenings.

Not that Chris was even home. In fact, he'd been gone all weekend, in Minneapolis for a series against the Twins. And before that, he'd been in Kansas City for the All-Star Game. He'd played well, too, and he'd texted her after the game saying that next year he was bringing her with him.

Next year.

She hadn't known what to think when she read the message, but later, after the shock wore off, she liked it. Liked it a lot.

Liked him a lot. And he was good about texting and calling and he'd made her install Skype on her phone, but she hadn't installed it right, so he promised to look at it when he returned.

Then he sent her flowers, masses of red roses, to the café, with a card saying he didn't want her to think he'd forgotten her.

She'd laughed and tucked the card into her apron and had later scolded him for the extravagance, but secretly, she loved the flowers.

She'd never received flowers before . . . at least, not like this. Lush, romantic, long-stemmed roses. Dozens of them. It was a statement, Bette had said.

Lauren didn't think she cared about roses or statements, but they mattered. Because he was making her feel as if she mattered. And it was doing something to her heart, making it skip . . . making it smile . . .

She'd forgotten hearts could smile.

Lauren stepped into the shower, turned the water on cold to stop thinking about Chris. They'd had dates, lots of them, and she'd stayed at his place, and they'd made out, a lot, but hadn't gone all the way. Come close a couple of times. And she'd come many times. But then, how could she not when Chris knew just what to do with his hands and tongue?

She was ready to do more.

Ready to make love.

And that's why they'd waited. Chris didn't want to have sex with her. He wanted it to be more than intercourse, wanted to be sure it felt right, not just in her body but in her heart and head.

She'd teased him for being old-fashioned. But truly, she was grateful. He was right, too. She needed the time to get to know him . . . her . . . them.

Out of the shower, Lauren blotted her hair and began blow-drying it. She was still drying it when a text came in on her phone.

Hey baby, hope you'll have a good day. Xoxox

Lauren smiled. *You too*, she answered.

He texted right back. *That was really romantic, darlin'. Thank you.*

She grinned, typed, *What should I have said, Steir?*

She had to wait a moment for his answer. *I want you and miss you. I am crazy about you. You are the hottest, sexiest man on earth and I can't wait for you to return and make sweet love to me.*

Lauren laughed, texted back. *But that would not be true.*

Which part? he asked.

The hottest, sexiest man on earth part. It should have read the hottest, sexiest man in the universe.

Damn girl, I'm rock hard right now.

Stier, not romantic.

It's better if I'm soft?

Lauren spluttered, texted *No!* before putting down her phone. She dried her hair for another minute or two, smiling into the mirror, and caught her reflection.

Her lips were curved, her eyes crinkled, her entire face glowing. She looked happy.

She looked . . . she looked as if she was in love.

Because she was.

Lauren put down the blow-dryer. Sent one more text. *Thank you for making me laugh again.*

His reply was immediate. *It's just going to keep getting better.*

I think I like you a lot, Steir.

I think I like you more.

You don't know.

I know what I know.

She paused, chewed on her lip, before texting *What do you know?*

That we're good together. You & me. It works.

And that, she thought, holding the phone in her hands, was the best text of all.

B oone was home from the three-day road trip, having arrived late the night before. Sarah woke up with his hands sliding slowly up her abdomen to cup her breasts, and she reached for him. They made love at two in the morning, and there was no urgency, no sound, just warmth, desire, love, skin.

When she fell back asleep, she was tucked into his arms, against his chest, and her last thought before sliding back to sleep was that she couldn't love anyone more than she loved him.

It was late morning now, and Boone was downstairs in the family room, sprawled on the big leather sofa with Ella leaning against him in a pink princess costume, watching one of her Disney princess movies. So sweet, Sarah thought, carrying freshly laundered, folded towels back up the stairs to each of the bathrooms.

She set three in the kids' bathroom and carried four to the master bath, shuddering as she exited from her "emerald" bathroom to her rose bedroom. Just a rental, she reminded herself, adjusting the duvet on the bed and then the pillows at the head.

Turning to leave, she spotted Boone's iPad on the nightstand, open. She moved to close the cover, saw his e-mail program was open. He never left it open.

It was through reading his e-mail that she'd discovered he was cheating.

Sarah reached for the iPad, scanning his in-box, and then realized what she was doing.

She stopped. Looked up. Away.

Did she really want to do this?

Know this?

Did she want to open herself to whatever it'd be . . . good or bad?

Because what she discovered wouldn't satisfy her. It wouldn't be enough. It was never enough. She knew. She'd been here, in this position, before.

She used to patrol his e-mail, patrol his life.

It made her sick. Made her hate him.

She didn't want to hate him.

And yet . . . it'd be nice to know there was nothing to worry about. Reassuring to know there was no one but her.

And yet . . . it wasn't that simple. It was never that simple. If she didn't find something in his in-box, she'd go to his sent box. And if she couldn't find anything there, she'd check trash. She'd check drafts. She'd check downloads for photos. She'd check—snoop, dig—until she found something, anything, and then she'd be right back in hell again.

She knew, because this is what she did. It's how she'd dealt with his affair. Spying. Monitoring. Policing.

But it never helped. It never resulted in anything good. She'd always find something, even if Boone hadn't initiated contact. Girls would send photos of themselves. Fan mail. Sexy fan mail. And there was so much of it.

No, she didn't need to climb back on the roller coaster. Didn't want to doubt him. Hate him. Hate herself.

And his affair did make her hate herself because she loved him, needed him, more than she loved herself.

More than she loved her self-respect.

More than she loved her sanity.

Sarah swiftly set the iPad down and walked away.

But as she went downstairs, the tight panicky feeling had settled into her chest and the rest of her had gone cold.

Fear. Anxiety. Dread.

She stopped in the hall and looked at him on the couch, Ella nestled against his chest, her arm wrapped confidently around his neck.

How lucky she was . . .

Sarah felt a wave of envy. She'd give anything to be Ella. She'd give anything to feel that safe and secure with Boone.

She moved on, back to the laundry room, and tears filled her eyes as she started a new load of wash.

I want to feel safe like that.

I want to feel loved like that.

I want—

"Hon?" It was Boone, in the doorway, Ella in his arms.

She straightened, knocking away tears. "Yes?"

"You okay?"

"Yeah. Got something in my eye. Lint or dust. It's fine." She forced a smile. "Are you hungry? Can I make you something before you go to the park?"

"No, that's okay. I'll grab something on the way." He moved toward her, putting Ella into her arms, freeing himself.

Sarah didn't like it. Didn't like that he was leaving already, didn't like that he would go out and eat rather than stay and eat with her. "I bought groceries yesterday. Have food—"

"I've got my routine." He grimaced. "It's working."

"I would love to make you a meal. Makes me feel good to take care of you."

"Babe, it's not personal, but I'm in a groove, and right now, since I'm hitting well, I'd just as soon not do anything that would jinx it."

"I've never known you to be that superstitious."

"Not going to take any risks," he said, closing the distance, kissing her. "But thank you. I appreciate it." And then he was gone, jogging upstairs to retrieve his bag and head out.

*D*on't be paranoid, Sarah told herself, after Boone left.

Don't be paranoid, she silently repeated, making it her mantra as she sat outside by the pool with Kit. Kit looked good, too, Sarah thought. She was playing on the steps with Ella while Sarah swam in the deep end with Brennan.

Brennan was a good swimmer. He'd learned to swim young, and he really liked the water. Sarah wondered if he'd enjoy being on a swim team. He couldn't do the butterfly yet, and his breaststroke was rough, but he could learn. Sarah made a mental note to look into it.

"How are things with Jude?" she asked, swimming back to the steps to avoid being splashed by Brennan, who was now doing cannonballs off the diving board.

"Good. His job has him working graveyard, and I'm teaching summer school, but I'm almost done, and he's hoping to get a week off in August so we can go on vacation." Kit sat lower in the water to stay cool. "I think we'll go to Texas."

"Texas?"

Kit floated up. "Go see Delilah." She saw Sarah's puzzled expression. "My student. Her stepdad was the one who was really abusive."

"That's right. He and her mother left her. Can't imagine just abandoning your child." Sarah reached for Ella and pushed soggy dark brown hair from her eyes. Ella was not as comfortable in the water as her brother. Somehow, in the pool, she always managed to resemble a drowned rat. "How is your student doing?"

"Getting by. Still hoping her mom will send for her. I hope her mom doesn't. Delilah's better with Shey and Dane. They're stable and loving and Delilah's safe there. They won't let anything happen to her."

"Where do you think her mom is?"

Kit shook her head. "I don't know. But we did learn that her stepdad, Howard, isn't working for Chevron anymore. Chevron won't talk about it, but they let him go."

"So you'll go to Texas, see Delilah . . . anything else you plan to do while there?"

"We're going to pick up a car at the airport, so we thought we'd do some exploring. Visit Fort Worth, drive down to Austin, see the Hill Country, end up in San Antonio. I've never been to San Antonio. Neither has Jude. We thought it'd be a fun hol—" Kit broke off, shrugged, smiling. "Fun."

Sarah studied her sister's pink face. Kit was literally glowing with happiness. "You're happy with him?"

Kit nodded, smile deepening, her blue eyes shining. "Yeah."

"He's sooooo different from you."

"But that's what makes it work. I already know all about books and rules and discipline. But I've never been the rebel. Never dated a rebel. And with him, I get to see into a different world, a new world, and it's exciting."

"You don't think there's going to be a point when you begin to miss your world?"

"But I still *have* my world. I'm still Kit Brennan, teacher; Kit Brennan, Sarah's sister. I have my house and my books and my energy-efficient car. And now I have the bad boy, too." Dimples fluttered at her mouth. "And he's not that bad, Sarah. He's actually really good."

"Humph." But Sarah was smiling and her heart felt tender. She might sound skeptical but she was actually happy for Kit. Happy that Kit was glowing and shining and living life. "Just know that if it ever goes south, I'm here for you." She paused, glancing up at the massive stucco house next to them. "Literally. Just down the street."

Kit laughed, and Ella started laughing, too, just for the pleasure of it.

And then Brennan cannonballed off the side of the pool, soaking everyone.

Boys.

That evening Sarah took the kids to the game against the Rangers, having texted Boone after they got out of the pool, asking him to put them on the pass list. She invited Kit to go with them, but Kit had other commitments, and so the three of them headed to the park early so they could watch warm-ups, and Brennan and Ella could go down to the field and wave to their daddy.

Boone spotted the kids, came to the fence, and talked to them, only to be mobbed by a dozen other kids.

He talked to all the kids and signed autographs for a few minutes before heading back to the cage for some additional batting practice.

Sarah and the kids took their seats, and Sarah had butterflies as the national anthem played. She still got nervous for him, and it was here, when sitting high in the stands with thirty thousand cheering fans, that she felt the pressure Boone lived with daily.

Fans weren't tolerant.

Fans quickly stopped cheering and starting booing and jeering if a player disappointed.

The game wasn't just physical. It was mental. And that's what separated the boys from the men. Boone had lasted because he was strong, tough. He was careful about allowing noise to enter his head. Careful to surround himself with the right people, positive people, and he'd learned to deflect the rest.

She liked that about him. And that trait of focusing on

positives and eliminating negatives had attracted her to him in the
first place.

Well, that and his beautiful face.

But humor aside, the athlete in her admired his drive, focus,
and discipline. She knew from playing collegiate sports that success wasn't just about what you did on the court or field during a
game, but about your commitment to the game even when you
weren't playing. It impacted everything. What you ate and drank,
how much you slept, how hard you trained.

And Boone was on fire tonight, going two-for-two and getting
ready to bat again when Sarah's phone buzzed with a text and
Ella announced she had to go to the bathroom.

"But Daddy's going to bat," Sarah said, glancing at the score-
board, then at Boone, who was now on deck, as she reached for
her phone. Bottom of the fifth. Two outs. Number seven for the
Athletics, Stier, was at bat. Two strikes, two balls. The fans were
on their feet, chanting his name. Steir, Steir, Steir. Apparently
Steir was a crowd favorite.

The pitcher wound up, threw, but lost control, striking Steir in
the shoulder. Steir dropped the bat, briefly doubling over. The
entire A's bench were on their feet, even as the Rangers' pitcher
ran toward him, apologizing. Steir nodded and jogged toward
first.

The players on the bench hesitated. The pitcher and catcher
talked. The pitcher returned to the mound. The A's sat back
down.

Fight averted.

Sarah glanced down at her phone as she heard Boone's name
called. He walked toward home plate.

She blinked as she read the message, not understanding. She
read it again. The text was from Olivia, one of the wives from
Tampa Bay.

Since you were friends with Alyssa, Olivia wrote, *I thought
you'd want to know Alyssa and Jeff are getting a divorce.*

Sarah shook her head. No way. There was just no way. She texted Olivia back even as the announcer called strike one.

What?? Why?? Sarah typed.

Alyssa found out he was cheating on her.

Sarah's heart fell, plummeting so hard and fast she nearly threw up. *With who?*

Are you kidding me?!? Who didn't he sleep with?

No, I don't believe it. Sarah's fingers trembled as she typed.

Strike two, the announced called.

Come on, Olivia wrote. *Everyone knew. Jeff never could keep his dick in his pants.*

Did this happen on the road?

It happened everywhere. He'd put these girls he was tapping on the pass list for home games. TJ said one of them sat next to Alyssa one game and she couldn't stop laughing cuz she was sitting next to her boyfriend's wife.

Sarah couldn't read more, didn't want to know more, and she turned off her phone and put it in her purse.

Ella danced back and forth. "I have to go, Mama, I have to go bad!"

Sarah nodded, took Ella's head in her hands, holding it tightly.

Dear God, don't let that be Boone.

Dear God, don't let him be like that.

Dear God, don't let him humiliate us all like that.

Strike three, the announcer called. The fans booed the umpire, shouting it should have been a ball. Brennan booed with them.

Boone tucked the bat under his arm and walked back to the dugout, peeling off his glove.

Sarah dragged Brennan with them to the bathroom. On the way back they stopped for ice cream. Sarah tried to concentrate on the game, but for the next couple of innings she could barely see the field, unable to focus.

They ended up leaving at the top of the seventh. Ella didn't mind. Brennan did. Sarah promised him a treat when they got

home, and then, as she drove him, wondering what she'd give
him . . .

Ella fell asleep in the car. Sarah put her to bed when they got
back to the house then found a minibag of M&M's for Brennan.
He ate them in his bed, munching away, leaning against his night-
light pillow, which glowed with different colors every few seconds.

"Good night, bud," Sarah said, kissing his forehead and leaving his room, making sure to keep his door open a crack.

In her room, she sat down at the foot of her bed, numb. She
chewed on her thumb, shocked.

Horrified.

Jeff and Alyssa were so sweet together. Alyssa was so devoted
to him. Jeff was a nice guy. A good guy. A great neighbor. Boone's
friend.

Sarah stripped, stepped into shorts and tugged on a camisole,
and climbed into bed. She didn't sleep, though.

She kept thinking about Alyssa. And Jeff. And the fact that
Jeff apparently had cheated on Alyssa right and left.

Boone had to have known. So why hadn't he told her?

Sarah was still awake when he came home three hours later.
She looked at the clock. Midnight. Her stomach hurt. It was late.
She knew the game hadn't gone extra innings. She'd left bed and
checked her computer to be sure.

Now she listened to him change in the hideous green bathroom. Listened as he turned out the light, opened the door,
walked to the bed in the dark.

He climbed into bed, mashed up a pillow under his head. He'd
brushed his teeth and used mouthwash, but she could still smell
alcohol on him. He'd been out in a bar. Drinking . . .

And doing God only knew what else . . .

Sarah's stomach churned, spewing acid. She swallowed,
and swallowed again, hating where her imagination was taking her.

* * *

The next morning, after Boone woke up and came downstairs, Sarah poured him a cup of coffee, doctored it with milk and sugar, and then handed it to him, asking if he'd heard about Alyssa and Jeff.

"Heard what?" he asked, taking a seat on one of the kitchen stools.

"They're divorcing."

Boone frowned. "No, I hadn't heard that. Who told you?"

"Olivia. Max Fenton's wife. She texted me last night."

"Have you talked to Alyssa?"

Sarah shook her head. "Wanted to talk to you first. See what you thought."

"I don't know. This is all news to me."

She leaned back against the counter. "Apparently he's been cheating on her. Olivia said everyone knew. That Jeff would even pick these girls on the pass list at home—"

"I don't know about that," Boone said, looking uncomfortable and rising from the stool.

Sarah crossed her arms, knuckles pressed to her ribs. "Would you tell me if you did know something?"

"About what?"

"You know what. About them. About him. About Jeff having affairs and making Alyssa look stupid."

"She doesn't look stupid."

"She does if everyone on the team knew her husband was screwing around with other women—"

"Why are you yelling at me?"

"I'm upset!"

"Baby, this isn't about us. We're not them. And we don't know what happened, and to be perfectly honest, I'm good with that."

She took a deep breath, lowered her voice. "I just can't believe Jeff would do that to her. I didn't think he was that kind of man."

Boone said nothing.

"Poor Alyssa." Sarah pressed her fist to her mouth, remembering her last conversation with her friend, sitting in the kitchen drinking wine, planning Alyssa's visit to California.

"I think you have to let it go," Boone said. "You're just going to make yourself crazy, and fretting about it, or fuming about it, won't change anything. It is what it is—"

"Which is *wrong*."

"But it's *not* your business."

"She's my friend."

"But it's her marriage. And who knows what happened, and why?"

Sarah's jaw jutted. "Olivia said he cheated, Boone, on Alyssa constantly."

"Olivia is a gossip. Even Max says his wife is a gossip."

"She might be a gossip, but if she says everyone on the team knew, she means it. And I have a feeling you knew, too, but you didn't tell me."

He said nothing, which just upset Sarah more.

"I can't believe it," she said under her breath. "Can't believe he'd do that to her, and I can't believe you wouldn't tell me."

A small muscle pulled in Boone's jaw. He exhaled slowly. "We've had a great couple of weeks . . . do we really want to go down this road?"

"What does that mean?"

"It means you're making a point—"

"I'm not."

"You are. You didn't think Jeff was the kind of man to cheat . . . whereas I am . . . ?"

"*No.*"

"Then what?"

"We're talking about Jeff and Alyssa."

"Are we?"

"Yes."

Boone gave her a long, searching look. "Sometimes I'm not so sure, babe."

He turned to leave, and Sarah stopped him, snaking an arm around his waist, feeling his warmth through his thin knit shirt, his lower back taut, thickly muscled like the rest of him.

She held on to him this morning out of love and desperation.

He must have felt it, too, because he pulled away from her, as if he couldn't wait to escape.

She didn't let go. "Don't be mad at me," she whispered. "This stuff scares me."

"But this stuff isn't us."

She nodded and lifted her lips for a kiss. He gave her one, a brief one, and then looking into her eyes, he kissed her again, his lips softening, giving the kiss heat.

Some of the cold, hard ice in her chest melted, and she pressed closer, craving comfort.

He knew how to make her feel good.

But he could also make her feel so bad.

"Got to go, babe," he said, easing back.

She looked at him, nodded, unable to smile.

"I'll see you after the game," he said.

She nodded again.

Boone gave her a good-bye pat on her ass and walked out.

He walked in.

Lauren straightened abruptly at the café counter, heart doing a quick double thump. God, he was gorgeous . . . and hers.

She smiled shyly as Chris sauntered toward her. "Hi," she said, nervous for no reason other than that she was excited, and he got her pulse going. "How's that shoulder? Heard you got a pretty nice bruise."

"It's sore, but whatever." He slid an arm around her waist and

pulled her up against him and kissed her, right in front of everyone. "So how are you, baby?"

"Good," she whispered, heart thumping like mad.

"You are so damn beautiful."

She blushed, grinned. "I should tell you to stop, but I like it."

He laughed, hugged her to him. "You're still coming to the game
tonight, right? It's the first game in our series against the Yankees."

Lauren's smile faded. "The Yankees?"

"Supposed to be a good series."

She hesitated. "I'm not sure I can make the game. I'm short on
waitstaff for closing. Can I meet you after?"

"Of course. No stress, darling." He cupped her cheek, warming it. "But you're still coming home with me tonight? You're
staying all night?"

Her face tingled, hot, and butterflies filled her middle, pushing
the Yankees and John Meeks from her mind. "Yes."

"Just making sure." He kissed her again. "I've got to be at the
park early for an interview, so I can't stay. But I'll see you tonight."

Lauren saw stars as he pushed the door open and disappeared
into the sunshine. Beautiful, sparkly stars everywhere.

She'd fallen, fallen hard, she thought. If this didn't work out—

No, wouldn't think that, not now, not today. She was happy.
She liked being happy. Why be sad when she could feel good . . .
and it'd been such a long time since she'd felt this good . . .

Lauren was still thinking about Chris and bussing the counter
when Boone entered the café fifteen minutes later, jaw set, expression hard.

Lauren had never seen him so upset. "You okay?" she asked as
he took a place at the counter.

He nodded once, expression still flinty.

She tipped her head, studying him. "Coffee?"

"Please. And your New York strip with three eggs scrambled."

She placed his order and brought him water and coffee, then
hesitated. "Feel like talking?"

"Only if you can explain women to me."

She smiled. "Well, I am one."

"Maybe I should have said 'explain women and drama.'"

"Hmm . . . maybe I should steer clear of this after all."

"Yeah, maybe," he agreed, sighing, running a hand through his hair. "This is just so hard. I love my wife. I do."

Lauren didn't doubt it for a moment. "Then whatever it is will get sorted out."

"I'm not so sure anymore."

"Why?"

"She can't let the past go."

Lauren grimaced. "Been there. Done that."

"But it's going to destroy us. It will. I can feel it already eating away at us . . . the doubts are poison . . . they are."

That did not sound good. Lauren glanced out across her section and then toward the front, making sure everything was okay. No fire, no chaos, no fuming customers. "What's happened?" she asked, dropping her voice.

He dropped his, too. "We've been together a long time, been through a lot. My career hasn't been easy for her."

"She doesn't like baseball?"

Boone hesitated. "I'm on the road a lot, and she's scared by the stories she hears . . . you know, about guys being dogs."

"But you're not one," Lauren said firmly.

He gave his head a small shake. "I've made mistakes. But I learned from them."

Lauren's heart thumped uncomfortably. Was he saying he'd been unfaithful?

Boone looked up at her, eyes blazing. "I screwed up. I did. I admit I was wrong, and I promised her it wouldn't happen again. And it hasn't. But she doesn't believe me."

"It's that trust thing," she said softly.

"Yeah. I know."

"That's a hard one."

His gaze was fixed to the counter, his expression somber. He nodded again.

Lauren saw Bette, gestured to her, and Bette nodded. She reached out and touched Boone's forearm. "Don't lose faith," she said, getting back to work.

Sarah hadn't gone through his e-mail, but yesterday after Boone left for the park, she went through his pockets, searching.

She dug deep into the jeans he'd worn yesterday, found a folded slip of paper in the front pocket. She unfolded the paper, heart skidding, then exhaled when she saw it was just a receipt for Mama's Café in Alameda.

Sarah skimmed the receipt, yesterday's. Steak and eggs, side of biscuits and sausage gravy, coffee. Nineteen dollars and change, plus tip, then unfolded the credit-card receipt attached. A fifteen-dollar tip. On a nineteen-dollar bill. Pretty generous. Must have been a pretty waitress.

She dug deeper into the other pockets. Nothing. Picked his wallet up off the dresser. Cautiously she opened his wallet, looked inside. Lots of receipts.

She opened them one by one. Mama's Café. Mama's Café. Mama's Café.

Sarah sucked in an uneasy breath.

What was it with him and this Alameda restaurant?

She needed to know. Had to find out. What was the attraction? Or more importantly, *who* was the attraction?

Lauren made dinner for Chris in his condo's kitchen. She enjoyed cooking in his kitchen. All the appliances were new, and the space was gorgeous and sleek, just the way the kitchen of a penthouse should be.

They ate on his couch watching the eleven o'clock news and highlights from tonight's game, which the A's had won.

"You have tomorrow off," Chris said, using the remote to turn the TV off. "Come to the game tomorrow night."

Lauren stacked their plates. "I'm not a big Yankees fan," she said hoarsely.

Chris took the plates from her and put them down on the coffee table. "I think you want to tell me something, but you don't know how."

She shot him a swift look, then glanced away. Did he know? If so, that meant someone in her family had told him. She couldn't imagine her dad saying anything, which meant it was either Mom or Lisa.

Chris pushed a long tendril of hair back behind her ear. "Just say it. I think you'll feel better when you do."

"Are we talking about the same thing?"

His gaze met hers and held. "Are we?"

She swallowed hard. "Blake's father?"

"Then we are."

"Who told you?" she demanded.

He shrugged. "Your sister made a comment once that Blake was truly talented . . . as good, if not better, than his father. But she gave me no name."

"So how did you figure it out?"

"She said he still played ball. You went to Napa High. I did a quick Google search and had my answer pretty easily."

"Do you know John?"

Chris hesitated. "We're not friendly, or friends."

"You don't like him?"

"Not a fan, no."

"Because . . . ?"

"He's a dick. And now that I know he fathered Blake but walked away from you . . . I'd like nothing more than to take him out."

She leaned close, kissed his lips. "Thank you."

Chris drew her onto his lap and kissed her back. It was a long, warm kiss but at some point he broke off long enough to ask, "So should I break Meeks's pitching arm or a leg?"

Lauren smiled against his mouth. "Neither. But I appreciate the offer."

Nineteen

Lauren finally attended the third game of the Yankees series Saturday night and was thrilled she decided to go as Chris homered and the fans went wild.

Goose bumps covered her arms as the stadium cheered Chris around the bases. Reaching home plate, he'd looked up into the stands for her and found her there in the section reserved for family and she'd blown him a kiss.

It had been a magical moment and now they were heading to dinner. Chris had made reservations for after the game at his favorite restaurant, Flora, which was in the historic Oakland Floral Depot, a city landmark with its lavish silver, gold, and blue tiled art deco design.

Lauren had been to Flora before with Chris, and they'd sat at the bar having cocktails and small bites, but tonight Chris wanted real food. He was hungry, and happy, and over steaks he predicted that they'd win tomorrow, too, sweeping the Yankees.

She sipped her wine, smiling at his confidence. She liked it. She wanted the Yankees swept, too, because tomorrow night John

Meeks was pitching, but she wouldn't be at the game. She didn't want to see John on the mound. Didn't want to have anything to do with him.

But she wouldn't think about John tonight. Didn't want to think about him ever.

"You played well," she said to Chris, putting her hand on his forearm and giving it a slight squeeze. "Three for four. Pretty sweet."

He lifted her hand to his lips, kissed the backs of her fingers. "I liked having you there, watching me. I like it when you're near me."

"Does your family ever come to games?"

"Until a couple of years ago they attended a lot of games, but now that my dad has some heart stuff going on, they mostly see me when I'm in Arizona, playing the Diamondbacks."

"Is your dad going to be all right?"

"His cardiologist is recommending a pacemaker, but Dad doesn't want it, which really stresses my mom out."

"I can imagine."

"He's a tough guy. Your dad reminds me of him."

She tried to picture his parents. She wondered who he took after, his mother or his father. "You get your height from your dad?"

Chris nodded. "Yeah. He's big. Bigger than me."

Her eyes widened. "Seriously?"

"Dad played football for almost thirteen years in the NFL."

"So sports are in your blood."

Chris didn't answer, his attention on something happening across the restaurant.

Lauren leaned toward Chris to see what he was looking at.

It took her a moment and then she saw.

John Meeks was here, along with several of his Yankees teammates.

Oh my God. Here. The same restaurant.

She hadn't seen him arrive. But then, when she was with Chris, she never noticed anyone else.

But now that she knew John was here, she felt sick.

To think she'd waited years, hoping he'd return for them . . . hoping he'd claim them, love them, provide for them.

What a fool she'd been.

Such a waste of time.

"Do you want to go?" Chris asked, his voice deep, pitched low.

She glanced at him. His mouth was set, his jaw hard. Chris wasn't happy.

"Don't let him ruin your dinner," she said softly, not wanting to let John spoil one more moment of her life.

"I'm done. You're the one still eating."

Her plate was still full. She'd taken her time tonight, eating and talking and savoring the meal. Savoring Chris's company. But the mood had changed.

Chris's mood had changed.

So had hers.

She didn't want to be here now. Didn't want to be anywhere near John. "Maybe we should go," she agreed, as the waitress cleared their plates. "It's late."

Chris handed the waitress his credit card. While they waited for the waitress to return, Lauren tried to make small talk, feeling a need to fill the silence, distract Chris as he seethed now with tension, aggression.

Not good.

She just prayed they could leave without John seeing them. Not that he'd recognize her. He hadn't seen her in over eighteen years, not since they'd found out she was pregnant.

As Chris added the tip and signed the receipt, Lauren grappled with anger and pain.

"You okay?" Chris asked, setting the pen down and looking at her.

She opened her mouth, but there were no words. The rage

went too deep. She nodded and managed a small, tight smile, shielding Chris from her chaotic emotions.

Chris didn't need to be drawn into this. It was her battle. Her problem. Not his.

He rose and extended his hand to her. As they moved through the tables to the entrance, he drew her closer to his side, his arm now circling her waist, resting on her hip.

They were almost through the crowded floor and several tables from John when he stood.

"Lauren?" he said in disbelief.

She turned and looked at him. Her heart thumped so hard she thought it would break free from her chest.

She didn't realize she'd moved, but suddenly she was there, standing in front of him and his table. "John."

John seemed nonplussed. He glanced past her to Chris. His brow creased. "You're . . . with Steir?"

"Yes," she answered, after a half beat of silence.

"Wow. Well." John obviously didn't know what to say.

Lauren had no desire to hear more. "Good night," she said coolly.

She was walking away when John spoke. "I'm sorry about the kid," he said.

Lauren froze. She blinked. Staggered.

The kid.

The kid, he'd called Blake.

Jesus.

She swayed. Chris's hand went to her elbow. He was standing close behind her, so close she could feel his warmth and the light pressure of his fingers at her elbow, reassuring her.

But she didn't want reassurance. And she didn't want to be calmed. Slowly she turned and stepped past Chris to retrace her steps. "So you knew?" she demanded, her voice barely above a whisper.

John had sat back down and he looked up at her, surprised. "Yes."

"You *knew* he'd died?" she repeated, her voice rising. She didn't care who heard her. She didn't care about the three teammates at his table. She didn't care about anything but the truth.

"My parents told me."

The ice inside her turned to fire. Heat raced through her. Her jaw worked, her eyes burned, it hurt to breathe. "And you did nothing? No call, no card, no flowers . . . no nothing?"

"I was on the road."

"I see." She was shaking, but she held her ground and stared hard into his eyes, eyes so much like Blake's eyes, the same shape, the same color it was unnerving.

"But I was sorry to hear about the kid's passing," he added.

Lauren saw red. "What did you say?"

John frowned, puzzled. "I said I was sorry about—"

"*Blake*," she said, interrupting him, jabbing a finger into his chest. "His name was Blake, and he wasn't *the kid*, you fucker. He was your son!"

John rose. "Hey, now wait—"

"Your son," she said again, jabbing his chest harder. "And he was amazing."

She stepped away. John rolled his eyes at one of the guys at his table. She saw but before she could react, Chris threw a punch, connecting with John's jaw, sending the Yankees pitcher to the floor, taking his chair with him.

John shoved the chair away and staggered to his feet.

"That was for Blake," Chris said quietly, gesturing to John's teammates to stay put, even as he nodded at John, inviting him to come back for more. "This next one's for Lauren."

John hesitated, uncertain.

But Chris wasn't. He threw another punch.

Lauren walked out. Chris followed.

They were silent in the car. Chris drove and Lauren stared blindly out the window, her insides churning, her dinner threatening to come up any minute.

It wasn't until they were nearing Chris's condo that he spoke. "I'm sorry if I embarrassed you, but I'm not sorry I did it."

Lauren looked at him, chest tight. Is that what he'd been thinking this whole time? That she was upset with him?

"I'm not sorry you hit him," she said quietly, fiercely. "I'm glad. I just wish I'd punched him myself."

Tuesday morning, Sarah sat on the foot of their bed and held her breath, her heart racing as she watched Boone pack for a six-day road trip.

He'd be back late on July 29, and then Tampa Bay arrived in town.

Yay, Tampa Bay.

Screw you, Jeff Neeley.

But she said none of this as she watched Boone prepare to go, already so nervous about him leaving that she felt sick—physically ill—as the panic and anxiety bubbled.

She didn't want the craziness, though. Didn't want the fear. It was too much, and it was getting too big.

Maybe bigger than her.

All the thoughts about what if . . . and who . . . and where . . .

"Be good," she said, putting a hand to her thigh, trying to look relaxed.

Boone didn't answer, intent on tucking clean boxers, briefs, and T-shirts into his suitcase.

"Behave," she added.

He walked to the closet, pulled out a couple of shirts still wrapped in the plastic from the dry cleaners, and hung them in his open garment bag, leaving them in plastic and on hangers.

"And tell the bad girls to stay away," Sarah added, folding her knees against her chest, feeling childish. Childish and afraid. He was the one who had to draw the line in the sand. Keep the groupies and girls away. At the very least at arm's length. Because the girls and groupies didn't care that he was married. They just wanted a sexy man, didn't matter that he had a wife and kids at home.

"I do," he said, looking up from the garment bag.

"I hope so."

"Nothing is going to happen."

"I love you, Boone."

"And I love you, Sarah."

She nodded, even as a lump filled her throat, making it hard to breathe.

He didn't know.

He didn't what it was like, always being left. He didn't know what it was like sitting home, waiting. Waiting for him to text. Waiting for him to call. Waiting for him to return, only to start waiting for the next road trip.

The time apart was getting harder, not easier.

If only he'd retire.

If only he'd get a normal job.

If only he'd be like other men, with nine-to-five jobs . . .

But come on, even a nine-to-five job didn't mean he wouldn't travel. It didn't mean he wouldn't flirt. And it didn't mean he couldn't cheat. It just meant he wouldn't be a professional athlete anymore. His mystique would be gone—that of being the big baseball player—but he'd still be six three. He'd still be handsome. And he'd still enter a room as if he owned it.

The fact was, women would always love him.

The fact was, women would always come on to him.

The fact was, Boone was the only one who could protect their marriage.

And those were all things Sarah couldn't control.

*   *   *

Three days down, and three to go before Boone returned. Sarah couldn't help counting the days as she laced up her running shoes. She wanted him home. Felt far more secure with him home. And yet, when he was home, it felt like he was always trying to escape.

Was he?

Did he feel trapped here with her? Did he wish he was with someone else? He said he loved her, but maybe he said it only to keep her calm . . . so she didn't freak out . . .

But no. He wasn't with her because he *had* to be with her. Boone loved her. He did. He loved the kids and his family . . .

But men could separate family love from sexual love. He could love Sarah as his wife and yet want another woman because she was more sexually desirable . . .

More free, more fun, more of an escape.

Sarah knew she wasn't much fun. Not anymore. Not when she was borderline crazy.

Stop this.

Sarah stood and pressed her hands to her eyes, trying to silence the noise and chattering in her head. She couldn't let these thoughts happen. Couldn't let her mind race, her thoughts wild and scattered and pulling her in every direction.

Just go for your run, she told herself. Run and burn off some of this nervous energy and then get your hair done and everything will be fine.

Sarah strapped her music to her arm, hung the earbuds around her neck, and headed out, into the upstairs hall, which had been sponge-painted in the early nineties the strangest peach color she'd ever seen. It was such a fleshy shade. Just walking down the hall to the stairs made her think of Hannibal Lecter in *Silence of the Lambs.*

The house was quiet downstairs and the lights off. Dad and

Brianna had arrived earlier and whisked Ella and Brennan out for the day. Sarah didn't know their plans but had overheard Brianna talking with Ella about the Oakland Zoo. Sarah was so grateful her dad and sister had come to give her a break.

She needed one. She also needed to get some things done for herself, including a color touch-up and a leg and bikini-line wax. Maintenance was a bitch, but essential. Which was why she was going for a run now before her hair appointment.

The run wasn't just for her body. Today she was running to burn off some of her endless, nervous energy. Boone had recently made a comment about her being a little too wound up, and he was right. She was tense. She felt as if she could go off any minute. And that wasn't her. She'd always been ambitious and focused, but she'd never been angry or prone to outbursts. Yet lately she felt like a walking powder keg.

She'd use exercise to help her deal with her anxiety. Exercise was better than pills and wine. Exercise was natural.

So while she was running, every time a disturbing thought popped into her mind, she ran faster, pushing herself harder. She ended up running five miles before she returned home, and entering the house, she kicked off her shoes, tired but calm.

As she showered, her thoughts were less frantic, and as she dressed for her hair appointment, she told herself Boone loved her and the kids. He wouldn't do anything to jeopardize the happiness of his family. He wouldn't.

But an hour later, as the color sat in her hair and she faced herself in the salon mirror, a little voice whispered that maybe Boone might not think that an affair would cost him his marriage.

He'd had that affair three years ago, and it'd been ugly. Very ugly. She'd cried. They'd fought. She'd yelled. He'd apologized. She'd yelled some more, threatened to leave.

He'd made promises. She'd stayed.

She'd stayed.

The stylist returned to peel the plastic back and check Sarah's roots. "Five more minutes," she said, tucking everything back into place before leaving Sarah in her chair.

Sarah stared at her reflection, into her eyes, wondering if Boone knew what she knew.

That she loved him too much.

And looking into her eyes, she wondered if that's why he'd had the affair in the first place.

Because he felt safe and secure, knowing she was the dependent one, knowing she couldn't leave him.

Sarah's eyes burned. She looked away, unable to look at herself.

Forty minutes later, she stood outside Mama's Café in downtown Alameda. So it'd come to this, she thought, disgusted with herself for driving here after her hair appointment instead of going home. It was midafternoon. Dad was expecting her soon. She ought to be home.

Instead she was here. Snooping. Spying. Craving peace of mind.

Sarah peeked through the window of the small café, checking out the interior. It didn't look like much. Long counter, old-fashioned ceiling fans, and big booths covered in burgundy red leather. Pies and cakes filled a bright glass cabinet. Matronly waitresses moved through tables, pouring coffee, refilling waters, clearing dishes.

She felt foolish now, being here, but she'd driven here today to assuage her curiosity. She should at least go in. Order a slice of pie. Observe people.

Sarah opened the door, felt the gust of chilled air. Shivering, she stepped in, hearing the small bell on the door jingle, and the clink of glass and clang of cutlery.

So normal, she thought, approaching the register, which was also a hostess stand. She could find nothing remotely sexy or threatening about the café.

Sarah smiled uncomfortably as one of the stocky gray-haired waitresses approached, menu in hand.

"Sit where you like, hon," the waitress said, gesturing toward the red booths and long Formica counter. "I'll follow you."

Sarah couldn't continue with this. It was wrong. She felt hideous. "Next time," she said, backing up, desperate now to escape. "But thank you."

She walked outside and then practically ran to her car. That evening, after the kids were in bed, Sarah opened a bottle of wine, drank a glass as she watched the TV, refilling her glass periodically, still in disbelief that she'd actually gone to the café.

As she drank, she leaned back in her chair, resting the wineglass on her stomach, the stomach she worked so hard to keep taut and toned and flat, as part of the body—the package—she was, so important to keep it beautiful and appealing . . .

Because after all, there was so much competition. Women—wives—were easy to replace when there were hundreds—thousands?—of women waiting to step into her empty shoes and bed . . .

Sarah sipped from her glass, letting the wine fill her mouth and warm her all the way down. She needed the alcohol as much as she needed security. Stability. Peace. She needed to know she wouldn't be replaced. And not just as the wife, but as the beloved, because that's what she needed most. To be the One.

She would fight for her man to the end, but would he fight for her?

She'd lay down her life for him—hadn't she already?—but did it mean anything?

Sarah drank again, throat aching, heart on fire.

Love was supposed to be patient and kind.

But love was also the most brutal thing in the world.

It'd been three years, but she still couldn't forgive him for wanting another woman. And he hadn't merely wanted her, he'd taken her, enjoyed her, enjoying her again and again over weeks . . . months . . .

He said it wasn't months. He said it was weeks. But weeks was almost the same thing. Weeks was bad enough.

Sarah headed for the kitchen and took the bottle of Chardonnay from the fridge, emptying the last little bit of wine into her glass.

But he hadn't just slept with her, that woman, Sarah thought, hand shaking as she tossed the empty bottle into the kitchen's recycling bin.

Boone had called her and sent her e-mails and texts. He'd told her things, said things, that had cut Sarah's heart wide open . . .

Want you . . .

Can't stop thinking about you . . .

Need you . . .

You and that beautiful body are all I can think about . . .

Fuck you, Boone, Sarah thought, knocking away the tears that fell before drawing a quick, shaky breath, aware that she was close to losing control.

She leaned against the counter and looked across her expansive kitchen to the sunken living room with its huge leather sectional that looked overpowering when empty of sitters but shrank the moment Boone stretched out on it, his six-three frame filling it, reducing it to something practical, functional.

She could picture Boone on the sofa, his big, muscular arm outstretched, gesturing for Ella to come to him, and how it always moved her, every single time, when Ella ran to him. Not walked. *Ran.*

Little girls and their daddies.

Little girls and their hero worship of men.

Sarah had told herself it was because of Ella, and Brennan, that she stayed after discovering Boone's infidelity. It was because of them that she'd fought to get through her anger and pain . . .

But it wasn't because of them.

She'd stayed for herself. She'd stayed because she loved him.

All the magazines said if you had self-respect you'd go. All the books and experts said once a cheater, always a cheater, and Boone was a cheater. The media loved to mock the women who stood by their men, whether politicians or actors or professional athletes. The media painted those women as weak. Maybe the media was right.

Or maybe the media was just plain mean.

Lots of people in the world were mean. Haters, Sarah thought, twirling the stem of the glass. The world was full of haters and she didn't want to be one of them. She wanted to forgive Boone and get past this. Wanted to move past the ugly and get back to love. Get back to happy. Get back to feeling like Sarah on the inside . . . but that was the thing she couldn't seem to do.

Who was she? What was she? Besides angry?

Sarah lifted her wineglass, inhaled the crispness of the wine, the tangy oak and sweet pear teasing her nose before she sipped, letting the wine sit in her mouth. It was cold and sharp and she waited until it warmed before swallowing.

She was drinking too much. She knew it. Wasn't proud of it. But she needed the wine, needed the softness it gave her, and the escape, blurring the edges of time and easing the endless minutes of night.

She glanced at her watch. Ten thirty. Boone was in Baltimore. What time would it be there? Twelve thirty? One thirty? Would he be in bed, or was he out having a late dinner . . . drinks . . . with his teammates . . . or with others.

Old friends. New friends. And were those friends female? Were they sitting with him somewhere, having a beer, having fun, while she was here, home, holding down the fort? Was he out there being handsome and sexy and male . . .

Virile.

Single.

Free.

Jesus. Sarah drew a sharp breath, her insides hurting, bruised.

Boone had promised her he'd never cheat again. He'd promised her he'd learned his lesson. But had he? How would she know if he was being unfaithful? She hadn't suspected before, and yet when she discovered the truth she was shocked by the heat of it, and how carnal it was between them, he and that woman . . . and when Boone had said it was nothing, that the woman meant nothing to him, that it was just sex . . .

Was that really supposed to make her feel better?

Did knowing that he could separate sex and love help?

Did knowing that men were—supposedly—different from women change anything?

No, and no, and no, and no.

If anything it made trust impossible.

How could she trust Boone not to stray when he could say it was exercise, an outlet, a release, and not something more, something important?

What kept her here, in this marriage, was the fact that love and sex were so intertwined. She couldn't sleep with Boone without loving him mind, body, and soul.

Perhaps the fault was hers. Not being able to have casual sex . . .

Abruptly Sarah dug into her skirt pocket for her phone and tapped Boone's number on speed dial.

He answered after a few rings. There was noise in the background—voices, music, cutlery. He was in a bar. Or a restaurant with a bar. Someplace lively for one thirty at night.

"What are you doing?" she asked, trying to sound unconcerned even as she pressed her hips against the counter's edge and felt the stone dig into the small of her back.

"Having a bite to eat with the guys," Boone answered, laughter erupting in the background. "What about you?"

Sarah strained to hear a female voice in the hum. *Please don't let there be a female voice. No girls or women hanging out with the guys tonight . . . no girls or women having a drink and feeling pretty, feeling fun . . . please God, keep it just the men . . .*

"Tidying things up before I go to bed," she answered before taking a sip from her glass, draining it. "Where are you having dinner?" she added, hearing the hoarseness in her voice, hoping he wouldn't. It'd be a dead giveaway, and Boone wouldn't like it. He didn't like her falling apart every time he left, but she didn't know these new guys, didn't know this team. Were these players *players*, or were they solid family men?

"We're at the hotel, in the bar. It's the only place we could order food this late."

"Ah." So they were in a bar. The hotel bar. "Any girlfriends or wives on this road trip?"

"One of the bench coaches is from Baltimore, so his wife came, but she's staying with her family."

Sarah stared into her empty glass, wishing it wasn't empty, and smiled bitterly, thinking it was funny, this conversation, knowing she and Boone were playing a game.

She wanted the truth and all the dirty, awful details, and he wanted to give her the truth, but he knew she couldn't handle it.

"So there are no girls at your table? No women joining you sexy men tonight?" Sarah asked, trying to sound teasing and aware it came out mocking.

There was the slightest hesitation on Boone's part, which told Sarah everything she wanted to know. "One is a sister of a player, and the sister's friend."

"And let me guess—they're twenty-two and smoking hot?"

"I don't know their age," he said flatly. "It's dark in here, can't see much of anything."

"Are they married?"

"I don't think so, but I don't know. How would I know?"

"You're having dinner with them."

"I'm not having dinner with them. I'm having dinner, and they're here to see Raul and visit with him."

"But you're all together at the same table."

"Sarah, I'm not interested in them."

Sarah tensed at another burst of laughter in the background, her gut churning, emotions running hot. She hated that he was out, night after night, having dinners in bars and restaurants with teammates and others, while she was home. "Just don't take anyone upstairs with you," she said, smiling again, feeling hateful, and petty, and mean.

"Babe, you know I won't."

Her eyes stung. "But I don't actually know that, Boone. That's the problem." And then she said good-bye quickly and hung up the phone.

For a moment she sat there, sick, the alcohol flooding her veins, alcohol and adrenaline.

She'd said too much.

Said more than she'd meant to say.

She went through their conversation, replaying the parts about being out with the guys, and being good and not taking girls up to his room . . .

He said he didn't. And she should know that.

And then she said something like . . . she didn't.

Sarah held her breath as the actual words came back to her. *I don't actually know that, Boone. That's the problem.*

Sarah exhaled, rubbed her temple, queasy. Why did she say that? Not good. Not smart. What was she thinking? Maybe she shouldn't be drinking.

Panic hit her, flooding her, and she called him back.

After the first ring she went straight to voicemail. He'd switched off his phone. Her stomach knotted, gutted.

She kicked herself, wishing she hadn't said anything, and tried to call again. Again, straight to voicemail.

The panic grew, exploding in her chest, shooting into every limb.

She tried him again. Voicemail.

She called back a fourth time, shaking, and left a virtually incoherent message. "Sorry, baby, sorry. I'm just . . . stupid. Emotional. I don't know what's wrong with me. Forgive me. Please forgive me."

Then she hung up, went to the sink, and threw up, again and again. She was drunk. And sick. And she hated herself.

I'm lost, she thought, clinging to the sink.

I need help.

I need a life.

I need an identity.

Something that has nothing to do with him.

"Mommy? Mama? Where are you?" It was Ella, crying for her from upstairs.

Sarah rinsed her face and then her mouth, realizing Ella must have had a bad dream. "Coming, baby," she said, going to the stairs and grabbing the banister, dizzy.

At the top of the stairs, she picked Ella up and discovered she was wet. Sarah changed her out of her wet pajamas, dressed her again in a clean nightgown, and took her to bed in the master bedroom, where Ella curled up against her in bed.

Lying on her back, staring at the ceiling, she stroked Ella's hair, wondering how her thirteen years of marriage to Boone had changed her from Sarah Brennan, all-star, to Sarah Walker, no one.

Boone returned from Baltimore in the middle of the night, sometime around two, but when he climbed into bed he stayed on his side. Usually he reached for her, or slid up against her and put an arm around her waist. He didn't. Sarah lay in the dark, wondering if she should go to him but feared being rebuffed. So she clung to the edge, too upset to sleep.

Now it was morning and he'd come downstairs, and entered the kitchen.

Sarah asked if he wanted coffee. But instead of answering, he walked past her and poured a cup for himself.

"Don't ignore me," she said, more sharply than she intended.

He just looked at her as he reached into the refrigerator for cream.

"I don't know why you're mad at me," she said, watching him add cream and sugar to his coffee.

One of his brows lifted. "You don't?" he drawled sarcastically.

She swallowed hard. He was still angry. Well, fine. She was still angry. They could both be angry, then. But he really had no right. He was the one who'd messed things up by having the affair. He was the one who sent that lady all those goddamn messages about how much he wanted her—

"I'm not cheating on you, Sarah," he said, setting his spoon down hard. "I told you I'd learned my lesson—"

"But how do I know that?"

"Because I'm telling you, Sarah. I'm telling you to trust me."

"And if I can't?"

"Then we're not going to make it. We're just not."

"Why not?"

He gestured, the sweep of his hand moving back and forth between them. "This," he said, gesturing again, "isn't working. This, isn't good."

"I'm having a hard time with your career right now."

"Why? What have I done?"

"It's what you did."

"Three years ago?"

"Yes."

"Sarah, I can't undo the past, and I'm sorry for what I did, but you have to believe me when I say there's no other woman in my life but you. You are my girl. You're it."

Her eyes searched his, wanting to believe him, needing to believe him, but there was a brittle part of her and it had broken off inside and was rattling and humming really loud. "I want to believe you," she whispered.

"Then do."

"It's not that easy."

"Why not?"

"I don't know."

He opened his mouth to say something else, then closed it, shook his head, looking away. Sarah studied his profile, seeing all the beautiful lines had gone hard and tight. Closed.

She was pushing him away.

She knew it, felt it, and yet felt helpless to stop it when she couldn't feel anything but anger and despair.

He'd loved someone besides her.

He'd made love to that woman, touching her body, exploring it, pleasuring it, the way he'd pleasured hers.

How could he do it? Their love had been sacred. Their love had been beautiful. Their relationship had been special . . .

"I don't understand how you could be with that woman," Sarah whispered. "I don't understand how you could tell her those things, and text her those things, and then come home to me."

Boone's jaw jutted. His shoulders shifted. "I was stupid and wrong."

"It still hurts, Boone."

"I'm sorry."

She looked at him sideways, wondering if he meant it. "It kills me that you'd do things with her . . . that you'd do with me."

"I love you. I never loved her."

"But the idea of you with her—"

"Stop going there. Stop thinking about it. You're torturing yourself. Torturing me. I'm not proud of what I did and I hate that I hurt you, Sarah. I hate that I've caused you so much pain, but you have to help us get through this, too. You have to help us move forward. You have to forgive me and move on."

"And if I can't?"

"Then maybe we stop trying to make this work. Maybe face the fact that we're not going to survive this, and then we move on."

Separately.

He hadn't said that last word, but it hung there between them, unspoken.

Sarah swallowed hard, suppressing the lump in her throat. "Would you like me to make you something for breakfast?"

He shook his head. "Not hungry. Just want coffee now."

She walked out, heading for the stairs, to go make the kids' beds and tidy their rooms.

In her next life she was coming back as a man, with a big dick, too.

An hour later, Sarah rapped lightly on the master-bathroom door and then opened it. Boone was naked, save for the towel wrapped around his lean hips, and leaning toward the mirror, shaving. He almost always shaved before games.

"Leaving soon?" she asked.

He nodded, drawing the blade down his cheek and over his jaw in a clean, smooth stroke. "Meeting up with some of the guys from the Rays for breakfast."

She watched him shave another section. "Will Jeff be there?"

"Probably."

Sarah crossed her arms over her chest. "I don't like him."

Boone tapped the razor in the sink before moving to the next section. "He's never done anything to you."

"You watch your friends' backs. Why can't I watch mine?"

"I don't want to fight with you right now."

"You want to fight later instead?"

His gaze met hers in the mirror and held. "I don't want to fight at all."

Sarah bit her lip, struggling to contain her anger. She kept thinking about what a man's world it was. At least Boone's world was. She despised it. And him.

Because he didn't have to take Jeff's side. He could have taken Alyssa's. He should have taken Alyssa's.

"She was going to come here for this series," Sarah said, chin lifting. "We'd planned for her and the boys to be here."

"You discussed it, back in June, before you moved," Boone retorted, rinsing his razor, "but you never discussed it since. It was just talk."

"You don't know that!"

"I do." His gaze met hers again, and she saw the anger in his eyes. He'd been hiding it earlier, but it was there now. He was still pissed off with her. "And I'm not going to discuss Jeff and Alyssa's marriage anymore. I'm sorry they're having problems. Marriage isn't easy. Now I've got to finish shaving, so if you'll excuse me . . . ?"

Sarah didn't budge. She wasn't going anywhere. She wasn't about to be dismissed like a naughty child. "You can't shave with me standing here?"

"I can't shave and argue."

"So let's not argue."

"Great. Let's not argue."

She watched as he drew the razor down in another long stroke before running the blade up the other direction, beneath his jaw, making sure the right side of his face was smooth.

He didn't even glance at her as he finished shaving the left side. Nor did he glance at her as he took a hand towel and wiped off the last foamy bit of shaving cream.

"Can you put the kids and me on tonight's pass list?" she blurted, not even sure why she asked since she hadn't even thought about attending the game until this very moment.

Boone dropped the towel into the hamper and faced her, expression incredulous. "You're not going to the game tonight."

"Why not?"

"It's not a good idea."

"Why?"

"It's where I work, and I don't need you making a scene."

Sarah's hand clenched. She could have smacked him just then. "Why would I make a scene?"

"Because it's what you do."

"*What?*"

"I know you're going through my things, checking up on me. Digging through my pockets, reading my e-mail—"

"I don't read your e-mail!"

"You do, too."

"I don't. How could I? I don't even know your password."

"But if you did, you'd be snooping there."

"Probably," she flashed, defensive and pissed. "And yes, I check up on you. Why shouldn't I? You didn't even tell me about Jeff and Alyssa and you knew. You knew how much I liked her and yet you never once said anything—"

"What was I supposed to say? Make an announcement that your friend's husband was screwing around on her?"

"Yes!"

"And what would you have done?"

"Told her! Protected her. She deserved to know, Boone."

"But it's none of your business."

"That's where you're wrong. Friends look out for friends."

"Exactly!" He was in her space, in her face now. "Jeff wasn't just a friend of mine, he was a teammate. We worked together, and we're paid to win."

"So?"

"So creating controversy isn't part of my job description. Creating controversy creates conflict that hurts the whole team. And I'd be one hell of a selfish player if I didn't try to protect my team."

"I think it's selfish not being honest."

"I do not—repeat do not—condone Jeff's behavior."

"So why didn't you tell me?"

"That he was cheating on Alyssa?"

Sarah nodded.

"Because, Sarah, I knew you'd react like this, and it's not good for either of us. It's not healthy. And I love you. So I try to protect you the same way I try to protect my team."

"By glossing over the truth."

"By minding my own business and focusing on what's important to me—which is you. And our family. And keeping our family intact."

When Boone returned from the park that night, Sarah was in bed. She'd tried reading but couldn't concentrate on the words and ended up putting the book away before Boone entered the room.

"Sorry about earlier," he said gruffly, seeing that she was still awake with the light on.

"I hate that we're fighting so much," she said.

"Me, too." He peeled off his shirt, dropped it on the chair in the corner, and stepped out of his pants, leaving him in his snug athletic boxers. He was such a beautiful man, and a genuinely kind man. She knew that. She knew he didn't mean to hurt her. But it had happened and she was beginning to realize it would never get better.

She might not be able to forgive him. She might not be able to let them move on . . . together. Which meant they'd have to move on apart.

"You okay?" he asked, standing there, gazing down at her, expression troubled.

Her eyes stung, gritty.

No, she wasn't okay. She was far from okay. But there wasn't anything either of them could do about it.

He wanted her to be happy. She couldn't be happy. She didn't trust him. And the inability to trust him was pure poison.

Their relationship had become toxic. She had no idea how to stop this . . . fix this . . .

Was it time to get help?

Time to go to counseling . . . see a therapist?

Did she need something for her anxiety and depression?

What would make her okay? What would make everything okay?

"I don't know," Sarah answered.

How strange that you could love someone so much that it made you . . . hate . . . them.

Or yourself, for allowing yourself to care so much in the first place.

"What's going on?" he asked, sitting down next to her on the side of the bed.

She shook her head once, tired, conflicted. Confused. And really tired of feeing conflicted and confused. "I don't like myself," she whispered.

"I don't—" Boone broke off, frowned. "What does that mean?"

There was so much tension in her. The pressure felt unbearable. "I think I'm going crazy."

"You're not." He reached down, stroked her shoulder and then her back. "You're tired and stressed. We've had all these changes, and then this last year with your mom . . . that was really, really hard."

She nodded halfheartedly. She *was* tired and stressed. And there had been changes, too many changes. She was good at weathering storms, but there had just been too many lately.

"It's just temporary," he added, now smoothing the hair from her face. His thumb followed the line of her cheekbone, up toward her brow. "It'll pass. You'll get your mojo back."

Her mojo. If ever an expression owed its roots to sports, there it was.

Sarah wanted to smile, but her eyes were burning and tears were forming. "You're right. Everything is fine. Everything will be fine." She said the words, wishing that by saying them, she could make them true.

His thumb followed her brow bone. "Maybe you need to go on vacation . . . do something for yourself. Have a girls' weekend, perhaps. You've certainly earned it."

"Trying to get rid of me?" she asked, attempting to laugh but failing, her voice breaking.

"No. Never. Why would I want to do that? You're my best friend, my wife, and the most beautiful woman I've ever met."

"But we're fighting constantly."

"We're fighting a lot," he agreed.

"You don't like fighting."

"I don't. I'm not good with negativity. Never have been. I work hard to stay positive and focused."

"It's my fault that we're having so many problems, isn't it?"

Boone chose his words carefully. "You seem tired. But I'm not surprised; you've had a lot to deal with these past couple of months, and most of the pressure of the move has fallen on you, right when you've lost your mom. I'm sorry about that. The timing sucks."

She struggled to smile. "I just want you happy."

"I am."

"I just want you happy with your career, and your kids—" She drew a breath. "And me."

His gaze met hers, held. "Don't I seem happy?"

She searched his eyes, trying to see shadows in them, secrets. Trying to see if he was honest. True.

The fact that she had to search his eyes terrified her. She should know these things. She should have confidence in him, in them. She should feel safe.

But she didn't.

And so she constantly monitored her marriage, patrolling the perimeter of her yard like a high-strung dog.

"Yes," she lied, hoping to protect him, just as he wanted to protect her.

He turned out the lights, and in bed, he reached for her and they started to make love. But Sarah felt numb as he touched her.

Normally she could relax into it, but the panic was there, and the pain and fear . . .

She wasn't young and fun anymore. Didn't laugh as much. Didn't tease and giggle. Didn't bat her eyes and work to make Boone feel like a million bucks.

"Not into it, baby?" Boone asked, kissing the side of her neck, feeling her detachment.

No, she wasn't into it, but she also didn't want to shut him down or reject him in any way. If he thought she wasn't willing, if he thought she wasn't into him, then he really might feel entitled to look for satisfaction some other place.

"Let's change position," she whispered. "Change it up a little."

He braced his weight on either side of her head, and his teeth scraped along her neck. "What do you want?"

To feel safe. To feel secure. To know I'll never be replaced.

She squeezed her eyes shut, trying desperately to block out the voices in her head. "What sounds good to you?"

"You pick a position. You know I like it all."

She was crying. She didn't want him to know. "How about doggie style?" she suggested. That way he couldn't see her face.

Twenty

The car, traveling. Fast. Bright lights, blindingly white, brakes scream. Headlights swing wildly, an arc of light. Metal grinds against metal. Smoke. Fire.

So much fire.

Help, help!

Help my baby. Save him. Save my son.

Jerking awake, Lauren sat up. Dark. Night. A dream.

She opened her mouth, gasping for air.

Just a dream, she repeated, even as Chris's hand came to her back, rubbing it lightly. "You okay, babe?" he asked, his voice husky with sleep.

"Yes." *No.*

She drew the covers back, swung her legs out to sit on the edge.

It'd felt so so real. The blinding lights, the screeching brakes, the smoke. She'd even felt the flames, the heat of them. Blistering.

Lauren stood up, legs shaking.

She'd stayed at his condo again, seemed to be staying there more and more lately, and one entire wall of his bedroom was glass, massive plate-glass windows that overlooked San Francisco Bay. Chris never closed the curtains at night since he had the penthouse condo on the forty-fourth floor and tonight the moon shone, the white lights of buildings and boats glimmering white and yellow below it.

"Where are you going?" he asked, pushing up on his elbow to look at her, naked to his waist, muscles bunching, contracting across his back, his thick blond hair tumbling loose to his shoulders.

A warrior, her Chris. So different from her.

"Just to get a drink of water," she said.

"Coming right back?"

"Yes." She leaned over the bed, kissed his cheek. "Go back to sleep."

He reached out to catch her hand, his fingers lacing with hers. "Were you having that bad dream again?"

"No. Just thirsty, baby. Go back to sleep."

But in the modern, sophisticated kitchen of Chris's condo, Lauren stared blindly out the window with its insane view of the Bay Bridge and the water and the city beyond, her heart still pounding, skin clammy and cold.

Ever since she'd visited Grandma's house on Father's Day, ever since she'd gone into Blake's room, she'd been having the dreams again. Dreams of Blake crashing and dying. Dreams of him calling for her.

It was too much.

She shouldn't have gone inside. Shouldn't have opened the door to his room. It had opened up her memories, and the past, and the grief had sucked her right back in.

Lauren filled her glass with chilled water, drank it slowly, trying to slow her racing pulse.

She hated the dreams. They were never exactly the same. In some, the accident happened at night. In others, it was sunny, the sun shining, just like it had been the day David, Blake's best friend, pulled a stupid teenage move, passing a slower car on the twisting country road, and discovered there was nowhere to go, killing three of the four kids in the car.

Stupid boys with their stupid teenage testosterone that made them feel immortal. But they weren't immortal. They were just kids . . . kids who played baseball and air guitar and played Xbox half through the night. Boys proud of their straggly stubble and their deepening voices and the fact that they now towered over their mothers . . .

Boys. Love. Life. Love. Boys. Dying. Boys.

"I'll make it through this, I will," Lauren whispered, exhaling again, panting, letting the pain out. Just like when she was in labor and had to breathe through the pain. Breathe out. Blow it out. Don't hold it in where it'll burn like the fire that swept through the car, taking her boy.

Let it go, let it go, let it go. She just had to keep working through the grief so one day she could remember the joy. Blake had been her joy. Blake wasn't the consequence of sin, but a gift. Being his mom had been the ultimate privilege.

Remember that. Remember the good.

Footsteps sounded in the hall. Chris padded into the kitchen in nothing but baggy gray sweatpants that were practically falling off his hip bones. She knew he'd only just pulled them on. He always slept naked.

Chris didn't speak, but came to her, and wrapped his arms around her, kissing the top of her head.

She slipped her arms around him and held tight. "You're so warm," she whispered.

"You did have one of those dreams," he said, his voice deep and raspy and so unbearably sexy.

She nodded and shivered, still sad and chilled.

If only she could see Blake one more time.

Just one more time to tuck him in. Tell him she loved him.

That's all she wanted. All she needed. Because this time she'd remember everything about him—his smell, his warmth, his skin.

Lauren hugged Chris tighter, her body curving against his, her throat squeezing closed with unspeakable grief.

If God would give her one last chance to say good-bye, she'd never ask for anything again.

If God would—

"It will get easier," Chris murmured, kissing the top of her head, then her temple, and down to her cheek.

She nodded against him, needing to believe him.

"Come on, darlin'," he said gently. "Come with me. Let's go back to bed."

She let him lead her back to his giant bed with its stunning view, but once she was under the covers, Lauren couldn't sleep, and she didn't think Chris was sleeping either.

She knew he wasn't sleeping when he began rubbing her back, making circles between her shoulder blades, and then higher over the little bones Blake had always called her chicken wings.

"I miss him," she said, her voice so soft it was more like a hiccup of sound.

"Of course you do. "

"He was so good. He deserved better. More."

"You were robbed," Chris said. "Both of you."

"You would have liked him," she said thickly. "And he would have loved you."

"I wish I could have met him."

"Me, too."

As he rubbed her back, her thoughts drifted, going to a distant place where she and Chris and Blake lived together, had a life together . . .

In her fantasy it all worked. It was good.

Lauren turned to face Chris, the moonlight illuminating his brow, the straight length of his nose, the firm line of his full lips.

She leaned close, her finger feathering across his mouth. Beautiful mouth. Beautiful man. "I'm glad you're part of my life. My life feels good with you in it."

"I feel the same way."

She grinned. She couldn't help it. "I'm glad. I like this . . . us."

"Me, too." Chris slid an arm around her and pulled her against him. He kissed her, deeply, making her head spin. "Marry me, baby."

Lauren jerked her head back. "What?"

"Marry me."

Suddenly it was hard to breathe. "Seriously?"

"Yes. I'm proposing to you. But if you'd rather wait for me to get down on one knee—"

"No! Yes."

"So what is it, darlin'? No or yes?"

Lauren knew her past but could see the future, the one she wanted, but she wasn't sure about Chris. "Before I answer, I have to ask a question." Her eyes met his, held. "Kids . . . do you want them?"

He was silent a long moment. "Do you? Would you ever have another child?"

"I want to know what you want."

"And I want to know what you need," he answered.

Her heart thumped uncomfortably. "It's hard to imagine replacing Blake."

"You won't ever replace him. You can't. He was your boy. And by all accounts, an amazing boy."

Her eyes filled with tears. "He would have been an amazing man. Not like his dad, though. He had a big heart." She struggled to smile through her tears. "A heart a lot like yours."

Chris wiped beneath her eyes, catching the tears before they fell. "I don't need kids, as much as I need you, with me."

"I'm not ready for a baby now, but one day . . . one day . . . I could be." She nodded. "I would be. I think—I know—one day I would be."

"So . . . you and me? Together?"

She nodded again, smiling through her tears. "Yes."

He rolled over, taking her with him, under him, his body above hers. He kissed her, then murmured against her lips, "Consider yourself engaged. We'll go ring shopping on my next day off."

Early the next morning Lauren baked her cakes and pies at Mama's Café feeling delirious from shock and lack of sleep.

Had Chris really proposed? Had she really said yes? Everything was moving so fast and yet she wasn't scared. She was excited. Blake's accident had changed her life overnight. Why couldn't she let her life be upended by joy? Life wasn't just bad things. It was also miracles and possibility and hope . . .

Marriage meant home.

Marriage meant love.

Marriage meant she and Chris would become a family.

Her head was still spinning when Boone entered the café later that morning, taking one of the few empty spots at the counter.

She headed over with a menu, water, and coffee. "'Morning," she said, grinning, feeling so full of brightness that she thought she'd burst. "Coffee?"

"Better not. Have already had too much." He also refused the menu. "How about a large orange juice instead?"

He also gave her his order, pork chops and eggs with plenty of country-fried potatoes, and she turned the order in, humming to herself.

She and Chris had agreed they wouldn't tell anyone until she had her ring. He also said this morning as she scooted from his bed that he wanted to speak with her father that evening, just to make sure he approved, which wasn't a given seeing as Chris played for the A's.

Lauren had laughed and kissed Chris good-bye. She'd driven to work, still laughing, and then the laughter gave way to a picture of her in a wedding dress, walking down the aisle to Chris.

She'd been a mother but never a wife.

She'd been a parent but never a bride.

She was going to get married.

Unable to stop smiling, Lauren carried a plate of three piping-hot beignets to Boone at the counter. "Here," she said. "Not as good as Café du Monde, but made with love. Thought you needed a little bit of New Orleans this morning."

Boone smiled reluctantly before taking a bite of one, his fingers now coated with fine powdered sugar. "Good," he said, wiping his mouth off. "You know, my mom would take me to Café du Monde for beignets on special occasions. If it was my birthday, I'd get to skip school for beignets and café au lait. We did it every year and then I hit puberty and hated the whole date-with-your-mom, found it embarrassing."

"So she stopped taking you?"

"No, she dragged me anyway."

Lauren laughed. "Your mom sounds wonderful."

"She's a character all right. It was fine to miss school for beignets, but not for baseball games." He shook his head. "I've been thinking about her a lot lately, and how I don't see much of her or my dad. If I'm not careful, they'll both be gone before I know it."

"Time passes quickly."

"Too quickly," he agreed. "When you're younger you're desperate to get away from your folks and have your own life, and then one day you wake up and realize they're old and will soon be gone. Not fair."

Lauren leaned across the counter to brush the dusting of sugar from his cheek. "Did Chris ever tell you . . . I had a son?"

Boone's gaze lifted, met hers. "No."

She nodded, hand resting on the counter, just in case she needed support. "He died last June. He was seventeen." She struggled to find the words. "He played baseball. He loved baseball. He was good, too. He had a future—" She counted to ten, then pressed on. "I don't say that boastfully, or lightly. Blake was good. But I never enjoyed watching him play. I was so angry at baseball."

"You've said you didn't like ball."

"Or baseball players." She struggled to smile. "It's because of his dad. I finally told Chris about him. Not sure why I've kept it a secret. Not sure why I felt so ashamed. But I did.

"I was a single mom," Lauren added. "With tremendous family support. But John—Blake's dad—was never in the picture. He wanted nothing to do with me, at least not after conception. I even signed this document stating I would never identify John as the father or come to him for child support." Her smile wasn't quite steady. "And I didn't."

"I don't think that's legal, and I can't imagine it'd stand up in court today."

"It doesn't matter, though. It's too late. Blake's gone." She took a quick breath. "It used to make me so angry that John wouldn't acknowledge Blake, but now I realize it was John who lost out. John had no idea what an incredible son we had."

"It was his loss." Boone reached for her hand, took it, gave it a squeeze. "Absolutely."

"Excuse me," a low breathless voice interrupted. "I'm sorry to interrupt, but I'd like a word with my husband."

Lauren jerked her head up. She blinked, recognizing Sarah Walker, Meg's sister. Boone's wife.

Boone released her hand. "Sarah," he said, swiveling in his counter seat. "What are you doing here?"

"Thought I'd join you," Sarah said brightly, chin lifting, lips pinched but still trembling. "But it seems you already have company."

Sarah glanced past Boone, leveled her gaze on Lauren, who stood behind the counter. "Not that it matters to you," she said quietly, fiercely, "but he's married. And the father of two."

Sarah looked back at Boone, pale, so pale. "I hate you," she whispered, teeth now chattering. "I hate you, and I'm done with you. Done. Got it? We're over. Through."

She turned and walked out, the heels of her tall sandals clicking against the floor.

Boone shot Lauren an apologetic, and rather desperate, look before chasing after Sarah, grabbing his wife's arm at the corner so she couldn't dash across the street.

"What the hell is going on?" he demanded, spinning her to face him.

"You tell me, Boone!"

"I was having breakfast, Sarah, like I do every morning."

"And now I know what the charm of Mama's Café is. It's not the food. It's that hot little mama in there—"

"Stop it."

"How long have you been fucking her?"

"You're out of your mind, Sarah. That's Lauren. Lauren Summer. She's a friend of your sister Meg's."

"Sure she is."

"You met her, Sarah. She was catering Jack's funeral. Lauren said you two talked while she was bartending, and you discovered you were both the same age."

Sarah was shaking from head to foot, shock giving away to heartbreak. "I'm not stupid, Boone. She's very pretty—in a skanky, skinny-girl sort of way—and you're into her. I could see it on your face."

"You don't know what you're talking about."

"I do, too. I stood outside watching, Boone, as she reached out and caressed your face and then you took her hand—"

"She was wiping powdered sugar off my face."

"The bitch had no right to."

"*Sarah.*"

"I'm serious. She had no business touching you. And you had no business holding her hand. Disgusting. Both of you."

"You're losing it, babe."

"Screw you! I'm tired of being played. Tired of being the irrational one. Tired of fighting so hard to keep our marriage together."

"Baby, you aren't the only one fighting to keep our marriage together. For the past three years all I've done is fight for you, but it isn't ever enough and just ends up as a fight with you—"

"You betrayed me!" she screamed, aware that they were standing on a busy street corner where everyone could see. But she didn't care. She didn't care who saw, who heard, because she was over it. Over all the anger and the fear and the pain. Over feeling only bad things and never good things. "You betrayed me and our marriage has never been the same!"

"You're right. I'm sorry, babe. I wish I could take it back, I wish I could go back and undo what I've done, but I can't. Jesus, I can't—"

"I hate it when you sound like the victim," she snapped, cutting him off, closing the distance between them to jab him in the chest. "You're not a victim! You brought this on us. You did this to us. You destroyed my trust, and I hope she was worth it. Hope the thrill or chase or novelty of new pussy was worth it—"

Sarah broke off at Boone turned around and walked away, cutting so swiftly across the street that a car had to slam on its brakes to avoid hitting him.

Sarah cringed at the squeal of brakes. Boone didn't even seem to notice. He just kept walking.

He was leaving her?

Pain surged through her, hot and sharp and livid. She chased after him, running across the street, lucky to have a green light. Her heels clicked against the sidewalk and she ran fast, around the corner to where she saw his black SUV was parked.

She reached him as he was climbing into the car. "If you walk away from me now, you're done," she screamed. "Got it? You're done. Gone. Out of here."

"Got it," he gritted, his gaze sliding over her contemptuously.

Sarah's legs wobbled. Her insides flipped. He didn't mean it. Couldn't mean it. So she pushed harder. "And you're not coming back. I don't want you back. I don't want you anywhere near me."

"I hear you, babe. Loud and clear." And then he slammed the door shut and started his car and pulled away, into the traffic without a single glance at her.

Sarah wrapped her arms around herself and clamped her jaw, teeth grinding together, to keep from screaming for Boone to come back.

He didn't come home that night.

Sarah had told herself he wouldn't, trying to prepare herself. But she'd hoped she was wrong. Hoped he'd prove her wrong. So she couldn't sleep, waiting, listening for the sound of his car pulling through the gates.

She'd pretend she was asleep when he walked in. Keep her back to him, give him the cold shoulder. Punish him for hurting her. He should feel how bad she felt . . .

But there was no car. She lay awake in vain. Boone didn't return that night. Didn't show up in the morning. He didn't call either.

Sarah walked around the house with the phone in her hand all morning, just in case.

She could call him. But she was so mad. And hurt. He hadn't come home. He'd walked away from her. Drove away from her.

Sarah stopped loading the dishwasher and straightened, staring out the kitchen sink out to the garden with the gated pool and hot tub.

Maybe he wasn't coming home. Maybe he was done. Maybe he meant what he had said.

Good.

Great.

Maybe now she could get on with her life.

She called him later that afternoon. He didn't call back. She texted. He didn't reply. She left angry messages. He ignored them. She left pleading messages. He ignored those, too. She went to bed, shattered, and spent the night wanting to die.

What had happened? What had she done? What had they done?

The next morning there was still no word from him. She sent him another text, asking him to please see her side, that it was confusing walking in, seeing him holding another woman's hand.

He finally texted back, *I do.*

So we're okay? she texted.

No.

Can you forgive me? she typed.

I am not Jeff. I am not cheating on you. And it's really difficult having a mistake I made three years ago thrown in my face. Daily.

Sarah read this one, again and again. She exhaled slowly, trying to calm herself. *So what do we do?*

You either leave the past in the past, or we end this. Because I can't live like this anymore. It's not good for you. It's not good for me. And it's not good for our kids.

Does that mean we're done?

He didn't answer.

Three hours later, after dropping her kids at Kit's house, Sarah showed up at the ballpark, talked to a security guard, telling him she was Boone Walker's wife and there was an emergency. She showed him her driver's license for proof of identity, adding that she had to see Boone immediately.

The security guard located team personnel, and the team personnel person escorted her downstairs, where she waited in an office for Boone to be found.

He practically broke down the door of the office racing to meet her. "The kids?" he demanded.

He was wearing shorts and a T-shirt. He'd been lifting weights, working out. She shook her head. He closed the door.

"Your father?" Boone asked.

"No." Sarah swallowed hard, thinking now maybe this wasn't the right thing, coming here like this. But he wasn't taking her calls. He wouldn't see her. She couldn't handle being shut out. "I'm not sure what's happening here, between us, so I've come to find out what we're supposed to do next."

"Do next?" Boone repeated.

"Are we divorcing or separating, are you moving out or am I? Have you hired a lawyer yet . . . ?"

"They told me this was an emergency."

"I don't know what's going on, Boone."

His jaw tightened, his eyes flashed. "I ran in here thinking my kids were hurt, Sarah, or maybe dead."

"You aren't returning my calls. You didn't come home—"

"Because I need space, Sarah! I need to figure out how to deal with you when you're completely irrational. You've snapped—"

"I haven't!"

"You went off on a woman in a restaurant because she was talking to me."

Sarah glanced up at him from beneath her lashes. "She's really Meg's friend?" she whispered, horrified that she'd been so caught up in her own rage and pain that she hadn't even really looked at the other woman, too focused on Boone. From the time she'd met him, she'd only had eyes for Boone.

"Yes."

"And you're not . . . sleeping . . . with her?"

"No. She's the girlfriend of Chris Steir, my teammate."

"But you two looked so cozy."

"We're friends, Sarah. We talk."

"But that's even worse because you don't talk to me! You don't have conversations with me."

"We used to, before you began acting paranoid and treating me like a criminal again, while you're the virtuous cop, determined to play parole officer."

She glared at him, arms folded across her chest. "I think I've seen that musical and you're no Jean Valjean."

He just stared back at her, expressionless. "What do you want, Sarah? Because I'm not doing this anymore. Won't be your whipping boy. Can't be. Makes me sick. Makes me hate you." His jaw eased a fraction. His voice dropped. "And I don't want to hate you, babe. I've spent too long loving you to hate you now."

Her eyes prickled, stung. She swallowed, fighting tears. What was she supposed to say now? She didn't know and the silence stretched, heavy, suffocating.

Sarah's gaze dropped to her feet. The carpet was old. Hideous. "I don't want you to hate me."

"Then stop throwing the past in my face. Forgive me—"

"I'm trying!"

"Not very hard."

She shook her head. "It's not easy to forgive something like this."

"You're telling me you wouldn't forgive Brennan if he shoplifted or played doctor with a little girl?"

"Of course I would. He's my child."

"And I'm your husband."

She said nothing. And it was Boone's turn to be quiet. He was quiet so long that it made her insides hurt. She finally looked up, into his eyes. He was studying her, his expression somber.

"You're never going to forgive me," he said at last.

She cringed at the roughness in his voice, his Southern accent suddenly pronounced. "I wish I could."

"If you loved me as much as you said you did, you would."

"I've thought that, too. But it's not that simple. I feel . . . different. Crazy. And my thoughts are just getting crazier."

"Why?"

She shrugged. "I wake up worrying about you, about us, about every woman on the street approaching you, hitting on you, stealing you from me. I wonder constantly where you are, what you're doing—"

"If I'm not home with you, I'm at the ballpark, or on the bus—"

"Or at a hotel, or in a bar, or in a bed . . . possibly a parked car."

He looked at her, appalled. "Is that really what you think of me?"

Her chest squeezed, her heart mashed. "See? It's crazy, I know. But it's how my brain works. It's where I go."

"To the worst-case scenario."

"Yes."

"Jesus."

The raw, raspy note of incredulity in his voice made her eyes burn. "I'm telling you this, Boone, because I'm scared. I'm scared of what's happening. I'm scared of who I've become."

He was silent so long that she thought he wasn't going to answer. "So am I, babe," he said after another long stretch of silence. "So am I."

She blinked and wiped her eyes, catching the tears before they fell. "You're not happy either. Are you?"

"Like this? *No.*"

She knew it. She'd known it. It was over, then. They both knew it. And they'd just been delaying the inevitable. "How do you want this to . . . play out? Should I go, or you? Who should keep the house?"

His shoulders squared. He looked remote, his expression blank, as if she were a stranger instead of his wife for the past thirteen years. "You stay in the house. With the kids. It's better for all of you."

She didn't speak, not right away, holding her breath, waiting for something to shift, give, but nothing happened. Just silence. Emptiness. Distance.

Crushing, she thought. And heartbreaking.

To think she'd come rushing to the stadium for this.

To think he'd raced into the office for this.

Brutal.

"What do we tell the kids?" she whispered.

"Whatever you think is best."

Suddenly hot tears were filling her eyes, falling. She knocked them away. "I can't imagine telling them we're divorcing. Can't imagine a future where they won't have both of us."

"I don't know what to tell you, babe. This is your idea, not mine."

"It's not my idea. It's not. But you won't fight for me—"

"Baby, I don't know what else I can do to reassure you besides put a GPS tracking device on me—"

"Would you?" she joked, wiping away more tears.

He gave her a sharp look. "No."

"I was kidding," she said.

"I don't think you were. But maybe it's better if we don't say a lot to the kids right now. There's no need to upset them. They've had enough change for the time being. Let them think I'm traveling and we'll make sure I see them when I'm in town. And then, at the end of the season, we'll sit down and come up with a custody plan and how we'll share them."

Sarah swallowed. "So you're not coming back to the house?"

"I'll stay at a hotel for now, and then sometime down the road, when you're not there, I'll move my things out."

So it really was all over.

Impossible.

Twenty-one

Sarah couldn't get out of bed. She told the kids she had the flu. The truth was, it'd been four days since she'd last seen Boone, four days since she'd last talked to him, and she couldn't breathe. Couldn't function.

Her head told her this separation was for the best.

Her heart refused to accept it.

Sarah knew that the only way she'd ever have peace was if she were on her own, away from Boone. She knew that eventually it would be easier, once she'd learned to live without him. It was just a matter of getting to the point where she could think of him without feeling like she was dying.

And the truth was, he could move on without her. He'd be fine. He was a man. Men compartmentalized. Within a year or two he'd have someone else. Be in love with someone else.

But the idea of him loving anyone the way he'd once loved her made her physically ill.

Sarah rushed into the bathroom, threw up into the toilet, and then crawled back into bed.

She cried, her face buried in her pillow. She was an addict. And Boone was her crack.

Reason told her it wasn't healthy to love someone this much. It wasn't normal to need someone this much. She had to stop this, regain control, regain independence.

Move forward.

Reclaim her life.

And she would.

She would.

As soon as she could stop crying.

They were supposed to go to her dad's house on Sunday for his birthday, but at the last second Sarah couldn't. She called Tommy and Cass, telling them she was sick and needed to go back to bed, and they came and picked up the kids, taking them to San Francisco for her dad's birthday party.

While Cass ushered the kids to the car, Tommy climbed the stairs to the master bedroom to check on his sister for himself.

"You okay?" he asked, from the doorway.

Sarah nodded. "Just queasy. I'll feel better sleeping."

"Is it a stomach flu or . . . ?"

Sarah stared at him, confused.

He sighed impatiently. "You're not pregnant again, are you?"

"No!"

"Okay. Just checking." He hesitated another moment. "Is Boone coming to the house after the game today? He'd said he was, when I talked to him yesterday."

Sarah's heart flip-flopped. "You talked to him? What did he say?"

"He wanted to know what Dad wanted for his birthday. Why? Were we not supposed to talk?"

"No. That's . . . good." She swallowed, pulled the covers up over her legs. "I think I'll just rest. Thanks for taking the kids."

"No problem. And if you need Boone here, after the game, just give me a call and I'll drive the kids home."

"Thank you."

It was five when Sarah got a text from Tommy. *We're bringing the kids home with us. We'll be there between six and six thirty.*

Sarah dragged herself out of bed on Monday to take Ella to her swim lesson and Brennan to a friend's house to play. She was back home with the kids by noon, and she crawled into bed for a nap, and slept for hours, only waking when Brennan asked her to make him either lunch or dinner because he was hungry.

She told him she would, soon.

They had a fight about frozen pizza.

She was stepping into the shower to try to wake up when Brennan screamed, "Fire."

Sarah tore down the stairs and there was a small fire, but it was limited to the microwave. Brennan had tried to microwave a personal pizza. Unfortunately, he'd wrapped it in foil.

Fire contained, disaster averted, Sarah made the kids turkey sandwiches for dinner, put on a TV show, and stumbled around picking up clothes, running a load of laundry, doing dishes, killing time until she put the kids to bed.

She went back to bed once they were sleeping in theirs, and she was lying there in the dark, thinking but not thinking, when she heard a door open and close and then footsteps on the stairs.

"What is going on?" Boone asked, flipping on the light as he entered the bedroom and came to stand at the foot of the bed.

Sarah sat up. "What are you doing here?"

"Brennan called me. Said you were sick and couldn't get out of bed. Not even when the kitchen caught fire."

"The kitchen didn't catch fire. The foil he wrapped the pizza in did. And I wasn't in bed when it happened. I was getting ready to take a shower."

"Why is our eight-year-old cooking his own pizza?"

"Because he didn't want to wait for me to make it."

"And why should he wait for his dinner?"

"Because in real life, people wait. They wait for things all the time, Boone. It's part of life."

"Oh, so you're going to tell me about life."

"Yeah."

He grimaced. "Have you been drinking?"

"No!"

"Not even a glass here and there?"

"*No.*"

"So what's going on?"

God, he sounded cold. "I've had a bug."

"Is that why you didn't go to your dad's house yesterday?"

"Yes." She picked at the comforter. "Why didn't you go?"

"Why do you think?"

She held her breath, trying to keep her cool.

"Brennan said you've spent the last four days in bed."

"I took them to swimming and a friend's house today."

"Why was Brennan cooking without supervision?"

"He was supposed to wait."

"He said he'd waited hours."

"Not hours."

"But more than an hour."

"He knows where the pantry is. He could get himself a snack—"

"Just like he could microwave his own pizza?"

"You're right. It's my fault the microwave caught fire. It's my fault he was hungry. It's my fault our marriage is over. Just like it's my fault that I gave up law school and all my dreams when I fell in love with you."

"What does that mean?"

Sarah's chin jerked up. She met his gaze, her expression just as furious and flinty as his. "It means I'm furious. I blame me. You never asked me to give it all up for you. I did it myself. I did it without thinking twice. And now I don't understand why . . . why did I give up what I wanted, what I needed, to be with you?"

"Wow. So that's how you feel."

"You know how I feel? Angry. Betrayed. Betrayed by what I thought it would be. Betrayed by what I thought it would mean. I loved you. I still love you. But somewhere in loving you I stopped loving me."

He looked at her for an endless moment before nodding. "Okay."

Okay.

She wanted to laugh if only to keep from crying.

Okay.

What the hell did *okay* mean?

"I'm saying this because I love you, Sarah. But you need to get away . . . get some rest. Pull yourself together so you can be a good mom to our kids, kids I know we both love very much." He paused, waiting for her to speak, and when she didn't, he continued. "I'm going to stay here with the kids until I leave Friday for the next road trip. I'll find someone to stay with them while I'm gone. If you're feeling better next week, come home. If you need more time to sort through things, then stay away. Just let me know by text or phone what you want. But I can promise you this, we're not going to tear those kids apart. We're not going to put them in the middle, not like Meg and Jack did. I'd rather cut off my right arm than have those kids hurt. They're good kids. They deserve to be protected. Can you agree with me on that?"

She nodded. Her eyes burned.

"And I'm not kicking you out, Sarah." He dropped his voice, his tone gentling. "This is your home, and you're a great mother, a very devoted mother, but you're clearly burned out. You need some time to take care of you now."

"But where do I go? What do I do?"

"You could travel, or go to a spa, or do a girls' trip somewhere."

Her shoulders shifted. "I don't know anybody here."

"You have your sisters."

Sarah blinked, taken aback. But he was right. She did have her sisters. Funny, she kept forgetting about them. Forgetting about her big, sprawling Brennan family.

How was that possible?

But then, how was it possible that she and Boone were divorcing?

Tears filled her eyes and she struggled to breathe through the heartbreak. A life without Boone . . . a life without the person she loved best . . .

"Maybe you go do one of your Brennan Girls' Getaways, where you go to Capitola," he said, still gentle, his expression kind. "You like the beach. You can sleep in. Drink."

Of course he'd mention drinking.

She turned her face away, brushed the tears from her eyes. "I'm sorry, Boone. Sorry about everything."

"I hear you, babe. So am I."

B oone called Kit.

Sarah had no idea what he said to her, but in the morning she and Cass were on her doorstep, hugging the kids, chatting with Boone in the family room, where they'd stumbled onto him sleeping on the sofa.

Fifteen minutes later Kit had packed a bag for Sarah, and then she and Cass were dragging Sarah out the door, hustling her into Kit's Prius, informing her they were heading to Capitola for a Brennan Girls' Getaway. Meg and Brianna would meet them there.

Sarah allowed herself to be pushed into the backseat, but she knew this was no Brennan Girls' Getaway. This was an intervention.

An intervention staged by Boone.

Kit drove, with Cass in the passenger seat. Sarah was fine being in the back. As the youngest, she'd been relegated to the backseat from birth. It wasn't until her brother and sisters had all gone off to college that she got to ride in the passenger seat, and by then, she'd gotten her driver's license and was driving herself everywhere.

But the backseat wasn't all bad. In the back, she didn't have to help navigate or keep the driver company.

In the back, you could sleep or cry. Which was what she did now.

"Almost there," Kit said as she took the ramp from 17 onto Pacific Coast 1 South.

Good, Sarah thought, closing her eyes. Soon the drinking could start.

Meg and Brianna were already at the beach house when they arrived.

Sarah glanced into the kitchen. From the boxes and bags in the kitchen, it looked as if Meg and Brianna had taken care of the groceries while Kit and Cass had taken care of her.

Sarah opened the refrigerator. No wine.

Seriously?

She closed the fridge, shouldered her overnight bag, headed upstairs, wondering what Kit had packed for her, and then shrugged, not caring.

It didn't matter. None of it really mattered.

But upstairs, on discovering that Meg had put her suitcase in the master bedroom, thereby claiming it as her own, Sarah felt annoyed and let it show. "Why do you get Mom's room, Meg?"

Meg had been unpacking her vanity bag, placing her toiletries on the dresser, and she straightened abruptly, glancing at Sarah, and then at the others, bewildered. "I'm sorry. I was just in here all summer."

Meg's expression made Sarah hate herself. But instead of backing off, she just came back, swinging harder. "Well, it's not summer, and this is the Brennan Girls' Getaway with your sisters, so you're stuck in the girls' bunk room with the rest of us."

Meg frowned. "But if we have an empty bedroom—"

"It's Mom's," Sarah said fiercely. "And it's empty because she's dead."

"*Sarah!*" Kit protested.

Bree put a hand on Sarah's arm. "That's not necessary."

And Sarah, who'd already opened her mouth to say more, because she had to say more, because she was burning on the inside with this rage she couldn't deal with, realized she was unleashing it on the wrong person.

She was venting here, because she was terrified she'd vented the wrong things at home.

She hadn't wanted to end her marriage. She'd wanted to end the pain. But ending the marriage seemed like the only way to end the pain.

But the pain was still in her, burning hotter and brighter than ever before.

"I'm sorry," she said, breaking away from Bree. She stumbled out the door, down the stairs to the front porch.

Cass and her sisters followed.

Sarah stared out at the sea, refusing to turn around when the screen door opened and banged closed.

"Sarah," Meg said. "It's okay."

Sarah held up a hand, jaw tight. "It's not. I was wrong. I'm sorry. I don't know why I'm being such a bitch—"

Meg came up behind her, wrapped her arms around her, and hugged her. "I miss Mom, too," she whispered in Sarah's ear. "I miss her so much. And there's nothing we can do."

Sarah covered Meg's hand, squeezed it, refusing to cry because tears would solve nothing now.

Tears wouldn't bring Mom back.

Or heal her marriage.

They were self-indulgent at this point, and something not to be tolerated.

It was Cass who coaxed them all off the front porch and into the tiny aqua-blue kitchen, where they were gathered now—well, squished was more like it—making the Brennan Girls' favorite, fresh strawberry margaritas, for their traditional happy hour.

They always had happy hour every day at the beach house during their getaways and today was no exception.

Kit sat crouched in front of the ancient oven, keeping a close eye on the tray of nachos she'd placed beneath the temperamental broiler, Cass hulled the strawberries, and Meg put the fresh crab and shrimp on a plate. Sarah observed all from her perch on the rickety step stool in the corner, looking forward to the first cocktail.

"I've got some news," Kit said casually as she rescued the nachos from the oven, the cheese bubbling and browning on top of the tortilla chips as she plunked the hot cookie sheet on top of the stove.

"What kind of news?" Brianna asked, dumping ice into the blender.

"Um . . . I think it's good," Kit said, pulling off her oven mitts and tossing them onto the counter. "I hope you will, too."

Cass had been in the middle of dropping the basket of washed, hulled strawberries into the blender and looked up abruptly, missing the blender, dropping berries onto the floor.

"Cass!" Brianna scolded. "We need those."

But even Brianna was looking at Kit, waiting to hear the news. Wondering.

At last year's Brennan Girls' Getaway their mom had news. It hadn't been good. It had changed everything.

"Wait," Brianna said, holding a finger up. She hit Puree on the blender. For a minute the only sound in the kitchen was the whine of the blender grinding ice.

While the blender whirred and chopped the ice, Sarah couldn't stop thinking about last year's Brennan Girls' Getaway and how Mom had said there was nothing she could do this time. Nothing she would do. Mom was gone ten months later.

The blender turned off.

"So what is it? Is that why we're here?" Sarah demanded. "It's not because Boone thinks I'm having a breakdown?"

"You *are* having a breakdown," Brianna said tartly, "and that *is* why we're here. But apparently Kit has news of her own." She looked at her twin. "You're pregnant. Right?"

Kit laughed. "Yes. How did you know?"

Brianna rolled her eyes. "Because your boobs are huge, and you're glowing."

Kit laughed again and blushed. "I've had to buy all new bras."

Sarah darted a glance in Cass's direction but Cass looked surprisingly serene.

"Cass knows," Kit added. "I told her a month ago. She was the first one I told." Her expression was protective. "I . . . know . . . it can't be easy for her."

Cass's blue eyes shimmered with tears but she smiled. "I'm thrilled for you, Kit. You will be an incredible mother."

"Thank you."

"So when is the baby due?" Meg asked, whipping out her iPhone to add the information to her calendar.

"He's going to be a Christmas baby." Kit, still blushing, was also beaming, radiating happiness. "December twenty-fifth."

"He?" Meg repeated.

Kit nodded again. "They saw a little penis on the ultrasound."

"Hopefully it'll be a big penis one day," Brianna deadpanned.

Everyone laughed, including Sarah. But then she thought of their father and how she'd missed his birthday just a few days ago.

That was bad. She owed him a makeup dinner. She'd have to make a point of doing something with him soon.

"Have you told Dad yet?" Sarah asked.

"Yes," Kit answered. "He knows."

Meg and Sarah exchanged glances.

"And what did he say?" Sarah demanded.

Kit smiled. "He's thrilled."

Meg and Sarah exchanged another swift glance. "He didn't have a problem with you . . . not being married?" Meg asked.

"No." Kit's cheeks were dark pink. "Because he was there with us at the courthouse when we got married."

It was Brianna's jaw that dropped this time, eyes enormous. "You're married?"

"At the courthouse?" Cass squeaked, incredulous.

Kit nodded. "We didn't want a big wedding. In fact, we didn't want a wedding at all. We just wanted to get married, so we did. And Dad was our best man."

"Whoa." Sarah was grateful for her rickety old stool. "And you're telling me Dad was cool with all of this?"

Kit couldn't stop smiling. "Yep." She reached into the pocket of her skirt, pulled out a sparkling diamond engagement ring, and slipped it onto her finger. "And Dad loves Jude. *Loves* him," she repeated, wiggling her fingers, showing off the ring. "And you will, too, when you know everything."

Meg frowned. Brianna's eyebrows arched. Cass still looked stricken. And Sarah didn't know what to think.

"What does that mean?" she demanded.

"It means that Jude isn't a mechanic. He's not a grease monkey. Or a drug dealer." Kit took a breath, chewed her lip. "Not really supposed to talk about it yet, but since we're married, you should know. He's a police officer . . . just an undercover one."

"A what?" Meg choked.

Brianna grinned. "A narc," she said, hugely amused. "Our

Kit's married a narc. And they've made a little undercover baby. What could be more perfect than that?"

They all slept in the next morning and then walked to Mr. Toots for coffee, where they sat on the saggy sofas in the window nook talking about their plans for the day.

Cass and Meg were going to take a walk. Brianna wasn't sure what she wanted to do. Maybe read, maybe see a movie. Kit had grading to do, behind on reading her students' journals, and Sarah just wanted to go back to bed and sleep.

They all pretty much did what they wanted, with the exception of Brianna, who found herself roped into Cass and Meg's walk.

Sarah went back to her upper bunk bed and napped the rest of the morning away. It felt good to be lazy. Felt good to not think.

Far better to not think. Or feel. Or look ahead.

But after a couple of hours of dozing, she headed downstairs, poured a glass of iced tea from the pitcher in the fridge, and stepped outside onto the front porch, where Kit sat in an old wicker armchair with a pile of notebooks on her lap. "Still grading journals?" Sarah said, appalled. "You've been at it for hours."

"I have one hundred and eighty-two students, which means I have one hundred and eighty-two journals to read," Kit answered, glancing up with a smile. But she placed the stack of notebooks on the wicker coffee table, freeing up her lap, and then patted the chair next to her. "Sit. Let's talk. We need to talk."

"Why?"

"Because something's obviously wrong. You've apparently come unglued."

Sarah didn't sit, just leaned against one of the columns and chewed her thumbnail. "I have," she agreed. "Completely unglued. I kept warning Boone, but he didn't listen."

"What did you tell him?"

"That I wasn't happy. That I wasn't doing well."

"And what did he say?"

Sarah shrugged. "That I was tough and strong and would soon get my mojo back."

"He was giving you pep talks."

"Yeah. But I'm not on his team. So it didn't help."

"You're not on his team?"

"Not anymore. It used to be Team Walker, but it's changed. I've changed." She opened her mouth, gulped in air, filling her lungs. "Boone and I are divorcing."

Boom. She'd said it.

Sarah held her breath, waiting for her Kit to jump on her. Waiting for Kit to protest and defend Boone, because of course, Kit loved Boone. All her sisters loved Boone. But loving Boone wasn't the problem.

She loved Boone.

But she didn't respect him. And a woman had to respect her man. She had to have confidence in him. And faith, too.

Sarah had tried to have faith, but it wasn't there, the trust wasn't there, and without it, it was like the biblical story of building your house on sand instead of rock. The sand washed away, fell away, destroying the house. Her house was the same.

"You haven't been happy for a long time," Kit said, her cautious expression matching her tone.

"But I want to be happy," Sarah said.

"You deserve to be happy," Kit agreed carefully, because as their parents had frequently lectured to them over the years, divorce didn't solve everything. In their eyes, it was just the start of a whole new set of problems. Maybe even bigger problems.

"It's not that I don't love him," Sarah added.

Kit nodded. "I know."

Suddenly Meg and Cass and Brianna were there as well, walking up the front steps, having returned from the beach.

"Are we interrupting something?" Meg asked, glancing from Sarah to Kit, seeing somber faces.

"Boone and I have separated," Sarah said wearily. She was worn out from months of worrying and resenting, never mind all that bottled-up self-loathing. "It's not working anymore, and I don't know that it's his fault. It may be mine. But regardless, I need to learn to love myself again. Because I don't. I don't even like myself. I don't even know who I am. Or what I am. Besides a failure."

"A failure?" Meg dropped into a faded wicker chair. "How are you a failure? I don't understand."

Sarah's shoulders twisted. "I spend my days obsessed with Boone and whether he is or isn't faithful. I think of him out on the road, playing ball, living the good life while I'm at home, holding down the fort, and I hate it. I hate him. I hate me. Mostly I hate me."

"But why would you hate yourself?" Bree asked, burying her hands deep in her swirling-cotton-skirt pockets.

"Because I'm a snoop. A sneak. A spy." Sarah smiled hard even as she ground her back teeth together. "You should see me, going through his wallet and pockets. His travel bag and desk drawers. I examine everything, even his damn restaurant receipts."

"You think he's cheating," Meg said.

Sarah nodded.

"And what have you found?" Cass asked softly.

"Nothing." Sarah laughed, slightly hysterical. "And that's just it. I can't find proof of anything . . . or he can explain everything . . . and then I just look stupid. I feel stupid. And the self-loathing kicks in."

"But if Boone was the one who cheated, why would you hate yourself?" Cass persisted.

Sarah fought for her composure. "Because I stayed with him. And I didn't stay because I was strong. I stayed because I didn't think I'd survive without him." Her lips curved, as she tried to hide the tears in her eyes. "Pathetic, huh?"

"That's so harsh," Cass protested.

"But true." Sarah's voice hardened "I used to be somebody. I used to have confidence, a sense of self-worth. But I don't anymore. I want it back. I need it back. Bad."

Sarah didn't drink that night. Not by choice. There was no wine, and the tequila was gone. She could have walked to the store on the corner and bought a bottle, but she didn't.

Instead she sat up, late into the night, on the front porch, wrapped in a blanket.

Sitting on the steps, she listened to the sounds of the night. The waves pounding the beach across the street. The voices of young kids racing down the back alley. The laughter of girls leaving a bar. A young couple murmuring, talking. Another couple arguing.

You said, she said.

You said, he said.

Sarah watched them walk past her, on their way to their car. They walked with space between them, their anger like a third person tagging along.

Boone and me, Sarah thought, ducking her head, closing her eyes, hating to be like the couple fighting.

She and Boone had always been more than that. Better.

Eyes closed, she could see him the day they first met. It'd been here in Capitola and he and two friends were in line at Pizza My Heart. She'd just come off the beach in nothing but a bikini and cropped T-shirt, having killed it in an aggressive beach volleyball game.

She was still sweating, and hot, her long hair in a messy ponytail high on her head, and she'd walked right past Boone, not seeing him at first, but then something—some energy—caught her attention and she stopped, looked behind her.

There were three men, but she saw only one.

Tall, lots of muscles, a gorgeous face, a golden tan.

She looked then at his friends. They both had muscles, too, that lean fit look that identified them as athletes.

She knew. She'd been an athlete.

She'd looked away, and then looked back, and Boone was staring at her, his gaze warm, intense.

He likes me, she thought. *He likes what he sees.*

She liked that, and she smiled, just a little, the corner of her lips lifting.

He'd liked that, too.

She'd lifted a brow, slightly mocking, and gave him a smile that was more challenge than anything else, and then turned around, giving him a view of her ass in its little red bikini bottom, and headed on home to the family beach house.

He caught up with her before she made it to the cottage's front door.

He had to leave soon, he said. He had a game that night at Candlestick Park. Could she come? He'd put her on the pass list . . .

Sarah had laughed and tugged the rubber band from her hair, freeing it. Her hair tumbled down over her shoulders to the middle of her back. She pushed her hand through it, lifting it. "I don't even know you," she'd said.

"I'm Boone Walker. I play baseball for the Braves."

"What position?"

"First base."

Impressive. She liked first base. "Where are you from?"

"New Orleans."

She liked his accent. Sounded hot, sexy. But then, he was pretty damn hot and sexy. "Do you put a different girl on the pass list every night?"

"Only ones who wear red bikini bottoms."

She tugged her T-shirt lower, but it did nothing to conceal her bare, flat stomach. "You're a flirt."

"You're beautiful."

She'd held his gaze, wanting to see what was in his eyes, appreciating his intensity. He was smart. Successful. He'd also be impossible to keep. She'd gone to school with guys like this. Had dated guys like this.

"Come tonight," he said.

She lifted a shoulder. "Can't."

"Why?"

"I have to work. I bartend across the street at Margaritaville."

"You bartend?" he repeated.

"I do. It's my job until school starts."

"You're still in school?"

"I start law school in September."

He was impressed. But she wasn't finished. "I also act as a bouncer when required," she added, leaning toward him, looking into his eyes. He took her breath away. It made her furious. "And I could kick your ass." She smiled. Sweetly.

Boone laughed. "Do you always play hard to get?"

"I *am* hard to get."

He laughed, again, and yet something had changed, something between them. She found herself staring at his mouth. She could barely breathe. *Kiss me,* she thought.

And he did.

He pulled her into his world, his hands sinking into her hair, his mouth covering hers. It wasn't a long kiss. Wasn't a hard kiss. But it still blew her mind.

"I'm in town for two more days," he said quietly, his mouth hovering just above hers. "Come see me tomorrow. Our team's staying in Burlingame."

And then he'd expect her to sleep with him.

And it'd be good. Maybe great. But then he'd be gone.

"Nope," she said, even as part of her was jumping up and down saying *yes yes yes*. But she knew. She couldn't just give herself to him. He'd never respect her if she did.

"Why not?" Boone persisted.

"I've a game tomorrow."

He brushed a long tendril of hair back from her cheek. He seemed fascinated with her skin. "What kind of game?"

"Beach volleyball." She gave him a look. "And I'm good."

"I bet you are. You have serious legs."

"They could kick your ass."

He laughed, hard. He wiped his eyes. She'd made him cry.

She smiled at him reluctantly. "So why don't you come down here tomorrow and watch me play?"

"I don't have a car."

"Then rent one."

"And if I do?"

She shrugged. "You'll see me crush the competition, and then maybe, if you're lucky, I'll have lunch with you."

"That's it? Just lunch?"

"Hey, bud—"

"Not bud. It's *Boone*."

She'd laughed now, too. She liked him. "So, Boone." Her lips twitched. "I don't have lunch with just anybody."

"I'm not just anybody."

"You're really confident."

He shrugged. "I know what I want."

Heat rushed through her. She knew what he meant. He wanted her.

Sarah called in sick the next day. The rest was history.

The wind blew, cool air off the sea, and sitting on the front steps of the old beach house, she shivered inside her blanket.

If she hadn't met Boone that day in Capitola, she would have gone to law school. But meeting him changed everything.

In retrospect, she shouldn't have dropped out of the law program.

She shouldn't have dropped everything for him. But he'd pursued her hard. And it'd been flattering, gratifying, to have a man like Boone want her. It'd made her important and incredibly desirable. And maybe it was good to enjoy being a desirable woman, but she'd taken it too far, dissolving her boundaries and melting—melding—into him.

Mistake.

She should have kept part of her separate. Part of her sacred.

Should have kept at least one of her goals . . .

Like law school.

Was it too late to go? Pursue a career? She was thirty-five. Law school would take a couple of years, and then she'd have to study for the bar . . .

But why not? Lots of people changed careers, reinvented themselves midlife. Why couldn't she?

Have work she found meaningful. Income of her own. An identity that was solely hers . . .

It would have been so much easier being Boone's wife if she hadn't felt like an accessory to his life.

Shivering, Sarah left the steps, returning to the house. She turned off the hall light, locked the front door, and climbed the stairs to the girls' bunk room on the second floor.

As she settled into her bed, she tried to imagine herself back on campus, a student.

It was an intriguing idea. A little scary. But she liked learning, she wouldn't mind studying. It'd be good to have something external—objective—to think about.

There were so many areas of law that interested her, too, but one immediately came to mind. Sports law. Having been married to Boone for thirteen years, she understood the world of professional sports, and the demands it placed on athletes. She'd find it fascinating to be on the other side of negotiations and contracts. Would love to work in an office and represent players. Would love to represent someone like Boone, someone so committed to the game.

She fell asleep dreaming about contracts and athletes and player lockouts.

* * *

arah woke late, discovered it was nearly noon. Everyone else had gone for breakfast already. She walked to Mr. Toots, got her coffee and a bagel, and returned home to eat.

"You slept in late," Kit said from her seat on the porch. She'd been grading papers all morning and looked sick of it.

"I couldn't sleep. Kept thinking about things."

"What sort of things?" Kit asked, leaving her chair and stretching.

"I need to work," Sarah said, sipping her coffee. "Need to contribute to life again. Do something with my brain."

"It doesn't have to be a job," Kit said, leaning against the railing. "You could volunteer, get involved with an outreach of some sort."

"I know. But I'd like to have income."

Kit glanced down at her hands and feet. "I'm swelling."

"It's probably just the heat. And you've been sitting for hours. You need to move."

"Want to go walk with me?" Kit asked hopefully.

"As long as I can take my coffee."

They left the house, walking at an easy pace. "Remember how I once wanted to go to law school?" Sarah asked as they crossed the street.

Kit nodded.

"I still want to go." Sarah glanced at Kit's profile, checking her reaction. "I think maybe this fall I should apply for next year. See what happens."

"I think that's a great idea." Kit nodded approvingly. "You're smart. Probably the smartest of all of us. And the most ambitious. And you've been a wonderful mom, and a good wife, but I think you need to use that brain of yours and channel your thoughts, harness your drive, so you can feel good about yourself again."

"And be someone," Sarah added under her breath.

"You are someone already," Kit retorted, "but there's no shame in wanting more. You'd always planned on working. And you know, Mom went back to school and earned her MBA at the same age you are now."

That's right, Sarah thought. Mom had gone back to school in her midthirties.

"And you are like her, Sarah. Not physically, but on the inside. You have her smarts, and strength—"

"I'm not strong."

"You're very strong. But you're self-destructing because you have no place to channel all your drive and energy."

They crossed the street and turned the corner, dodging a woman walking five different-sized dogs on very long leashes.

"Did you ever read 'The Yellow Wallpaper' by Charlotte Perkins Gilman in any of your women's studies classes?" Kit asked as they stepped back off the path to avoid a speeding cyclist.

Sarah shook her head, walking next to Kit again as they headed for the eighty-six stairs to Depot Hill.

"The story was first published in 1892; it's written in first person, about a young woman who is also a new mother. She's suffering from depression and needs an outlet. Instead of allowing her to be active and physical and work, her doctor and her husband confine her to an attic room to recuperate, but the confinement backfires. It makes her obsessive, and pushes her over the edge."

They were climbing the stairs now and Kit slowed, taking the steps one at a time. "I'm not saying you're mad, but you aren't seeing the big picture anymore, just the patterned wallpaper in your mind."

The patterned paper in her mind being Boone.

Sarah stopped midstep. "I obsess about Boone. Where he is, what he's doing. I don't even care about the rest of the world anymore . . ." She frowned. "That's not right. Not normal."

"As you said, it's time to figure out what you want. Will you be happier with him? Or without him? Regardless of your decision, the obsessive stuff has to end. It's not healthy."

Sarah glanced past Kit to the sea, which could be glimpsed through the buildings and trees. "I just wish I knew definitively that he was faithful. Wish I could know once and for all."

"You know Jude has a dangerous job," Kit said after a moment, tugging on her auburn braid. "His dad died on the job. Jude could, too. And I could spend every day thinking about him dying and leaving me and our baby. I could imagine the horrible things that could happen to him, but why? How does it benefit me to imagine terrible scenarios?"

"You're preparing yourself. In case."

"Yes. But let's be honest. He probably won't die. He could very well live to ninety-five. And then wouldn't it be pointless for me to spend all these years we have together worrying and obsessing about something that might not ever happen? And I'm not taking Boone's side, but I think it's important to consider the possibility that he is innocent. And since you're the one who once wanted to go to law school, let's entertain the possibility that since screwing up so badly three years ago, he's been absolutely faithful to you." She paused, her gaze resting on Sarah's face. "Wouldn't it be terrible to go through your life fearing the worst, tormenting yourself, only to find out at the very end that Boone was a good husband? That he was faithful and he did protect you?"

Sarah didn't answer.

Kit started climbing the stairs again. Sarah trailed after. They reached the top in silence, and as they walked to Grand Avenue, Sarah was thinking about everything Kit had said.

It would change everything if Boone was faithful.

It would mean she could relax. She could stop obsessing. She could just love him, and feel good about them again.

Kit picked up the pace. Sarah lengthened her stride to catch up. "I just wish I knew for sure," she insisted. "It would change everything."

"So let's play prosecutor," Kit said. "Let's build a case against him. Tell me all your incriminating evidence, and what we know so we can convict him."

"He cheated three years ago. Had an affair that lasted a couple of months."

"Yes, we have that. And that was bad. He didn't come clean willingly. You found out. He denied it. You did some research and confronted him with evidence, and then and only then did he confess and apologize."

Sarah hated the facts. "That alone would influence a jury."

"Yes, if that's the only evidence presented. But now you're the defense attorney. What would you say about Boone in his defense?"

Sarah sighed. "He's a good father. For the most part a thoughtful husband. He is affectionate. Compliments me. Is great in bed. But that could work against him in a courtroom, too."

"Is he reliable? Does he show up when he says he will, fulfill his commitments, support you and your family?"

"Yes. And yes and yes and yes."

"Do you have any evidence at all that he's been unfaithful these past few years?"

"No."

"Nothing?"

"Nothing that couldn't be explained. The receipts for breakfast that were for two, were actually for Boone and a team member. The waitress he likes turns out to be a teammate's girlfriend."

"So there is nothing in the past three years to make you doubt him? It's just the past."

"The past *haunts* me."

"You're still angry."

"And hurt."

"You haven't forgiven him."

"I don't know how."

"I think you could figure out how, Sarah, if you decided you *wanted* to forgive him. The real issue seems to be, do you *want* to forgive him?"

They'd turned onto Hollister.

"I'm not sure," Sarah admitted.

Kit glanced at Sarah. "Maybe you should talk to Meg about that."

"Why?"

"Jack couldn't forgive her for what she did, and it broke her heart."

"But Meg's . . . Meg. She's a really good person."

Kit's eyebrows arched. "And Boone's not?"

B ack at the house, Sarah showered and changed into a sundress, and then called her dad, who Brianna said was staying at the house with the kids so Boone could go to the park each night.

"Hi, Dad," she said.

"How are you doing?" he asked.

"Okay." She hesitated. "I'm sorry about missing your birthday."

"You weren't feeling so hot."

"I was upset. Not sick."

"You were heartsick. Worse than flu sick, babe."

Her throat swelled shut. "You know Boone and I are . . . not . . ." Her voice faded. She couldn't say "divorcing," not to her dad. "Not . . . doing so good?"

"He told me that he was moving out of the house permanently before he leaves this weekend."

Sarah didn't even know what to say.

"Sarah, people make mistakes," her dad said gruffly.

"I don't want to be hurt like that ever again."

"And I don't want you hurt again. I don't like my girls getting hurt. I don't like my kids hurting. I don't want anyone I love to hurt. But it's part of life. To live . . . to love . . . you take risks. You have a child . . . there's a risk. They walk across the street. Risk. They put pizza wrapped in foil in the microwave—"

"Boone told you."

"Brennan told me. He thought that as a fireman, I should know."

Sarah smiled faintly. "As Mom always said, there are no guarantees."

"That's right. There are no guarantees. And you, of all people, know that. You grew up playing every sport there was. You even played lacrosse before anyone here in the city had heard of it. And why did you play it? Because someone said that girls couldn't play. So you begged for a stick and that was that.

"Sarah, you're the competitor in the family. And yet you, who love your husband so passionately, have walked off the field in the middle of the game, claiming defeat. But the game's not over. It's not even the fourth quarter."

"He's so mad at me, Dad."

"He wants off the leash."

"He's not on a leash."

"You're snooping and sneaking and checking up on him—"

"I'm trying to protect us."

"Listen to me, babe. Trust on a leash isn't trust."

Sarah hung up, wandered outside, wandered across the lawn, then crossed the street to the beach, watched the waves break on the sand and the kids jumping waves. The sun was beginning to drop into the sea, a bright orange ball that turned the horizon copper. Families were gathering towels and blankets. Teenagers flirted by the volleyball nets.

She could see the place where Boone had sat, watching her play volleyball that second day. She'd worn a pink bikini, the bottom so tiny her mother had almost had a heart attack.

God, she'd been so confident then.

She'd fallen for Boone, but she didn't let him know it, keeping him guessing, making him work.

She'd loved the chase, and the challenge. It'd been thrilling. Those long-distance calls. Her first visit to him in Atlanta. Her first night there, and how they'd made love for hours.

With Boone, she felt like the most amazing thing in God's creation.

He proposed before the end of summer. They married at Thanksgiving. She left San Francisco to be with him. They were only in Atlanta another year before he was traded to Houston.

It had been a good life.

They'd had a great marriage.

And if she closed the door on the past, they could have a good future.

If she could close the door. That was the key. She had to trust him, and let him go.

A virtually impossible thing for a competitive girl like her.

Maybe that's why she hadn't forgiven him. It was her pride. She was angry he'd embarrassed her. Humiliated her. Played her.

"It's going to be a beautiful sunset," Meg said, joining her at the beach wall.

Sarah glanced at her sister. Meg wore a colorful tunic, Tory Burch, Sarah thought, recognizing the red and blue and ivory pattern.

"You doing okay, Meg?" Sarah asked, remembering what Kit had said about Jack not forgiving Meg, and how it'd crushed her.

"It's not my favorite year."

Sarah would have to agree with that.

"I wouldn't say this to anyone else," Meg said after a moment. "But I know you're struggling, so I'm going to be honest with you. I wish I'd done things differently. With Jack." She pursed her lips, considered her next words. "I wish I'd asked for a divorce."

Sarah's jaw dropped.

Meg nodded. "I wish I'd taken more time to think about what I really needed before I insisted we stay together and work it out. But I didn't take time. I was scared and ashamed. Worried about what everybody would think."

"So you really did want to be with Chad?"

"I really wanted to be happy."

Sarah didn't know what to say to that.

Meg studied her youngest sister. "I don't know what's best for you. Only you know that. So here's my advice: don't worry about what other people think. This—your marriage—it's *your* marriage. This is your life. Those other people . . . they have their own lives. They have their own relationships. They don't get to have a say in yours. They don't get to vote. My opinion . . . Dad's . . . Kit's . . . Boone's parents' . . . none of our opinions matter because none of us are in your marriage. None of us are in your bedroom, or your bed. You are. And you, and only you, know what's best for you."

Sarah drew a deep breath. There was a great deal to process, but Meg's words resonated with her. What her sister said made sense.

"Dad said I'm an athlete who's walked off the field in the middle of the game, forfeiting the game," Sarah said. "I'm not quitting because the ref made a bad call. I'm quitting because Boone cheated."

Meg smiled at her. "But you love the game."

Sarah frowned. "Do you mean, I love Boone?"

"I mean you love it all. Boone, life, challenge. You love to play. You love to put it out there. You're dangerously competitive, you take risks, you go for it. And you did. Always. In school, on the volleyball court, with Boone."

"Dad wants me to work it out with Boone."

"Dad wanted me to work it out with Jack. That's Dad. He's old-fashioned. He likes his girls married. He likes everything tidy and safe. And yet he's the retired firefighter. His only son is a firefighter. His dad and brothers and grandfather and great-grandfather were all firefighters, too. This risk thing is in the genes, Sarah. It's part of our DNA."

"Well, Kit was sure risk averse."

"Until she met Jude. And now she's risk happy."

Sarah snorted, amused. "Does that mean you wish you'd tried to make it work with Chad?"

"It doesn't really matter now. He's dating someone else," Meg said. "It's serious. Craig thinks they'll be engaged before the end of the year."

"You talked to Craig recently?"

"He called and offered me my job back."

"Did you take it?"

Meg shook her head. "Couldn't go back, couldn't work there. Too much water under the bridge."

"You did love Chad, then."

"I loved the idea of being loved."

"You risked your marriage for the idea of being loved?"

"I risked—" Meg broke off, brow creasing as she thought. "Yes. I risked my marriage because I wanted more. I needed more. It didn't work out. Now I'm focused on helping the kids through their loss, helping them adjust to life without their father. It's probably a good thing Chad is involved elsewhere. If we got together now, it would be for the wrong reasons."

"Wrong reasons?"

"I can't make him a crutch. Can't lean on him because I'm scared or lonely."

Sarah saw herself kicking Boone to the curb and then kicking him while he was down. She saw her just go at him in her mind, kicking, kicking, kicking . . .

Sarah was fighting with Boone for the wrong reasons.

"I'm punishing him," she said. "I'm punishing Boone because he hurt me."

"I found out just recently that Jack had . . . someone . . . on the East Coast. I don't know all the details. I don't want to know the details. It's enough to know he was leaving me for someone else. They must have been together for at least a couple of months. He'd bought a house right before Christmas. He put her name on the deed. She's living in the house now in D.C., mourning my husband. Who she thought would be her future husband."

"So Jack was having an affair?"

"From what I gather, it started last summer, while I was here in Capitola. Jack thought we were over, and he was back in Virginia and fell in love with this Nancy. But who knows. And does it matter? Does keeping score help anything?"

Sarah had to think about it. "Only if you want to know who won."

"But marriage isn't about winners and losers. It can't be. The moment you start keeping score, you will lose. It'll be over."

"It's hard to remember that when you're hurt."

"Damn hard to remember anything when you're licking your wounds." Meg paused. "Jack and I never had an easy marriage. I loved him. He was brilliant. Interesting. I loved his mind. But he was never really there for me the way I'd hoped he'd be. But I made it work. I wanted us to work. I changed my expectations. Managed my needs. Mom helped me a lot with that. She made me realize that there is no right way to love. No right way to do anything. There's just the way that works for you."

Meg looked at Sarah, smiled faintly. "So I stopped wanting the perfect marriage and settled for a good marriage. I stopped thinking I had to be the perfect wife and accepted that I was doing my best, and being a good wife."

Meg returned to the house to finish her card game with Cass, and Sarah walked down to the water and watched the waves crest and break before one crashed higher than the others, the white surf rushing up, surging across her feet.

The water felt cold. The air smelled tangy, salty, and the sun had almost sunk all the way into the ocean. Just a little bit of orangy-red glowed on the horizon, an arc of persimmon against the purple sea.

So many colors, she thought, color everywhere, not black and white.

And yet she'd always viewed life as black and white. Good and bad. Right and wrong.

It's how sports were played. It's why there were umpires and referees in sports. They were there to enforce the rules. Make sure everyone played fair.

She'd liked having umps and refs. It was convenient. They made life easy.

But life wasn't easy. It was messy. Messy color. Layer upon layer of color like Ella's globby finger paintings.

And Sarah framed those finger paintings. And Brennan's art projects. She framed them not because they were perfect, but because her children had made them. And her children mattered.

Boone mattered.

Just as she mattered.

They were all important, not because they were perfect and right and orderly, but because they *were*.

They existed.

They were part of creation.

Of course creation needed order. She'd been attracted to law for a reason. But couldn't she find order and meaning at home? Couldn't she find herself without leaving the people—the person—who mattered so very much to her?

Perhaps what she needed to do was not leave Boone, but to shift her focus off of him and onto herself.

She needed goals. Dreams. Work she could do.

There was no reason to limit herself. She could have lofty goals. How did it hurt to set the bar high?

If they stayed in the Bay Area, she could apply to Berkeley's law school.

If they moved to New Orleans, she could apply to Tulane.

Tulane had an outstanding law school. It'd be fun—interesting—to go to school in New Orleans. It'd be fun to live there. It'd be a new adventure. Sarah liked adventure. And challenges.

She'd fallen in love with Boone because he'd challenged her.

She was a risk taker. She'd always been a risk taker. She just needed to get out of her head and back into life.

Sarah fished her phone from her sundress pocket. She hit Boone's name under favorites. She went to voice mail. She expected it. It was a little after seven. He'd be on the field, under the stadium's bright lights, with forty thousand fans cheering in the stands.

"Hey, Boone, it's me," she said, leaving him a message. "I know you're heading out of town Friday for a six-day road trip. I hope it'll be a great trip. You guys are doing really well. If things continue like this, you'll be in the playoffs, which would be so cool."

She drew a quick breath, her heart pounding, her voice less steady. "I love you. I love you so much that I kind of lost myself a bit, but it's going to be okay. I know it's going to be okay. Because you're right. We can't change the past, but we have now, and I'm thinking about the future. I'm excited about the future. You know I once wanted to go to law school. Maybe it's not too late. Both Berkeley and Tulane have prestigious law schools. I know you wouldn't tell me no. You've never discouraged me from anything. But I'd still like to get your thoughts. Hear what you think. Anyway. Call me later, if you want. Or whenever you want. No pressure. There's been enough of that lately."

She hung up. Clutched the phone between her hands and started walking back to the beach house.

She was almost to the porch when her phone buzzed with a text.

My girl would be an incredible lawyer.

Sarah blinked back tears. *You have your phone in the dugout?*

Not supposed to. I'll get fined if I get caught. But I've been missing you. Was hoping you'd call. And you did.

You still love me a little bit?

He texted, *I love you more now than ever.*

So can we please forget the whole separating thing?

Consider it forgotten.

Her heart turned over. She sat down on the front steps of the beach house. *Easier said than done. I was pretty crazy.*

Shit happens. But it doesn't mean I don't love you.

Sarah took a deep breath, grateful, so grateful he was strong. *The past is the past. I'm focusing on us, now, and in the future.*

That's my girl. Knew you could do it. You've got your mojo back.

Twenty-two

The restaurant Plum was dark. Heads turned as Boone and Sarah moved between the tables in the dining room, the hostess leading the way.

Sarah was glad Boone held her hand as they wove between the thick wood tables. She was nervous. They were meeting Chris and Lauren for a late dinner following tonight's game.

The dinner had been her idea. She wanted to apologize to Lauren. Needed to apologize. She'd been horrible to Lauren the day in the café. Her behavior embarrassed her. It also made her sad. She knew better. She might be Boone's wife, but she was still a Brennan. She'd always be a Brennan.

Boone gave her fingers a squeeze. "Don't be nervous," he said.

She looked up into his handsome face. His expression was warm. A smile lurked in his beautiful eyes. "I just wish I'd apologized sooner. It's been over two weeks—"

"We've been on the road a lot. Lauren works a lot. It's okay. Trust me."

She nodded, relaxing, because she did trust him. She would

trust him. That was the vow she'd made in Capitola. She'd focus on being positive, focus on forgiveness, focus on what lay ahead, not that which was behind.

Suddenly they were at the table where Chris and Lauren waited. Chris and Lauren rose. Boone shook hands with Chris, kissed Lauren's cheek, and then Lauren was turning to Sarah, and she opened her arms and hugged Sarah. Warmly.

"I'm sorry," Sarah whispered, eyes burning. "I shouldn't have—"

"Meg's my friend," Lauren interrupted huskily. "That makes you my friend." She pulled back, smiled at Sarah. "It's all good."

And it was all good, Sarah thought, as the four of them lingered at the dinner table two hours later, talking, laughing, discussing life, love, and baseball.

It was past midnight. They were closing the restaurant tonight, but the waitstaff didn't seem to mind. It was just that kind of a night. Mellow.

Special.

Great food. Great company. Great conversation.

Boone suddenly turned to look at her, and his warm gaze held hers. His lips curved. Heat flared in his eyes.

She blushed, knowing what he was thinking.

He leaned close, whispered, "I want you."

Her cheeks burned. Her pulse quickened. She nodded. She wanted him, too.

"You and me," he said, voice pitched low, sliding an arm around her shoulders.

"Together," she added, huskily.

He smiled.

He'd taken her to see the Dave Matthews Band in concert and this was her favorite song. It was her anthem. Their anthem. She'd always felt like it'd been written just for them.

"Can do anything," Boone finished.

She smiled unsteadily, blinking back tears.

It was true, she thought, reaching for his hand under the table and holding it tightly. Together they could do anything.

Together anything was possible.

Together.

That was the key word.

That was the important piece.